"A R

"Neill creates a strong-minded, sharp-witted heroine who will appeal to fans of Charlaine Harris's Sookie Stackhouse series and Laurell K. Hamilton's Anita Blake." —*Library Journal*

"Smart, sexy and delightful . . . a must read!"
—Candace Havens, Author of *Take It Like a Vamp*

"Chloe Neill owes me a good night's sleep. With her wonderfully compelling reluctant vampire heroine, and her careful world building, I was drawn into *Some Girls Bite* from page one and kept reading far into the night."
—*USA Today* bestselling author Julie Kenner

"The kind of sassy heroine readers love to root for—add to that a fun cast of characters and smokin'-hot sexual tension and you've got a stunning combination."
—Tate Hallaway, national bestselling author of *Dead If I Do*

"Packed with complex subplots, embittered family members and politics, this is an excellent first installment to what should be an outstanding series in a crowded field."
—*Monsters and Critics*

"There's a new talent in town, and . . . she's here to stay . . . an indomitable and funny heroine . . . truly excellent."
—*Romantic Times*

"Engaging, well-executed and populated with characters you can't help but love. It was impossible to set down."
—*Darque Reviews*

continued . . .

PRAISE FOR THE
CHICAGOLAND VAMPIRES SERIES

Friday Night Bites

"Wonderfully entertaining, and impossible to set down."
—Darque Reviews

Twice Bitten

"The pages turn fast enough to satisfy vampire and romance fans alike." —*Booklist*

Hard Bitten

"A fast and exciting read." —Fresh Fiction

"Fantastic from beginning to end, with one of the best endings in urban fantasy history." —*Romantic Times*

Drink Deep

"A completely unpredictable read that left me more than satisfied." —A Book Obsession

Biting Cold

"Chloe Neill keeps readers right on the precipice of anticipation." —Fresh Fiction

"[Merit's] a character I fully root for." —Hardcore Heroines

House Rules

"*House Rules* is the book that keeps on giving with lightning-fast pacing, a masterful web of plotlines, and a steadfast heroine who refuses to give up." —Rabid Reads

Biting Bad

"There is heart-pounding danger, high-stakes drama, and excitement as Merit, Ethan, and crew take on a treacherous new enemy!" —*Romantic Times*

A CHICAGOLAND VAMPIRES NOVEL

SOME GIRLS BITE

CHLOE NEILL

A ROC BOOK

ROC
Published by the Penguin Group
Penguin Group (USA) LLC, 375 Hudson Street,
New York, New York 10014

USA I Canada I UK I Ireland I Australia I New Zealand I India I South Africa I China
penguin.com
A Penguin Random House Company

Published by New American Library, an imprint of New American Library, a division
of Penguin Group (USA) LLC. Previously published in a Roc trade paperback edition.

First Roc Mass Market Printing, March 2014

ROC REGISTERED TRADEMARK—MARCA REGISTRADA

ISBN 978-0-451-46905-2

Printed in the United States of America
10 9 8 7 6 5 4 3 2 1

ACKNOWLEDGMENTS

I owe a debt of gratitude to (at least) the following people:

Jessica and the staff at Penguin for a phone call I will always remember, and for taking a chance on a new author;

Lucienne, my agent, for patiently reading would-be chapters and offering fabulous advice;

Melissa, for explaining the architecture of the University of Chicago's English Department;

Jess and Jill, for being the guinea pigs in my writing experiment;

Jess and Jenny, for being fabulous shower hostesses;

Ryan, for reading the fight scenes and repeating the moves until I figured out how to write them;

My friends and colleagues, including Julie, Sandi, Anne, Amy, Heather, Tory, Matt, and Kevin, who read the draft, helped with the search for a title, and/or offered advice on contracting, history, character development, and editing (and who patiently listened to my incessant lectures on the virtue of vampires);

D.J., for information on weapons and tactics;

The Murphy family, for their hospitality, advice, and inspirational sarcasm;

Baxter, for keeping me company;

Nate, for making me smile more and laugh harder than I thought humanly possible; and

Dusan and Mom, for always believing in me.

Want to learn more about the vampires,
the Houses, the *Canon*, or Chloe?
Visit chloeneill.com.

"It is better to be hated for what you are,
than to be loved for what you are not."

—André Gide

CHAPTER ONE

THE CHANGE

Early April
Chicago, Illinois

At first, I wondered if it was karmic punishment. I'd sneered at the fancy vampires, and as some kind of cosmic retribution, I'd been made one. Vampire. Predator. Initiate into one of the oldest of the twelve vampire Houses in the United States.

And I wasn't just *one* of them.

I was one of the best.

But I'm getting ahead of myself. Let me begin by telling you how I became a vampire, a story that starts weeks before my twenty-eighth birthday, the night I completed the transition. The night I awoke in the back of a limousine, three days after I'd been attacked walking across the University of Chicago campus.

I didn't remember all the details of the attack. But I remembered enough to be thrilled to be alive. To be shocked to be alive.

In the back of the limousine, I squeezed my eyes shut and tried to unpack the memory of the attack. I'd heard footsteps, the sound muffled by dewy grass, before he grabbed me. I'd screamed and kicked, tried to fight my way out, but he pushed me down. He was preternaturally strong—supernaturally strong—and he bit my neck with a predatory ferocity that left little doubt about who he was. What he was.

Vampire.

But while he tore into skin and muscle, he didn't drink; he didn't have time. Without warning, he'd stopped and jumped away, running between buildings at the edge of the main quad.

My attacker temporarily vanquished, I'd raised a hand to the crux of my neck and shoulder, felt the sticky warmth. My vision was dimming, but I could see the wine-colored stain across my fingers clearly enough.

Then there was movement around me. Two men.

The men my attacker had been afraid of.

The first of them had sounded anxious. "He was fast. You'll need to hurry, Liege."

The second had been unerringly confident. "I'll get it done."

He pulled me up to my knees, and knelt behind me, a supportive arm around my waist. He wore cologne—soapy and clean.

I tried to move, to give some struggle, but I was fading.

"Be still."

"She's lovely."

"Yes," he agreed. He suckled the wound at my neck. I twitched again, and he stroked my hair. "Be still."

I recalled very little of the next three days, of the genetic restructuring that transformed me into a vampire. Even now, I only carry a handful of memories. Deep-seated, dull pain—shocks of it that bowed my body. Numbing cold. Darkness. A pair of intensely green eyes.

In the limo, I felt for the scars that should have marred my neck and shoulders. The vampire that attacked me hadn't taken a clean bite—he'd torn at the skin at my neck like a starved animal. But the skin was smooth. No scars. No bumps. No bandages. I pulled my hand away and stared at the clean pale skin—and the short nails, perfectly painted cherry red.

The blood was gone—and I'd been manicured.

Staving off a wash of dizziness, I sat up. I was wearing different clothes. I'd been in jeans and a T-shirt. Now I wore a black cocktail dress, a sheath that fell to just below my knees, and three-inch-high black heels.

That made me a twenty-seven-year-old attack victim, clean and absurdly scar-free, wearing a cocktail dress that wasn't mine. I knew, then and there, that they'd made me one of them.

The Chicagoland Vampires.

It had started eight months ago with a letter, a kind of vampire manifesto first published in the *Sun-Times* and *Trib*, then picked up by papers across the country. It was a coming-out, an announcement to the world of their existence. Some humans believed it a hoax, at least until the press conference that followed, in which three of them displayed their fangs. Human panic led to four days of riots in the Windy City and a run on water and canned goods sparked by public fear of a vampire apocalypse. The feds finally stepped in, ordering Congressional investigations, the hearings obsessively filmed and televised in order to pluck out every detail of the vampires' existence. And even though they'd been the ones to step forward, the vamps were tight-lipped about those details—the fang bearing, blood drinking, and night walking the only facts the public could be sure about.

Eight months later, some humans were still afraid. Others were obsessed. With the lifestyle, with the lure of immortality, with the vampires themselves. In particular, with Celina Desaulniers, the glamorous Windy City she-vamp who'd apparently orchestrated the coming-out, and who'd made her debut during the first day of the Congressional hearings.

Celina was tall and slim and sable-haired, and that day she

wore a black suit snug enough to give the illusion that it had been poured onto her body. Looks aside, she was obviously smart and savvy, and she knew how to twist humans around her fingers. To wit: The senior senator from Idaho had asked her what she planned to do now that vampires had come out of the closet.

She'd famously replied in dulcet tones, "I'll be making the most of the dark."

The twenty-year Congressional veteran had smiled with such dopey-eyed lust that a picture of him made the front page of the *New York Times*.

No such reaction from me. I'd rolled my eyes and flipped off the television.

I'd made fun of them, of her, of their pretensions.

And in return, they'd made me like them.

Wasn't karma a bitch?

Now they were sending me back home, but returning me differently. Notwithstanding the changes my body had endured, they'd glammed me up, cleaned me of blood, stripped me of clothing, and repackaged me in their image.

They killed me. They healed me. They changed me.

The tiny seed, that kernel of distrust of the ones who'd made me, rooted.

I was still dizzy when the limousine stopped in front of the Wicker Park brownstone I shared with my roommate, Mallory. I wasn't sleepy, but groggy, mired in a haze across my consciousness that felt thick enough to wade through. Drugs, maybe, or a residual effect of the transition from human to vampire.

Mallory stood on the stoop, her shoulder-length ice blue hair shining beneath the bare bulb of the overhead light. She looked anxious, but seemed to be expecting me. She wore flannel pajamas patterned with sock monkeys. I realized it was late.

The limousine door opened, and I looked toward the

house and then into the face of a man in a black uniform and cap who'd peeked into the backseat.

"Ma'am?" He held out a hand expectantly.

My fingers in his palm, I stepped onto the asphalt, my ankles wobbly in the stilettos. I rarely wore heels, jeans being my preferred uniform. Grad school didn't require much else.

I heard a door shut. Seconds later, a hand gripped my elbow. My gaze traveled down the pale, slender arm to the bespectacled face it belonged to. She smiled at me, the woman who held my arm, the woman who must have emerged from the limo's front seat.

"Hello, dear. We're home now. I'll help you inside, and we'll get you settled."

Grogginess making me acquiescent, and not really having a good reason to argue anyway, I nodded to the woman, who looked to be in her late fifties. She had a short, sensible bob of steel gray hair and wore a tidy suit on her trim figure, carrying herself with a professional confidence. As we progressed down the sidewalk, Mallory moved cautiously down the first step, then the second, toward us.

"Merit?"

The woman patted my back. "She'll be fine, dear. She's just a little dizzy. I'm Helen. You must be Mallory?"

Mallory nodded, but kept her gaze on me.

"Lovely home. Can we go inside?"

Mallory nodded again and traveled back up the steps. I began to follow, but the woman's grip on my arm stopped me. "You go by Merit, dear? Although that's your last name?"

I nodded at her.

She smiled patiently. "The newly risen utilize only a single name. Merit, if that's what you go by, would be yours. Only the Masters of each House are allowed to retain their last names. That's just one of the rules you'll need to remember." She leaned in conspiratorially. "And it's considered déclassé to break the rules."

Her soft admonition sparked something in my mind, like the beam of a flashlight in the dark. I blinked at her. "Some would consider changing a person without their consent déclassé, Helen."

The smile Helen fixed on her face didn't quite reach her eyes. "You were made a vampire in order to save your life, Merit. Consent is irrelevant." She glanced at Mallory "She could probably use a glass of water. I'll give you two a moment."

Mallory nodded, and Helen, who carried an ancient-looking leather satchel, moved past her into the brownstone. I walked up the remaining stairs on my own, but stopped when I reached Mallory. Her blue eyes swam with tears, a frown curving her cupid's bow mouth. She was extraordinarily, classically pretty, which was the reason she'd given for tinting her hair with packets of blue Kool-Aid. She claimed it was a way for her to distinguish herself. It was unusual, sure, but it wasn't a bad look for an ad executive, for a woman defined by her creativity.

"You're—" She shook her head, then started again. "It's been three days. I didn't know where you were. I called your parents when you didn't come home. Your dad said he'd handle it. He told me not to call the police. He said someone had called him, told him you'd been attacked but were okay. That you were healing. They told your dad they'd bring you home when you were ready. I got a call a few minutes ago. They said you were on your way home." She pulled me into a fierce hug. "I'm gonna beat the shit out of you for not calling."

Mal pulled back, gave me a head-to-toe evaluation. "They said—you'd been changed."

I nodded, tears threatening to spill over.

"So you're a vampire?" she asked.

"I think. I just woke up or . . . I don't know."

"Do you feel any different?"

"I feel . . . slow."

Mallory nodded with confidence. "Effects of the change,

probably. They say that happens. Things will settle." Mallory would know; unlike me, she followed all the vamp-related news. She offered a weak smile. "Hey, you're still Merit, right?"

Weirdly, I felt a prickle in the air emanating from my best friend and roommate. A tingle of something electric. But still sleepy, dizzy, I dismissed it.

"I'm still me," I told her.

And I hoped that was true.

The brownstone had been owned by Mallory's great-aunt until her death four years ago. Mallory, who lost her parents in a car accident when she was young, inherited the house and everything in it, from the chintzy rugs that covered the hardwood floors, to the antique furniture, to the oil paintings of flower vases. It wasn't chic, but it was home, and it smelled like it—lemon-scented wood polish, cookies, dusty coziness. It smelled the same as it had three days go, but I realized that the scent was deeper. Richer.

Improved vampire senses, maybe?

When we entered the living room, Helen was sitting at the edge of our gingham-patterned sofa, her legs crossed at the ankles. A glass of water sat on the coffee table in front of her.

"Come in, ladies. Have a seat." She smiled and patted the couch. Mallory and I exchanged a glance and sat down. I took the seat next to Helen. Mallory sat on the matching love seat that faced the couch. Helen handed me the glass of water.

I brought it to my lips, but paused before sipping. "I can— eat and drink things other than blood?"

Helen's laugh tinkled. "Of course, dear. You can eat whatever you'd like. But you'll need blood for its nutritional value." She leaned toward me, touched my bare knee with the tips of her fingers. "And I daresay you'll enjoy it!" She said the words like she was imparting a delicious secret, sharing scandalous gossip about her next-door neighbor.

I sipped, discovered that water still tasted like water. I put the glass back on the table.

Helen tapped her hands against her knees, then favored us both with a bright smile. "Well, let's get to it, shall we?" She reached into the satchel at her feet and pulled out a dictionary-sized leather-bound book. The deep burgundy cover was inscribed in embossed gold letters—*Canon of the North American Houses, Desk Reference*. "This is everything you need to know about joining Cadogan House. It's not the full *Canon*, obviously, as the series is voluminous, but this will cover the basics."

"Cadogan House?" Mallory asked. "Seriously?"

I blinked at Mallory, then Helen. "What's Cadogan House?"

Helen looked at me over the top of her horn-rimmed glasses. "That's the House that you'll be Commended into. One of Chicago's three vampire Houses—Navarre, Cadogan, Grey. Only the Master of each House has the privilege of turning new vampires. You were turned by Cadogan's Master—"

"Ethan Sullivan," Mallory finished.

Helen nodded approvingly. "That's right."

I lifted brows at Mallory.

"Internet," she said. "You'd be amazed."

"Ethan is the House's second Master. He followed Peter Cadogan into the dark, so to speak."

If only Masters could turn new vampires, this Ethan Sullivan must have been the vamp in the quad, the one who bit me during round two.

"This House," I began. "I'm, what, in a vampire sorority or something?"

Helen shook her head. "It's more complicated than that. All legitimate vampires in the world are affiliated with one House or other. There are currently twelve Houses in the United States; Cadogan is the fourth-oldest among those." Helen sat up even straighter, so I took a wild guess that she was also a flag-flying member of Cadogan House.

Helen handed me the book, which must have weighed ten pounds. I centered it in my lap, distributing the mass.

"You won't need to memorize the rules, of course, but you'll want to read the introductory sections and have at least a passing familiarity with the content. And of course you can refer to the text if you have specific questions. Make sure to read about the Commendation."

"What's the Commendation?"

"The initiation ceremony. You'll become an official member of the House, and you'll take your oaths to Ethan and the rest of the Cadogan vampires. And speaking of, payments typically begin two weeks after take the oath is taken."

I blinked. "Payments?"

She gave me one of those over-the-glasses looks. "Your salary, dear."

I laughed nervously, the sound strangled. "I don't need a salary. I'm a student. Teaching assistant. Stipend." I was three years into my graduate work, three chapters into my dissertation on romantic medieval literature.

Helen frowned. "Dear, you can't go back to school. The university doesn't admit vampires as students, and they certainly don't employ them. Title VII doesn't cover us yet. We went ahead and removed you, just to avoid the squabble, so you won't have to worry about—"

My pulse thudded in my ears. "What do you mean, you removed me?"

Her expression softened. "Merit, you're a vampire. A Cadogan Initiate. You can't go back to that life."

I was out the door before she was done talking, her voice echoing behind me as I rushed to the first-floor bedroom that served as our office. I wiggled the mouse to wake my computer, brought up a Web browser, and logged into the university server. The system recognized me, and my stomach unclenched in relief.

Then I brought up my records.

Two days ago, my status had been changed. I was listed as "Not Enrolled."

The world shifted.

I went back to the living room, my voice wavering as I fought through the quickly rising panic, and faced Helen. "What did you do? You had no right to take me out of school!"

Helen turned back to her satchel and pulled out a sheath of paper, her manner irritatingly calm. "Because Ethan feels your circumstances are . . . particular, you'll receive your salary from the House within the next ten business days. We've already arranged the direct deposit. The Commendation is scheduled on your seventh day, six days from now. You will appear when commanded. At the ceremony, Ethan will assign your position of service within the House." She smiled at me. "Perhaps something in public relations, given your family's connections to the city."

"Oh, lady. Wrong move, bringing up the parents," Mallory muttered.

She was right. It was exactly the wrong thing to say, my parents being one of my least favorite topics. But it was at least jarring enough to wake me from my daze. "I think we're done here," I told her. "It's time for you to leave."

Helen winged up an eyebrow. "It's not your house."

Brave of her to piss off the new vampire. But we were on my turf now, and I had allies.

I turned to Mallory with an evil grin. "How about we find out how much of the vampire myth is actually myth? Don't vampires have to have an invitation to be in someone's home?"

"I love the way you think," Mal said, then went to the door and opened it. "Helen," she said, "I want you out of my house."

Something stirred in the air, a sudden breeze that blew through the doorway and ruffled Mallory's hair—and raised goose bumps along my arms.

"This is incredibly rude," Helen said, but yanked her satchel up. "Read the book, sign the forms. There's blood in the refrigerator. Drink it—a pint every other day. Stay away from sunlight and aspen stakes, and come when he commands you." She neared the door, and then, suddenly, like someone had flipped the switch on a vacuum, she was sucked onto the stoop.

I rushed to the doorway. Helen stood on the top step, glasses askew, staring back at us in disheveled shock. After a moment, she straightened her skirt and glasses, turned crisply, and walked down the stairs and toward the limo. "That was—very rude," she called back. "Don't think I won't tell Ethan about this!"

I gave her a pageant wave—hand cupped, barely swiveling.

"You do that, Helen," Mallory dared. "And tell him we said to fuck off while you're at it."

Helen turned to look at me, eyes blazing silver. Like, supernaturally silver. "You were *undeserving*," she sniped.

"I was *unconsenting*," I corrected and slammed the heavy oak door shut with enough force that it rattled the hinges. After the *scritch* of rocks on asphalt signaled the limo's retreat, I leaned back against the door and looked at Mallory.

She glared back. "They said you were on campus by yourself in the middle of the night!" She punched my arm, disgust obvious on her face. "What the hell were you thinking?"

That, I thought, was the release of the panic she'd suffered until she learned that I was coming home. It tightened my throat, knowing that she'd waited for me, worried for me.

"I had work to do."

"In the middle of the night?!"

"I said I had work to do!" I threw up my hands, irritation rising. "God, Mallory, this isn't my fault." My knees began to shake. I moved the few steps back to the couch and sat down. Repressed fear, horror, and violation overwhelmed me. I covered my face with my hands as the tears began to fall. "It wasn't my fault, Mallory. Everything—my life, school—is gone, and it wasn't my fault."

I felt the cushion dip beside me and an arm around my shoulders.

"Oh, God, I'm sorry. I'm sorry. I'm freaked out. I was so scared, Mer, Jesus. I know it's not your fault." She held me while I sobbed, rubbed my back while I cried hard enough to hiccup, while I mourned the loss of my life, of my humanity.

We sat there together for a long time, my best friend and I. She offered Kleenex as I replayed the few things I could remember—the attack, the second set of vampires, the cold and pain, the hazy limo ride.

When I'd sobbed my body empty of tears, Mallory stroked the hair from my face. "It'll be okay. I promise. I'll call the university in the morning. And if you can't go back . . . we'll figure something out. In the meantime, you should call your grandfather. He'll want to know you're okay."

I shook my head, not yet ready to have that conversation. My grandfather's love had always been unconditional, but then again, I'd always been human. I wasn't ready to test the correlation. "I'll start with Mom and Dad," I promised. "Then I'll let word trickle down."

"Tacky," Mallory accused, but let it go. "The House, I guess it was, did call me, but I don't know who else they contacted. The call was pretty short. 'Merit was attacked on campus two nights ago. In order to save her life, we've made her a vampire. She'll return home tonight. She may be dizzy from the change, so please be home to assist her during the first crucial hours. Thank you.' It sounded like a recording, to be real honest."

"So this Ethan Sullivan's a cheapo," I concluded. "We'll add that to the list of reasons we don't like him."

"Him turning you into a soul-sucking creature of the night being number one on that list?"

I nodded ruefully. "That's definitely number one." I

shifted and glanced over at her. "They made me like them. *He* made me like them, this Sullivan."

Mallory made a sound of frustration. "I know. I am so effing jealous." Mal was a student of the paranormal; as long as I'd known her, she'd had a keen interest in all things fanged and freaky. She put her palm to her chest. "I'm the occultist in the family, and yet it's *you*, the English lit geek, they turn? Even Buffy would feel that sting. Although," she said, her gaze appraising, "you will make damn good research material."

I snorted. "But research material for what? Who the hell am I now?"

"You're Merit," she said with conviction that warmed my heart. "But kind of Merit 2.0. And I have to say, the phone call notwithstanding, this Sullivan's not a cheapo about everything. Those shoes are Jimmy Choo, and that dress is runway-worthy." She clucked her tongue. "He's dressed you up like his own personal model. And frankly, Mer, you look good."

Good, I thought, was relative. I looked down at the cocktail dress, smoothed my hands over the slick, black fabric. "I liked who I was, Mal. My life wasn't perfect, but I was happy."

"I know, hon. But maybe you'll like this, too."

I doubted it. Seriously.

————— ✦ —————

CHAPTER TWO

RICH PEOPLE AREN'T NICER—
THEY JUST HAVE BETTER CARS.

My parents were new-money Chicago.

My grandfather, Chuck Merit, had served the city for thirty-four years as a cop—walking a beat in Chicago's South Side until he joined the CPD's Bureau of Investigative Services. He was a legend in the Chicago Police Department.

But while he brought home a solid middle-class living, things were occasionally tight for the family. My grandmother came from money, but she'd turned down an inheritance from her overbearing, old-Chicago-money-having father. Although it was her decision, my father blamed my grandfather for the fact that he wasn't raised in the lifestyle to which he thought he should have been accustomed. Burned by the imagined betrayal and irritated by a childhood of living carefully on a cop's salary, my father made it his personal goal to accumulate as much money as possible, to the exclusion of everything else.

He was very, very good at it.

Merit Properties, my father's real estate development company, managed high-rises and apartment complexes throughout the city. He was also a member of the powerful Chicago Growth Council, which was made up of representatives of the city's business community and which advised the city's newly reelected mayor, Seth Tate, on planning and development issues. My father took great pride in, and often remarked upon, his relationship with Tate. Frankly, I just thought that reflected poorly on the mayor.

Of course, because I'd grown up a Chicago Merit, I'd been able to reap the benefits that came with the name—big house, summer camp, ballet lessons, nice clothes. But while the financial benefits were great, my parents, especially my father, were not the most compassionate people. Joshua Merit wanted to create a legacy, all else be damned. He wanted the perfect wife, the perfect children, and the perfect position among Chicago's social and financial elite. Little wonder that I worshipped my grandparents, who understood the meaning of unconditional love.

I couldn't imagine my father was going to be happy about my new vampiric identity. But I was a big girl, so after I washed my face of tears, I got into my car—an old boxy Volvo I'd scrimped to pay for—and drove to their home in Oak Park.

When I arrived, I parked the Volvo in the drive that arced in front of the house. The building was a massive postmodern concrete box, completely out of place next to the more subtle Prairie Style buildings around it. Money clearly did not buy taste.

I walked to the front door. It was opened before I could knock. I glanced up. Dour gray eyes looked down at me from nearly seven feet of skinny white guy. "Ms. Merit."

"Hello, Peabody."

"Pennebaker."

"That's what I said." Of course I knew his name. Pennebaker, the butler, was my father's first big purchase. Pennebaker had a "spare the rod" mentality about child rearing and always took my father's side—snooping, tattling, and generally sparing no details about what he imagined was my rebellious childhood. Realistically, I was probably lower than average in the rebellion department, but I had perfect siblings—my older sister, Charlotte, now married to a heart surgeon and pumping out children, and my older brother, Robert, who was being groomed to take over the family business. As a single twenty-seven-year-old graduate student, even though studying at one of the best universities in the country, I was a second-class Merit. And now I was coming home with a big ol' nasty.

I walked inside, feeling the *woosh* of air on my back as Pennebaker shut the door firmly behind me and then stepped in front of me.

"Your parents are in the front parlor," he intoned. "You are expected. They've been unduly concerned about your welfare. You worry your father with these"—he looked down disdainfully—"*things* you get involved in."

I took offense to that, but opted not to correct his misunderstanding of the degree to which I'd consented to being changed. He wouldn't have believed me anyway.

I walked past him, following the hallway to the front parlor and pushing open the room's top-hinged door. My mother, Meredith Merit, rose from one of the room's severe boxy sofas. Even at eleven p.m., she wore heels and a linen dress, a strand of pearls around her neck. Her blond hair was perfectly coiffed, her eyes pale green.

Mom rushed to me, hands extended. "You're okay?" She cupped my cheeks with long-nailed fingers and looked me over. "You're okay?"

I smiled politely. "I'm fine." Relative to their understanding, that was true.

My father, tall and lean like me, with the same chestnut hair and blue eyes, was on the opposite sofa, still in a suit despite the hour. He looked at me over half-cocked reading glasses, a move he might as well have borrowed from Helen, but it was no less effective on a human than a vampire. He snapped closed the paper he'd been reading and placed it on the couch beside him.

"Vampires?" He managed to make the single word both a question and an accusation.

"I was attacked on campus."

My mother gasped, clutched a hand to her heart, and looked back at my father. "Joshua! On campus! They're attacking people!"

My father kept his gaze on me, but I could see the surprise in his eyes. "Attacked?"

"I was attacked by one vampire, but a different vampire turned me." I recalled the few words I'd heard, the fear in the voice of Ethan Sullivan's companion. "I think the first one ran away, was scared away, and the second ones were afraid I was going to die." Not quite the truth—the companion feared it might happen; Sullivan seemed supremely confident it would. And that he could alter my fate when it did.

"Two sets of vampires? At U. of C.?"

I shrugged, having wondered the same thing.

My father crossed his legs. "And speaking of, why, in God's name, were you wandering around campus by yourself in the middle of the night?"

A spark fired in my stomach. Anger, maybe mixed with a hint of self-pity, not uncommon emotions when it came to dealing with my father. I usually played meek, fearful that raising my voice would push my parents to voice their own long-lived desires for a different younger daughter. But to everything, there is a season, right?

"I was working."

His responsive huff said plenty.

"I was working," I repeated, twenty-seven years of pent-up assertiveness in my tone. "I was heading to pick up some papers, and I was attacked. It wasn't a choice, and it wasn't my fault. He tore out my throat."

My father scanned the clear skin at my throat and looked doubtful—God forbid a Merit, a *Chicago* Merit, couldn't stand up for herself—but he forged ahead. "And this Cadogan House. They're old, but not as old as Navarre House."

Since I hadn't yet mentioned Cadogan House, I assumed whoever had called my parents mentioned the affiliation. And my father had apparently done some research.

"I don't know much about the Houses," I admitted, thinking that was more Mallory's arena.

My father's expression made it clear that he wasn't satisfied by my answer. "I only got back tonight," I said, defending myself. "They dropped me off at the house two hours ago. I wasn't sure if you'd heard from anyone or thought I was hurt or something, so I came by."

"We got a call." His tone was dry. "From the House. Your roommate—"

"Mallory," I interrupted. "Her name is Mallory."

"—told us when you didn't come home. The House called and informed us that you'd been attacked. They said you were recuperating. I contacted your grandfather and your brother and sister, so there was no need to contact the police department." He paused. "I don't want them involved in this, Merit."

The fact that my father was unwilling to investigate the attack on his daughter notwithstanding, my scars were gone anyway. I touched my neck. "I think it's a little late for the police."

My father, evidently unimpressed by my forensic analysis, rose from the couch and approached me. "I've worked hard to bring this family up from nothing. I will not see it torn down again." His cheeks were flushed crimson. My mother, who'd moved to stand at his side, touched his arm and quietly said his name.

I bristled at the "again," but resisted the urge to argue with my father's assessment of our family history, reminding him, "Becoming a vampire wasn't my choice."

"You've always had your head in the clouds. Always dreaming about romantic gibberish." I assumed that was a knock against my dissertation. "And now this." He walked away, strode to a floor-to-ceiling window, and stared out of it. "Just—stay on your side of town. And stay out of trouble."

I thought he was done, that the admonishment was the end of it, but then he turned and gazed at me through narrowed eyes. "And if you do anything to tarnish our name, I'll disinherit you fast enough to make your head spin."

My father, ladies and gentlemen.

By the time I made it back to Wicker Park, I was red-eyed and splotchy again, having cried my way east. I didn't know why my father's behavior surprised me; it was completely in keeping with his principal goal in life: improving his social standing. My near-death experience and the fact that I'd become a bloodsucker weren't as important in his tidy little world as the threat I posed to their status.

It was late when I pulled the car into the narrow garage beside the house—nearly one a.m. The brownstone was dark, the neighborhood quiet, and I guessed Mallory was asleep in her upstairs bedroom. Unlike me, she still had a job at her Michigan Avenue ad firm, and she was usually in the Loop by seven a.m. But when I unlocked the front door, I found her on the couch, staring blankly at the television.

"You need to see this," she said, without looking up. I kicked off the heels, walked around the sofa to the television, and stared. The headline at the bottom of the screen read, ominously, *Chicagoland vamps deny role in murder*.

I looked at Mallory. "Murder?"

"They found a girl dead in Grant Park. Her name is Jennifer Porter. Her throat was ripped out. They found her tonight, but think she was killed a week ago—three days before you were attacked."

"Oh, my God." I dropped onto the sofa behind me, pulled up my knees. "They think vamps did this?"

"Watch," Mallory said.

On screen, four men and a woman—Celina Desaulniers—stood behind a wooden podium.

A swath of print and broadcast reporters huddled before it, their microphones, cameras, recorders, and notepads in hand.

In perfect sequence, the quintet stepped forward.

The man in the middle of the group, tall with a spill of dark hair around his shoulders, leaned over the microphone.

"My name," he said in a wine-warm voice, "is Alexander. These are my friends and associates. As you know, we are vampires."

The room erupted in flashes of light, reporters frantically snapping images of the ensemble. Seemingly oblivious to the flash of the strobes, they stood stoically, side by side, perfectly still.

"We are here," Alexander said, "to extend our deepest sympathies to the family and friends of Jennifer Porter, and to promise to do our part to assist the Chicago Police Department and other law enforcement agencies in any way that we can. We offer our aid and condemn the acts of those who would take human life. There is no need for such violence, and it has long been abhorred by the civilized among us. As you know, although we must take blood to survive, we have long-established procedures that prevent us from victimizing those who do not share our craving. Murder is perpetrated only by our enemies. And rest assured, my friends, they are your enemies and ours, alike."

Alexander paused, but then continued, his voice edgier. "It has come to our attention that a pendant from one of Chicago's Houses, Cadogan, was found at the crime scene."

"Oh, my God," Mallory whispered.

I kept my eyes on the screen.

"Although our comrades from Cadogan House do drink from humans," Alexander continued, "they are meticulous in ensuring that the humans who donate blood are fully informed and fully consenting. And Chicago's other vampires do not, under any circumstances, take human blood. Thus, it is our belief, although only a hypothesis at this early time, that the medal was placed at the scene of the crime solely to inculpate the residents of Cadogan House. To suggest otherwise is unjustified supposition."

Without another word, Alexander fell back in line next to his comrades.

Celina stepped forward. At first, she was silent, her gaze scanning the reporters in front of her. She smiled softly, and you could practically hear the reporters' sighs. But the innocence in her expression was a little too innocent to be believable. A little too forced.

"We are devastated by the death of Jennifer Porter," she said, "and by the accusations that have been leveled against our colleagues. Although Navarre House vampires do not drink, we respect the decisions of other Houses to engage in that practice. The resources of Navarre House are at the city's disposal. This crime offends us all, and Navarre House will not rest until the killer is caught and prosecuted."

Celina nodded at the bank of reporters, then turned and walked offscreen, the rest of her vampires falling in line behind her.

Mallory muted the television and turned back to me. "What the hell have you gotten yourself into?"

"They say the Houses aren't involved," I pointed out.

"She says Navarre isn't involved," Mallory said. "She seems pretty willing to throw the other Houses to the wolves. And besides, vampires were involved when you turned up almost dead. A vampire attacked you. That's too many fangs to be coincidental."

I caught the direction of her thoughts. "You think I'm, what, number two? That I was supposed to be the second victim?"

"You *were* the second victim," she said. She used the remote to turn off the television. "And I think it's an awfully big coincidence that your throat was ripped out on campus. It's not exactly a park, but it's close enough. Look," she said, pointing back at the television.

A picture of Jennifer Porter, a small shot from an ID card, filled the screen. Dark brown hair, blue eyes, just like me.

We shared a moment of silence.

"And speaking of heinous people," Mallory finally said, "how was the visit home?" Mallory had met my parents only once, when I couldn't hold off an introduction any longer. She'd just adopted the blue-hair regimen. Needless to say, they weren't impressed. Creativity, even if benign, was not tolerated in the Merit house. After the one visit, during which Mal had barely avoided socking my father in the jaw, I decided not to force them on her again.

"Not great."

"I'm sorry."

I shrugged. "My expectations were low going in, just not as low as they should have been." I took a long look at the giant leather *Canon* on top of the coffee table, then reached out and pulled it into my lap. "They were concerned, I guess, but mostly I got a lecture about embarrassing the family." I put my hands in the air, waggled my fingers for dramatic effect. "You know, the Chicago Merits. Like that means anything."

Mallory snorted softly. "Unfortunately, it does mean something. You only have to look at the *Trib* to know that. Did you go see your grandpa?"

"Not yet."

"You need to."

"I will," I quickly replied, "when I'm up to it."

"Bullshit," she said, grabbing the cordless phone from its cradle next to the couch. "He's more of a father to you than Joshua ever was. And you know he's always up. Call him." She handed the receiver over, and I clutched it, stared down at the rubbery blue buttons.

"Damn it," I muttered, but punched in his number. I lifted the phone to my ear, clenching my hand to control the shaking, and silently prayed that he could be understanding. The phone rang three times before the machine kicked on.

"Hi, Grandpa," I said at the beep. "It's Merit. I wanted to let you know I'm home and I'm okay. I'll come over as soon as I can." I hung up the phone and handed the receiver back to Mallory.

"Way to be an adult," she said, reaching across the couch to return it to its cradle.

"Hey, I'm pretty sure I can still kick your ass, undead or not."

She snorted disdainfully. She was quiet for a moment, then cautiously offered, "Maybe something good could come from this."

I slid her a sideways glance. "Meaning?"

"Meaning, maybe you could get laid?"

"Jesus, Mallory. So not the point," I said, but gave her points for the hit on my nonexistent dating life. Mallory blamed the cold spell on me, said I "didn't put myself out there." What was that supposed to mean? I went out. I hung out in coffeehouses, went to English department FACs. Mallory and I went out almost every weekend to catch bands, Chicago being a hub for touring indies. But I also had to focus on finishing my dissertation. I'd assumed there'd be time for boys after. I guess I had an (undead) eternity for it now.

Mallory put an arm around my shoulder, squeezed. "Look. You're a vampire now. A *vampire*." She looked me over, took in the Cadogan makeover. "They've definitely improved your fashion sense, and pretty soon you'll have this whole goth-chic-undead thing going on."

I lifted brows.

"Seriously. You're tall, smart, pretty. You're like eighty percent legs." She cocked her head and frowned at them. "I hate you a little for that."

"You've got better boobs," I acknowledged. And just as we'd done each time we'd had this boobs-versus-legs conversation, we looked down at our chests. Ogled. Compared. My boobs were fine, if a little on the small side. Hers were perfect.

"So I do," she finally said, but waved a hand dismissively. "But that's beside the point. The point is, you're great-looking, and although it personally irks you, you're the daughter of Joshua Merit. Everyone knows his name. And for all that, you haven't had a date in, what, a year?"

Fourteen months, but who was counting?

"If you're out there doing your hot new vampire thing, it could open up a new world for you."

"Right, Mal. That's a phone call home I'm gonna make." I raised my hand, arched my fingers to mimic a telephone receiver. "Hi, Dad. It's the daughter you barely tolerate. Yeah, I know you're disappointed I'm the walking undead, but vampire guys are seriously hot." I mimicked hanging up the phone. "No, thanks. I'm not going to date a vampire."

She put her head on my shoulder. "Hon, you *are* a vampire."

I rubbed my temples, which were beginning to throb. "I know, and it sucks. I don't want to talk about this anymore."

Mallory sighed impatiently, but didn't say anything else about it. She pushed back into the couch cushions and tapped the cover of the guide to vampire life, still closed in my lap, with a finger. "So, you're going to read it?"

"I should probably understand the ground rules. And since I have all night . . ."

"Well, I don't have all night." She rose and stretched. "I've got to get some sleep. I've got an early meeting. Have fun with your vampire book."

"Night, Mal. Thanks for waiting up."

"No problem. I'll call U of C tomorrow and let you know what they say about reenrolling." She walked out of the room, but peeked back in, her hand wrapped around the oak doorframe. "Just to review, you're pissed about being made a vampire, and we hate this Ethan Sullivan guy, right?"

I thumbed through the *Canon*'s thick, ancient-looking pages, scrolling through the acknowledgments and table of contents, my drifting gaze stilling when I reached the title of chapter two: "Servicing Your Lord."

"Oh, yeah," I assured her. "We hate him."

I slept on the couch, book in my hands. I'd spent the final hours of the evening, long after Mallory had dragged herself upstairs, poring through the *Canon*. I was wide-awake for the review, the transition to vampire already reversing my sleep schedule, at least until the wave of exhaustion hit me at sunrise. As dawn approached, I could feel the sun creeping up, preparing to breach the horizon. As it rose, so did the weighty drowsiness. What was it that Carl Sandburg had said about fog? That it crept in like a cat? That was how the exhaustion came. It crept in, silent but assuredly there, and covered me like a heavy velvet blanket.

But where falling asleep was incremental, I woke suddenly, finding myself wrapped in an ancient musty quilt. I unraveled my limbs, and looked out to see Mallory on the love seat in jeans and a Cubs T-shirt, staring at me curiously.

"Were you trying to mummify me?"

"There are windows in the room," she pointed out, "and you were too heavy to get upstairs. I leave you exposed to the sun all day and I definitely don't get this month's rent." She rose, walked closer, and looked me over. "No burns or anything?"

I threw the blanket on the floor and surveyed my body. I was still in the slinky cocktail dress, and the parts of skin that showed looked fine, maybe better than they had before the change. And I felt a helluva lot better than I had the night before, the sluggishness having finally cleared. I was now a healthy bloodsucking vampire. Yay!

"Nah," I told her, sparing her the internal monologue. "I think I'm good. Thanks."

Mallory tapped nails against her thigh. "I think we need to spend a little time tonight, you know, checking you out. Figuring out what we're dealing with, what your needs are. Write down stuff you might need."

I lifted my brows skeptically. Mallory was brilliant, without a doubt. Case in point: She'd landed the job as an advertising executive at McGettrick-Combs right after college—literally the day after she graduated from Northwestern. Said Mallory: "Mr. McGettrick, I want to work for your firm." Said grumpy, balls-to-the-wall Alec McGettrick: "Be here at eight a.m. Monday morning."

But Mallory was an idea person, not a detail person, which was probably why she was so valuable to Alec and crew. For her to suggest that I make a list—well, that just wasn't typical Mallory.

"You feeling okay, Mal?"

She shrugged. "You're my best friend. Least I can do." Mallory cleared her throat, looked blankly at the wall. "That said, the refrigerator is now filled with blood that was delivered before you woke up, and there's an eight hundred number on the side to order more." Her mouth twitched, and I could tell she was trying not to laugh.

"Why are you chortling at my food?"

She closed her eyes. "The company that does this vampire delivery thing? It's called 'Blood4You.' Unoriginal much? I mean, they've got a captive audience, but still, take your branding seriously, for Christ's sake. They need a new name, new image, repackaging. . . ." Her eyes glazed over, probably as potential logos and mascots danced in her head to the sound track of the jingle she'd no doubt already conceptualized.

"Never mind," she finally said, shaking her head as if to clear it. "I'm not at work. In more important news, I bought a leather curtain for your bedroom. It's huge, so it completely covers the window. That should give you a safe place to crash, although it totally clashes with the decor." She looked critically around the room. "Such as it is."

When Mallory moved in, she hadn't made any changes to the brownstone beyond divvying up bedrooms, stocking the fridge, and adding electronics. So the decor, such as it was, remained Aunt Rose–ish. The woman took her name seriously, and covered virtually every free surface with flowered doilies or throw rugs. Even the wallpaper was dotted with cabbage-sized roses.

"Again, thanks."

"In case it matters, you were actually sleeping."

I grinned at her. "You checked?"

"I held a finger under your nose. I didn't know if you were breathing, or if you just kind of . . . died. Some books say vampires do that, you know, during the day."

And Mallory, being a student of the occult, would know. If she hadn't been so well-matched to her job at a Chicago ad agency, she would have dedicated her life to vampires and the like—and that was even before she knew they were real. As it was, she put in the time during her off-hours. And now she had me, her own little in-house vampire pet. Vampet?

"It felt like sleep," I confirmed, and stood, laying the book on the floor between us and realizing what I was still wearing. "I've been in this dress for twenty-four hours. I need an excruciatingly long shower and a change of clothes."

"Knock yourself out. And don't use all my conditioner, dead girl."

I snorted and walked to the stairs. "I don't know why I put up with you."

"Because someday you want to be as kick-ass cool as me."

"Please. You're a total fang hag."

Laughter issued from the living room. "We're going to have some serious fun with this."

I doubted that, too, but I'd wallowed enough, so I swallowed my doubts and padded upstairs.

I avoided looking at the bathroom mirror just in case, fearful that I'd find no reflection there, but stood beneath the showerhead until the hot water ran out, cherishing the prickles of heat, and thinking about my new . . . existence? Helen had mentioned the basics—stakes, sunlight, blood—but she'd avoided the metaphysics. Who was I? *What* was I? Soulless? Dead? Undead?

Forcing myself to face at least part of the issue, I brushed a hand over the fogged mirror, praying for a reflection. The steam swirled in the small bathroom, but revealed me, damp and mostly covered by a pink bath sheet, the relief in my expression obvious.

I frowned at the mirror, tried to puzzle out the rest of it. I'd never been explicitly religious. Church, to my parents, was an excuse to show off Prada loafers and their newest Mercedes convertible. But I'd always been quietly spiritual. I tried, my parents notwithstanding, to be grateful for the things I'd been given, to be thankful for the things that reminded me that I was a small cog in a very big wheel: the lake on a moodily cloudy day; the gracious divinity of Elgar's "The Lark Ascending"; the quiet dignity of a Cassat painting at the Art Institute.

So as I shivered, naked and damp, in front of the bathroom mirror, I raised my eyes skyward. "I hope we're still okay."

I got no answer, but then, I didn't really expect one. Answer or not, it didn't matter. That's the thing about faith, I guess.

Twenty minutes later, I emerged downstairs, clean and dry, and back in jeans. I'd settled for a favorite low-waisted pair and teamed it with two thin, layered T-shirts in white and a pale blue that matched my eyes, and a pair of black Mihara Pumas. At three inches short of six feet, I had no need for heels. The only accoutrement missing from the ensemble was the black elastic I kept on my right wrist for hair emergencies. Today, I'd already pulled my dark hair up into a high ponytail, leaving the fringe of straight-cut bangs across my forehead.

I found Mallory downstairs in the kitchen. She sat on a stool at the kitchen island, a Diet Coke on the counter before her, a copy of *Cosmo* in her hands.

"What'd you learn last night in your vampire bible?" she asked, without looking up.

Preparing myself for the retelling, I nabbed a soda from the refrigerator, popped the tab, and slid onto a stool next to her. "Like Helen said, there're twelve vampire Houses in the United States; three in Chicago. The House arrangement is kind of . . . Well, think feudal England. Except instead of a baron, you've got a Master vampire in charge of everything."

"Ethan," she offered.

I nodded my agreement. "For Cadogan, Ethan. He's the most powerful vamp in the House. The rest of the vampires are basically his minions—we have to take an oath to serve him, swear our allegiance, that kind of thing. He even gets a fancy title."

She looked up, brows lifted.

"He's my 'Liege.' "

Mallory tried unsuccessfully to hide a snicker—which ended up sounding strangled and anemic—before turning back to her magazine. "You have to call Darth Sullivan your 'Liege'?"

I grinned. "Only if I expect him to answer."

She snorted. "What else?"

"The Houses are like"—I paused to think of a good analogy—"company towns. Some vamps work for the House. Maybe guards or public relations folks or whatever. They've got administrators, docs who work outside the House, even some historic positions. All of them get a stipend."

"Historic positions?"

I took a sip of my soda. "Ethan has a 'Second,' like a second-in-command or something."

"Ooh, like Riker?"

Did I mention she also loved *Star Trek: The Next Generation*? "Sure. There's also a 'Sentinel,' which is like a guard for the House."

"For the brand?"

I nodded at the apt metaphor. "Exactly. And the House itself is in Hyde Park. Think mansion."

Mallory looked appropriately impressed. "Well. If you're going to be attacked and unwillingly made a vampire, let it be a rich and fancy vampire, I guess."

"That's an argument."

"How many Cadogan vamps?"

"Three hundred and eight nationally. Eighty-six actually live in the House proper. They get dorm rooms or something."

"So these vamps live in a mansion-slash-frat house, and you get a stipend just for having pointier teeth." She cocked her head at me. "How much cash is it, exactly?"

"Decent. Better than TA-ing."

"Minus the free will."

"There is that."

Mal cleared her throat, put the can on the counter, linked her hands together, then looked over at me. I guessed I wasn't going to like whatever confession she was about to make.

"I called the university."

The tone of her voice made my heart sink. "Did you tell them none of this was my choice?"

Her gaze dropped to the counter. "Merit, they don't admit vampires. They don't have to do it legally, and they're afraid of the lawsuits if one of you was to, you know"—she frowned, waved a hand in the air—"with the teeth and the biting. Honestly, if Helen hadn't done it, the university would have dropped you when they found out."

That seed of hatred unfolded, sprouted. "But I wouldn't have told them," I persisted. "How else would they have known? I could have rearranged my schedule, taken night classes. . . ."

Mallory shook her head, handed me, with somber expression, a folded newspaper that lay on the tabletop. It was the morning's *Trib*, open to a page that bore the word "CONGRATULATIONS!" in bold Gothic letters across the top.

I popped the paper open. The banner topped off a full-page ad in the lifestyles section. A list of names, twelve columns of them, a dozen names in each column. The text read: *The North American Vampire Registry congratulates the following new Initiates. May your service be fruitful and fulfilling.*

I scanned the Houses: Navarre, McDonald, Cabot, Cadogan, Taylor, Lincoln, Washington, Heart, Lassiter, Grey, Murphy, Sheridan. My name was listed in the Cadogan column.

My stomach clenched.

"Some reporters called," Mallory quietly said. "They left messages on the machine. They want to talk to you about being a vampire. A Merit vampire."

"Reporters?" I shook my head and chucked the paper back onto the table. "I can't believe this. I can't believe they'd do this. That they'd *out* me." I scrubbed hands across my face, tried to contain the anger that was beginning to well.

"Are you okay?" Mallory asked.

I dropped my hands and looked at her, willing her to understand. "I could have pretended, made sure no one knew. All I had to do was take evening classes, which wouldn't have been so hard. My committee would have worked with me. Goddamn it! I didn't even get a chance to try!"

The fury rose, quick, hot, and strong. It itched beneath my skin like my body was one size too small to contain it. Like my body didn't fit. I rolled my shoulders in irritation, the anger still swelling.

I wanted to hit something. Fight something. *Bite* something. I slowly turned my head, cast a covetous glance at the refrigerator.

"Jesus H., Merit."

I flicked a glance her way. Mallory's eyes were wide, her hands clenched at the edge of the countertop. I heard the quick, flat double-thudding of a drum, and realized it was the thump of her heartbeat.

"What?" I whispered.

She reached out a hand, but snatched it back. "Your eyes. Your irises are completely silver."

I ran from the kitchen to the first-floor bathroom, flipped on the light, and stared at myself. She was right. The blue of my eyes had become gleaming silver, the pupils dilated to pinpricks.

Mallory squeezed into the tiny powder room behind me. "You got angry. It must happen when you get angry."

Angry or thirsty, I silently amended, since I'd just considered drinking blood as a means of stress relief.

"Open your mouth."

My eyes still silver, our gazes met in the mirror. I hesitated for a moment, having to work up the courage for it, knowing what I'd see when I did.

I opened my mouth, saw the fangs that had descended from my upper jaw. My eyeteeth had lengthened, the tips becoming longer, sharper. That must have happened when I'd considered raiding the refrigerator. I'm not sure what it said about who I was now that I hadn't noticed at the time.

I murmured a worried curse.

"Those weren't there before."

"I know," I bit out.

"I'm sorry, but that's wicked fucking cool."

I snapped my mouth shut, and pointed out through a clenched jaw, "Not so cool the first time I get the urge to make you an afternoon snack."

"You wouldn't do that."

Her tone was easy, wholly confident, but I had no such faith. "I hope not."

She picked up a lock of my straight, long hair. "Your hair is darker." She cocked her head at me. "Maybe 'sable,' instead of 'chestnut.' And your skin is paler. You have this kind of . . . undead glow."

I stared at my reflection. She was right—darker hair, paler skin, like the stereotypical vamp.

"What else do you feel? Stronger? Better hearing? Eyesight? Any of that?"

I blinked at my reflection. "I see the same stuff, and my hearing level is the same." I thought of the smells of the house, the richness there. "Maybe a little better sense of smell? And I'm not bombarded or anything, but when I got excited, I could kind of sense new things." I didn't mention the prickle in the air I'd felt around her, or the fact that the new things I could sense included the resounding thud of her heartbeat.

Mallory leaned against the doorframe. "Since my hands-on experience with the walking dead is, like, eighteen hours old, this is just a guess, but I bet there's an easy way to take care of this silver-eyes problem."

This should be good. "And that would be?"

"Blood."

We put it on the island, along with a martini glass, an iced tea glass, a food thermometer, a bottle of Hershey's chocolate syrup, and a jar of olives, both of us unsure how best to attack. Mallory jabbed the bag with the blunt end of a bamboo skewer. It gurgled, and the depression in one side of the medical-grade plastic slowly filled back in. She made a sound of disgust and looked at me with sympathetic eyes. "Jesus, Merit."

I nodded and looked down at the bag of type O. It was one of the seven that had been delivered. There was one of each type—A, B, AB and O—and three extra bags of O. It was supposed to have universal appeal, I guessed.

"Liquid, liquid everywhere and not a drop to drink," I observed.

"Ugh. English lit geek much?"

"Corporate oppressor."

"Nerd."

"Blue-haired weirdo."

"Guilty as charged." She picked up the iced tea glass and handed it to me. "Now or never, Merit. She said you needed a pint every other day."

"I'm kind of assuming that's an average. You know—four pints a week, give or take, averaging to one every other day. And I probably had one before they dropped me off yesterday. So I don't really need to open it until tomorrow."

Mallory frowned at me. "You don't want to even try it? It's blood, and you're a vampire. You should be ripping at the plastic with those sharp-ass teeth just to get to the stuff." She held up the bag between two fingers, waggled it in the air. "Blood. Yummy, delicious blood." The crimson liquid shuffled back and forth in the bag as she waggled it, making little waves in a tiny, self-contained ocean. And it was making me seasick.

I put a defensive hand over my abdomen. "Just put the bag down, Mallory."

She did, and we stared at it for another few minutes until I looked up at her. "I think I'm just not hungry for it. Surely it would be more appealing if I really, really wanted it."

"Are you hungry for anything?"

I scanned the library of cereal boxes on top of the refrigerator, the stash owing in part to Mallory's preparations for the rumored vampire apocalypse. "Hand me the box of Chunkee Choco Bits. The marshmallow kind."

"Done and done," she said, and slid off her stool. She went to the refrigerator, reached up, grabbed the box, and walked back to hand it over. I opened and reached into it, grabbing a handful of cereal, then picking through it to get to the marshmallows, which I popped into my mouth. "None for you?"

"Mark's coming over," she carefully said, "if that's okay with you."

Mark was Mallory's sweet but aimless boyfriend. I gave them two more weeks. "Fine with me. Make him bring Chinese. But if he annoys me, I'll probably have to bite him."

She rolled her eyes. "Vampire bitch."

I shrugged and picked through another handful of cereal. "I'm just warning you, I'm probably going to be a total hard-ass vamp."

Mallory snorted and walked out of the kitchen, calling out, "Yeah, well, you've got a purple marshmallow on your chin, hard-ass vamp."

I peeled it away and, between my thumb and index finger, flicked it into the kitchen sink. Stuff like that was going to ruin my reputation.

At twenty-five, Mark Perkins decided he wanted to swim the English Channel. At twenty-six, he decided he wanted to climb Everest. Then it was Machu Picchu, base-jumping, ghost-hunting in New Orleans and racing the Utah salt flats. Unlike Mallory, who rarely planned, Mark planned with a vengeance.

He just never actually *did* anything.

Tall and thin with short brown hair, he blew through our front door like a tempest, arms laden with guidebooks, maps, and two paper bags with greasy bottoms.

"Chinese!" Mallory squealed, leaping to the door when he came in. She pecked his cheek, grabbed a bag of food, and headed to the kitchen. I'd been reading again, so I returned the book to its spot on the coffee table.

He nodded in my direction, dumped his own books on the love seat, and followed Mallory. "Merit."

"Hi, Mark." I gave him a little finger wave and rose from the couch, but I paused before following him to check his literature. On the couch, their glossy, mountain-pictured labels read: *The Greatest Adventure Book Ever*, *Climbing for Dummies*, and *Your Big, Fat Swiss Adventure*. The Matterhorn, apparently, was next on Mark's list. Poor, sweet, dumb Mark.

"She's gone fang, Mark," Mallory called out. "So be careful."

Halfway to the kitchen, Mark stopped midstride and turned to face me, grinning like an idiot. "Kick. Fucking. Ass."

I rolled my eyes and snatched the remaining bag of Chinese. "Kick your own ass. Did you get crab rangoon?"

He frowned. "What do vampires need with crab rangoon?"

We moved into the kitchen. I put the bag on the kitchen counter and picked through it until I found the paper box of fried crab-and-cream-cheese-stuffed dough and a container of sweet-and-sour sauce. I popped them both open, dipped a wrap in the sauce, and bit in. They were still hot—and I groaned happily at the taste: sweet, salty, crispy, creamy. Everything a newly changed vampire could want.

"Orgasms, apparently," Mallory snarked, and pulled out her own containers of food. She pulled one open, then broke open a set of chopsticks, stared into the container, pulled out a chunk of broccoli, and munched.

"So, how long have you been the walking dead?" Mark asked.

Mallory choked. I thumped her, ever so helpfully, on the back.

"I'm on day two," I told him, and pulled out another bit of fried wanton heaven. "So far, it's been uneventful."

Famous last words, those.

We'd been eating about ten minutes when we heard glass shatter in the front of the house. Our heads snapped up at the sound. We stood simultaneously, but I motioned Mark and Mallory back down. Mallory's eyes widened, and I guessed what she'd seen: My blood hummed with adrenaline, and I knew my eyes had gone silver.

"Stay here," I told them, and walked across the kitchen. I flipped off the overhead light and moved into the unlit hallway. There were no other sounds in the house, and I didn't hear anything outside—cars revving, people screaming, sirens blaring. Carefully hugging the walls, I crept into the living room. The living room window—a picture window made up of a single sheet of glass—had been shattered from the outside in. A brick lay on the floor, wrapped in white paper, a breeze fluttering one corner of it. First things first, I thought, ignoring the missile to pick my way across the glass to the front door and check the peephole. The yard was empty and quiet. It was dark out, so theoretically our attackers could have been hiding in the shrubbery, but I knew no one was there. I could kind of . . . tell. There were no sounds, no smells, no indications that anyone had been near the house beyond the light, acrid scent of car exhaust. They'd driven by, done the deed, and moved on.

I went back to the brick, reached down to pick it up, and pulled away the band of paper. In scraggly black script, it read:

Think U/R 2 good 4 us, Cadogan bitch?
Next time U die.

The threat was clear enough, and I guessed that I now qualified as the "Cadogan bitch." But "too good for us" stumped me. It sounded like a choice—like I'd chosen Cadogan out of the catalog of vampire Houses. It was profoundly untrue, and a good clue—the vandal didn't know me, at least not well enough to understand how inaccurate the statement really was. How little choice I'd had.

Mark's voice rang out. "Merit?"

I looked up, found them huddled in the doorway, and felt my chest tighten protectively. It took me a moment—a surprising one—to realize that the tingle in my limbs wasn't fear, but adrenaline. I beckoned them forward with a folded hand. "It's okay. You can come in. Just watch the glass."

Mallory stepped carefully into the room, tiptoed through the fragments. "Jesus. The window—what happened?"

"Holy crap," Mark agreed, surveying the damage.

Mallory looked up at me, eyes bright with fear. "What happened?"

I handed her the note. She read it, then met my gaze. "You're the bitch?"

I shrugged. "I assume so, but I don't understand the threat."

Mark walked to the door, opened it slowly, and looked

outside. "Nothing else out here," he called out, "just some glass." He drew back in, his gaze moving between us. "You've got some plywood or something I could hang over the window?"

I looked to Mallory, who shrugged. "There might be something in the garage."

He nodded. "I'll go check. I'll be right back."

When the front door shut behind him, Mallory looked down at the note in her hands. "Do you think we should call the cops?"

"No," I told her, remembering my father's admonition. But an idea dawned. I took the note back from her and stuffed it into my pocket. "I think we should go to the House."

Ten minutes later, Mark was balancing on the edge of the stoop, securing an old sheet of particleboard over the window, and Mallory and I were pulling the car out of the garage, Hyde Park address in hand. Mark wasn't thrilled that Mallory was planning to visit a den of vampires in the middle of the night, but I think that stemmed mostly from the fact that he hadn't been invited to tag along. His blusters about her safety didn't read sincere given the awestruck expression on his face.

To mollify him, we promised to keep our cell phones in hand. Apparently thinking extra precautions were warranted, Mark ran down the driveway as we pulled out, and when Mallory rolled down the passenger-side window, he stuffed a good-luck charm into her hands.

"What's this?" she asked him.

"Garlic." He slid a glance to me, then winged his eyebrows at Mallory. *"Vampires,"* he whispered through a tightly clenched jaw, as if the movement of his lips was the Rosetta stone that was gonna key me into his secret code.

"I can still hear, Mark," I reminded him.

He blushed and shrugged apologetically. Mallory shook the plastic take-out container of organic prepeeled garlic and held it beneath my nose. I sniffed, waited for a reaction, and when nothing happened, shrugged.

"I'm not sure Whole Foods is what Buffy had in mind, hon, but thanks for the thought." She blew a kiss to Mark, and we watched him return to his station at the window. As I pulled the Volvo out of the driveway, Mallory threw the plastic bin into the backseat. "I'm not sure how long this thing with Mark is going to last."

"Huh," I remarked, trying to remain supportively neutral. "Not going well?"

"He's well-meaning, I guess, and we have fun." She shrugged. "I don't know. There's just not much there—beneath the camaraderie, I mean."

I nodded. "I get that."

She waved a hand in the air. "More important issue at hand." She swiveled in her seat to face me. "Before we hit Hyde Park, I want to be sure what we're doing. Are we going to kick vampire ass, or are we just going to ask about this death-threat issue?"

I gnawed the inside of my lip as I considered her question. We were walking into a nest of trouble, and had only ourselves—an ad executive and a not-quite-two-day-old vampire—as weapons. And while Mallory spent an hour in the gym every day, and I had ten years of ballet lessons and a lot of jogged miles under my belt, I doubted either of those would help significantly. They certainly hadn't helped a few days ago.

"We're going to talk to them calmly and rationally," I decided.

"And you're not going to tell Darth Sullivan you reject his fascist assumption of authority?"

I stifled a laugh. "Maybe not at this first meeting, no."

Traffic was light; the drive didn't take long. Mallory served as navigator, checking the directions we'd printed off the Web. "We're getting close," she finally said, and instructed me to turn left. When we reached the address, we gaped.

"Oh, my God."

"I know. I see it." I parallel parked in an empty slot on the street—between a Beemer and Mercedes, incidentally—and we got out of the car. The House, and it was a mansion, took up a whole block. The building was surrounded by an intricately wrought, ten-foot-high, black iron fence. The interior of the fence was lined with shrubs and hedges, so the lawns were shielded from public view. The House itself was gigantic, three pale limestone stories leading to a slate mansard roof. There was a turret on one corner and tall rectangular windows ringed the floors. Gabled dormer windows and widows' walks gave the top floor a Gothic look. But overall, while the building was imposing and the lot larger than those nearby, it looked at home beside its Hyde Park neighbors.

Well, except for the vampire thing.

Mallory squeezed my hand. "You ready?"

"No," I admitted. "But I need to do this."

We followed the sidewalk to a gap in the iron fence where two black-clad men stood, swords belted at their sides. Both were tall and lean, with long, straight dark hair, tied back tightly. They looked alike, the guards, their just-this-side-of-gaunt facial features fraternally similar.

The one on the left whispered something into his mouthpiece, then touched his earpiece, and finally nodded at me. "You can go in," he told me, then shifted his gaze to Mallory. "But she can't."

Easy decision. "She goes, or I don't."

He turned his back on us, and I heard faint whispering as he touched the headset again. When he turned back again, a nod was the only affirmation we got.

As we walked up the sidewalk, Mallory took my hand and squeezed it. "Chatty fellows. They had swords."

Not just swords, I thought, glancing back at the lean, slightly curved scabbards and long, straight handles.

"I think they're katanas." These were the swords of the samurai, a fact I'd learned while researching weaponry for my dissertation. Although I was interested in the romantic side of medieval literature—think Lancelot and Tristan—the genre was heavy on the war and weapons.

"Do you think you'll get a sword?"

"What the hell would I do with a sword?" We reached the front door, which was unguarded. The portico that covered it was arched, and four symbols, the lowest one a stylized "C," hung above the door.

"Hmm," I said. "Knock or just go in, do you think?"

We were saved the decision. The door was opened by a tall, exquisitely handsome man with caramel-colored skin. His hair was short, his eyes a pale green. He wore a black suit that was perfectly fitted to his frame, and a crisp white dress shirt beneath. He extended a hand. "Malik."

This was the second vampire. Not the one who turned me, but his colleague.

"Merit," I said, taking his hand. "And Mallory."

His nostrils flared as he looked at Mallory, and his brows lifted. "Magic?"

Mallory and I looked at each other. "I beg your pardon?" I asked. He didn't respond, but moved aside to let us enter.

The interior of the House was as impressive as the outside. Contrary to what I'd expected—black tulle, leather furniture, red candles, pentagrams—the House was very tastefully decorated. Actually, it looked like a five-star hotel. The floors were gleaming wood, the high ceilings girded by ancient beams of thick oak. The decor—lots of inlaid woods, urns of flowers, carefully selected lighting—was sophisticated and French-inspired. Malik escorted us past one parlor and into another.

"Stay here," he instructed in a tone that brooked no argument. We obeyed, Mallory and I standing shoulder to shoulder in the doorway so we could survey the room. Ten or so men and women, all dressed in trendy black suits, milled around, some with PDAs in hand, others on couches perusing laptop computers. I felt incredibly gauche in jeans and a T-shirt, especially when their gazes began to fall on Mallory and me.

"New girl," Mal whispered. "It's like your first day at school."

I nodded. "Feels like that."

"Do you think he's in here? Sullivan, I mean?"

I looked around, which was futile. "Maybe?" I offered. "I don't know what he looks like." I hadn't gotten a good look at his face when he bit me, and if he'd been there while I was recuperating, I had no memory of it. I had an inkling that he belonged to the distinctly green eyes I remembered, but that was only a hunch.

"Use your spidey sense."

I chuckled. "Even if I had a spidey sense, I wouldn't know how to use it."

A voice suddenly echoed through the parlor—louder than the quiet whispering of the working vamps. "That's fine, Celina. I appreciate your calling me."

The words belonged to a man with a cell phone at his ear who'd stepped into the doorway on the opposite side of the long room. He was tall, two or three inches over six feet, and lean like a swimmer—narrow waist, broad shoulders, long legs. His hair was straight, shoulder-length, and golden-blond. His face was chiseled—knife-edge cheekbones and a firm jaw, his brow strong, his lips worth calling home about. He was dressed in a black suit that fit his body like a glove, beneath which was an impeccably white dress shirt, top button unclasped, no tie.

"He's prettier than Beckham," Mallory breathlessly whispered. "Jesus."

I nodded in silent agreement. He was incredibly handsome.

The blond was accompanied by an equally attractive redhead, her skin luminously pale. She wore only a slim burnt orange cocktail dress, the toes of her bare feet painted red. Her arms were crossed over her chest, and while she stood intimately close to the blond, she scanned the room with an almost mechanical precision. She looked around, saw Mallory and me, and tensed. Then she leaned toward the blond and whispered something. He raised his head, a lock of golden hair across his brow, and looked up.

Our gazes locked. He stared, and I stared back.

A chill raced up my spine, an eerie premonition of something I couldn't quite discern. Vampires definitely had some sort of spidey sense, and mine was sending up flares—enormous, fiery flares that put the Fourth of July fireworks at Navy Pier to shame. I pushed down the sensation and the disturbing, burgeoning sense of familiarity. I didn't want him to be familiar. I didn't want him to know me, to know who I was, to have taken part in my change. I wanted this beautiful man to be new to the House, a regular vampire doing a hard night's work for the Master he secretly loathed. I wanted him to approach me, introduce himself, be pleasantly surprised that I was a vampire and that I'd just joined his cool kids' club.

I couldn't tear my eyes away. I stared. He stared back, lips parted in shock or surprise, his knuckles white around the file folder he held in his free hand.

The rest of the room stilled and quieted as the vampires watched us, probably waiting for cues—*Should we jump the new girl? Mock her for wearing jeans and sneaks? Welcome her into the ancient brotherhood of vampires with a pancake breakfast and mixer?*

Making some decision, the blond snapped his cell phone shut and walked toward us, his stride confident and swift. Each step seemed to make him more handsome—his perfectly sculpted features coming into sharper relief.

Before that moment, before watching him walk toward me, I'd been a normal girl. If I saw a boy I found attractive, I might smile. I might, on the rare occasion, say hello or give someone my phone number. I wouldn't say I was forward, but I made a move when I was interested. But something about this boy, maybe mixed with the fact that I'd recently become a vampire, made every molecule in my body tingle. I wanted to sink my fingers into his hair and push my lips against his. I wanted to claim him for my own—the rising of some deep-seated, instinctual need. Time seemed to speed up, to zip by, my body driving me toward a fate my head didn't understand. My heart thudded, hammerlike inside my chest, and I could feel the blood rushing through my veins.

Mallory leaned toward me. "FYI, your eyes are silver. I'll just add 'horny' to the list of reasons that happens."

I nodded absently.

My beautiful blond moved closer, until he stood in front of me, until, looking up, I could see the color of his eyes.

They were a deep, translucent, emerald green.

Impossibly green.

And as my heart sunk, I realized, *familiarly* green.

"Shit," was all I could think to say.

Our rangy Beckham look-alike was my sworn enemy.

CHAPTER THREE

YOU GOTTA FIGHT FOR YOUR RIGHT.

"Merit?"

Pulled from my fantasy by the sudden flood of adrenaline, I clenched my hands into fists. I'd heard about the fight-or-flight instinct—the animalistic drive to dig in and fight for survival or to run away, seek shelter or cover. Before tonight, it had always been an abstract construct. Biological trivia. But I felt it after the attack on our house, and as I faced Ethan Sullivan for the first time, I felt it intimately. Some previously absent part of my psyche awoke and began to evaluate surroundings, to debate whether to set heel to the ground and get as far away from him as possible, or face him, stand against him, and even if the effort was doomed, to see what I was made of.

This was one of those moments, I thought, one of those make-or-break moments that set the direction of your life, that remind you about courage and free will.

I felt a nudge at my ribs, and heard a fierce whisper. "Merit!" I looked beside me, where Mallory stood, eying me curiously. "Are you okay? Ethan was just saying hello. Did you have something you wanted to say to him, maybe regarding an eath-day eat-thray?"

I slid my gaze back to Ethan, who watched me cautiously,

then let my focus shift to the vampires, who stood at attention in the room. They'd stopped tapping the keys of their PDAs and were outright staring. Without looking at him, I asked, "Can we speak privately?"

He paused, apparently surprised, and then said in a voice smooth enough to send a second chill down my spine, "Of course."

His hand at my elbow, Ethan escorted me through the crowd of gaping vampires, back into the hallway, and then into the room next door. It was an office, masculine and well-appointed. His office. To the right was a sizable oak desk; to the left was a seating area of brown leather furniture. At the end of the room was a long, oval-shaped conference table, which stood just before a bank of windows covered by navy blue velvet curtains. Both side walls were lined with built-in shelves covered in books, trophies, photographs, and memorabilia.

Mallory followed us in, and Ethan closed the door. He waved his hand in invitation at two chairs that sat in front of his desk, but Mallory moved to the shelves at the far end of the room and, hands crossed behind her back, began to peruse the mementos. She gave us privacy without leaving me alone with him. Appreciating the gesture, I remained standing.

Ethan crossed his arms and gazed at me expectantly. "Well? To what do I owe the pleasure, Merit?"

I stared at him blankly for a moment, trying to remember why I thought visiting the Hyde Park office of a Master vampire was a good idea, when my mouth, which apparently wasn't privy to the internal debate, suddenly blurted out, "I didn't give you permission to change me."

Ethan stared at me for a moment before turning his head. He walked away, moving with self-assurance to the leather chair behind his desk. For all the tailored clothes and impeccable looks, his power was obvious. He fairly hummed with it, and while his movements were crisp and elegant, they hinted at something darker, something menacing beneath the surface—a shark arcing below deceptively smooth water.

He shuffled papers on his desk, then crossed his legs and looked up at me with those obscenely emerald eyes. "Frankly, that's not what I expected to hear. I was hoping for something along the lines of 'Thank you, my Liege, for saving my life. I do so enjoy being alive.' "

"If saving me had really been your goal, you could have taken me to a hospital. A doctor could have saved me. You unilaterally decided to make me something else."

He furrowed his brow. "Do you think the vampire who bit you first intended to let you live?"

"I didn't have a chance to ask him."

"Don't be naive."

I'd seen the press conference about Jennifer Porter's death, knew about the similarities between our attacks. So, unable to argue that point, I made another. "My life will never be the same."

"Yes, Merit," he said, frustration in his voice, "your human *life* will never be the same. It was, regrettably, taken from you. But we've given you another."

"It should have been my decision."

"I was a little short on time, Merit. And given that you are fully aware of the choice I had to make, this petulant attitude is beneath you."

I didn't disagree, but who was he to tell me that? My throat constricted with emotion. "Excuse me for not having adjusted to the fact that my life has been turned upside down. Excuse me for not reacting to that with grace."

"Or gratefulness," he muttered, and I wondered if he knew he'd been loud enough for me to hear him. "I gave you a life. And I made you like me. Like the rest of your brothers and sisters. Are we such monsters?"

I wish I could have said yes. I wanted to say yes, to feign horror.

But a tear ran down my cheek, propelled by some combination of rage and guilt that I wasn't as repelled by Ethan Sullivan as I'd planned to be. I wiped away the tear with the back of my hand.

Ethan looked at me for a long time, and I could read the disappointment in his eyes. It bothered me, that disappointment, more than I cared to admit.

He steepled his fingers together on the desk, leaned forward. "Then perhaps I made a mistake. Cadogan House was allowed twelve new vampires this year, Merit. That makes you one-twelfth of my allotment. Do you think you were worth it? Do you think you can contribute to Cadogan in sufficient measure to repay that investment? Was my bringing you into the House a better decision than saving someone else to whom I might have given a new life?"

I stared at him, the value of the gift he'd given me, however much I hadn't wanted to become one of them, sinking in. I slid into the chair before me.

Ethan nodded. "I thought that might do it. Now, your objections to having been changed have been duly noted. So for the moment, what say we move on? I don't want that between us, even if you have decided I'm your mortal enemy." He lifted brows in challenge. I didn't bother to deny it.

I paused, then asked, "Duly noted?"

Ethan smiled knowingly. "Noted and recited in front of a witness." His gaze flicked to the corner of the room, and he gazed at Mallory with curiosity. "I haven't met your companion."

"Mallory Carmichael, my roommate."

Mallory glanced up from the thick book she was perusing. "Yo."

"And your backup, I presume," he said, rising and walking to a bar tucked into the bank of bookshelves on the left side of the room. He poured amber-colored liquor into a chubby glass and watched me over the rim as he sipped its contents. "I've met your father."

"I'm sorry to hear that."

He cradled the glass in his hands. "You aren't close to your family?"

"My father and I don't get along. We have different priorities. He's solely focused on building his financial kingdom."

"While Merit's not," Mallory offered from her corner. "She's perfectly happy dreaming about Lancelot and Tristan."

"Lancelot and Tristan?" he asked.

Embarrassed at the love-struck-teen implication, I stammered out, "I am—was—working on my dissertation. Before."

Ethan finished his drink and put the glass on the bar, then leaned back against it, arms crossed. "I see."

"Honestly, I doubt that you do. But if you hoped changing me would help you access Merit money, you're out of luck. I don't have it—either the money or the access."

Ethan looked momentarily startled, and didn't meet my gaze when he pushed off the bar and moved back to the desk. When he was seated again, he frowned at me—not in anger, I thought, but in puzzlement. "What if I said that I could give you things? Would that ease the transition?"

Across the room, Mallory groaned.

"I'm not my parents."

I was the recipient of another long stare, but this one held a glimmer of respect. "I'm beginning to see that."

Finally finding my footing—he may have been a vampire, but he was subject to human prejudices just like everyone else—I relaxed back into the chair, crossing my legs and arms, and arching a brow at him.

"Is that what you thought? That I'd see the Armani and the Hyde Park address, and I'd be so excited I'd forget that I hadn't consented?"

"Perhaps we've both misjudged the situation," he allowed. "But if there's such animus in your family, why do you go by 'Merit'?"

I glanced over at Mallory, who was picking a bit of lint from one of the heavy velvet curtains that lined the windows.

She was one of only a handful of friends who knew the entire story, and I wasn't about to add Ethan Sullivan to that group.

"It's better than the other option," I told him.

Ethan seemed to consider that before averting his gaze to a pile of papers on his desk. He shuffled them. "And you aren't undead. You aren't undead, or the walking dead, and *Buffy* isn't a reliable anatomical resource. You didn't die that night. Your blood was taken and replaced. Your heart never stopped beating. You're better now, genetically, than you were before. A predator. The top of the food chain. I've made you an immortal, assuming you manage to keep out of trouble. If you follow the rules, you can have a long, productive life as a Cadogan vampire. Speaking of, did Helen give you everything you need? You received a copy of the *Canon*?"

I nodded.

"Have you had blood yet?"

"Bagged blood was delivered to the house, but I haven't had any. To be honest, it didn't look that appetizing."

"You got plenty during the transition, so the thirst hasn't hit you yet. Give it another day. You'll want it badly enough when First Hunger strikes." Ethan's lips tipped up, and he smiled. It was a little disarming—that smile. He looked younger, happier, more human. "Did you say bagged blood?"

"That's what was delivered. Why is that funny?"

"Because you're a vampire of the Cadogan line. You can drink directly from humans or other vampires. Just don't kill anyone."

I put a hand across my stomach, as if the touch could still the greasy wave that suddenly rolled through it. "I'm not going to bite someone. I don't want to drink at all, bagged or otherwise, people or not. You can't just go around and"—I waved a hand in the air—"chew on people."

Ethan clucked his tongue. "And to think—we were so close to having a normal conversation. Merit, you're an adult. I suggest you learn to accept your circumstances, and quickly.

Like it or not, your life has changed. You need to come to terms with exactly who you are."

"I know who I am," I assured him.

A golden eyebrow winged upward. "You know who you *were*. I know who you are, Merit, and who you'll come to be."

"And what is that?"

His face was completely, serenely confident. "Mine. My vampire. My subject."

The possessiveness called my anger, and it rose, flowered and rushed across my body with a warmth that curled my toes. That warmth was delicious, and yet the emotion felt strange—separate, somehow. As if it wasn't my anger, but an anger inside me. Whatever the source, it was pervasive, strong, and thrilling.

I stood up and asked him, my voice huskier, lusher, "Would you like to test that theory?"

Ethan's gaze dropped to my lips, and he wet his own, but when he responded, seconds later, his tone was chill. Composed. The tone of Master-subduing-rebellious-peon. "You forget yourself, Initiate. You're two days old. I've three hundred and ninety-four years. Do you really want to test your mettle against me?"

I wasn't completely stupid. I knew my answer to that question should have been a resounding no. But that didn't stop my body, which I was beginning to learn was operating on a completely different frequency from the rest of my brain, from responding with all the bravado it could muster, "Why not?"

A heavy silence descended, the only sound penetrating it the solid thud of my heart. Ethan pushed back his chair. "Come with me."

"What did you just do?"

Mallory and I followed Ethan back through the first floor of Cadogan House.

"I don't know," I whispered back. "Vampire Merit's a lot braver than People Merit."

"Yeah, well, you better figure out a way to reconcile the genetics, 'cause Vampire Merit just landed you in some serious shit."

We took a right, descended a flight of stairs, and followed Ethan through another hallway to a set of antique wooden doors. The room we entered was huge and bright, the center of its wooden floor covered with a set of tatami mats. Half the height of the twenty-foot-high walls was covered in gleaming wood; the remainder, up to an overhanging balcony supported by massive wooden columns, showcased an impressive collection of antique weaponry, including swords, maces, bows, axes, and wicked-looking knives.

This was a room for sparring.

It took a moment for the implication to settle in.

"You're kidding, right?" I asked, turning to him. "You can't actually think I'm going to fight you?"

Ethan regarded me coolly and began unbuttoning his shirt. Question answered, I thought, and averted my eyes after the first peek of toned chest.

I walked into the middle of the floor, thinking I'd feel better if I had a better grasp on my surroundings. Ethan's arsenal was impressive—a set of crossed pikes, blue ribbons hung from their ends; a hefty broadsword; a black wooden shield bearing a golden oak tree, the acorns painted red; rows of unsheathed katanas.

"Experience?" Ethan called out behind me.

"Ballet and jogging. And whatever extra strength two days of being fanged will give me." I made the mistake of turning around just as he was pulling the button-up shirt over his head. My mouth went dry. His shoulders were broad and perfectly sculpted, as was the rest of his torso. His chest was firm, his stomach flat and lean, dotted only by the pucker of navel and a thin line of dark blond hair that disappeared into the waist of his trousers. Around his neck was a thin gold chain, on which hung a tiny oval of gold with a design stamped into it. It looked like a saint's medal, although I doubt any saints would have approved of a Master vampire wearing it.

Ethan caught me staring and lifted a brow, and I looked quickly away. Mallory yelled my name, waving me frantically toward where she stood at the edge of the mats. When I reached her, she shook her head at me.

"You cannot seriously think you're going to fight this guy. He could kick your ass with one arm tied behind his back, much less with all his voluminous vampire powers. He's probably stronger than you, faster than you. He can probably jump higher. Hell, he can probably glamour you into making out with him right there on the mats."

We simultaneously looked over to where Ethan, half naked, was toeing off black leather loafers. The muscles in his abdomen clenched as he moved. So did the lines of corded muscle across his shoulders.

God, but he was beautiful.

I narrowed my gaze.

Beautiful but evil. Wicked. The repugnant dregs of foul malevolence. Or something.

"Jesus," Mallory whispered. "I want to support your quest for revenge and all, but maybe you should just let him glamour you." She looked at me, and I could tell she was trying not to laugh. "Either you're fucked, or you're *fucked*, right?"

I rolled my eyes at her. "You're not helping."

The shuffle of footsteps rang through the room. We looked up. Vampires were filling the balcony, all dressed in black, all throwing hateful looks at me and Mallory. As I took in their obvious disdain, the weight of the risk I'd taken settled into my bones. According to the aptly named *Canon*, vampire society was based on antiquated notions of feudalism, including unfailing loyalty to a House and its Master. I'd walked into my House—into Ethan's House—spouted off, and challenged him to a fight. Twenty-seven years of trying to live under my parents' radar, of never causing enough trouble to raise their notice, and I'd made two very big mistakes in a matter of days. Walking across campus had nearly killed me. Challenging Ethan . . . Well, we'd find out soon enough.

"Probably this wasn't the best decision I've ever made," I admitted.

"No," Mallory agreed, but when I looked at her, her eyes shone bright with appreciation. "But it's ballsy. And you've needed to make a ballsy decision."

"Just a minute ago you said—"

"Forget it. I know what I said," she interrupted. "I've changed my mind. Geniuses are entitled. This is the right thing to do. This is the new Merit." She hugged me quickly, then stepped back. "Kick his ass, dead girl."

Ethan joined us and made a gallant bow. When he straightened again, he clucked me beneath the chin. "Don't lose that courage now, Initiate."

"It wasn't *my* courage—the vampire challenged you."

"You *are* the vampire, Merit, now and forever. But sometimes the mind needs a chance to catch up with the genetics," he allowed.

I cast a worried glance to the balcony. "I hope that happens soon."

He chuckled. "I'm not going to hurt you, and despite the fact that you've broken virtually every rule in the *Canon*, I'll make you a deal."

I faced him again, forced myself to meet his green eyes, despite the trembling of my hands. "What?"

"If you manage to land a blow, I'll relieve you of your obligations to me."

It was the opposite of what I'd have predicted—which was something of the "If you survive this, I'll let you heal before punishing you for challenging me" variety. By those standards, it was a good deal, if improbable-sounding. I searched his face, not sure if he was serious. "How do I know you'll keep your word?"

Ethan lifted his gaze to the balcony of vampires above us. "They know."

When our gazes met again, I nodded. I handed the crumpled death threat, which I'd been too busy being stupid to bring up, to Mallory, tugged at the bottom of my T-shirt, and followed Ethan into the middle of the room. He turned and bowed slightly. "One hit. That's all you need to do."

With no further ado, he kicked, an elegant roundhouse that would have brought his bare foot across my face had I not fallen back. I hit the mat on my back, my breath rushing out with the impact.

As I lay there, the gallery tittering above me, I wasn't sure which scared me more: the fact that he'd nearly kicked me in the face, or the fact that I'd been fast enough to avoid it.

I *had* changed.

"Nice reflexes."

I looked up to find Ethan a few feet away, peering down at me curiously. He wasn't the only one with questions. I wondered how much more I could do, so I pushed my palms flat behind me, brought up my legs, rolled back, and popped onto my feet in a quick bounce.

"Very nice."

I shrugged off the compliment, but I was thrilled by the motion. I hadn't danced classically in years, but I'd always relished the few seconds of being airborne in a *grand jeté*—the brief sensation of fighting gravity . . . and winning. This was similar, but infinitely more satisfying. My body felt even lighter, sprightlier than when I was in top dancing form. Maybe there were advantages to being a vampire.

I grinned back at Ethan. "Just taking her for a test spin." Then I circled, looking for a weakness. Ethan bounced on the balls of his feet and crooked his hand at me in invitation. "Then let's see what you can do."

Someone started music, and Nine Inch Nails' "The Hand That Feeds" spilled into the room.

"Apropos," he muttered, and crooked his hand again.

NIN was an interesting choice for a nearly four-hundred-year-old vampire. Whatever his issues, I couldn't fault his taste in music.

Back to the challenge at hand, I tried a punch. I swung forward, rotating my wrist as I tried to catch him in a jab, but he avoided it, followed the motion of my hand, and swung his leg into a low sweep that nearly brought my feet out from under me. But I jumped just in time and arched my back into a handspring, which put me a few feet away and out of his range.

Or so I thought, until he rushed forward so quickly, the motion was blurred. I flipped back again, then again, the motion nearly effortless, but he kept coming. When I popped up the last time, I instinctively crouched, which put the cross he'd directed at my jaw out of range. He struck air, and I reached out arms to grab his knees, but he flew over me, landing behind me with a gentle thud.

I pushed to my feet again and turned to see him grinning wildly, his eyes blazing green. "I'm impressed. Let's do it again." Then his expression went solemn, and he bounced on the balls of his feet and crooked a hand again in invitation. Rolling my eyes at the *Matrix* replay, I tried a butterfly kick. I'd once seen a kickboxing instructor try it, but as a human I hadn't had the power or stretch to execute it.

Being a vampire changed the rules. Now I had the strength to push myself into the air and swing my legs around, to spin my body horizontally.

Still, Ethan's reflexes were faster than mine, so I missed him again. He threw his torso back nearly 180 degrees, all the while keeping himself upright, and completely avoided my extended legs.

"So close," he offered breathily.

"Not close enough." But I grinned when I said it, thrilled that I'd managed the move. It pleased the crowd, too, and they hooted appreciatively. "Careful, Liege!" someone called out. "She might scar that pretty face."

Ethan laughed good-naturedly. "God forbid," he told the gallery. "Then I'd only have fabulous wealth and canny instincts to rely on." The vampires chuckled together, and he tipped his head up to smile at the crowd.

That was my chance, and I took it. Ethan was distracted, so I rushed him, but the sneaky bastard anticipated my move. He edged to the left just before I could take him down. I braced my arms to hit the ground as I flew past him, but before I made contact, he grabbed my arm, spun me around midair, and pushed me to the ground. I landed flat on my back with Ethan above me, his body stretched atop mine. He neatly captured my wrists in his hands and pushed them—despite my squirming—to the mat above my head.

The crowd erupted into catcalls and lewd suggestions.

"You baited me!" I accused.

His lips scant inches from my face, he smiled wolfishly. "And so easily." I squirmed, but he pushed me harder against the mat and slid a knee between mine. "Initiate, you can guess exactly where that's going to lead."

I growled in irritation.

At least, I told myself it was irritation, and not at all the fact he smelled delicious, a clean combination of linen, cotton, and soap. Not the fact that the weight of his body on mine felt completely natural—a languid heat suddenly flowing through my chest, like the union of our bodies had closed a circuit.

I tried to tune out the sensation and, embarrassed at the silvering of my eyes—I have to admit, I had a sudden, new sympathy for men faced with hiding their arousal—I squeezed them shut. Ethan let me calm, and when I finally opened my eyes, his face was blank.

"Do you agree that you failed to land a blow?"

I paused, but nodded. "Unless you're willing to give me a freebie?"

For a heartbeat, his gaze dropped to my lips. I wondered if he'd kiss me, if he thought about it, if he felt the pull like I did. But he looked away, then loosened my wrists and pushed himself up. He offered me a hand, which I took, and let him pull me to my feet . . . to the boos and general disappointment of the peanut gallery.

"Is this why you came?" he asked when we were both upright again. "To fight me?"

Mallory must have heard the question over the mumbling of the crowd, as she stepped forward, the note in her outstretched hand. "We came for this."

Ethan wiped his brow with the back of a hand, then took the note. He read it, his expression blanking. "Where did you get this?"

"It was wrapped around a brick that was thrown through our living room window," I said.

His gaze snapped up. "Were you hurt?" He scanned my body, looking for injuries.

"We're fine. There were three of us in the house, and we're all fine."

"Three?"

"Mallory's boyfriend was there."

"Ah."

I thumped the note with a finger. "What's this about? Is there a vampire war I don't know about? Did changing me piss someone off?"

He frowned as he perused the note again. "Perhaps your initial attacker is bitter about not having finished the job, or about my having finished it for him. We believed he, the one who bit you, was a Rogue—a vampire living outside the House system. The note would suggest that's true. It's also possible there's a connection between your attack and the attack that killed Jennifer Porter."

It wasn't the first time I'd considered that connection, but the idea was more unnerving coming from his lips. It gave legitimacy to the possibility that I was the intended victim of a vampire-turned–serial killer. But it also raised other questions.

"You know, it's quite a coincidence that you were trolling across campus at the same time I was attacked by a vamp."

He lifted deeply green eyes to mine. "There was a considerable amount of luck involved."

We looked at each other for a moment.

"Ethan," I softly said, "you didn't kill Jennifer Porter, did you?"

His lashes fell, crescents of long, dark blond against golden skin. "No, I didn't kill her. Nor did anyone from my House."

I wasn't sure if I believed him, although I had no reason to doubt his honesty, not when he'd dealt with me, even I could admit, generously. I'd openly challenged the head of my House, and all I'd suffered for it was a little embarrassment before a cadre of vampires I didn't know. I opened my mouth to ask about the note, but before I got anything out, something set off the gallery. They began to yell down at us, the general consensus being that I deserved a beating.

"Liege!" one yelled. "You can't let her get away with challenging you!"

He raised his gaze to his vampires. "You're right. I'll send her to her room without dessert and take away her cell phone!"

The crowd snickered, but Ethan raised a hand again, and as if he was conducting the symphony of their voices, they quieted immediately. Whatever my issues with his authority, they were clearly much less reticent.

"Friends, she made a good-faith effort to best me. And since she hasn't yet taken the oaths, she hasn't"—he glanced at me—"*technically* breached the *Canon*. Besides, she rose a mere two days ago, and nearly managed to catch me. She will make an undeniably important addition to the House, and we all know how . . . delicate our alliances are."

There were fewer titters now, mixed with reluctant nods.

"More important, she came here in fear for her life." He held up the note. "She rose a mere two days ago, and she's been threatened."

The redhead who'd accompanied him in the parlor stepped to the edge of the balcony. "Are you sure she hasn't brought war to us, my Liege?"

If I had any question as to what she was to him, her cannily cocked hip and bedroom eyes were answer enough. Girlfriend. Lover. Consort, if we were sticking with feudal terms. I expected to see Ethan's emerald eyes on her lush curves, but when I turned back to him, his gaze was on me, his smile cocky, like he knew I'd been appraising his mistress.

I shrugged. "She seems nice enough, if you like the busty, voluptuous, gorgeous type."

"Much to my dismay"—and that rang clear in the irritably flat tone of his voice—"I find I have a sudden taste for stubborn, lithe brunettes with horrible fashion sense."

He might as well have been parroting lines from *Pride and Prejudice*, for all the disdain that rang through his voice, his obvious aversion at being attracted to a woman so déclassé. Self-conscious again of my casual clothes—but cognizant of the fact that I looked good in them—I managed not to tug at my T-shirt or jeans. Instead, I slipped thumbs into my belt loops and tapped fingers against my flat hips. Ethan watched the movement intensely. When his eyes lifted again, I arched an eyebrow. "Not even in your dreams, Sullivan."

He only grunted in response.

I smirked.

The door to the sparring room opened, and Malik entered with a tall man. This one wore his slacks and dress shirt with discomfort, and from the strong set of his jaw, broad shoulders, and tousled sun-kissed hair, I guessed he'd be more comfortable in jeans and cowboy boots. I let my gaze drop, checked his shoes. Sure enough, they were black alligator with silver-tipped toes. Called that one.

It also occurred to me that I hadn't yet seen an unattractive vampire. They were all fit, tall, impeccably groomed, undeniably handsome. Flattering, I guess, that they'd made me one of them, unless you thought too hard about the circumstances.

Ethan approached the men and handed over the note. They reviewed it in turn, chatting and occasionally glancing over at me and Mallory. She linked an arm through mine.

"I've decided this is going to be a treat to watch."

I slid her a dubious glance.

"I've known you for three years. That entire time, you've been puttering around the little ivory tower you built for yourself. You need to be rescued. And if you can't be rescued by Prince Tall, Sexy, and Alive"—she looked over at the trio of deliberating vampires and scanned Ethan's half-naked body—"he's certainly the next best thing." She made an evil-sounding chuckle. "And you complained about your oral exams. This boy's gonna be the biggest challenge of your life."

"Calling him a 'challenge' assumes I'm interested. And I wasn't puttering around. I was writing a dissertation."

"You're interested," she declared. "And given that possessive look in his eyes, I'd say he's interested, too."

"He thinks I'm unsophisticated."

She looked over at me. "You're you. Unapologetically you. And he can't do any better than that."

I kissed her cheek. "Thanks, Mal."

"Yup." She released me and ogled the threesome of vamps, who stood in a tight knot in front of us, discussing our fate. Then she rubbed her hands together. "Now. Which one do I get? How about Cowboy Pete?"

I was saved formulating an answer (which, incidentally, would have been something along the lines of "Don't you have a boyfriend?") by Ethan, who motioned us closer with a single crooked finger. When we reached the group, he gestured to his comrades. "Malik, my Second, who I believe you've met, and this is Luc, Captain of my Guards." He motioned toward us. "Merit, two-day-old Initiate, and Mallory, her roommate, who likely has the patience of a saint."

Mallory chuckled, the traitor, but then got exactly what was coming to her. Although Malik and Luc nodded in greeting, Luc then frowned down at her from his towering six feet and change.

"You have magic."

Mallory blinked. "What's that now?"

Ethan ran a finger delicately over her hair as she flinched beneath it. "Ah," he said, nodding. "I'd wondered."

"Wondered what?" she asked.

"Who brought in the magic," Malik said so casually you'd have thought he was discussing the weather.

Mallory put hands on her hips. "What the hell are you people, and I use that term loosely, talking about?"

Luc inclined his head toward Mallory, but looked at Ethan. "Is it possible she doesn't know?"

"Doesn't know what?" I asked, irritation rising. "What the hell is going on?"

As if I hadn't spoken, Malik shrugged at Luc. "If she's not union yet, it's possible the Order hasn't yet picked up on her postadolescence. This is Chicago, after all."

"True," Ethan said. "We should call the Ombud, tell him there's a new witch in town."

"New witch?" Mallory asked, paling. "Time out. Who's a witch, hoss?"

Ethan glanced at her, brow arched, and his tone couldn't have been more bland. "You, of course."

While Mallory came to terms with that little revelation, Ethan and his staff filled me in on the current state of vampire relations in Chicago. While most vampires in the world—all the registered vampires—were affiliated with Houses, a minority were categorized as Rogues, vampires who had no ties to a House and no loyalty to a particular Master. There were a number of ways this could happen—being bitten by a vampire who wasn't a Master and thus wasn't strong enough to command the newly changed; by defecting from a House; or by being bitten by an unaffiliated vampire who required no oaths of loyalty or fealty.

Because of the implicit danger they posed to the House structure, they were treated as outcasts. And because they were rarely strong enough individually to take on House vampires, they were usually ignored by the Houses unless they'd chosen, somewhat ironically, to band together into anarchistic units.

Chicago's vamps believed Jennifer Porter's death was the work of a Rogue, maybe one unsatisfied with living in the shadow of Chicago's Houses. This possibility posed two problems.

First, humans didn't know Rogue vampires existed. They knew about the Houses, and seemed to take some comfort in the fact that vampires were organized into political bodies, were supervised by their Masters, and lived by a code—the *Canon.* That was a kind of existence that humans could relate to. And that was why vamps were tight-lipped about Rogues, about the fact that vampires with no House ties, no supervision, and no laws were living in their midst.

Second, as the vamps in the press conference had pointed out, a Cadogan medal, identical to the one Ethan (and, I belatedly realized with a glance around the room, the rest of the Cadogan vamps) wore snug around his neck, had been found at the site of Porter's death. Ethan was confident no one from his House was involved, and he'd agreed to cooperate fully in the Chicago Police Department's investigation. The CPD had interviewed him, and he'd agreed to interview each and every vampire in residence at Cadogan House to assure himself and the CPD detectives that his House, and his vampires, were innocent. He suspected, as did the representatives of Navarre House with whom he'd spoken (including Celina Desaulniers, its Master), that a Rogue was to blame for Porter's death. But that didn't explain *why* she'd been killed, especially since the Greenwich Presidium, the organization that regulated vampires in North America and Western Europe, would mete out its own punishment to the offender. Before the death of Jennifer Porter, the possibility of death-by-aspen-stake had been strong enough to protect humans. Now—who knew?

Whoever the perpetrator, the threesome believed my attack was the second attempt by the killer, and the note evidence of his bitterness at having failed to kill me.

"My name was in the paper today," I reminded them, "so the person who threw the brick wasn't necessarily the one who bit me."

"But it was only your last name," Malik said. "It's doubtful he'd have been able to figure out who you were simply because of that."

Ethan shook his head. "She's a Merit. For better or worse, as often as the family appears in the papers, he'd have been able to figure out which Merit was involved. Robert and Charlotte are older and have children. They're not the typical candidates for change."

Disturbing, I thought, that he knew so much about my family. "But if he meant to kill me," I asked, "why the note? The language suggested a choice, like I picked Ethan over the vampire who attacked, picked Cadogan over whatever group he was affiliated with. If he was going to kill me, why would it matter?"

Luc frowned. "So maybe this isn't related to the Porter girl's death?"

"Maybe it is, and maybe it isn't," Ethan unhelpfully pronounced. "Without more information, we can't discount either possibility. What we do know is that we were the second vampires at the scene of the attack. The language of the threat suggests that whatever plans had been made for Merit—death or otherwise—they'd been unable to follow through. They blame that on her and, to a more general extent, us. Given the tone of the note, maybe the House system more generally."

"So we're definitely thinking Rogues, then," Malik summed up, "or a House with some unspoken animosity toward us. Grey?"

Luc snorted. "Opening day was last week. Scott's attention is on completely different things right now, namely the Cubs' chance at a pennant. It's unlikely he'd be involved in this even if they cared about House politics, which they don't. What about Navarre?"

Ethan and Malik shared an undecipherable glance. "Doubtful," Ethan said. "As old and prestigious as Navarre is—"

"Or so they think," Malik interjected.

With an amused expression, Ethan finished, "Navarre would have little to gain from warring with us. Celina's strong, the GP loves her, and she's positioned herself as poster child for Chicago vampires. There's simply no reason for her to worry about Cadogan."

"Which means we've got investigating to do," Luc concluded.

Ethan nodded at me. "Luc will station sentries at your house. We'll continue looking into the threat, and perhaps as we gain information about the Porter death, we'll learn more about this. If you see anything suspicious, or if you're attacked again, call me immediately." He pulled a card from his trouser pocket and handed it to me. It read, in tidy block letters:

CADOGAN HOUSE

(312) 555-2046

NAVR NO. 4 | CHICAGO, IL

"NAVR number four?" I asked, card between my fingers.

"That's our registry number," Malik explained, and I remembered the NAVR tag under the announcement in the *Sun-Times*. "We were the fourth vampire House established in the United States."

"Ah." I slid the card into my pocket. "Thanks. We'll call if something comes up."

"Not that this visit hasn't been educational," Ethan said, eyes on Mallory, "but we need to get back to work. I believe we've had plenty of excitement for one evening." He dismissed Malik and Luc and motioned us toward the training room door.

The gazes of the vampires we passed still edged toward hostility, but at least they were tempered with curiosity. On the other hand, I'm not sure if that was better or worse; I generally preferred staying under the radar of people-sucking predators.

Or I would have, if I'd given that kind of thing any thought.

Ethan escorted us back through the House. When we reached the front door, he put a hand on my arm. "Mallory, could I have a word with Merit, please?"

"It's your pitch," she replied, and bounced through the doorway to the steps below.

He looked at me. "My pitch?"

"It's a soccer thing. What did you need?"

His mouth tightened into a grim line, and I could tell he was preparing to speechify. "What happened tonight is unusual," he said. "For an Initiate to challenge a Master is virtually unheard of, as is the Master not punishing an individual who has challenged his or her authority. I'm giving you a break because you didn't choose to rise as a vampire, because our laws mandate consent, and you weren't in a position to offer it." He gazed down at me with frigidly green eyes.

"That said, should you ever pull a stunt like this again, you will be disciplined. If you ever raise a hand to me again, you'll rue that decision. I am the Master of this House and in command of three hundred and eight vampires. They look to me for protection, and they give me their loyalty in exchange for it. Should any not understand that bargain, I'm fast, I'm strong, and I'm willing to demonstrate those qualities. Next time, I won't pull my punches. Do you understand what I'm telling you?"

The chill in his glare tamped down my instinct for sarcasm. I nodded.

"Good." He held out his hand toward the sidewalk, inviting me out of the House. "You have five days yet before the Commendation. The *Canon* will explain the oaths, the ceremony and the manner in which I will call you to service. Prepare yourself."

Giving him another acquiescent nod, I stepped down to the sidewalk.

"And do something about your clothes," he ordered, just before closing the heavy oak door behind me.

We silently walked back to the car, where I found a club flyer beneath my windshield wiper. I lifted the wiper, scanned the sheet, which advertised Red, a club in River North. I got into the car, unlocked Mal's door, and stuffed the flyer into the glove box. Partying wasn't really on my agenda right now.

The ride back home was quiet as we both, I imagine, mulled over the night's events. I certainly did, especially the enigma of Ethan Sullivan. For the few seconds I hadn't known who he was, I'd been awed by his face and form, intrigued by his nearly tangible sense of power and determination.

Thinking he was pretty was one thing. Infinitely more disconcerting was the fact that after I discovered who he was—and even knowing what he'd taken from me—I could admit to a lingering attraction. His arrogance was irritating, but he was handsome, intelligent, and respected by his subjects. Ethan wore his power—his mantle of confident self-possession—as well as his designer clothes. But danger, I knew, lurked underneath that perfect facade. Ethan demanded complete and utter loyalty with no exceptions and, it seemed, had little willingness to compromise. He was skilled, strong, fast, limber, and confident enough to prove his mettle against an unknown opponent in front of a gallery of observers. And while he might have found me attractive—his flirting was proof enough of that—he wasn't thrilled about the attraction. Quite the opposite—he seemed as eager to be rid of me as I was of him.

For all that, I hadn't been able to banish the memory of my first glimpse of him. An after-image of green irises ghosted across my retinas when I closed my eyes, and I knew nothing would wipe away the visual. The impact had been that strong—like a crater furrowed into my psyche, leaving an empty space that a mortal man seemed unlikely to fill.

I muttered a curse when I realized the anatomical direction that line of thought was headed, and renewed my attention to Chicago's dark streets.

Mallory cleared her throat. "So that was Ethan."

I turned the Volvo down a side street as we neared home. "That was him."

"And you're thinking what?"

I shrugged, unsure how much I wanted to admit to my feelings, even to Mallory. "I should hate him, right? I mean, he did this to me. Changed everything. Took away everything."

Mallory stared out the car window. "You were due for a change, Merit. And he saved your life."

"He made me the walking undead."

"He said you aren't dead. It was just a genetic change. And there are benefits, whether you want to admit them or not."

Just a genetic change, she'd said, like it was a small, simple matter. "I have to drink blood," I reminded her. "Drink. Blood."

Mallory slid me an unpleasant glance. "At least be honest about it—you can drink whatever you want. You eat whatever you want, and you'll probably never gain an ounce on those mile-long legs. Blood's just a new"—she waved a hand in the air—"vitamin or something."

"Maybe," I allowed. "But I can't put toe one in the sun. I can't go to the beach, or drive around with the top down."

And then something incredibly disturbing occurred to me. "I can't go back to Wrigley, Mallory. No Cubs games on a warm Saturday afternoon."

"You're Irish way back. You get splotchy in the sun, and you haven't been to Wrigley in, what, two years? You'll watch the Cubbies from your bedroom television set, just like you always do."

"I can't go back to school. And my family hates me."

"Hon, your parents have always been horrible. At least this way," she gently said, "you get to feed them a steady diet of inappropriate vampire behavior."

Pleasant as that thought was, it didn't completely assuage the grief. I knew I needed to buck up, to let go of what I'd lost and find a way to survive, to thrive, in my new world. But how do you let go of a lifetime of plans? Of assumptions about your life, about who you were and who you were going to be?

While Mallory was more than willing to dole out advice and urge me to get over "my little quibbles" about having been made a vampire, she wouldn't discuss the trio's bizarre conclusion that she'd brought magic to Cadogan House, that she was a witch. I knew nothing about magic beyond what I'd learned from television and in the tidbits Mallory, in her fixation with the occult, managed to slip into conversation. And it scared me that my normally chatty roommate was avoiding the discussion. So, as I pulled the car into the garage, I tried again.

"Do you want to talk about the other thing?"

"As far as I'm concerned, there is no other thing."

"Come on, Mallory. They said you have magic. Do you feel like you're . . . different? I mean, if they're right, you must have felt something."

She got out of the car and slammed the door shut, and I winced on the Volvo's behalf as Mallory stormed to the sidewalk. "I don't want to talk about it, Merit."

I closed the garage door and followed her, both of us ignoring the black-clad guards who flanked the front door. They were virtually identical to the guards who stood point at the Cadogan gate, tall and gaunt with sleek swords at their sides. Whatever Ethan's faults, he was damn efficient.

We went into the house, which was comfortingly quiet and, present company excluded, vampire-free. Mallory faked a yawn and trudged toward the staircase. "I'm going to bed."

"Mallory."

She stopped at the bottom stair, turned, and looked at me with very little patience. "What?"

"Just—try to be careful. We don't have to talk about it now, but if this threat thing continues, or if Ethan learns anything more about who you are . . ."

"Fine."

As she started up the stairs, desperate to comfort her as she'd done for me, I threw out, "This could be a good thing, Mallory. You could have some special powers, or something."

She stopped and glanced back, her smile sardonic. "Given how I feel right now, I can only assume that my giving you the same bullshit platitudes earlier didn't help you, either." She walked up the stairs, and I heard the slam of her bedroom door. I went to my room and lay on my back on the double bed, staring at the rotating ceiling fan until dawn claimed me.

CHAPTER FOUR

THE THINGS THAT GO BUMP IN THE NIGHT . . . ARE PROBABLY REGISTERED VOTERS IN COOK COUNTY.

Having avoided my granddaughterly duty for two days, when I rose at sunset the next evening to an empty house, I showered, dressed in jeans and a fitted T-shirt that bore the image of a ninja (and certainly would have embarrassed Ethan), and drove to the West Side to my grandfather's house.

Unfortunately, even fight-happy Vampire Merit feared rejection, so I'd been standing on his narrow front stoop, unable to make myself knock, when the door opened with a creak. My grandfather peered out through the aluminum screen door. "You weren't going to come by and talk to your pop?"

Tears—of doubt, of relief, of love—immediately spilled over. I shrugged sheepishly at him.

"Ah, jeez, baby girl. Don't start that." He pulled open the screen door, held it open with his foot, and opened his arms. I moved into them, clenched him in a fierce hug. He coughed. "Easy now. You've got a little more push in those muscles than the last time we did this."

I released him and wiped the tears from my face. "Sorry, Grandpa."

He cupped my face in his bear-paw hands and kissed my

forehead. "No worries. Come on in." I moved into the house and heard the closing of both doors behind me.

My grandfather's house—once my grandparents' house—hadn't changed in all the years I remembered it. The furniture was simple and homey, the walls adorned with family pictures of my aunts and uncles—my father's brother and two sisters and their families. My aunts and uncles had endured their upbringing with significantly more grace than my own father, and I envied their easy relationships with their children and my grandfather. No family was perfect, I knew, but I'd take imperfection over the farce of my social-climbing parents any day.

"Have a seat, honey. You want some cookies? I've got Oreos."

I grinned at him and sat down on the floral sofa. "No, thanks, Grandpa. I'm fine."

He sat on an ancient recliner positioned kitty-corner to the sofa and leaned forward, elbows on his knees. "Your father called me when the House called him." He paused. "You were attacked? Bitten?"

I nodded.

He looked me over. "And everything's okay now? You're okay?"

"I guess. I mean, I feel okay. I feel the same, except for the vampire part."

He chuckled, but his expression sobered fast enough. "Do you know about the attack on Jennifer Porter? That it was similar to your attack?"

I nodded again. "Mallory and I saw the press conference on television."

"Sure, sure." My grandfather started to speak, but seemed to think better of it. He was silent for a moment, the ticking of the wall clock the only sound in the house. He finally raised concerned eyes to mine. "Your father has asked that the police not be involved in your attack. But your name was in the paper, so the city will know that you were changed. That you're a vampire now."

"I know," I told him. "I've already gotten calls from reporters."

My grandfather nodded. "Of course. I would have expected that given your father's notoriety. Frankly, Merit, I'm not going to hinder a police investigation, not for crimes of this magnitude. I can't in good conscience do that, not when a killer is still out there. But I have enough pull to keep the nature of your transition under wraps but for a select few detectives. If we can limit access to that information, keep it on a need-to-know basis, you won't be called out as a potential victim of this killer. We can keep the press from hounding you about it, and you can learn to live as a vampire, not just as an attack victim. Okay?"

I nodded, tears beginning to well again. Say what you wanted about my father, but I loved this man.

"Now that said, while I'm not going to parade you through a bureau office, we still need an official interview for the record." He put a gnarly hand on my knee. "So why don't you tell me what happened in your own words?"

My grandfather, the cop.

I gave him the entire tale, from my walk across campus to my conversation with Ethan, Luc, and Malik, including their Rogue-vampire hypothesis. The general public may not know about the Rogues' existence, but I wasn't about to hide that fact from my grandfather. When I was done, he asked thoughtful questions—essentially walking me through the entire few days again, but this time pulling out details Ethan, Luc, and Malik hadn't discussed, like the fact that the attacker bailed upon seeing Ethan, apparently aware of who he was and unwilling to risk a one-on-one confrontation. When we'd walked through the events twice, he sat back in his recliner and scratched what little hair remained on the perimeter of his head. For all that his mind was impeccably sharp, he looked so much the grandpa—tucked-in flannel shirt, twill trousers, comfortable thick-soled shoes, gleaming pate.

He sat forward again, elbows on his knees. "So the Cadogan folks have concluded that Porter's death is connected to your attack?"

"I think they're willing to consider it a possibility."

After nodding thoughtfully, Grandpa rose and disappeared into the kitchen. When he returned, there was a manila folder in his hand. He sat down again and opened it, then flipped through some documents. "Twenty-seven-year-old white female. College educated. Brunette. Blue eyes. Slim build. She was attacked just after dusk, walking her dog through Grant Park. Her blood was drained, and she was left for dead." His pale blue eyes, which matched mine in color, watched me intently. "There are undeniable similarities."

I nodded, not thrilled that Grandpa agreed with Ethan's conclusion. But what was worse, the first vampire probably had meant to kill me. Which meant I was supposed to be his second victim and would have been—death by exsanguination in the middle of the quad—had Ethan not come along.

I really did owe Ethan for saving my life.

And I really didn't want to owe Ethan anything.

My grandfather reached out and patted my knee with a large callused hand. "I'd really like to know what you're thinking right now."

I frowned and picked a fingernail against the nubby fabric of the couch. "I'm alive. And I really do have Ethan Sullivan to thank for it, which is . . . disturbing." I looked up at my grandfather. "Someone was gunning for me. Because I look like Jennifer Porter? If so, why send the brick through my window? This guy wanted me dead, maybe for himself, maybe on someone else's behalf. And he's still out there." I shook my head. "Vampires coming out of the closet was bad enough. The city is not going to be prepared for this."

Grandpa patted my hand again, then rose from his chair

and grabbed a jacket that lay across its arm. "Merit, let's go for a drive."

My grandfather, the man who cared for me for much of my childhood, announced to the family four years ago, following the death of my grandmother, that he was taking partial retirement. He told my sneering father that he was off the streets and would instead man a desk in the CPD's Detective Division, helping the active detectives with unsolved homicides.

But as we drove south in his gigantic Oldsmobile—think red velveteen upholstery—he confessed that he hadn't exactly told us the truth about his role with the CPD. He was still working for the city of Chicago, but in a wholly different capacity.

As it turned out, when vampires came out of the closet those eight months ago, my grandfather wasn't the least bit surprised.

"Chicago has had vamps for over a century," he said, hands at ten and two as he drove through the city's dark streets. "Navarre's been here since before the fire. Of course, the administration hasn't been in the know that long, only a few decades. But still, the Daleys knew about you. Tate knows about you. There aren't many in the upper echelon who don't." Eyes on the road, he leaned slightly sideways. "By the way, Mrs. O'Leary's cow had nothing to do with it."

"All that time and no one thought to tell the city that vampires were living among them? All that time, and no leaks? In Chicago? That's kind of impressive, actually."

My grandfather chuckled. "If you think that's impressive, you'll love this. Vamps aren't even the tip of the supernatural iceberg. Shape-shifters. Demons. Nymphs. Fairies. Trolls. The Windy City has pretty much every entry in the sup phone book. And that's where I come in."

I glanced over at him, brows raised. "What do you mean, that's where you come in?"

My grandfather started to speak, but stopped himself. "Let me start at the beginning?"

I nodded.

"All these supernatural contingents—they have disputes, too. Sniping between the Houses, fairy defections, boundary disputes among the River nymphs."

"Like, the Chicago River?"

My grandfather turned the car onto a quiet residential street. "How do you think they get the river green for St. Pat's?"

"I'd assumed dye."

He huffed out a sardonic sound. "If it were only that easy. Long story short, the nymphs control the branches and channels. You have River work to do, you call them first." He held up a hand. "So you see, this isn't just domestic disputes and petty theft. These are serious issues—issues the majority of the boys in blue don't have the training, the experience, to deal with. Well, Mayor Tate wanted a way to funnel these issues down to a central location, a single office. Folks who could handle the disputes, take care of things before they could affect the rest of the city. So four years ago, he created the Ombudsman's office."

I nodded, remembering Ethan's reference. "Ethan mentioned that, said something about having Mallory talk to the Ombud. They think she has magic. That she's a witch or something."

Grandpa made a sound of interest. "You don't say. Catcher will be interested to hear that."

"Catcher?" I asked. "Is he the Ombudsman?"

My grandfather chuckled. "No, baby girl. I am."

I froze, turned my head to stare at him. "What?"

"The Mayor likes to call me a 'liaison' between the regulars and the sups. Personally, I think 'liaison' is a bullshit bureaucrat word. But the Mayor asked me to serve, and I said yes. I'll admit it—I never came across any vamps or shifters when I walked the beat, and I was curious as all get out to meet these folks. I love this city, Merit, and don't mind making sure everybody gets a fair shake."

I shook my head. "I don't doubt that, but I don't know what to say about the rest of it. You were retired, Grandpa. You told us—you told me—that you were retired."

"I tried retirement," he said. "I even tried a stint in the evidence locker, a desk job. But I was a cop for thirty years. I couldn't do it. Wasn't ready to give it up. Cops have lots of skills, Merit. We mediate. We problem solve. Investigate." He shrugged. "I just do it for some slightly more complicated folks now. I started at a desk in City Hall, and now I have my own staff."

He explained that he'd hired four people. The first was Marjorie, his secretary, a fifty-year-old woman who'd become battle-hardened by twenty-five years of staffing phones in one of the city's more crime-ridden police bureaus. The second was Jeff Christopher, a twenty-one-year-old computer prodigy and, as it happened, a shape-shifter of as-of-yet-unidentified shape. The third was Catcher Bell. Catcher was twenty-nine and, my grandfather said, gruff. Warned my grandfather: "He's pretty, but he's wily. Give him a wide berth."

"That's only three," I pointed out when my grandfather paused.

Silence, then, "There's a vampire. Housed, but his colleagues don't know he works for me. He avoids the office unless absolutely necessary. They do the groundwork," my grandfather continued, "so all I have to do is step in and play good guy." I doubted he was as uninvolved as all that, but—especially in contrast with my father—the humility was refreshing. "You won't believe this," he said on a gravelly chuckle, "but I'm not as spry as I used to be."

"No!" I exclaimed, feigning shock, and he laughed in response. "I can't believe you've been keeping this from us. I can't believe you've been playing with magic for four years and didn't tell me. *Me!* The girl who wrote about King Arthur for a living."

He patted my hand. "It wasn't you that I was trying to keep the information from."

I nodded in understanding. My father's discovery of my grandfather's secret would have led to one of two results: arranging to have my grandfather fired or trying to manipulate my grandfather to get closer to the Mayor. Ever scheming was my father.

"Still," I said, watching through the window as the city passed by, "you could've told me."

"If it makes you feel any better, I'm now *your* Ombudsman. And I'm taking you to our secret headquarters."

I looked over at him, watched him try unsuccessfully to hide a smile. "Secret, huh?"

He nodded, very officially.

"Well, then," I said. "That makes all the difference."

The office of the Ombudsman was a low, unassuming brick building that stood at the end of a quiet block in a middle-class neighborhood on the city's South Side. The houses were modest but well tended, the yards surrounded with chain link fence. My grandfather parked the Olds along the curb, and I followed him up a narrow sidewalk. He tapped buttons on an alarm keypad on the wall next to the door, then unlocked the front door with a key. The interior of the building was equally unassuming, and looked like it hadn't gotten a style upgrade since the late 1960s. There was a lot of orange. A *lot* of orange.

"They work late," I noted, the interior well lit, even given the hours.

"Creatures of the night serving creatures of the night."

"You should put that on your business cards," I suggested.

We walked past a reception area and down a central hallway, then into a room on the right. The room housed four metal desks that were placed at intervals, two back-to-back set out from each facing wall. The front and back walls were covered by rows of gunmetal gray filing cabinets. Posters lined the white walls, most of gorgeous, scantily clad women with flowing hair. The prints looked like they were part of a series: Each featured a different woman wearing a tiny scrap of strategically placed fabric, but the "dresses" were cut in different colors, as were the pennants they held in their hands. One woman was blond, her dress blue, and she held a pennant that read "Goose Island." A second had long, raven-dark hair and was dressed in red. Her pennant read "North Branch." These, I surmised, were some of the Chicago River nymphs.

"Jeff. Catcher."

At my grandfather's voice, the men who sat at two of the desks looked up from their work. Jeff looked every bit the twenty-one-year-old computer prodigy. He was fresh-faced and cute, a tall, lanky guy with a mop of floppy brown hair. He wore trousers and a white dress shirt, unbuttoned at the top, the sleeves rolled halfway up his lean arms, long fingers poised over an expansive set of keyboards.

Catcher had a solidly ex-military look about him—a muscular body beneath a snug olive T-shirt that read "Public Enemy Number One" and jeans. His head was shaved, his eyes pale green, his lips full and sensuous. Had it not been for the annoyed look on his face, I'd have said he was incredibly sexy. As it was, he just looked disgruntled. Wide berth, indeed.

Jeff grinned happily at my grandfather. "Hey, Chuck. Who's this?"

My grandfather put a hand at my back and led me farther into the room. "This is my granddaughter, Merit."

Jeff's blue eyes twinkled. "Merit Merit?"

"Just Merit," I said, and stuck out a hand. "It's nice to meet you, Jeff."

Rather than reaching out to take my outstretched hand, he stared at it, then looked up at me. "You want to shake? With me?"

Confused, I glanced back at my grandfather, but before he

could answer, Catcher, his gaze on a thick ancient-looking book in front of him, offered, "It's because you're a vamp. Vamps and shifters aren't exactly friendly."

That was news to me. But then, up until twenty minutes ago, so were the existence of shifters and the rest of Chicago's supernatural citizens. "Why not?"

Catcher used two fingers to turn a thick yellowed page. "Aren't you the one who's supposed to know that?"

"I've been a vamp for three days. I'm not really up on the political nuances. I haven't even had blood yet."

Jeff's eyes widened. "You haven't had blood yet? Aren't you supposed to have some kind of crazy thirst after rising? Shouldn't you be, you know, seeking out willing victims for your wicked bloodlust?" His gaze made a quick detour to the stretch of T-shirt across my chest; then he grinned up at me through a lock of brown hair. "I'm O neg and completely healthy, if that matters."

I tried not to grin, but his enthusiasm over my notably unbuxom chest was endearing. "It doesn't, but thanks for the offer. I'll keep you in mind when the wicked bloodlust hits." I looked around for a chair, found an avocado green monstrosity behind one of the two empty metal desks, and sank into it. "Tell me more about this vamp-shifter animosity."

Jeff shrugged negligently and went back to tinkering with a vaguely octopus-shaped stuffed animal on his desk. A buzz sounded, and my grandfather pulled a cell phone from a hip holster, took a look at the caller ID screen, then glanced up at me. "I need to take this. Catcher and Jeff will get you started." He looked at Catcher. "She's trustworthy, and she's mine. She can know everything that's not marked Level One."

At my smile and nod, he turned and disappeared through the door.

I had no idea what Level One was, but I was pretty sure that was the stuff I'd really want to know. Or it was the stuff that would scare the crap out of me, so it was probably better not to press the point today.

"Now you can get the real scoop," Jeff said with a grin.

Catcher snorted and closed his book, then slid back in his chair and linked his hands behind his head. "You met any vamps yet? Beyond Sullivan, I mean?"

I stared at him. "How did you—"

"Your name was in the paper. You're Cadogan's vamp, which means you're Sullivan's vamp."

My skin prickled. "I am not Sullivan's—"

But Catcher waved a hand. "Babe, not the point. The point is, and I'm guessing from that bristly tone you've met Sullivan and you understand at least the basics of vamp politics, that your people, and I use that term loosely, are a little particular."

I gave him a sly smile. "I've gotten that sense, yeah."

"Well, shifters aren't. Shifters are happy. They're people; then they're animals; then they're people again. What's not to be happy about? They live with their friends. They drink. They ride their Harleys. They party in Alaska. They have hot shifter sex."

At that revelation, Jeff winged up his eyebrows at me, an invitation in his eyes. I bit down on a grin and shook my head sternly in response. Apparently unruffled, he shrugged and turned back to his computer. Happily.

"Vampires, on the other hand," Catcher continued, "play chess with the world. Should we let people know about us, or shouldn't we? Are we friends with this House or that one? Do we bite people, or don't we bite people? Eek!" He bit down on a crooked finger dramatically.

"Wait," I said, holding up a hand, remembering something Ethan had said about Cadogan vamps. "Stop there. What's the story with the biting?"

Catcher scratched absently at his head. "Well, Merit, a long, long time ago—"

"On a continent far, far away," Jeff threw in.

Catcher chuckled, the sound low and sensual. "Way back when, Europe got pissy about its vamps. Figured out that aspen stakes and sunlight were the best treatment for an over-abundance of vamps and took out most of the fanged population of Europe. Long story short, vamps eventually formed the precursor to the Greenwich Presidium, which made the survivors take an oath never to bite another unwilling human." He smirked. "Instead, in true, manipulative vamp form, they found people who could be blackmailed, bribed, glamoured, whatever into giving it up for free."

"Why buy the cow?" I asked.

He nodded with approval. "Precisely. When the technology was developed to preserve blood, to bag it, most vamps turned away from humans. Immortality makes for long memories, and some Houses thought they'd be safer if they cut contact with humans almost completely, relied on bagged blood, or shared blood with each other." At my raised eyebrows, he added, "It happens. The vamp biology needs new blood, a new influx, so it's not a reliable source of nutrition. But it happens—sometimes ritually, sometimes to pass along strength."

Jeff's throat clearing filled the brief pause in Catcher's explanation. "And there's the other thing," he prompted, a flush coloring his cheekbones.

Catcher rolled his eyes. "And some vamps find there to be a . . . sensual component in sharing." I felt a blush cross my own cheeks and nodded studiously, trying not to think about the details of that act—or any green-eyed vamps it could be performed on.

"Anyway," Catcher continued, "as times changed, a few Houses, Cadogan included, gave their members the choice."

"To drink or not to drink," Jeff put in.

"That was the question," Catcher agreed. "Some vamps think humans are dirty and biting's a little too throwback. Cadogan takes heat on it. Not that doing it in secret is any better."

"Raves," Jeff said, with a knowing nod.

"What are raves?" I asked, leaning forward, eager to

gather as much information as they were willing to pass along.

Catcher shook his head. "We'll save that sordid little chapter for another time."

"Okay, then what about vamps being particular?"

"Vamps think their politics, this House bullshit, is the biggest issue in the world. They think it outshines human concerns, world famine, whatever. And a lot of supernatural folks agree. Vamps are predators, alpha predators, and where vamps go, a lot of fey follow."

"Fey?"

"You know—sups. *Supernaturals,*" he testily added, at my confused expression. "Anyway, angels, demons, your heavier sorcerers, they pay attention to the Houses. Who's screwing who, who's allied with who, all that crap. Shifters, on the other hand, could give a shit. They're just too laid back."

"And we're too neurotic?"

Catcher smiled. "Now you're getting the picture. Vamps don't appreciate that shifters are lackadaisical about their problems. Vamps want alliances. They collect friends they can rely on, especially the older ones that remember the European Clearings. Next time you're at Cadogan House, check the symbols above the front door. Those are alliance insignia; they show who Ethan's got signed up as allies. Really, they're backup in case humans get pissed or other Houses decide Cadogan's drinking is a little too risky. And because shifters don't play those kinds of games—Keene's never gonna post insignia over Ethan Sullivan's front door—vamps ignore them." Catcher sighed. "There are also rumors that shifters had the chance to step in during the Second Clearing, but chose not to act, not to become involved."

"Not to save lives?" I asked. Catcher nodded heavily, his expression tight, his gaze on Jeff, who looked to be working to ignore the direction of the conversation.

"I see. And who's Keene?"

"My pack leader," Jeff offered, looking up from his keyboard with a bright expression. "Gabriel Keene, Apex of the Central North American. He lives in Memphis."

"Huh." I stood up and paced from one end of the room to the other, then back again. The feast of information he'd just thrown at me needed to be digested. "Huh."

"Verbal, this one," Catcher said. Then quickly added, "Jeff, quit staring at her ass."

There was throat clearing behind me before typing started again in earnest.

This was so much more complicated than I'd imagined. Granted, before the change, I hadn't thought much about vamps. The few thoughts I'd had—especially after watching Celina Desaulniers seduce her way through a Congressional hearing—weren't flattering. The few I'd had since— *Well*, they involved too much Ethan Sullivan and too little anything else.

"I'd love to know what you're thinking right now, babe."

I looked around, saw Catcher grinning knowingly, brows lifted as he waited for a response. I felt the blush to the roots of my hair, but waved a hand negligently. "Noth—nothing. Just thinking."

His "Uh-huh" didn't sound convinced, so I turned the tables. "Where do you fit in all this?"

No response until, abruptly, Catcher sat up and began flipping through his book again. That was answer enough, I thought.

My grandfather stepped back into the office, and since Catcher was no longer broadcasting, he took the floor, giving his crew the basic facts on recent relevant events in my life— the bite, the threat, the challenge. When he'd given the full replay to Jeff and Catcher, he updated me on the investigation into Jennifer Porter's death. As a potential victim—and the three of them agreed that I'd been next in line—he thought it important to keep me informed.

Unfortunately, a lack of communication was standing in the way of progress on the investigation. Although the Navarre vamps promised to work with the CPD in solving the crime, they'd been tightlipped about their findings, if they had any. Grandpa's vampire connection helped fill in some blank spots, but in Catcher's words, the vamp was an enlisted man, not an officer, so his access to information was limited. Plus, the vamp was skittish about being labeled a traitor by his House, so he reported to the Ombud, not the CPD. That meant any information he did uncover had to be passed through channels. And even when it found its way to an investigator's desk, CPD detectives were still suspicious. Cops were old school; they didn't trust information from supernatural sources. Even my grandfather's thirty-four-year service record didn't immunize him from the prejudice. Many of the cops he worked with, served with, just thought he cavorted with phony weirdos.

More important, all the communication in the world couldn't help the fact that the only evidence recovered in Porter's death was the Cadogan medal. Detectives found no other physical evidence, no witnesses, and even the medal had been wiped clean of fingerprints. Unfortunately, with little else to go on, and plenty of prejudice in their favor, the CPD was loath to ignore Cadogan House as the source of their suspect.

By the time we'd gone over all that, I was seated at one of the empty desks, tapping a pencil absently against its top. I looked up, met Catcher's eyes. "Do we agree that he didn't do it?" I assumed I didn't need to specify who "he" was.

"He didn't do it," was Catcher's immediate response. "But that doesn't mean someone in Cadogan House wasn't involved."

Elbow on the desk, I put my chin on my hand, frowned at him. "He said he was interviewing the vamps that live in Cadogan House. He doesn't think Cadogan vamps were involved."

"Catcher didn't say a vamp *from* Cadogan House," my grandfather clarified. "He said someone *in* Cadogan House. We know a medal was taken from Cadogan. The House probably keeps extra medals on hand in case a vamp from another House defects or a pendant gets lost. And Commendation's coming up. That's when the medals are handed out to new vamps. They're there."

"And for the taking," Jeff pointed out.

Catcher stood up and stretched, his T-shirt riding up to reveal washboard abs and a circular tattoo on his stomach. Gruff was Catcher, but a little delicious.

"Vamps date out of their House," he said, dropping his arms. "And sometimes they bring their dates home. If the medals weren't properly secured, any of the visitors could have snagged one. And if Sullivan wasn't such a goddamn tight ass, he'd consider that."

"You two don't get along?" I asked.

Catcher chuckled and sat down at his desk again, the chair squeaking beneath him as he adjusted himself. "Oh, we get along fine. Sullivan and I go way back."

"How so?

He shook his head. "We don't have time for that story tonight. Suffice it to say"—he paused thoughtfully—"Sullivan appreciates my unique talents."

"Which are?"

Catcher chuckled gravelly. "Never on a first date, sunshine." He ran a hand over his buzzed skull and reopened the book on his desk. "And just because Sullivan and I are friends doesn't mean he's not a tight ass. And that doesn't mean he's willing to admit that he's wrong."

That being the most profoundly accurate statement I'd heard in days, I laughed heartily. "Oh, yeah," I said, patting my heart. "That gets me right here. Ethan said something about Rogue vampires being involved," I offered. "But it doesn't sound like they could have gotten into the House. I mean, security looked pretty tight."

"Rogues are one theory," Grandpa said. "And we've passed it along to the bureau."

"So that's your role in all this?" I asked. "Passing information along?"

"We're not investigators," Grandpa confirmed. "This office works more like a diplomatic corps. But since our vamp doesn't talk to cops, we've got access to information the cops don't have. The Mayor said to pass the info along, so we passed."

"And to be fair," Catcher added, "you and your little sorceress are involved now. That gives us incentive to pay attention and to get this wrapped up—and this psychopath off the streets—sooner rather than later."

I lifted an eyebrow, wondering how he'd learned about Mallory's secret identity, but he looked away. Sullivan, I guessed, had made a phone call.

My grandfather settled a hand on my shoulder. There were bags under his eyes I only just recognized, and I felt suddenly guilty for having waited so long to talk to him, for worrying him needlessly, even as I knew it wasn't me, but the loosed killer, who put the concern in his eyes now.

"That's all we've got," my grandfather said. "I know it isn't very satisfying, not when you've been a victim. When your life has been turned upside down."

I squeezed his hand, appreciating the validation. "Anything helps," I said, meeting each of their eyes to get my appreciation across. "It helps."

After a round of goodbyes, Grandpa walked me outside to await my cab. He locked up the building, then guided me to a wooden park bench that sat in one corner of the building's small, neatly clipped lawn.

"I still can't believe you're involved in all this," I told him. "There's so much going on in the city, and people think vamps are the sum total of it." I glanced over at him, worry in my gaze. "And you're right on the front lines."

Grandpa chuckled mirthlessly. "Let's hope it doesn't come

to front lines. It's been eight months. Sure, the coming out was a little rocky, but things have been stable for months now. I wouldn't say humans have accepted vamps, but there seems to be a kind of . . . curiosity." He sighed. "Or we're in the eye of the hurricane. The lull before more rioting, chaos. And there's no telling what that might do to the balance of power. Like Catcher was saying, a lot of sups take the vamps' superiority for granted. They see them—*you*," he corrected, looking at me over his glasses, a move so much like my father's, it tripped my heart nervously, "as alpha predators. Sups tend to follow the vamps' lead because of that. But that loyalty, if you want to call it that, was conditioned on vamps staying out of the limelight. Keeping under the radar, keeping human eyes off the supernatural world. They've never had good PR, the vamps. And you saw those nymph posters in there?"

I nodded.

"Who's to say, if the nymphs set out to control Chicago, they couldn't?" He chuckled. "They'd have a pretty easy time getting the male population behind them. Although shifters are probably the only group with the numbers and power to take a national stand against the vamps. I don't think they're interested in that, but then again, we're dealing with unknowns." He shrugged.

"The truth is, Merit, this is the first supernatural outing in modern history, and it happened in the post–Harry Potter era. In the post–*Lord of the Rings* era. Humans are a little more comfortable thinking about supernatural beings, supernatural happenings, than they were in the days when witches and vampires burned. Hopefully, things will be different this time." He was quiet for a moment, giving us both the chance to consider that possibility—the possibility that we could all just, to put it tritely, get along. That was certainly better than imagining the worst-case scenario. Burnings. Lynchings. Inquisition-like proceedings. The kind of mob violence that arises when a majority fears the loss of its power, the unbalancing of the status quo.

When my grandfather began talking again, his voice was quieter. More solemn. Weighed down, maybe.

"There's just no precedent. I didn't make thirty-four years on the force by making random guesses, so I can't say what will happen or, if worse comes to worst, who would win. So we'll keep our eyes and ears open, hope the sups keep trusting us, and hope the Mayor steps in if it comes to that."

"It's a hell of a time to've been changed into a vampire." I sighed.

He laughed cheerfully—the sound sweeping away the sudden melancholy—and patted my knee. "That it is, baby girl. That it is."

The door opened behind us, and Catcher stepped outside, his boots clacking on the sidewalk. "Can I have a minute?" he asked my grandfather, inclining his head in my direction. Grandpa looked at me for permission, and I nodded. He leaned in and kissed my forehead, then put his hands on his knees and rose.

"I brought you here because I wanted you to know that you always have a safe place, Merit. If you need help or advice, if you have questions—whatever. You can always come here. We know what you're dealing with, and we'll help you if we can. Okay?"

I stood and gave him a hug. "Thanks, Grandpa. And I'm sorry it took me so long to come by."

He patted my back. "That's no problem, baby girl. I knew you'd call when you'd had a chance to come to terms."

I didn't think I'd come to terms, but I didn't argue the point.

"Give her some cards," Grandpa directed and, after a quick wave, shuffled back into the building. Catcher pulled a handful of business cards from his pocket and handed them over. They bore only a phone number with the label "OMBUD."

"Consider it a 'Get Out of Jail Free' card," Catcher explained, then sat down on one end of the slatted bench seat.

He stretched out, slouching low and crossing his feet at the ankles. "So, you challenged Sullivan," he finally said.

"Not on purpose. I went to Cadogan to show him the note. I was pissed about being changed, but I didn't intend to argue with him about it."

"And what happened?"

I bent down to pluck a dandelion from the dewy grass next to the bench and twirled it in my hand, sending a cloud of ephemeral seeds into the air. "Ethan said something inordinately possessive, and it got to me. I challenged him. I think the vamp genetics were a little more eager for a fight than I was, but he offered me a deal—to release me from my obligations to the House if I landed a punch."

Catcher slid me a glance. "I take it you didn't?"

I shook my head. "I ended up on my back on the floor. But I got a few moves in. I held my own. And he didn't land a blow either. He seemed surprised that I was strong. That I was fast."

Catcher blew out a breath while he nodded. "If you held your own against Sullivan, your reflexes are better than they should be for a baby vamp. And that means, Initiate, that you're going to have some power. What about smell? Hearing? Any improvement?"

I shook my head. "Not much above normal, unless I get angry."

Catcher seemed to consider that, tilting his head to regard me. "That's . . . interesting. Could be those powers aren't on-line yet."

A motorcycle raced down the dark street, and we were quiet until it disappeared around the block.

"If you want to harness your power," Catcher continued, "whatever that power may be, you'll need training. Vamps have their own traditions of sword work—offensive moves, defensive patterns. You need to learn them."

Having depleted the dandelion of its seeds, I dropped the

empty stem to the ground. "If I'm stronger, why do I need training?"

"You're going to be a power, Merit, but there's always someone stronger. Well, unless you're Amit Patel, but that's not the point. Trust me—there's going to be lots of vampire kiddies who want to take you for a spin. You'll invite challenges from good guys and bad guys alike. To stay healthy, merely being stronger or faster won't be enough. You need moves." He paused, nodded. "And until the CPD brings this murderer in, it'd help if you could handle yourself. It'd make Chuck feel better, and if Chuck feels better, I feel better."

I smiled collegially, appreciative that my grandfather had Catcher at his back. "Can Jeff handle himself?"

Catcher made a sarcastic sound. "Jeff's a fucking shifter. He doesn't need martial arts to get around in the world."

"And you? Do you need martial arts?"

In lieu of answering, he flicked his hand in my direction. A burst of blue light flew from his open fingers, aiming straight for my head. Immediately, I dropped into a crouch again, then angled to the side as he shot a second burst. With an electric sizzle, the bursts exploded a shower of sparks.

I snapped my gaze back to the low-slung man on the bench, muttering a string of curses that would have turned even my grandfather's ears red. "What the hell are you?"

Catcher stood and extended a hand to help me up. I took it, and he pulled me to my feet. "Not people."

"A witch?"

His eyes narrowed dangerously. "What did you just call me?"

I'd obviously offended him, so I backtracked. "Um . . . Sorry. I'm a little unclear on all the . . . right labels."

He watched me for a moment, then nodded. "Accepted. That's a pretty big insult for someone like me."

I didn't tell him that the vamps threw the word around with casual ease. "And what is that, exactly?"

"I am—*was*—a fourth-class sorcerer, proficient in the minor and major, greater and lesser Keys."

"Keys?"

"The divisions of power. Of magic," he added at my blank stare. "But because I made the Order's shit list"—he pointed down at the words on his T-shirt—"I've been excommunicated."

"The Order? Is that a church?"

"More like a union. I was a member."

Although I understood the words he used, I had no context in which to place anything he'd said, so none of it made sense. (I needed a guidebook. A big, thick, illustrated, tabbed, and indexed guidebook to the sups of Chicago. Did they make those?) But the part about his being excommunicated was clear enough, so I focused there. "You're a magical rogue?"

He shrugged. "Close enough. Back to you. I'll train you."

"Why?" I looked back at the building, then flicked him a suspicious glance. "You can shoot blue lightning from your hands, but you're working in a run-down building on the South Side with my grandfather. Training me will take time away from your work"—I pointed at his T-shirt—"and whatever other supernatural business you've got going on. Besides, isn't that the vamps' job?"

"Sullivan will clear it."

"Why?"

"Because he will, Nosy. Weapons, objects of power, are the second Key. That's my bag, my specialty, and Sullivan knows it."

"And why do you care who trains me?"

Catcher looked at me for a long time, long enough that crickets began to chirp around us. "Partly because Chuck asked me to. And partly because you have something of mine. And the time will come when it's up to you to protect it. I need to know you'll be ready for that."

I took my own pause. "Are you serious?"

"Very."

I stuffed my hands into my pockets, tilted my head at him. "What am I protecting?"

Catcher just shook his head. "Not the time for that."

It was "not time" for all the good stuff, I thought as my cab turned onto the block and stopped at the curb before us.

"Tomorrow at eight thirty," Catcher said, then gave me an address I guessed was in River North. I walked toward the waiting cab and opened the back door.

"Merit."

I glanced back.

"She needs training, and a lot of it. The last thing I need is another misguided neophyte screwing around with the lesser Keys."

Sullivan had definitely made a call about Mallory. "How do you know that?" I asked him.

Catcher snorted. "Knowing things is what I do."

"Well, then, you know she's not taking the news well. Maybe you should give her a call. What with the fangs and serial killer, I'm full up on supernatural drama at the moment."

He grinned at me, white teeth flashing. "Babe, you're a vampire. Deal with it."

Mallory was asleep when I got home, tucked safely into bed. And why wouldn't she be safe with a pair of armed guards outside? I headed straight for the fridge. The bags of blood still held no appeal, so I grabbed an apple and munched at the kitchen counter, flipping through the day's paper. The front page featured a picture of Mayor Tate, tall and darkly handsome, under the headline *Mayor Announces New Anticrime Measures*.

I snorted, wondering what the readership would think if they understood the anticrime measures being employed in a small brick building on the South Side.

After flipping through the paper, I checked the clock. It

was two a.m., hours before sleep would pull me under. I was debating a hot bath when a knock sounded at the door. I headed to the living room, chucking the apple core on the way, and checked the peephole. The nose and hair were distorted by the angle, but there was no mistaking a blond, pissed-off vampire in black Armani. I flipped the locks and pulled the door open.

"Good evening, Ethan."

His gaze immediately dropped to the ninja print across my chest. I got an arched brow for the fashion choice—at least, that was how I chose to interpret the disdain—before he raised flame green eyes to mine.

"You think to bring down my House by spying on us?"

Anticipating Fight Number Two, I sighed but invited him in.

CHAPTER FIVE

just a quick bite

Sullivan walked in, followed by Luc and Ethan's redheaded consort from the sparring room. Since I hadn't officially met Ethan's flame, I stuck out my hand as she sauntered through the front door in hip-high leather pants and a pale blue tank she'd unfairly burdened with the task of holding up her pendulous breasts.

"Merit," I said.

She looked at my hand and ignored it. "Amber," she said before turning away.

"Nice to meet you," I muttered and shadowed the trio to the living room. I found Ethan standing, while his pretty vampire accoutrements fanned out on the sofa.

"Merit."

Playing it safe, I opted for the honorific. "Liege."

He arched an eyebrow. "What do you have to say for yourself?"

I opened my mouth, then closed it again, trying unsuccessfully to figure out what I'd done. "Why don't you go first?"

There was a two-part groan from the couch.

Ethan planted his hands on his hips, sweeping back the sides of his suit jacket in the process. "You've been to see the Ombud."

"I went to see my grandfather."

"I warned you yesterday—about your role, your place—and I thought we'd agreed that you weren't going to challenge my authority. Agreeing to spy on the House, to betray my House, clearly falls into the 'challenging my authority' category." He stared down at me. A moment passed as I tried to wrap my mind around the accusation.

His nostrils flared. "I'm waiting, Merit."

The tone was condescending. Patronizing. Profoundly irritating. And from what I'd seen so far, typical Sullivan. I tried to be the bigger person and explained, "I haven't agreed to spy on anyone, and I resent the implication. You may not like me, Sullivan, but I'm no traitor. I've done nothing that justifies the accusation."

This time, he blinked. "But you admit you were at the office?"

"My grandfather," I carefully began, controlling my voice to keep from screaming at him, "took me to his office to meet his staff, to tell me about Chicago's other supernaturals. I didn't agree to spy on anyone or to betray anyone. And how could I? I've been a vampire for three days, and I'm willing to admit that I'm still pretty ignorant."

Amber *humph*ed. "She has a point, Liege."

I gave him credit—he kept his eyes on me. I got a long look before he spoke again. "You don't deny that you went to the Ombud's office?"

I grappled to discover the logic underlying the questions, found nothing. "Sullivan, you're going to have to help me here, because, contrary to the information you've been given, I haven't agreed to do anything for the Ombud's office. I went there to learn, to visit, not to get an assignment. I haven't agreed to spy, to sneak notes, to give updates, anything." I narrowed my gaze and crossed my arms. "And I don't see what's wrong with visiting my grandfather at his office."

"What's wrong," Ethan said, "is that your grandfather's

office is trying to pin the Jennifer Porter murder on *my* House."

"The Chicago Police Department is trying to pin the murder on your House," I corrected. "From everything I've heard, my grandfather and everyone else in his office think you're innocent. But you know there was a Cadogan medal at the crime scene. Assuming the forensics unit didn't plant that evidence, that medal came from your House. Cadogan is involved, regardless of what my grandfather does, and whether you like it or not."

"No one from my House would do this."

"Maybe not the murder," I agreed. "But unless you hand those medals out as party favors, someone from your House has a part in it. At the very least, someone let in the person who *did* take it."

I didn't expect his reaction.

I expected another rant, an outburst about the loyalty of Cadogan vamps. I didn't expect his silence. I didn't expect him to walk to the love seat and sit down, elbows on his knees, his hands clasped together. I didn't expect him to run his hands through his hair, then rest his head in his hands.

But that was what he did. And the move, the posture, was so humble, so tired, and so very, very human, that I had the sudden, surprising urge to reach out, to touch his shoulder, to comfort him.

It was a moment of weakness, of yet another breach in the defenses I'd tried to erect against Ethan Sullivan.

And that, of all the goddamn times, was when the hunger rose.

I nearly lost my breath from the sudden race of fire through my limbs, and had to grip the back of the love seat to stay upright. My stomach clenched, pain radiating in waves through my abdomen. I went light-headed, and as I touched my tongue to the tip of an eyetooth, I could feel the sharp bite of fang.

I swallowed instinctively.

I needed blood. *Now.*

"Ethan." Luc said his name, and I heard rustling behind me.

A hand gripped my arm, and I snapped my head to look. Ethan stood next to me, green eyes wide. "First Hunger," he announced.

But the words meant nothing.

I looked down at his long fingers on my arm, and felt the warm rush of fire again. I curled my toes against it, reveled in the heat of it.

This meant something. The feeling, the need, the thirst. I looked up at Ethan, dragging my gaze past the triangle of skin that showed through the top, unfastened button of his shirt, then the column of his neck, the strong line of his jaw, and the sensuous curves of his lips.

I wanted blood, and I wanted it from him.

"Ethan," I whispered in a voice so husky I barely recognized it.

Ethan's lips parted, and I saw the flash of silver in his eyes. But it was gone in an instant, replaced by smoky green. I edged closer to his body, wet my lips, and then, without a single thought as to the consequences or what the act admitted, pressed them to his throat. He smelled so good—clean, soapy, everything male and masculine. He *tasted* so good—of power and man. The ends of his hair brushed my cheek as I kissed the long line of his neck.

"*Ethan,*" I whispered again, his name an invitation.

A promise.

He went statue-still as I pressed a kiss to the skin just below his ear. I could hear blood singing in the veins that lay millimeters below the press of my teeth. Then he sighed, and the sound echoed through my head, an acknowledgment of shared passion, of mutual desire.

The others around us began to talk. I didn't want talk. I wanted action. Heat. Motion. I scraped my teeth against his neck—not breaking skin, just enough to hint at what I wanted.

Of the direction I would take. His pulse raced, and I fought not to bite in too quickly, not to rush the pleasure of it.

But through the burn of arousal, something cold, un- wanted pricked. I shook my head and pushed it back.

"Liege, you can't feed her the first time. She needs human or Novitiate blood. You've got too much power for a first feeding. She's strong enough as it is."

Ethan growled but didn't move. He stayed exactly where he was, beneath my lips, a silent submission. Pleased, I slid my hands around his waist.

"Get her off him, Lucas!"

I felt the cold touch again—a drop of chilled water against my heated skin. Irritating. Unwelcome. It was my con- science, I realized, begging me to wake up, to shoulder through the hunger. But superego warred with deep-seated instinct and latent attraction.

Id won.

I growled and flicked the tip of my tongue against his ear, ignoring my own warnings. *"Ethan."*

"Luc, you'll have to—I haven't—" He groaned earthily— and God, what a sound, thick enough to touch—as I trailed a line of kisses down his neck. "I haven't fed in two days. Merit, you have to stop." Given that he was leaning into my body when he said it, his words lacked conviction.

A hand grasped my arm. Ever so slowly, I turned my head to find coral-painted nails digging into my biceps. The touch was enough to distract me, to make me realize, my lips still against Ethan's neck, that I was acting out the *Canon*. De- spite his protests, I'd pushed on and was preparing to bite him. I was preparing to rip down his clothes and take him on the floor.

I was preparing, in every conceivable fashion, to service my lord.

That insight did it, pushed me through the hunger with an ice-cold hand, pushed me through the desire to the other side—back to the land of rational thought and good choices.

Gathering all the strength I had, I inhaled and pushed myself away from him and from her, needing space to regain control of my body. I hunched over, hands on my knees, gasping for breath. The hunger left me sweating even in my thin T-shirt and jeans, goose bumps prickling my arms as my body cooled again. I could still feel the hunger, a caged tiger prowling through my body, eager for sustenance, waiting to rise again. I knew any control I displayed was temporary. Illusory.

But in some deep, new core of me, I reveled in that knowledge. The tiger paced and was thrilled to be merely biding her time. She would have her chance.

She would drink.

Luc asked, "Blood?"

"Kitchen," Ethan hoarsely answered. "They delivered bagged. Amber, go with him. Give us a minute."

"Lot of control for seventy-two hours," Luc observed. "She reined it back in."

"If I wanted observations, I'd ask for them." His voice was firm, obviously troubled. "Go into the kitchen and ready the blood, please."

When we were alone, when I'd slowed my breathing, I stood straight again and dared to meet his eyes. I waited for a sarcastic response, but he merely looked back at me, his expression carefully blank.

"It's fine," he said, his tone clipped. "To be expected."

"Not by me."

Ethan pulled at the edges of his shirt collar, then smoothed the lapels of his jacket. Regaining his composure, I thought, maybe because he'd wanted something from me, as well. The silvering of his eyes demonstrated that, however much he protested.

"First Hunger can arise suddenly," Ethan said. "There's no need to apologize."

I arched a brow at him. "I wasn't going to apologize. If it wasn't for you, there'd be no thirst."

"Don't forget your place, Initiate."

"As if you'd let me."

"Someone has to remind you," Ethan said, stepping closer so that the cuffs of his trousers topped my sneakers. "You promised me submission. You agreed that your rebellious behavior was done. You agreed not to challenge me again. And yet you're poised to bring the walls of Cadogan House down around us."

"Master or not," I said, glaring up at him, "take it back, or I'll challenge you again." I'd been betrayed enough times in my life to know the value of honor and honesty, and tried to live by that code. "I have given you no reason to doubt my loyalty, which is a fairly tremendous thing given how you changed me."

His nostrils flared, but he didn't challenge the statement. "Merit, so help me, if you support Tate's office over my House . . ."

I looked at him blankly. "Tate? *Mayor* Tate? I don't even know what that means, supporting his office. Why would I be supporting his office?"

"The Ombud is a creation of the Mayor."

I still missed his point. "I understand that. But why would the mayor care what I do? Why would he care if one of his employees brings a grandkid to work?"

Ethan gazed down at me. "Because even if you're estranged from your father, he's still Joshua Merit, and you're still his daughter. On top of that, you're the granddaughter of one of the most influential men in the city. And, in case we needed additional fuel, you're clearly stronger than average." He flicked a hand in the direction of the kitchen. "Even they recognize that."

Ethan stuffed his hands into his pockets and moved away, turning to look at a row of books on the shelf next to the front door. "Tate's not trustworthy," he said. "He knows about us—has known about us—and even though his appointment of your grandfather seems well-intentioned, the man's secretive. We understand that he knows about Rogue vampires, but he hasn't released that information to the public. That raises questions—is he trying to avoid more public panic, or is the information a bargaining chip he'll use against us later on? And, he won't speak to the heads of the Houses; instead, he works through the Ombud's office. As helpful as he may be"—he turned back—"as well-intentioned as he may be, your grandfather still works for Tate. Tate controls the purse and the policy direction. That means he pulls the strings."

"My grandfather is his own man."

Ethan stepped back from the bookshelf, crossed his arms, and looked at me. A line creased his forehead. "Think about it, Merit: Vampires announced their existence here, in Chicago. We're the first Houses in the U.S. to do so. Tate stands first among Mayors in that regard—first in terms of setting supernatural policy, in terms of making alliances with the Houses, maintaining security. A man can use that power, that position. But whatever he has planned—and rest assured the man has plans, probably has had them as long as he's known about us—he's not being forthright. I can't afford for you to become part of his plans, or for my House to be caught in the eddies. So until you've learned enough to act appropriately, to use discretion when discussing our concerns, you'll stay away from the Ombud's office."

I wouldn't stay away, and he probably knew that, but there was no sense in belaboring the argument. Instead, I cocked my head at him. "How did you know I went to his office?"

"I have my sources."

I didn't doubt it. But while I wondered which source he'd tapped—Catcher, Jeff, the undercover vamp who serviced the Ombud's office, or someone else assigned to watch me—I knew better than to ask. He'd never tell me.

But someone had given him information about my activities, someone who hadn't been close enough to know exactly why I was there. That was worth passing along.

"Some free advice," I said. "The person who's giving you

information wasn't inside the building. If they had been, they'd have known why I was there, what was discussed. And more important, what *wasn't* discussed. They made deductions and managed to convince you those deductions were fact. They're playing you, Sullivan, or at least trying to puff up sparse information to increase their own cachet."

For a moment, Ethan didn't speak. He just looked at me, like he was seeing me for the first time, had suddenly realized that I was more than his newest rebellious underling, more than the daughter of a financial mogul.

"That's a nice analysis."

I shrugged. "I was in the room. I know what went on. She, or he, doesn't. And back to the point, he's my grandfather. Other than Mallory, he's all I've got. He's my only real family tie. I can't cut that tie. I won't, even if you think it's a challenge. Even if you think it's rebellious and goes against your sovereign authority."

"You have other ties now, Initiate. Cadogan House. Me. You're my vampire now. Don't forget that."

I think he meant it as a compliment, but the tone was still too possessive for my taste. "Whatever happened six days ago, I belong to no one but myself, Sullivan, and least of all you."

"You are what I made you."

"I make myself."

Ethan took a step forward, then another, until I was stepping away to avoid him, until he'd backed me against the living room wall, until I felt the cold slickness of painted plaster behind me.

I was caught.

Ethan braced his hands against the wall, one on each side of my head, boxing me in, and stared down at me. "Do you want disciplining, Initiate?"

I stared at him, a flame igniting in my core. "Not especially." *Liar.*

His eyes searched mine. "Then why do you persist in taunting me?"

The eye contact felt too intimate, so I turned my head away and tried to swallow down the reluctant arousal, uncomfortably aware that I couldn't blame my actions, my interest, on the vampire lurking inside me. On the genetic change. She and I were one and the same—same mind, same genetics, same unwanted, *undeniable*, attraction to Ethan Sullivan.

But I reached out for that whisper of denial, wrapped hands around it, and held it like a life preserver. In that second, I dreamed of running away, of beginning again with a new name, in a new city, where I didn't long to clench fingers into his hair and push my mouth against his until he capitulated and took me against the cold white wall, pushed his body into mine to alleviate the need, to warm the chill.

Instead, I said, maybe honestly, "I wasn't taunting you."

He didn't move, not until he lowered his head, his lips even closer to mine than before. "You wanted me a moment ago."

This time, his voice was quiet, his words not the challenge of a Master vampire, but the entreaty of a boy, of a man: *I am right, aren't I, Merit? That you wanted me?*

I forced myself to be honest, but I couldn't force myself to speak. So I stayed silent, and let the silence stand for words that I couldn't bring myself to say: *I want you. Despite myself, I want you. In spite of what you are, I want you.*

"Merit."

"I can't."

He dropped his head so that his lips hovered just above mine, his breath on my cheeks. "Give in to it."

I flicked my eyes up to meet his, which were the deep, dark green of primeval forests—ancient, unknowable, and hiding monsters in their wooded depths. "You don't even like me."

He smiled a little evilly. "That doesn't seem to matter."

A slap wouldn't have pulled me out of the trance any

faster. I twisted beneath his braced arms, then moved away.
"I see."

"I'm not happy about this either."

"Yes, I get that you don't want to be attracted to me, that
you think I'm beneath you, but thank you for pointing it out
anyway. And in case you haven't realized it, I'm not thrilled
about it, either. I don't want to like you, and I certainly don't
want to be with someone who's appalled by me. I don't want
to be . . . desired begrudgingly."

He stepped toward me with the grace of a slinking pan-
ther. And just as dangerous.

"Then what do you want me to say?" His voice was low,
thick with lambent power. "That I wanted you to taste me?
For all that you're stubborn, sarcastic, completely unable to
take seriously my authority, and patently disrespectful, that I
want you? Do you think this is what I would choose?"

There it was again—the list of flaws. The reasons he
shouldn't have been attracted to me. The reasons he hated the
chemistry that, against both our wills, flared between us. My
voice quiet, the sound oddly far away, I told him, "I don't
want anything from you."

"*Liar,*" he accused, and lowered his mouth to mine.

He kissed me, and the circuit closed again.

His lips were soft and warm, and implored a reaction,
challenged me to join in, to give in, even if only briefly, to the
chemistry. My limbs loosened, my body daring me to sink
into it, to revel in it. But I'd come close enough to the fire,
when I'd nearly jumped him to pull the blood from his veins.
That had been enough. That had been too much. So I kept my
lips together and tried to turn my head away.

"Merit," he intoned, "be still." Ethan's fingers slid along
my jaw, knotted into my hair, and he used his thumbs to tilt
up my chin. He took a small step forward, our bodies align-
ing, just touching.

He dipped his head and kissed me again, thumbs stroking my cheeks as he moved his lips across mine, caressing, calming, not coercive. Then, when his tongue slipped between my lips and stroked mine, when the electric thrill slid up my spine, I gave in.

Tentative at first—and only responding after promising myself that I'd never, *ever* touch him again—I kissed him back. I gave back his kiss, sucked on the tongue he offered me, responded to his nips and bites with my own.

I couldn't seem to help it. I couldn't *not* kiss him. He tasted so good, *smelled* so good. He was heaven, a golden beacon in the supernatural darkness that spindled around me. But this wasn't something to blame on magic. This was much more elemental, much more powerful. It was want, desire in its most basic form.

But I couldn't afford that, not to want someone who didn't want me. Not really.

So I put my hand on his chest, and felt the thud of his heart beneath the soft cotton of his dress shirt before I pushed him away. "Stop."

He took two halting steps backward, his chest rising and falling as he pulled in air, and stared down at me.

"That was a mistake," I said. "It shouldn't have happened."

He wet his lips, then ran a hand across his jaw. "No?"

"No."

Silence, then, "I could offer you more."

I blinked, looked up, met his eyes. "What?"

"Power. Access. Rewards. You'd need be available only to me."

My lips parted, words momentarily failing me, the shock of it was so overwhelming. "Are you asking me to be your mistress?"

He paused, and I had the sense that he was deciding if that was, in fact, what he was offering me. Likely weighing the costs and benefits, deciding if easing his erection was worth the trouble I'd cause. A flush crossed his sculpted cheek-bones. "Yes."

"Oh, my God." I dropped my gaze, put a hand at my abdomen, wondering how this night had suddenly become so bizarre. "Oh, my *God*."

"Is that a yes?"

I looked up at him again, saw the flash of panic on his face. "No, Ethan, Jesus. Definitely not."

His eyes flashed, and I wondered if he'd ever been turned down before, if any woman in his nearly four hundred years of existence had rejected the opportunity to service him. "Do you understand what I'm offering you?"

"Do you understand that it's not 1815?"

"It's not unusual for Masters to have Consorts."

"Yes," I said, "and your current Consort's in my kitchen right now. If you need . . . *relieving*, talk to her." The shock—the sheer shock of his offer—was beginning to wear off, replaced by a little bit of hurt, a little bit of insult that he didn't like me enough to offer me something else, and that he thought I'd be flattered by the little he did offer.

"As much as it pains me to say it, Amber isn't you."

I stared at him. "I don't even know what that means. Should I— What? Be flattered that while you don't like me, you're willing to sacrifice just to get into my pants?"

His nostrils flared, a tiny line appearing between his eyebrows. "You're crude."

"*I'm* crude?" My voice, the whisper that came out, was fierce. "You just offered to make me your whore."

He took a step closer, his jaw clenched, the muscle trembling. "To be the Consort of a Master vampire is an honor, Initiate, not an insult."

"It's an insult to me. I'm not going to be your—anyone's—sexual outlet. When that . . . happens for me, when I meet *him*, I want partnership. Love. You don't trust me enough for the former, and I'm not even sure you're capable of the latter."

He flinched, and I immediately regretted the words.

I took a breath and took some space, moving to the couch.

It was a long moment before I could stand myself enough to meet his eyes again. "I'm sorry. That was a really horrible thing to say. It's just— I live in a different time," I told him, "with different expectations. I wasn't born to serve someone indiscriminately, without thoughts of my own. Whatever else my father may have done, he raised me to be independent. To find my own way." He just didn't believe my own way was the correct one most of the time.

"I'm trying to be myself, Ethan. To keep some sense of myself in the middle of all this"—I raised a hand, made an abstract gesture with my fingers—"chaos. I can't be that kind of girl." There was more to that statement, I thought, than just my response to his offer, than a response to being his mistress. I wasn't sure I could ever be what he wanted—the acquiescent vampire, the perfect little soldier in his Cadogan army.

Ethan's expression, already shuttered, completely blanked, his green eyes going flat. "Then we're done here. I've explained the situation to you. Whether you like it or not, we're not human. You're not human. Not any longer. Our rules are different than those you're used to, but they are the rules. You can decry them, deny them, but they are the rules." His eyes shone with power. "And if you disobey them, if you balk, you defy *me*."

"I'm not rebelling," I said, as calmly as I could, realizing how many lines I'd already crossed, we'd already crossed, in the span of the evening. "Nor am I trying to usurp your authority. I'm just trying to"—I searched for words—"avoid it."

Ethan straightened the cuffs of his shirt. "We have rules for a reason, Merit. We have Houses for a reason—for a multitude of reasons, regardless of your opinion, regardless of whether you find . . . *merit* in the idea. Like it or not, you are my subject. If you deny your House, there will be repercussions. You'll be deemed an outcast. A Rogue. You'll be rejected by all vampires—ignored and ridiculed because you chose not to trust me. You'll have no access to the Houses, to the members, or to me."

I looked up at him. "There has to be something between anarchy and subjection."

Ethan glanced up at the ceiling, then closed his eyes. "Why do you think of it as subjection? You saw the vampires at my House. You saw the House. Was it a dungeon? Did they look miserable? When you challenged me, was I unfair to you? Did I treat you cruelly or give you a fair chance to prove yourself? You're smarter than this."

He was right, of course. The vampires in the House clearly respected him and looked, at least to my eyes, to be happy in their acquiescence to his leadership. But that didn't mean I was able, blindly, to put my trust in him, or any of them. I didn't have a cache of faith big enough for that.

We stood silently until Ethan made a final, frustrated sound and called for Amber and Luc. As they moved through the living room, Amber skewered me with a look that was both knowing and victorious. She somehow knew, had probably heard, what he'd offered me, and that I'd turned it down. But I hadn't just taken myself out of the running; I'd secured her position. She winked jauntily, and I felt a sudden, unwelcome stab of jealousy. I didn't want his hands on her. I didn't want her touching him. But I'd had my chance to take her place, and I'd refused. The decision had been made, so I ignored the irritation and looked away.

"Let's go," Ethan said.

Luc nodded at me. "There's blood on the counter. It's warm and ready to drink."

Ethan didn't look at me as he turned for the door, and I felt the weight of his disappointment. However illogical, I wanted him proud of me, proud of my fight and my strength, not disappointed that I'd failed to meet the basic criteria for vampire behavior. On the other hand, I shouldn't have to apologize for not crawling into bed with the head of my House.

Luc and Amber preceded him outside. There were two vehicles at the curb—a black Mercedes roadster that I guessed was Ethan's, and a heavy black SUV. Luc and Amber headed for the latter. Traveling security, I assumed.

When he reached the first step, Ethan turned and glanced back at me, his face carefully blank.

"I would have asked you if I could have, Merit. I'd have asked for your consent, and had you make the decision then and there. But I didn't. Couldn't have, without your dying. There certainly wasn't time for you to debate the merits of affiliation. Would that I had. Would that I had, so the choice would have been made."

After a pause, he continued, his voice suddenly tired. "The clock is ticking. You have four days until the Commendation, until your formal initiation into the House. The time is coming when you'll have to take a stand, Merit. One way or the other, you'll decide whether you want to accept the life you've been given and make the most of it, or run away and live on the fringes of our society, withstand the humiliation of being rejected by the House, by everyone else like you. By everyone who understands what you are. Who you are. How you thirst." His gaze intensified. "Your desire. And that decision, such as it is, is yours." With that, he trotted down the stairs.

I followed him outside, and flanked by the two guards at my door, I stood on the stoop and called his name. He glanced back.

"About the . . . hunger. Will it always be like that?"

He gave me a rueful smile. "Rather like being a Cadogan vampire, Merit, it will be what you make it."

I had to give him credit—he was right about one thing. The time had come for me to make a decision. To make a choice, either to accept the life he'd given me, such as it was, or eschew Ethan, the House, the community of vampires. I could choose to live as a member of the American Houses or make a life for myself on the outskirts. But an eternity of watching friends, the world, change around me while I stayed the same, was going to be lonely enough. Watching while Mallory aged, while my grandfather aged, while I looked eternally twenty-seven. What kind of life would it be, to also reject the House, to pretend at being human, and outlive my family, no companions but musty books and medical-grade plastic bags?

Still, I wasn't ready to take that next step. Not yet. There were loose ends to be wrapped up. Well, one major loose end. And that was what put me in the car at four o'clock in the morning, leaving the sanctum of Wicker Park for the neighborhood of vampires.

This time, I wasn't headed for the House. I was headed for the university. And I was a woman on a mission, so when I arrived, I ignored the permit warnings, parking in the first empty on-street spot I could find. I got out of the car, locked it behind me, and walked to the main quad, empty satchel over my shoulder.

I stood at the edge of the quad and stared at the expanse of grass, sidewalks and trees, my hand at my neck. I'd always loved this spot, had usually paused before heading into the Walker Building, which housed the English department, so that I could get a taste of grass and sky. I walked to the spot where I'd been attacked, crouched in the spot where my blood had been shed, and touched a hand to the grass. There was nothing here, no blood, no trampled grass, no indication at all that the few square yards of lawn had been witness to birth, to death. To me. To Ethan.

The tears I thought I'd finished shedding began to fall. I dropped to my knees, knotted fingers in the carpet of grass, wishing that things had gone differently. That I hadn't made the regrettable decision to leave the house, to walk the quad. I sobbed there on my knees, the frustration, the regret, nearly overwhelming.

There was laughter across the lawn. I knuckled away tears, lifted my head. Two students, a couple, walked hand in hand down the sidewalk, before disappearing between buildings. Then the night was quiet again, most of the windows dark, no breeze to stir the trees that dotted the quad.

I closed my eyes. Inhaled. Exhaled. Opened my eyes again. But for the cloak of grief, it was a beautiful night. One of an eternity of nights I'd have the opportunity to see. But in order to see those nights, I'd have to figure out a way to deal with loss, to mourn lives that would end, even as mine continued. A way to deal with my obligations to Cadogan.

A way to deal with Ethan.

I'd have to figure out how to support Mallory, how to keep my relationship with my grandfather in spite of our positions. I'd have to figure out how to tell the good guys from the bad guys in the strange, new world I'd been dropped into.

More important, I'd have to figure out whether I was one of the good guys. Whether Ethan was one of the bad guys.

I realized the means to that end. It had to be a *choice*. I'd been made a vampire without my consent—attacked and violated, of course, without my consent. The only way I'd be able to move on, to build a new life, to take ownership of my new life, would be to make that conscious decision for myself, for better or worse. To live, or not to live, as an acknowledged vampire.

I could make that choice. Here and now, I could take ownership, take back my life again.

"Vampire it is," I whispered. It wasn't much, but it was enough to get me off my knees in the middle of the night, in the middle of the quad.

And this time, I rose on my own terms.

My direction decided, I resituated the empty satchel diagonally across my chest and headed for Walker. The building was dark, locked. I pulled out my key, unlocked the door, and made my way up the stairs.

Each graduate student had a mailbox. I used mine like a scrapbook, kept in it the detritus of my time at Chicago. A ticket stub from a midnight screening of *Rocky Horror* I'd watched with fellow TAs and lecturers. A ticket stub from a basketball game we played against NYU, where I did my undergraduate work.

I opened my satchel and loaded papers, memorabilia, mementos into the bag. Tangible memories. Evidence of my humanity.

But also in my box was something new—a pink envelope, sealed but unsigned. I unhitched my bag, placed it on the floor at my feet, and slipped my thumb under the seal.

Inside was a scalloped pink card, glittery letters congratulating a girl for her sixth birthday. I grinned, opened it, and found inside, beside an equally glittery unicorn, the signatures of a good chunk of the grad students in the department, most with smart-alecky well wishes for my new, fanged life.

I didn't realize until I saw the card that I'd needed it. I needed the connection between my old life and my new one. I needed them to know why I'd disappeared, why I'd stopped showing up to class. It was closure of a kind. It didn't excuse the fact that I hadn't called my friends in the department, hadn't called my mentor or my committee chair. God only knew when I'd have the strength to do that.

But it was something.

For today, it was enough.

So I grabbed my bag, left the key in my mailbox, and walked away.

I returned to the brownstone to find, as promised, a glass of now-cold blood on the kitchen counter. The house was quiet, Mallory still asleep. I was alone, and glad that she wasn't there to witness what I was about to do.

I stared down at the thin orange-red liquid in its glass, and felt the hunger rise again—signaled by the humming of my blood. My pulse quickened, and I didn't need a mirror to know that my eyes had silvered. Still, it was blood. My mind rejected it, even while my body craved it.

Craving won.

I wrapped a hand around the glass, fingers shaking, and raised it, knowing this was truly the end of my life as a human, and the beginning of my life as a vampire. There'd be no more justifications, no more rationalizations.

I lifted the glass to my lips.

I drank.

It took mere seconds for me to empty the glass, and it still wasn't enough. I drained two more bags that I pulled straight from the refrigerator—bags I hadn't bothered to heat or prepare. I drank the liquid—more than I'd ever put into my body at one time—in minutes, finally stopping when I felt my own blood slow again. Three bags of blood, and I'd ingested them like I'd been starved for food and water, denied sustenance for weeks.

When the hunger was sated, I caught sight of the discarded bags on the floor. I was appalled at the act, at the substance, at the fact that I'd actually drunk—willingly drunk—blood. But I clamped a hand over my mouth, willing myself not to bring it up again, knowing that if I did, I'd just have to drink more. I slid to the floor, my back against the side of the island, and clutched my knees to my chest, forcing myself to breathe. Forcing my brain to catch up with my body—to accept what it needed.

To accept what I was.

Vampire.

Cadogan Initiate.

That was where Mallory found me—sitting on the kitchen floor, empty medical bags at my feet—minutes before the sun began to rise. She was prepped for work—black suit, heels, chunky jewelry, sassy handbag, blue hair a frame around her face.

Her smile faded. She crouched in front of me. "Merit? Are you okay?"

"I just drank three bags of blood."

Dropping her purse at my feet, Mallory picked up an empty plastic bag with the tips of two fingers. "So I see that. How do you feel?"

I giggled. "Fine, I think."

"Did you just giggle?"

I giggled again. "Nope."

Her eyes widened. "Are you drunk?"

"On blood? No." I swatted the idea with a hand. "It's mother's milk to me."

Mallory picked up the other bag, then walked them both to the trash can and tossed them in. "Uh-huh."

"And how are you? Feeling witchy?"

She went to the refrigerator and pulled out a soda, then popped the tab. "I'm adjusting. I guess I can say the same for you?"

I frowned, considering, then began counting off the events on my fingers. "Well, I found out my grandfather's been lying for four years about his job. I met a sorcerer, met a shape-shifter of indeterminate origin, got propositioned by said shifter, found out I was almost the victim of a serial killer, almost got hit by these magical electric blast things, made out with Ethan, rejected Ethan, was threatened by Ethan." I shrugged. "Pretty average day."

Her mouth fell open, and she gaped at me until closing it with a click of teeth. "I don't know where to start on all that. How about, your grandfather's been lying?"

I pulled myself up from the floor, hands on the countertop to steady myself. It took a moment for my head to stop spinning—the aftereffects, I presumed, of drinking so much blood at one time. "Drink, please?"

Mallory went back to the fridge and grabbed another soda, held it up for my approval, and when I nodded, popped the top.

After she handed it over, I took a long pull, discovering to my delight that diet grape soda was a refreshing chaser to three pints of human blood. I thanked her for the drink, then filled her in on the Ombud and his slate of employees. I didn't tell her about Catcher's recommendation that Mallory get training. I decided the safer course of action was just to put the two of them in a room together—all that beauty and stubbornness—and watch the fur fly.

"I have to train tonight," I told her. "I'm meeting Catcher at a gym on the Near North Side. You want to come along?"

She shrugged. "I could do that."

"Do we need to talk about something? I mean, are we okay?"

Mallory smiled ruefully. "We're fine. It's not your fault I'm . . . whatever I am."

"I bet Catcher has some answers for you."

"That'd be nice."

I finished my drink and tossed the can. "I need to be at the gym by eight thirty. But first I have to sleep. Dawn's coming, you know." I yawned, pointed out, "You haven't asked me about kissing Ethan."

She rolled her eyes. "Why would I need to? It's obvious you have the hots for him."

"No, I don't."

She gave me an obviously skeptical glare, in response to which I shrugged, lacking the energy to argue the point . . . and it would have required a heavy bit of lying and thickly laid self-denial anyway.

"Fine," she said. "I'll indulge you since you recently became the walking dead. Was he good?"

"Unfortunately."

"Technique? Skill? Hands?"

"High passes in all categories. Of course, after four hundred years, the boy's gonna have some skills."

"Quite a résumé," she agreed. "And it wouldn't matter if he was inexperienced and inept. Just being in the same room, you two melt the drapes. All that heat, it's not surprising you came to blows again," she added. "Didn't land one, did you?"

I went silent.

"Merit?"

"He asked me to be his mistress."

She just stared at me, openmouthed.

"Yeah."

We stood quietly for a moment, until she moved to the refrigerator and grabbed a pint of ice cream from the freezer. She found a spoon, popped the ice-cream top, and handed the duo to me. "No one has ever deserved this more."

I wasn't sure that was true, but I took them both anyway and helped myself to a dose of Chunky Monkey.

Mallory leaned against the countertop, tapped a manicured finger against it. "You know, it's kind of flattering in an ass-backward way. Even if he's conflicted about it, he clearly finds you attractive."

I nodded around a spoonful of ice cream. "Yeah, but he doesn't like me. He admitted it. He's just . . . kind of . . . accidentally attracted."

"Were you tempted?"

I shrugged.

"That doesn't answer my question, Merit."

What could I have said? That even in the midst of it, some tiny bit of me, some little secret room in my heart (or more accurately, my loins), wanted to say yes? To finish out that kiss with caresses and something more, anything more, than a lonely day beneath cool, empty sheets?

"Not really."

She cocked her head at me, seemed to evaluate that. "I can't tell if you're lying or not."

"Neither can I," I admitted around another spoonful of ice cream.

She sighed and rose, patting my back before grabbing her purse and heading toward the front door. "You give that some thought while you're hibernating. I'll see you tonight. I'll go with you to train."

"Thanks, Mallory. Have a good day."

"I will. You sleep good."

Maybe unsurprisingly, I didn't.

CHAPTER SIX

IF AT FIRST YOU DON'T SUCCEED,

FALL DOWN, DOWN AGAIN.

It was raining when I woke the next evening, the fourth day of my new life, tucked beneath the ancient quilt that covered my bed. I stretched and rose and walked to the window, flipping back the black leather curtain that kept sunlight off my body while I slept. The evening was gray, the window cold against the flat of my palm. Heavy drops of spring rain patted against the glass. It was seven thirtyish, and the evening stretched before me. I had only one thing planned—training with Catcher, as arranged the night before.

I made myself stop obsessing about the kiss. After all, I should have been thrilled to death that I hadn't been weak enough to say yes to Ethan's offer. I was still Merit, still Mallory's friend and still my grandfather's granddaughter. So when I rose, I put it behind me and focused on the night ahead.

I wasn't sure of the appropriate dress code for my first night of training as Cadogan House Initiate, especially given the weather, so I opted for black yoga capris, a T-shirt, running shoes, and a fleece jacket to ward off the chill. When we met in the living room, Mallory was out of her business suit and tucked into jeans and a T-shirt. She linked her arm in mine as we stepped onto the stoop, nodding to the guards at the door before darting to the garage.

Mallory flipped open the garage door and we walked inside. "You ready for your big vampire adventure?"

"You ready to find out who you are?" I countered.

"Honestly, I'm not yet sure if knowing is better than not."

I made a sound of agreement, unlocked the car, and slid inside. Mallory joined me after I reached over to pop the lock. The car started on the first try—not always a guarantee with a car nearly older than I was—and I backed her carefully out of the garage and onto the street.

"Can you believe we're wrapped up in this?" she asked. "Not even a few months ago, no one knew vampires existed. Now we're in the middle of it, as deep as you can get. And this Catcher. He's what?"

"He said he was a fourth-grade sorcerer until he was kicked out of the Order. I don't know what that—"

"It's the governing body for sorcerers," Mallory interjected.

I slid her a quick glance. "And you'd know that because?"

"I've done some homework. I made some calls."

"I see. And a fourth-grade sorcerer? That would be what, exactly?"

"Top of the line."

Not really surprising given the fireworks display. A little scary, but not surprising. "Gotcha."

When we reached the warehouse district, we found parking in front of the brick building bearing the address Catcher had provided. The building was four squat stories tall and ringed at the top with equally spaced square windows, like a coronet of glass. A substantial red door sat in the middle of the facade. We dodged raindrops to reach it, then pushed it open, revealing an impressive atrium that stretched the full height of the building. The room itself was shaped like an inverted T, with a long hallway punched through the middle. An empty demilune reception desk stood in the juncture.

Having gotten no instructions beyond the time and address, I gave Mallory a shrug, and we ventured toward the hallway. Doors marked both walls, but there was no sign of our sorcerer or a gym. Rather than testing each door, which felt a little too Alice in Wonderland, we decided to wait and hope that someone would eventually come looking for us. We debated whether they'd come from the right or the left.

"Left side?" I offered.

Mallory shook her head. "Right. Loser buys dinner."

"Done," I agreed, seconds too early. Mallory nailed it—a door opened on the right, and Jeff's head popped out of the doorway. He grinned at me, waved, and widened his eyes when he saw Mallory.

"You brought magic," he said, his voice a little dreamy, and beckoned us in. Mallory grumbled a few choice words about "magic," but we followed obediently.

The room was enormous. The walls were concrete, the floor dominated by blue gymnastics mats. A gauntlet of punching and speed bags hung in one corner. The contrast between this room—sterile, equipped for precision training—and the Cadogan sparring room—ceremonial, equipped for flashy moves—was easily apparent. This place lacked the gravitas, but it also lacked the ego. There, you showed off. Here, you worked out. You prepared. The music, though, was weirdly mellow—John Lee Hooker's "You Talk Too Much" flowed through the space.

"I'm Jeff," he said, sticking out a hand toward Mallory. She shook it.

"Mallory Carmichael."

"I'm a shifter," he said. "And you're magic."

"That's what I hear," she flatly said.

"Have you joined the Order yet?"

Mallory shook her head.

Jeff nodded. "Talk to Catcher. But don't let him blind you to the benefits of being unionized."

As if on cue, a door on the far side of the room opened

with a metallic scrape. Catcher emerged, stalking toward us in bare feet, jeans, and a T-shirt that read *Real Men Use Keys*. It was a good look for him—sexy, rough, a little dangerous. It was the look of a man who'd just crawled out of bed, leaving a very satisfied woman beneath the sheets.

I watched his eyes survey the room, saw his gaze move from Jeff, to me, to Mallory. And that was when I saw the blink, the tiny hitch in his composure when he took in the petite frame, the blue hair, the gorgeous face. I turned, saw the same awestruck expression on her face, and watched them stare at each other. The force of the attraction seemed to warm the air. I grinned.

"You're late," Catcher said when he reached us, crossing his arms over his chest.

Jeff, the sweetheart, defended my honor. "She was here on time. I found 'em standing in the hallway, staring at the architecture."

"It's a great building," I said.

"Thanks," Catcher replied, his gaze on Mallory. "I don't have time to deal with you tonight." I guessed introductions were unnecessary.

Mallory huffed. "I don't recall asking you for help."

The air seemed to prickle around us, drawing goose bumps along my arms. Jeff took a couple of steps backward. Since he undoubtedly knew more than I did, I followed suit.

"You don't have to ask," Catcher said. "You're practically drenched in power, and you obviously have no clue what to do with it."

Mallory rolled her eyes and crossed her arms. "You don't know what you're talking about."

"I know you're a fourth-grade," Catcher said, gazing at her through half-lidded eyes. "And I know you know what that means. I know you put in a call. But Merit doesn't have magic, and I need to make sure, first and foremost, that she can handle what's coming. So not now, okay?"

Mal's eyes flared, blazed. But after a moment, she nodded.

Catcher inclined his head, then looked me over. He pinched the sleeve of my fleece jacket. "This won't work. You're wearing too many clothes. You need to watch your body move, learn how your muscles work." He crooked a thumb toward the door in the back of the room. "Head back. There're clothes in the locker room. And lose the shoes."

"You're kidding, right?"

"Do you want a speech, too?"

I didn't, but I was a little sick of being bossed around by supernatural boys with ego problems, so I satisfied myself by muttering a few choice curses on my way back.

The locker room was bright, empty, and clean, but like all locker rooms, it carried the ubiquitous scent of sweat and cleaning products. There were two pieces of black fabric on a bench. I picked them up.

Catcher had been serious about watching my muscles work. The "clothes" were barely scraps—an eight-inch band of spandex to cover my breasts and a pair of spandex shorts that would just reach the tops of my thighs. It looked like a beach volleyball uniform, although I think even Gabrielle Reese got more clothing than this.

"You have got to be kidding me," I muttered, but stripped and pulled on the workout gear. They fit well, at least the little skin they covered. I folded and piled my clothes, placed my shoes on top, then pulled my hair into a ponytail. A quick survey in the mirror above a slate of sinks revealed a lot of pale vampy skin, but the effect wasn't bad, actually. I'd always been lean, but my muscles seemed more defined now, vampire genetics doing more for my body than miles on the treadmill. I blew the bangs out of my face, wished myself luck, and walked back into the training room.

For my trouble, I got catcalls from Mallory and Jeff, who grinned at each other in delight. I rolled my eyes, but curtsied to both of them, then walked to where Catcher stood, arms folded across his chest, a glower on his face, in the middle of the mats.

"Push-ups," he said, pointing at the floor. "Start now."

As commanded, I went to the floor, extended my arms and legs, and started lifting my body. The move was nearly effortless; while I certainly couldn't do push-ups indefinitely, I had noticeably more upper-body strength. I felt muscles clench and flex as I moved, and reveled in the sensation of blood flowing faster than before. I saw feet come into view, then circle me.

Catcher called Jeff's name, and the music changed—it became harder, louder, more rhythmic.

"The first step," Catcher said above me, "is evaluation. The vampire's powers are based in the physical—strength, speed, agility. The ability to jump higher, to move faster, than prey. Enhanced smell, sight, hearing—although those might require a little maturing before they kick in. And most important, the ability to heal wounds, to repair damage, which ensures that the body stays in top form." Thus, the unmarred skin on my neck.

As I steadily lifted and lowered my body, Catcher crouched before me, a finger under my chin pausing me, arms extended, in the middle of a push-up. He searched my eyes, but called Jeff's name. "Jeff?"

"She just finished push-up one hundred thirty-two."

Catcher nodded. "You're stronger than most." Hands on his knees, he rose again. "Sit-ups. Begin."

I swiveled my body into position, started a course of sit-ups. Those were followed by lunges, squats, and a set of yoga positions Catcher said were intended to test my flexibility and agility. They were all relatively easy, my body fitting into positions that—even years removed from serious dance-level fitness—should have been impossible. But I did King Dancer and Warrior poses, Wheel poses and Forearm Stands as effortlessly as if I'd been simply standing there. My muscles worked to maintain the positions, but the sensation was wonderful—like a full-body stretch after a long nap.

"So far, you're easily a Very Strong Phys," he commented.

I was in a headstand when he said it, and I lowered my feet to the floor and stood. "Meaning what?" I asked, straightening my ponytail.

"Meaning, just in terms of your patent physical strength, you're in the highest echelon. Vamps are rated on a three-prong basis. Phys—physical strength, stamina, skills. Psych— psychic and mental abilities. Strat—strategic and ally considerations. Who your friends are," he explained. "And within those categories, there are levels. Very strong at the top, very weak at the bottom, a range in between."

I frowned at him. "Give me a comparator. What are humans?"

"In strat and psych, 'very weak' by vampire standards. In physical strength, they might vary from a weak to a very weak. Many vamps aren't much stronger than humans. They need blood, and they have that nasty sunlight allergy problem, but their musculature remains essentially unchanged. Some will get powers, but even then it's later on. It's only been, what, four days since your change? Of course, even the vamps who don't get appreciably stronger get a boost metaphysically—the ability to glamour humans, mental communication, once your Master initiates the link."

I put my hands on my hips. "Mental communication? You mean like telepathy?"

"I mean telepathy," he confirmed. "Ethan will call you, initiate the link. You'll only be able to communicate with him—as your Master—but it's a handy skill to have."

I glanced at Mallory, thinking of her similar words before I took the floor with Ethan at Cadogan House. She nodded at me.

"You'll have Phys," Catcher continued. "Psychic, maybe. Those probably haven't come online yet. They may not until you and Ethan connect." Catcher moved a step closer and gazed into my eyes, his brow furrowed, like he was peering through my pupils. "You'll have something," he quietly said. Then his eyes focused again, and he stepped backward. "And those powers will move you up. You'll be a Master vampire, Merit. You'll have your own House one day."

"You're serious?"

He shrugged casually, like the possibility that I was going to be one of the most powerful vampires in the world was no big deal. "It's up to you, of course. You could stay a Novitiate, stay under Ethan's wing."

"You do know how to motivate a girl."

He chuckled. "Why don't you take five, and then we'll start you on the moves? There's a water fountain in the hallway."

I walked toward Mallory, who jumped up, grabbed me by the elbow, and pulled me out into the empty hall. I found the water fountain and latched on, my body suddenly aching for water. That was when she started yelling.

"You said 'sorcerer'! Sorcerer!" She pointed back into the training room. "*That* was not a sorcerer."

I guessed meeting Catcher did have an effect on her. I lifted my head and wiped water from my chin, then peered back into the room, where Catcher was sparring with a surprisingly sprightly Jeff.

"Uh, yeah, *that* was. Is. And believe me—I know. I was almost a victim of these little fingertip blast things he can do."

"But he's young! What is he, twenty-eight?"

"He's twenty-nine. And what did you think he was going to look like?"

She shrugged. "You know—old. Grizzled. Long white beard. Scruffy robes. Lovable. Smart, but a little absentminded professorish."

I bit back a grin. "I said 'sorcerer,' not 'Dumbledore.' So he's hot." I shrugged. "It could be worse. He could be a pretentious centuries-old vampire who's decided you're his latest project."

Mallory paused, then patted me on the arm. "You win. That's worse."

"Uh, *yeah*," I agreed, and led her back into the training room.

We worked for two more hours. He positioned me in front of a bank of mirrors along one wall and began teaching me how to move, how to defend myself. We spent the first hour—well, I spent the first hour—learning how to fall down.

Seriously.

Anticipating that I might be the object of an overhead toss or a clumsily executed jump, Catcher taught me how not to injure myself when I hit the ground—how to roll, to balance my weight, to use the momentum to push into a different move. The second hour we worked on the basics—kicks, punches, blocks, hand attacks. The building blocks that he'd eventually combine into katas, the combination sets that defined vampire fighting. The patterns had their origins in various Asian martial arts forms—Judo, Iaido, Kendo, and Kenjutsu—European vampires having learned the systems from a nomadic swordsman. But Catcher explained the moves had evolved into a unique form of fighting because, as he put it, "Vampires and gravity have a special relationship." Vamps could jump higher and keep their bodies in the air for longer than humans, so vampire moves were more complicated than the original human katas. Showiness, Catcher said, was encouraged.

It wasn't until the end of the second hour, after he'd begun to teach me defensive sword-fighting poses, that Catcher even let me see a sword. The sheathed blade had been wrapped in slinky indigo silk, and he unfolded it with careful concentration. It was a katana, much like the belt-bound blades worn by the guards outside Cadogan. It was sheathed in a black lacquer scabbard and had a long handle wrapped in black cord. He unsheathed it with a whistle of steel, the long, gently curved blade catching the glow of the overhead fluorescent lights.

As I admired the sword, tracing a finger in the air an inch above the blade—loath to sully the surface—Mallory asked, "Why swords? I mean, if vamps can be killed, why not just use guns? It's faster, certainly easier than carrying around a three-foot-long sword. Those things aren't exactly inconspicuous."

"Honor," Catcher said, gripping the sword just below the hilt and rotating it in his hand in a figure-eight pattern. He glanced over at me. "You're immortal, meaning you'll live forever if you aren't killed. But if someone decides it's your time to go, they have three options. Sunlight is, of course, the easy way." He gripped the sword in both hands, the blade pointing to the ground, and thrust it down. "Two— pierce the heart with a stake. Destroy the heart and you destroy the vampire. Aspen is the traditional wood."

"Why aspen?" I asked.

Mallory lifted a finger. "There's a theory chemicals in the fibers prevent the heart from regenerating."

"And you know this because . . . ?"

"Oh, please," she said, waving me off with a hand. "You know I read a lot."

Catcher swung the sword above his head, then sliced the blade through the air, the steel whistling as it fell. "Three— destroy the body. Remove the head, remove the limbs, the body dies. Slicing and dicing will weaken the body, as will guns. But guns are too easy. Bullets too easy. If you want to take out an immortal, you do it carefully, precisely, and after battle. You take out an immortal because you've fought them, used the old traditions, earned the right." Pommel up, he gripped the sword and sliced it beside his body, a move that would have gutted an enemy behind him. Then he looked up at me. "Honor among thieves," he concluded, brows lifted, and I wondered, not for the first time, how Catcher knew so much about vampires, and what put that intent gleam into his eyes.

He glanced back at Mallory. "That's why they don't use guns."

"How do you know all this?" she asked.

Catcher shrugged matter-of-factly. "Weapons are what I do."

"That's how he works his mojo," Jeff said.

"It's the second Key," I added, enjoying the surprised expression on Catcher's face. "I am capable of learning."

"Color me surprised," he snarked, then moved to his knees, resheathed the blade, and placed the sword in front of him on the floor. Solemnly, he bowed to it, then rewrapped it in the silk. "Next time, I'll let you hold her."

"Next time? What about your job? My grandfather?"

"Chuck doesn't mind that I'm ensuring your safety." When the scabbard was covered again, he rose, cradling it in his arms, and surveyed us all. "Who wants eggs?"

CHAPTER SEVEN

WHAT'S IN A NAME?

"Eggs," it turned out, meant a deliciously greasy breakfast. After I'd showered and changed back into my street clothes, Mallory and I followed Catcher and Jeff to a tiny aluminum diner situated in the shadow of the El in a commercial neighborhood that had seen better days. An electric blue neon sign blinked "Molly's" in one of the round windows.

Once inside, we piled into a booth and surveyed the breakfast-only menu. After a gingham-clad waitress took our orders—eggs, sausage, and toast all around—we lapsed into a companionable silence, marred only by the intense stares that Mallory and Catcher couldn't seem to help but exchange.

When the plates arrived minutes later, laden with greasy breakfast necessities, I tore into the sausage. I sucked down three links immediately and made doe eyes at Mallory, who handed me a fourth.

Catcher chuckled. "You're craving protein."

"Like a shifter," Jeff put in, grinning wolfishly. And that made me wonder something.

I nibbled the edge of my toast. "Jeff, what kind of animal do you change into?"

He and Catcher exchanged a glance, wary enough that I

guessed that I'd made another supernatural faux pas. I mentally reiterated my interest in getting a guidebook. Hell—writing one, if that was what it came down to.

"Did I ask the wrong question again?" I asked, taking another bite, social clumsiness clearly not affecting my appetite.

"Asking about someone's animal is the shifter equivalent of pulling a ruler and asking a guy to whip it out," Catcher said.

And down went toast into my trachea. I choked, had to swallow half my glass of OJ to get my breath back. "I'm okay," I said, waving Mallory off. "I'm fine." I gave Jeff a sheepish smile. "Sorry."

He beamed at me. "Oh, I'm not offended. I could show you. I think you'd be pretty pleased."

I held up a hand. "No."

Jeff shrugged and chewed a mouthful of eggs, apparently unruffled.

Catcher took a sip of his coffee, then dunked a corner of toast in the remnant of gooey egg yolk on his plate. "There's an easy way for you to remedy your ignorance, you know."

"What's that?" I asked him, pushing back my plate. I'd finished off five links of sausage—three of my own, two pilfered—three eggs and four triangles of toast, and I'd just taken the edge off the hunger. But two thousand calories or so of grease, carbs, and protein was my limit at one sitting. I'd catch a snack later, and wondered how late Giordano's was open. Or how late Superdawg stayed open. A hot dog and fries—how good did that sound?

"Read the *Canon*," Catcher answered, interrupting my meat reverie. "It's your best source for information on sups, including all the shit you're already supposed to know about vampires. There's a reason they give those out, you know."

I drummed fingers on the table—well on my mental way through a Hackneyburger with bleu cheese—and made a face. "Yeah, well, I've been busy—getting death threats, kicking my Master's ass, getting training."

"You finally have an excuse to buy that BlackBerry," Mallory pointed out, sipping at her diamond-patterned plastic tumbler of orange juice. I scowled at her, then batted my eyelashes at Catcher. "So, what's the story with Mallory?"

Mallory growled. Catcher ignored her. "Now that she's been identified, the Order will contact her. She'll get her training, be assigned a mentor—not me," he clarified, giving her a look, "and will be asked to swear never to use her magic for the forces of evil"—he crossed a hand over his heart—"but only for good."

"Is that what you did?" I asked him. "Used magic for evil instead of good?"

"Nope," was all he said, tossing his napkin onto his plate.

"Why now?" Mallory asked. "If I'm so powerful, why the interest only now? Why wasn't I identified before?"

"Puberty," Catcher said, relaxing back into the booth. "You've just come into your powers."

I snorted out a laugh. "And you thought the weird body hair and pimples were the end of it."

Mallory elbowed me in the gut. "What powers? It's not like I'm out there waving a magic wand or something."

"A sorcerer's power doesn't work like that. We're not spell casters—no charms, no recipes, no cauldrons. We don't have to invoke it or ask for it. We don't draw it through a wand or the combination of words and ingredients. We pull it through our bodies, merely by the strength of our own will." Catcher crooked a thumb at me. "She's a predator, a genetically altered human, tempered by magic. Her magic is accidental; vamps notice it more than humans, have a greater awareness of it than humans, but can't control it. We are vessels of magic. We keep it. Channel it. Protect it."

At Mallory's blank expression, Catcher said, "Look, have you recently decided that you wanted something, and then got it? Something unexpected?"

Mallory frowned and nibbled on the end of a sausage link, a move I noted was watched with avidity by Jeff.

"Not that I can think of." She looked at me. "Something I wanted and got?"

That was when it hit me. "Your job," I answered. "You told Alec you wanted the job—next day, you had it."

Mallory paled and turned to Catcher. "Is that right?" There was sadness in her expression, probably dismay at the possibility that she hadn't gotten the job at McGettrick because of her qualifications or creativity, but because she'd made it happen, the result of some supernatural force she could flick on like a light switch.

"Maybe," Catcher said. "What else?"

We frowned, considered. "Helen," Mallory said. "I wanted her out of the House—virulently. I opened the door, told her to get out, and poof, she's on the stoop." She gazed up at Catcher. "I thought if you revoked a vampire's invitation they got sucked out?"

Catcher shook his head, his expression radiating quiet concern. They'd be good for each other, I decided. Her energy, expressiveness, impulsiveness, creativity, matched against his smart-ass solidity.

"They leave by rule, by paradigm. Not by magic. That was your doing."

Mallory nodded and let the sausage fall back to her plate.

"You can try it, if you want. Right now, while I'm here." Catcher's voice was soft, thoughtful. Mallory's gaze on the table, she wet her lips. Finally, after a long silence, she looked up.

"What do I do?"

Catcher nodded. "Let's go," he said, reaching back into his jeans pocket. He pulled out a beaten black leather wallet, then slipped cash from the center fold and laid it on the table. After he'd leaned forward to push the wallet back in, he rose from the booth and held his hand out to Mallory. She paused, looked at it, but let him help her up and out. They headed for the door.

Jeff swallowed the remaining inch of his orange juice,

then put the empty tumbler back on the table, and we both followed.

Outside, the rain had finally stopped. Catcher led Mallory, her hand still in his, around the restaurant. Jeff and I exchanged a glance, but hurried to keep up.

Catcher walked a block or so until he and Mallory stood directly beneath the El, then positioned her body so they stood facing each other. Jeff stopped five yards from them and put a hand on my arm to stop me, too.

"Close enough," he whispered. "Give them room."

"Give me your hands," I heard Catcher tell her, "and keep your eyes on me."

She hesitated, but held out her hands, palms up.

"You're a channel," he said. "A conduit for the energy, the power." He held out his own hands, palms down, over hers, a little space between them.

For a second, there was nothing but the sounds of the city. Traffic. Conversation down the street. The thud of a hip-hop bass line. The drip of water from the tracks above us.

"Wait for it," Jeff whispered. "Watch their hands."

It happened simultaneously, the roar of the train overhead and the glow that began to gather in the space between their outstretched fingers.

Mallory's eyes widened; then Catcher mouthed something and her eyes lifted. They gazed at each other, Catcher telling her things I couldn't hear over the grate and rumble of the El.

The glow built, grew into a sphere, a golden orb of light between them.

The train completed its pass, the sudden silence a vacuum of sound.

"I can feel it," Mallory said, gaze dropping to her hands and the light between them.

"What do you feel?" Catcher asked.

She looked up at him, their faces illuminated by the glow.

Chemistry, I thought, my lips tilting into a smile at the mix of joy and surprise on her face.

"Magic," Jeff whispered beside me.

"Everything," Mallory answered.

"Close your eyes," Catcher told her. "Breathe it in."

She gave a hesitant nod. Her lids fell, and then she smiled. The orb grew, engulfed their hands, arms, torsos until it was a yellow bubble of light encasing them both. The air electrified, the breeze of magic fluttering my bangs and Jeff's floppy hair.

And then with a *pop*, it was gone, a plane of yellow mist dissipating into the air around them.

Mallory and Catcher, arms still outstretched, stared at each other.

He lifted his gaze. "Not bad at all."

"As if you've had better, Bell."

I grinned. That was my girl, magic funnel or not. She'd be okay, I decided.

They dropped their arms and rejoined us.

"So, what the hell was that, exactly?"

Catcher looked my way. "Need-to-know basis, vamp. And you do not need to know right now."

The magic demonstration concluded, we headed back to the block on which we'd left our cars, my chunky Volvo, Catcher's hipster sedan, and Jeff's old hatchback.

"Plans?" Catcher asked.

Jeff grinned. "It's a Friday night, I'm off work early, and I'm gonna chat with this cute kid from Buffalo. She's blond and curvy in all the right places, so I need to get home and get online." He elbowed Catcher. "Right, C.B.?"

"I told you not to call me that."

"It's, you know, so we have a thing, the two of us. You know."

Catcher gazed at Jeff. "I don't know, Jeff. I really, really don't." But when Jeff began to explain, Catcher held up a hand. "Nor am I interested." He looked at Mallory and me. "Plans?"

We shook our heads.

"There's a club in River North that looks cool." Catcher pulled a flyer from his pocket. It was similar to the one that had been left beneath my wipers when my car was parked outside Cadogan, advertising Red. "It's not too far from the gym."

I pointed at it. "I got one of those, too. They must be papering the city."

Catcher shrugged, refolded the paper, and stuffed it back into his pocket. "Anyone wanna dance?"

"Oh, Jesus," Mallory muttered.

"Dance?" I asked. "I could dance. I need to change, but I can dance." I could always dance. My hips didn't lie.

Mallory tucked her tongue into her cheek, then gave Catcher a look of mock irritation. "Nice going, Gandalf. You'll rile her up, and I'll never get her tucked in. You wanna give her candy and caffeine while you're at it?"

Catcher smiled at her, and even though the smile wasn't for me, it was hot enough to curl my toes. "Sorcerer, not wizard. Yes?"

After a beat, she nodded, a flush high on her cheeks.

I'd have nodded, too, if I was her. Probably even thrown in an eyelash batting for good measure.

"I'll let you two deal with him," Jeff said, and unlocked the doors of his hatchback. "Have fun dancing. And if you get bored later"—he winged up his eyebrows—"you give me a call." He winked, then climbed into the car and drove away.

"One of these days, I'm going to kiss him just for the principle of the thing," I told Mallory as we walked toward the Volvo.

"You should have done it just then. You'd have made his weekend."

I walked around and unlocked the door. "But his cute blonde would have missed out. Can't have that."

Mallory nodded solemnly. "True. You're so munificent."

I slid into the car, unlocked the passenger door, and waited while Mallory and Catcher argued over something. Issue apparently decided, Mallory slid inside, blushing furiously. I nearly asked what they'd argued about, but the subconscious way she touched her fingers to her lips answered the question. I stifled a laugh, pulled the car out of the parking lot, and headed home.

Catcher, who'd followed us to Wicker Park, camped on the couch in front of the television while Mallory and I switched outfits. We both came downstairs in trendy jeans and heels and cute, club-worthy tops. Mine was black with tiny white dots and cap sleeves—a bargain vintage find. Mallory wore a sleeveless, high-collared top with a long tie at the neck that glinted silver in the light.

"Great shirt," she told me, fingering a sleeve as we strode down the stairs. "It's like you've blossomed style overnight."

I was taking serious hits on my fashion choices this week, probably not surprising for a girl whose dressing decision was usually between colors of layered T-shirts. I wasn't a shopper, much to my mother's (and Mallory's . . . and Ethan's) chagrin.

But I thanked Mallory anyway and had the satisfaction of watching her flick fingers self-consciously through her shoulder-length hair as we neared the living room.

"I'm sure he'll like your hair," I poked, then grabbed keys and stuffed my wallet into a small black clutch purse. Mallory stuck out her tongue. We gathered up Catcher—who guiltily flipped off a Lifetime movie—and headed out.

Red was located in a stand-alone building, a three-story brick structure that looked, architecturally, like it might house a design studio. The facade was dominated by three rows of high, arched windows, each topped with an intricately carved relief. We parked the car on a side street and approached the door, bass thumping through the walls. We were headed for the back of the short waiting line, but the guard at the door—bald, clad in a black T-shirt and fatigues, and wearing a headset—waved a clipboard at us.

"We aren't on the list," Catcher told him.

"Names?" he asked anyway, his voice flat and deep.

"Catcher Bell, Mallory Carmichael, and Merit," Catcher told him. Face bunched, the bouncer flipped through the sheath of paper clipped to his board. But then his gaze rose, and he stared blankly ahead and nodded as, I imagined, he listened to someone on the other end of the headset. Then he stepped back from the door and waved us inside.

Weird, but who were we to argue with VIP service?

We entered to the rhythmic thump of a slow bass beat that carried enough power to vibrate my core. But while the music was raucously loud, the decor was chic. Elegant. Drinks were served from an enormous mirror-backed bar that was tucked against the building's front wall, while the side walls were lined in curtain-edged mirrors and red leather booths, tables in front of them. Tiny lamps lit the tables and reflected against the mirrors, giving the club the look of a European coffeehouse. A wrought-iron spiral staircase was positioned near the bar, and a small but completely filled dance floor dominated the back of the room. The clientele was as classy as the decor—chicly dressed couples in the booths along the wall, chatting over martinis and cosmopolitans. They were all oddly attractive—lots of Louis Vuitton bags and Manolo Blahnik shoes, carefully coiffed hair and perfectly tailored clothes.

Some, I knew, were vampires. I'm not sure how I knew that—although the fact that they were all, to a one, weirdly attractive was a sure tip-off. They just had a different vibe, a different sense about them. And here they were, sipping ten-dollar drinks, flirting, and swaying to the music just like people.

Catcher took our drink orders—vodka tonic for Mal, gin

and tonic for me—while we headed for the last available mirror-backed table. We slid against the wall, leaving the outside seat for Catcher.

"Gorgeous place," Mallory yelled over the din, surveying the room. "I can't believe we haven't been here before."

I nodded, watching the dancers move, taking the drinks Catcher handed us when he returned. One song ended and a second began instantaneously, the opening beats of Muse's "Hysteria" ringing through the club. Eager to dance, I took a quick sip of my drink and grabbed Mallory's hand, pulling her to the dance floor. We shuffled through the throng, finding a gap in the crush of designer-clad bodies, and danced. We shifted, moved, swayed hips and arms, and let the music overtake us, swallow us, beat the worries from our minds in time to the raging synthesizer. We stayed on the dance floor through that song and another, and another, and another, before tunneling back through the bodies for a break, a seat, a drink. (And we'd left Catcher guarding our purses, so we felt a little duty-bound to go back.)

Mallory slid into the chair next to him, filling him in on her fabulous dance experience, his eyes alight with amusement as she chatted with vital animation, pushing her hair behind her ears as she talked. I sipped at my cocktail and downed the water that waited for us.

Suddenly, the song ended and the club became silent, even as strobes flashed around us. A haze of fog began to flow around our feet, a prelude to the ominous beating vibe of Roisin Murphy's "Ramalama," which began to spill through the room. The club's dancers, who'd paused tremulously between songs, waiting for the signal to move again, screamed joyously, and began thrusting to the music once again.

We rested for a few minutes, chatting about nothing in particular, when Catcher took the drink from Mallory's hand, deposited it on the table, and led her back to the dance floor. When she turned back to me, her face radiating shock that he'd had the nerve to expect her to follow without a fuss, I winked back.

I rolled the ice around in my drink, watching Mallory blush as Catcher swayed against her, when a voice next to me suddenly asked, "Good song, don't you think?"

I looked over, surprised to find a smiling man with his arm stretched along the booth behind me. His hair was cropped, vaguely wavy, and dark brown, framing cut cheekbones, a cleft chin, and a strong jaw dotted with a day's worth of stubble.

But for all that he was handsome, it was the eyes that pulled me in, that focused the attention. That accelerated the pulse. His were dark and set beneath long, dark eyebrows. He peered at me beneath long, black lashes, his gaze seductively masked. The lashes rose, fell, rose again.

Sexy Eyes wore a fitted black leather jacket—trim lines, Mandarin collar, very alt-rock—over a black shirt that snugged his lean torso. Around one wrist was a watch with a wide leather wrap-band. Altogether, the look was urban, rebellious, dangerous, and damn effective on a vampire. And he was *definitely* a vampire.

"It's a great song," I answered, having finished my looksee, and inclined my head toward the dance floor. "And the kids seem to like it."

He nodded. "So they do. But you aren't dancing."

"I'm taking a breather. I was out there for nearly an hour," I told him, practically yelling to ensure that he could hear me over the pulsating music.

"Oh? Like dancing, do you?"

"I get around." Realizing how that sounded, I waved my hands. "That's not what I meant. I just mean I like to dance."

He laughed and settled a bottle of beer on the table. "I was going to give you the benefit of the doubt," he said, smiling softly and giving me a full-on look at his eyes. They weren't brown, as I'd first thought, but a kind of mottled navy blue.

And I was struck by the thought that when he finally

kissed me, they would flash and deepen, silver pulsing at the edges—

Wait. When he *finally* kissed me? Where in God's name had that come from?

I narrowed my gaze at him, guessing the source of the trickery. "Did you just try to glamour me?"

"Why do you ask?" His expression was innocent. Too innocent, but a corner of my mouth twitched anyway.

"Because I'm not interested in finding out what color your eyes turn when you kiss."

He grinned wickedly. "So it's the condition of, what, my mouth that's on your mind?"

I rolled my eyes dramatically, and he laughed and tipped back his beer, taking a swallow. "You're wounding my ego, you know."

I gave his body, at least the portion that wasn't hidden under the table, a quick appraisal. "I doubt that," I told him, and took a heartening sip of my own cocktail. A quick glance around the club confirmed the suspicion, revealing more than a few women—and a handful of men—whose eyes were glued to the man beside me. Given the intensity of their gazes—and my penchant for stepping on toes—I wondered if he was some kind of vampire celebrity I was supposed to know about. Afraid of being gauche again, I didn't want to come right out and ask, so I decided to carefully steer my way toward an introduction. "You come here a lot?"

He wet his lips and looked away briefly, then back at me, grinning wildly like he knew a special secret. "I'm here quite a bit. I don't remember seeing you before."

"It's my first time," I admitted. I inclined my head toward Mallory and Catcher, who swayed at the edge of the crowd, their bodies mashed together from the waist down, their hands at each other's hips. Quick work, I thought, grinning at Mallory when she caught my eye.

"I'm here with friends," I told him.

"You're new—newly made, I mean."

"Four days. And you?"

"It's impolite to ask someone his age."

I laughed. "You just did!"

"Ah, but this is my place." That explained the secret smile, but since I knew nothing about the club, it didn't give me any helpful information about who he was.

"Can I get you a drink?"

I held up the half-full cocktail in my hand. "I'm good. Thanks, though."

He nodded and sipped his own beer. "How are you finding vampiredom?"

"If it were a house," I answered after some serious consideration, "I'd call it a fixer-upper."

He snorted, then covered his nose with the back of his hand while sliding me an amused glance. It made me smile to think that even cute vampire boys got beer up their noses. "Well said."

I grinned at him. "We do try. How do you find vampiredom?"

He crossed his arms, cradling the beer against his chest, and gave me a once-over. "The perks are nice."

"Oh, come on. Surely you've got better lines than that."

He looked heartbroken. "I'm pulling out all my best material."

"Then I'd hate to see the bottom of that barrel."

He put a hand on my shoulder and moved closer, the motion sending little sparks across my skin, then panned an outstretched hand in front of us. "Imagine a landscape of nothing but astrology references and naughty limericks. That's what you're going to reduce me to."

I covered my heart in mock sympathy. "I'd say that I'm sorry to hear that, but mostly I'm sorry for the women who have to listen to it."

"You're killing me here."

"Oh, don't blame this on me," I said on a laugh. "It's the material that needs work."

"Oh, I blame you," he said solemnly. "I'm going to die a lonely man—"

"You're immortal."

"I'm going to live a long, lonely life," he quickly corrected, slouching down a little in the booth, "because you're being overly critical about my pickup lines."

I patted his arm, the muscle firm beneath my hand, and felt a sympathetic blush cross my cheeks. "Look," I told him. "You're a nice-looking guy." Under. Statement. "I doubt you need pickup lines. There's probably a desperate woman out there just waiting for you to come along."

He mimicked pulling a knife out of his chest. "Nice-looking? *Nice?!* That's the kiss of death. And you think a desperate woman is the best I can do?" He made a frustrated sound, the effect of which was dampened by the impish tilt of his mouth. Putting the bottle back on the table, he stood up. I thought I'd managed to scare him away, until he held out a hand. I raised questioning brows.

"Since you've wounded me, I figure you owe me a dance."

There was no room for debate in the pronouncement, no space for error or adjustment. Was it the male vampire mind, I wondered, that precluded the possibility of discussion? That couldn't comprehend a challenge to authority? Or maybe it was an authority issue. Based on what I'd heard about his sports fixation, I didn't think this was Scott Grey, the head of the House that bore his name. Whoever he was, he exuded that same sense of purpose as Ethan. He was high on the ladder, whatever House claimed him.

And I, of course, was but a lowly Initiate. But a lowly, *single* Initiate, so I stood and took his hand.

"Good," he said, eyes twinkling, then linked our fingers together and led me to the dance floor, which gave me another chance to appraise. He was a couple of inches taller than me, maybe right at six feet. His bottom half was as rock-and-roll as his top—dark, distressed jeans that perfectly encased his long legs, black boots, and a thick leather belt that held the jeans at his hips. And best of all, a divine tush that was perfectly framed by the designer denim. The man was a walking Diesel ad.

When he found a spot for us, he turned back to me and lifted my hands around his neck, put his hands at my hips, and moved in perfect syncopation to the music. He didn't try complicated dance steps—no twirls, no bends, no demonstrations of his prowess. But he moved his hips against mine in time to the throbbing beat, all the while staring down at me with a quirky half smile. Then he wet his lips and leaned forward. I thought he meant to kiss me, and I flinched, but instead he said, his lips close to my ear, "Thanks for not refusing me. I'd have had to slink out of my own club."

"I'm sure your ego would have withstood it. You're a big, strong vampire, after all."

He chuckled. "Somehow, you don't seem all that impressed with vampiredom, so I wasn't sure I had that to recommend me."

"Fair enough," I gave him. "But you've got really nice . . . shoes."

He blinked, then cast a dubious glance at his boots. "They were in my closet."

I snorted and plucked at the sleeve of his jacket. "Please. You've been planning this outfit for a week."

He burst out laughing, throwing his head back to revel in the moment. When he settled down again, occasionally wracked by aftershocks of laughter, he smiled keenly down at me. "I admit it. I give a shit what I look like." Then he plucked at the thin cap sleeve of my shirt. "But look what it got me."

There was no response I could give to that other than to beam back at him for the compliment, so that was exactly what I did. He smiled back and put his hands at my hips, and

I settled mine to the firm curves of his shoulders, and we danced. We danced until the song changed, jumping immediately to something faster, something stronger, and then we kept dancing—silently, intently, as bodies moved around us.

I realized then that part of the buzz, of the vibration of my limbs, wasn't from the raucous music. It came from him, from the tangible hum of power that rode beneath that trim, stage-ready form in front of me. He was a vampire, and a powerful one.

The music changed again, and he leaned forward. "What if I asked for your phone number?"

I grinned up at him. "Wouldn't you like my name first?"

He nodded thoughtfully. "That's probably important information."

"Merit," I told him. "And you are?"

His response wasn't what I expected. His cheery grin faded, and he froze in place, even as people moved around us. His hands dropped from my hips, and I self-consciously tugged my hands back from his shoulders.

"Morgan. Navarre, Second. Which House are you?"

That explained the vibe of power. I had a bad feeling about his reaction to my answer, but offered anyway, tentatively, "Cadogan?"

Silence, then: "How did you get in here?"

I blinked at him. "What?"

"How did you get in here? My club. How did you get in here?" His gaze took on a steely glint, and I guessed that flirty, getting-to-know-you time was over. Then I remembered Catcher's words, his warning that Cadogan was looked down upon for drinking from humans.

I scanned his face, trying to read his expression, trying to gauge if that was where the sudden anger had come from—some irrational bit of House discrimination. "Are you joking?"

He grabbed my hand and yanked me through the dancers off and away from the dance floor. When we were back in the club proper, he forced me to a stop and glared at me. "I asked how you got in here."

"I came in through the front door just like everyone else. Would you just tell me what's wrong?"

Before he could answer, his troops arrived, a cadre of vampires who clustered around him. Front and center was Celina Desaulniers, Chicago's most famous vampire. She was as beautiful in person as she was on TV. A pinup-worthy, comic book–curvy vampire—slim build, long legs, tiny waist, voluptuous bosom. She had long, wavy black hair that set off bright blue eyes and porcelain skin. Hiding very little of that skin was a short sheath dress of champagne-colored satin, which was gathered into intricate folds at the bodice. Her heels matched the shade perfectly.

She looked at me with obvious disdain. "And who is this?" Her voice was honey, thick-flowing and effective, even on boy-crazy me. I felt a brief, insistent urge to fall to her feet, to beg her for forgiveness, to move closer just so I could brush a hand against her skin, which I knew would be soft as silk. But I clenched my hands against what I belatedly realized was another Navarre attempt to glamour me, my resistance strengthened by the fact that Mallory and Catcher had joined us and stood behind me supportively. Celina's eyes widened, and I guessed she was surprised the trick hadn't worked.

"Merit," Morgan crisply said, the tattletale. "Cadogan."

"Would someone please explain to me what the problem is?" I got no response to the question. Instead, Celina looked at me, looked me over, arching a delicately shaped eyebrow. She repeated Morgan's name, an implicit demand.

"You need to leave," Morgan said. "We've got humans here, and we don't allow Cadogan vamps in the club."

I stared at him. What did they think I was going to do? Start munching on dancers? "Look, the guy at the door let my friends and me in here," I said, intent on making them understand, on pushing through blind prejudice. "We weren't causing any trouble—we were dancing. We certainly weren't harassing humans."

I looked to Morgan for support, but he only looked away. That small act of rejection, of denial, pricked. Frustration began to give way to anger, and my blood began to fire. I moved to take a step forward, but a hand at my elbow stopped me.

"The fight's not worth it," Catcher whispered. "Not for this." He gently tugged me back in the direction of the door. "Let's get out of here."

Celina looked at me again, and for a moment we were the only two vampires in the room. Whatever power she had— and it was far beyond anything I'd yet felt—crept toward me in slow amoebic tendrils. The length of a heartbeat, and I was wrapped inside it, enveloped by it. At first, I wasn't sure what she was trying to do—the impulse wasn't physically threatening, but it was aggressive. I didn't think she could injure me, but she tried to slink inside me, looking for weaknesses, feeling out my strengths. She was sizing me up, here in front of her Second and her patrons, in front of Catcher and Mallory. She was assessing me, testing me, waiting for me to cry out, to step back, to fall beneath that barrage of power.

I knew I wasn't strong enough to put up a wall against it, but neither would I give in, beg her to stop, cry uncle. And even if I had been strong enough, I didn't know how to fight it, how to battle against it. So I did the only thing I could think of—absolutely nothing. I blanked my mind, thinking that if I didn't fight her, if I put up no walls, it would slip and flow around me. That was easier said than done—I had to fight not to hold my breath as the air thickened, as it fairly pulsed with energy.

But I managed to keep my thoughts clear, stared back into her blue eyes, and let a corner of my mouth curve up.

Her eyes flashed silver.

In vampire terms, she blinked.

"Celina."

Morgan's voice broke the spell. I saw her concentration

waver, watched her body relax as the magic dissipated around us. She took a breath and slid her gaze to Morgan, schooling her features into haughty impermeability. "You've competition, pet, from Ethan's little plaything."

I nearly growled, and nearly jumped forward to get to her (although God only knows what I would have done), but Catcher's fingers, still around my arm, tightened.

"Merit," Catcher softly said, "let it go."

"Take the advice, little toy," Celina told me.

I wanted to snark back, but that would give her what she wanted. I decided I wasn't going to throw back anger or snarky words. No—this was my chance to play the better vampire. To play the cool, calm, collected girl. To play the Initiate who still remembered what it was to be human.

I kept my gaze on Celina, and copied a move I'd seen Ethan make: I slid my hands into the pockets of my jeans, kept my posture businesslike, and let my voice go a little deeper, a little smokier. "Not a toy, Celina. But rest assured—I know exactly what I am." That the words fairly mimicked Ethan's didn't occur to me until much later.

"Good girl," Catcher whispered, and tugged my arm, leading me away. I followed with what little pride I had left, and managed not to throw back a glare at the brown-haired boy who'd sold me out to his Master.

I kept quiet until we were a block from the club, and Catcher, apparently having deemed us a safe enough distance away, offered, "Okay. Let her loose."

And I did. "I cannot believe people would act that way! It's the twenty-first century, for God's sake. How is it okay to discriminate? And what the hell was with Celina testing me?" I turned to Catcher, my eyes probably wild, and grabbed his arm. "Did you feel that? What she did?"

"You'd have to be completely oblivious not to feel it," Mallory put in. "The woman's a piece of work."

"I thought you said vampires didn't have magic?" I asked him. "What the hell was that?"

Catcher shook his head. "Vamps can't *do* magic. They can't perform it. They can't bend and shape it. But you're still born of that magic, that power, whether you call vampirism genetic or not. You can sense it. Test it. And vamps can always do what vamps do best—manipulate." He pulled the Red flyer from his pocket again.

"They baited us," I realized. "They identified our cars, planted the fliers."

Catcher nodded and replaced the paper again. "She wanted a look."

"At me?"

"I don't know," he said, eyes on Mallory. "Maybe. Maybe not."

"And then there's Bedroom Eyes," I said. "I can't believe I fell for that pickup, actually danced with him. Do you think it was all a ploy?"

Catcher sighed, linked hands above his head, and gazed back at Red. "I don't know, Merit. Do you think he was plotting?"

He'd seemed sincere. Genuine. But who could tell? "I don't know," I decided. "But you know what the moral of this story is?"

We'd reached the Volvo, and I paused in the process of unlocking the doors, waiting to ensure I had their attention. When they both looked at me, I offered, "Never trust a vampire. *Ever.*"

I was about to squeeze into the front seat when I noticed that the Hummer parked in front of my car bore a vanity plate that read "NVRRE." Grinning impishly, I darted toward it and kicked one oversized tire. When the car's alarm began chirping wildly, I scrambled into my car, started it, and hit the gas.

It didn't do much to the Hummer, but the catharsis was nice.

When we were on our way and blocks from the club, I met Catcher's gaze in the rearview mirror.

"All that drama because we drink?"

"In part," Catcher said. "The flyer got you into the club for a look; drinking got you kicked out. It's a convenient way for Celina to survey the city, have folks come unwittingly to her door."

"Unwittingly to her web," Mallory muttered, and I nodded. It was pointless, I suppose, to rue the House I'd been born into, but what a way to enter the world of vampires. Four days out of the change and a chunk of Chicago's population decided they didn't like me because of my affiliation. Because of what others did. It stank of human prejudice.

Catcher stretched out in the backseat. "If it makes you feel any better, both of them will get what's coming to them."

I tapped fingers against the steering wheel as I drove, then met his gaze again. "Meaning what, exactly?"

He shrugged and averted his gaze, looking out the side window. Apparently he was psychic, too, our former fourth-grade sorcerer.

"Catch, did you know this was going to happen? Did you know it was a Navarre bar?"

Catch? I looked over at Mallory, surprised that they'd already progressed to nicknames. Apparently I'd missed some serious bonding on the dance floor. But her expression showed nothing.

"Yes, *Catch*," I parroted, "did you set this up?"

"I wanted to check out the club," he said. "I knew it was a Navarre club, but it hadn't occurred to me that we'd been baited. I certainly didn't intend for us to get thrown out, to become actors in Celina's morality play, although I suppose it shouldn't surprise me. Vampires," he said with a tired sigh, "are fucking exhausting."

Mallory and I exchanged a glance as she twirled a lock of hair around her finger. "Yes, dahling," she said, doing a lovely Zsa-Zsa Gabor imitation, "vam-piahs ah exhausting."

I faked a smile, and drove us home.

* * *

I was brushing my teeth in ratty pajamas—an ex-boyfriend's pale green T-shirt that read *I'M A ZOMBIE* and a pair of frayed boxers—when Mallory, still in her club clothes, rushed into the upstairs bathroom and slammed the door shut. I paused midbrush, and looked at her expectantly.

"So, I have to break up with Mark."

I grinned. "That may not be a bad idea," I agreed and resumed brushing. Mallory stepped next to me in front of the counter and met my gaze in the mirror.

"I'm serious."

"I know. But you were talking about breaking up with Mark before you met Catcher." I finished brushing, splashed a little water in my mouth, and spit. Thank God for friends who were close enough to watch you brush without getting grossed out.

"I know. He's not right for me. But it's really late, and I need sleep, and I feel really weird about this I-got-my-job-because-I-wished-for-it thing. And then there's Catcher."

She quieted, obviously thinking, and her silence left a space for strains of noise from the downstairs television, which floated through the house. A narrator was describing the plight of a battered woman who'd overcome adversity, cancer, and desperate poverty to start a new life with her children.

I wiped my mouth on a towel and looked at her. "And the fact that he's downstairs watching the Lifetime channel again."

She scratched her head. "He finds it inspiring?"

I leaned a hip against the bathroom counter. "You should go for it."

"I'm just not sure. All of a sudden, about this, I'm not sure. Work, I'm sure about. Your fangs, I'm fine with. But this boy. He's got baggage, and magic, and I don't know. . . ."

I hugged her, understanding that this wasn't just about Catcher, but her acknowledgment of the new shape of her life. Of the fact that her interest in the occult, in magic, had become something much, much more personal.

"Whatever you do," I told her, "I'll be here."

Mallory sniffed, pulling back to dab carefully at the tears that lay beneath her blue eyes. "Yeah, but you're immortal. You've got the time."

"You're such a cow." I walked out of the bathroom and flipped off the light, leaving her in the dark.

"Uh, who ate her weight in sausage earlier tonight?"

I laughed and walked into my bedroom. "Have fun with Romeo," I told her, and shut the door behind me. In the cool quiet of the bedroom, it still being a couple of hours from dawn, I snagged back the blankets, lit the lamp next to the bed, and settled in with a book of fairy tales. It didn't occur to me that given the current shape of my life, I didn't need to read them. I was living them.

CHAPTER EIGHT

FANGS MEAN NEVER HAVING

TO SAY YOU'RE SORRY.

At sunset I woke to the smell of tomatoes and garlic, and trundled downstairs in my pajamas. The television blared, but the living room was empty. I shuffled into the kitchen and found Mallory and Catcher at the kitchen island, both tucking into plates of spaghetti with meat sauce. My stomach growled. "I don't suppose there's any of that left?"

"Stove," Catcher said, gnawing on the end of a piece of baguette. "We left it out. Knew you'd be down."

Did *we*? I wondered with a smile, and shuffled to the stove. I wasn't sure how I felt about spaghetti for breakfast—or breakfast at nearly eight at night—but my stomach suffered no qualms, grumbling loudly as I poured the remains of the pot onto a plate. Seeking a drink, I went to the refrigerator to grab a soda. But my hand paused over the bags of blood, my teeth suddenly pulsing with the urge to sink into a bag. I touched my tongue to my teeth, felt the prick of my descended eyeteeth. Gone, though, was that raging, aggressive hunger I'd felt two days ago. Still, I pulled out a bag of type A and looked tentatively at Mallory and Catcher.

"I need blood," I told them, "but I can take it somewhere else if you're grossed out."

Mallory chuckled and chewed a forkful of spaghetti. "You're asking for permission to bite me? 'Cause you should know I don't care about the other thing."

I smiled gratefully and, permission granted, pulled a clean glass from the cabinet and filled it from the bag. I wasn't sure how long to heat it, so I set the microwave timer for just a few seconds, popped it in, and closed the door. When it dinged, I nearly lurched forward in eagerness to get to it, and drained the glass in seconds. The blood had a faintly plasticky aftertaste, presumably from the bag, but it was well worth the trouble. I repeated the move—pour, heat, sip—until I'd drained the bag, then patted my stomach happily, took my plate of spaghetti, and pulled out a stool next to Catcher.

"That took all of three minutes," he pointed out, sprinkling red pepper across his noodles.

"And was kind of anticlimactic," Mal said, "since you just stared at the microwave the entire time. I figured you'd at least give some kind of invocation, maybe some gnawing the plastic. Growling." She ate another forkful of spaghetti, then offered, "Clawing the ground. Barking."

"I'm a vampire, not a corgi," I reminded her and tucked into my own spaghetti. "So," I offered, when I'd chowed a couple of tasty forkfuls. Say what you wanted about Catcher's attitude, the boy could cook. "What happened around here today?"

"Mark's going to start skydiving," Catcher said. "Fortunately, we don't have to care anymore."

Mallory gave him a skewering glance. "I really wish you wouldn't put it like that. He has feelings, you know."

"Mmm-hmmm."

"You could also temper that attitude a little," Mallory warned, sliding off her stool. She dumped her plate in the sink and stalked out of the kitchen.

"Trouble in paradise?" I asked when she was gone, sliding Catcher a glance.

He lifted a shoulder. "She had Mark come over so she could break up with him in person. He was pretty upset. They both cried."

"Ah."

We ate silently until we'd cleaned our plates, and he put both in the sink. "Let's give her some space. We'll go to the gym. I'll give you a couple of hours. Then I need to get to the office."

"On a Saturday?"

He only shrugged in response. Catcher, I was learning, was a careful guard of information. The skill probably made him invaluable to my grandfather.

As we left the kitchen, I asked, "Can I hold your sword today?"

Catcher glanced back over his shoulder and lifted a brow.

"*The* sword," I corrected. "*The* sword."

"We'll see."

We trained for two hours, skipping the fitness evaluation and moving right into the basic moves Catcher had begun to teach me the day before. I'd always been a fast learner, a skill honed from the necessity of picking up dance routines quickly, but my muscle memory solidified even faster now, and the moves were nearly automatic by the time the session was done. That didn't mean I was elegant or graceful, but I'd learned what to do, at least.

Catcher made halfway good on his promise to let me hold the sword. He wouldn't let me touch the unsheathed blade, but he allowed me to strap on the belt that held the scabbard, before taking it away again to demonstrate how to draw and sheath the sword from a kneeling position. The moves he taught me, he explained, were similar to those in Iaido, and were designed to allow the sword bearer to react to a surprise—and thus dishonorable—attack. I almost asked why, if a surprise attack was so dishonorable, he needed to teach me how to defend against it. But I guessed the chip on his shoulder would color his answer, and I'd get a response about dishonorable vampires. So I didn't bother to ask.

When Catcher was done with me, I changed back into street clothes and said my goodbyes. He left for my grandfather's South Side office, while I opted to play the good little Cadogan vamp. I drove to Hyde Park with the intention of updating Ethan on the events of the day before. I wasn't thrilled about seeing him again, not after our last encounter, but I had no doubt he'd come to hear about our activities at Red. And that tale, I thought, would be better coming directly from me. I wasn't sure how to broach the issue of Morgan, of the fact that I'd flirted with a Navarre vamp not even twenty-four hours after our shared kiss and Ethan's ignominious proposal, and decided as I walked into Cadogan House, his domain, that it was probably best not to mention it at all.

Ethan, the guards informed me, was in his office. I walked directly back and knocked on his door, although I was sure he'd been informed of my arrival. He barked out a Picard-worthy "Come," and I walked inside and closed the office door behind me. Ethan, in his uniform á la Armani, was behind his desk, an open file folder in front of him. He stared intently at its contents, his eyes tracking across the page as he read.

"Look who's come willingly into my den of iniquity."

I relaxed incrementally, more than happy to accept sarcasm as the prevailing mood, and stopped in front of his desk. "Can I have a minute?"

"What have you done now?"

Evidently we were going to avoid the topic of our kiss altogether. Fine by me.

"Nothing, but thanks for that ringing vote of confidence. My ego's all swelled up."

"Hmmm," he muttered with obvious doubt, his gaze still on the papers on his desk. "If you're here willingly, and I didn't hear any screaming from Malik's having dragged you down the hallway, I assume you've"—he paused contemplatively—"resigned yourself to your fate?"

"I'm working on accepting the fact that I'm a vampire," I said, perching on the edge of his desk.

"Our hearts are simultaneously aflutter," Ethan responded, finally looking up, those haunting green eyes on me. He relaxed into his chair. "Although I can't see that your wardrobe has improved."

"I was training with Catcher Bell. He's introducing me to the katas."

"Yes. We've spoken about that. What brings you by?"

"An unpleasant run-in with Navarre vamps."

Ethan watched me quietly for a moment, then folded his arms across his chest. "Explain."

"I went to Red last night. You know the place?"

He nodded. "It's the Navarre club."

If only Catcher had mentioned that going in, I ruefully thought. But no sense in dwelling. "They let us in, Mallory, Catcher and me, but kicked us out when a Navarre vamp discovered I was from Cadogan."

Ethan's brow furrowed. "Since I doubt you spread the information yourself, how did they find out you were from Cadogan?"

"I met a vampire from Navarre—Morgan?"

A careful pause; then Ethan nodded again.

"He introduced himself, offered his House affiliation, and I did the same."

"Introduced himself?"

I nodded. "That's when he found out I was from Cadogan, and when he became a complete jackass. Celina and some other vamps were called out, and they kicked us out of the club. I wanted to tell you in case you heard about it from someone else and assumed I'd been out—I don't know—wreaking vampire havoc and giving Cadogan a bad name." Or a worse name, I mentally corrected.

Ethan's gaze narrowed. "Would I assume that?"

"Why lay blame where it belongs when you can use me as a scapegoat?"

"Touché," he allowed, one corner of his mouth tipped into a smile. I inclined my head.

Ethan rose from his chair, hands linked behind his back, and walked to the conference table at the end of the room. Then he turned and leaned back against it between two of its matching chairs. The move put distance between us, and I found it interesting that he was so eager to get away.

"And yet they let you into the club in the first place. Why?"

"They may have known who I was. We found flyers, Catcher and I, for Red on our cars. He suggested we give it a whirl, and they let us in at the door."

"She wanted a look at you."

I nodded. "That was Catcher's theory."

"Celina likely knew your family name, saw the registry list in the paper, and arranged a very passive-aggressive hello."

"She sounds like a treat."

"Celina isn't the most . . . philanthropic of vampires," Ethan said. "But she's smart. She's focused, determined, and very, very protective of her vamps. Navarre has flourished under her leadership, and the GP loves her. Added to that is the fact that she's one of the most powerful vampires in the U.S."

I met his gaze, and thought about the test she'd given me, thought about the fact that I'd withstood enough of it to put a sulky look on her face.

"Her psychic skills are particularly noteworthy," he continued. "She has an amazing ability to glamour. It's rather like the stories of old about mortals who go dopey-eyed after ill-timed eye contact."

He cocked his head at me, gave me an appraising look. I felt—just as I'd felt with Celina the night before—the subtle flow of a testing magic. But where Celina's investigation was

pushy, aggressive, Ethan's moved like water over rocks—
slipping, trickling, checking the shape of what lay beneath.

"You'll measure up," he finally concluded.

I nodded, opting not to tell him that she'd tried to glamour
me, or that she'd failed. That I'd felt the pull, but shaken it
off. If that was a sample of my burgeoning powers, he'd find
out soon enough.

Without elaborating, Ethan moved across the room to the
wall of bookshelves behind the leather couches, and pulled
out a slim book. "Come here, Merit."

I pushed off the desk and followed, stopping a few feet
shy of him. Ethan flipped through the red leather volume
until he found a particular page, then handed the book, the
pages spread open between his long fingers, to me. When I
met his gaze, he tapped the book with a finger. A sense of
dread coiled in my abdomen, but I made myself look.

They were as horrible as that bit of prescience predicted.
On each side of the page were woodcut prints, their black
lines stark against thick linen paper. Each woodcut depicted
a vampire, or medieval imaginings of vampires anyway. The
left-hand print showed a busty maiden lying beneath a for-
est tree. An animalistic caricature of a male vampire, his
inch-long fangs bared and ready to bite, reached over her.
The vampire was naked from the waist up, and he wore no
shoes. His fingers were tipped by claws, his hair long, dark
and mangy. Perhaps most telling, his feet were cloven
hooves. Beneath the woodcut, in elaborate script, were the
words: *Beware Ye the Vampyre, Whose Luste Tempts the
Chaste*.

But the industrious peasant who'd carved the original
block had offered not only a problem—the virgin-despoiling
vamp—but a solution: On the facing page, the vampire stood
alone, his hands bound behind the tree to which he was also
tied at the ankles and neck. His neck had been cut, his head
tipping precariously to the side, and his gut had been split,
organs spilling from a gaping wound in his belly. Through

his heart, which lay on the ground beside him, was a wooden stake.

Perhaps worst of all, his eyes were open, tears streaming from the corners, his gaze on something just off the page, his expression one of terror, pain, and loss. This wasn't caricature. This was portraiture, an image of the vampire in the depths of agony. The artist, if that was the appropriate word for the creator of something so gruesome, had offered little sympathy. This woodcut bore the inscription *Rejoice in the Terror Cut Downe*.

"Jesus," I mumbled, suddenly trembling enough to shake the book in my hands. Ethan took it back, closed it, and slid it carefully back into place.

I glanced up at him. His expression was unsurprisingly solemn. "We are not at war," he said. "Not *today*. But that could change at any moment, so we do what we must to protect peace. We've learned to be careful to distinguish our friends from our enemies, and to be sure that our enemies understand who our friends are."

That, I mused, echoed Catcher's sentiments regarding the state of vampire-shifter relations. It made sense to me that shifters, who'd opted for anonymity over stepping in to protest the massacre of vampires, weren't a popular bunch among the Houses. It also explained the vamps' tendency to band together, to nest into Houses, to form explicit alliances and view outsiders with wariness.

"Did you see"—I groped for an appropriate word— "punishments like that?"

"Not exactly like that. But I lost friends in the Second Clearing, and barely lived through it myself."

I frowned and worried my bottom lip with my teeth. "But if that's true, wasn't it ill advised to hold a press conference? To announce our existence at all? What did anonymity risk?"

Ethan didn't answer. His expression didn't change. He just looked at me, as if willing me to reach a conclusion he was unwilling to speak aloud.

The conclusion wasn't hard to reach: Coming out of the closet put us front and center before humans, endangered our survival, even, as my grandfather put it, in the post–Harry Potter era. We'd been lucky so far—Congressional investigations and minor rioting notwithstanding. Curiosity had generally won out over vampiricide. God willing, our luck would hold, but the fact that a vampire killer was loose in Chicago and that our House was suspected of involvement didn't bode well. The tide could so easily turn.

I was suddenly eager to be home again, safe inside my locked house, safe behind wood and stone and sword-bearing guards.

"I should go," I told him, and he walked me to the office door. "Do you think you'll hear from Celina about the club incident?"

"I'll hear from Celina." When we reached the office door, he opened it and waved an invitational hand. "Thank you for informing me about your . . . escapades."

I objected to the phrasing, but could tell he was trying to lighten the heavy mood, so I just smirked in response. "No problem. Thanks for the history lesson."

Ethan nodded and began, "If you'd only read—" but I held up a hand.

"I know. I've been advised to read the *Canon*. I'll hit the book when I get home." I held up two fingers to my brow. "Scout's honor."

A corner of his mouth tipped up. "I'm sure if you only applied yourself, you could find some use for that intellect beyond sarcasm."

"But what would be the fun of that?"

Ethan leaned out the door. "I realize that obedience would be a novelty to you, but I'd find it thrilling. You've two days left before the Commendation, the oaths. You might spend that time contemplating your allegiance."

That stopped me, and I turned on my heel to see him again. "If I'm one of twelve, have you given the rest the same speeches you're giving me? Made the same threats? Doubted?" *Made the same offer?*

I wondered if he'd lie to me, give me some speech about duty and being the Master of the House. But instead he said, "No. The stakes aren't so high with the rest of your cohort. They're foot soldiers, Merit."

When he didn't elaborate, I prodded, "And I'm . . . ?"

"Not." With that enigmatic response, he went back into his office and closed the door behind him.

It was nearly midnight when I returned to Wicker Park. The house was empty, and I wondered if Mallory and Catcher had reached some kind of peace after the dinnertime fight. I was starving, so I made a ham sandwich, layered on some tortilla chips, squished the concoction into a napkin, and carried it into the living room. I turned on the television for background noise—and it was unfortunate that I now lived in the hours of infomercials, B-movies and syndicated garbage—and pulled the *Canon* into my lap. I ate as I read, filling an hour of time and finishing chapter one, then moving on to the "Servicing Your Lord" tutorial. Luckily, the text was a little less connubial than the name sounded. Where the first chapter was a kind of introduction to vampirism, chapter two offered more detail about the duties of the Novitiate vampire—loyalty, allegiance, and something the book referred to as "Grateful Condescension," which was as ass-backwardly Jane Austen–esque as its name suggested. I was supposed to offer Ethan my "Polite Regarde," treating him with deference and respect and generally meeting his requests and demands with gratefulness that he'd deigned to make them of me in the first place.

I chuckled, realizing the degree to which my unacquiescent behavior probably shocked him and wondering why the *Canon* hadn't been substantively updated since, what, Regency England?

I'd just balled up my napkin and tossed it on the coffee table when a knock sounded at the door. Mallory, maybe, having forgotten her keys, or Ethan with a demand that I Gratefully Condescend to his Honored Personage. A little too comfortable with the guards out front, I made the mistake of opening the door without checking the peephole first. He stuck a black boot in the door before I could slam it shut in his face.

"I'm sorry," he offered through the three inches of open space.

"Get your foot out of my house."

Morgan shifted, peering through the crack. "I'm here to apologize profusely. And I'm willing to genuflect." His voice turned softer. "Look, I'm really sorry about the scene last night. I could have handled it better."

I pulled open the door and offered him my haughtiest stare. "You 'could have handled it better'? In the sense of not humiliating my friends and me? In not backing me up when I said—when you knew—that we hadn't been causing problems? Or in not treating us like trash because I'm from a different House than you? Which part of it could you have handled better? *Specifically*."

Morgan smiled sheepishly, an expression that was irritatingly cute on a dark-haired, bedroom-eyed boy. He was in jeans again tonight, this time paired with a smoky blue quarter-sleeved T-shirt that snugged his torso. I noted a hint of gold around his neck, and I guessed it was the medal of Navarre House, similar in style to the one worn by Ethan, but, as last night had shown, symbolizing a very, very different philosophy.

I stared him down, but he met my gaze, one corner of his mouth tipped into a charmingly lopsided smile. "Please?"

I blew out a slow breath that ruffled my bangs, but stood back to let him in. "Come in."

"Thanks."

I walked into the living room, assuming he'd follow, dropped onto the couch and crossed my legs. I looked up at him expectantly while he closed the door behind us. "Well?"

"Well, what?"

I waved a hand at the room. "Start genuflecting. Let's see some knee action."

"You're serious."

I lifted my brows. He responded in kind, but finally nodded his head, then walked between the couches. He dropped to one knee, then held out his hands. "I'm monumentally sorry for the pain and humiliation that I caused you and your—"

"Both knees."

"Pardon?"

"I'd prefer to see both knees on the ground. I mean, if you're going to grovel, be the best groveler you can, right?"

Morgan watched me for a moment, mouth twitching, the smile threatening to break, but acquiesced with grave solemnity. He bent both knees to the ground, then looked up at me through those navy blue eyes with an expression that would have worked on a loyal hound. "I'm really sorry."

I watched him for a moment, let him linger there on the floor, then nodded. "Okay."

So I wasn't immune to a cute boy with a sappy expression. Really, what twenty-seven-year-old ex-graduate-student-cum-Cadogan-vampire was?

Morgan rose and dusted off his knees, then took a seat on the love seat behind him. Just as I was wondering why, exactly, he'd decided to play contrite, he offered, "There's a lot of talk in Navarre about Cadogan. About Houses that drink. There are a lot of vampires with long memories, and a lot of them are affiliated with Navarre. It's not you personally—it's more like decades of inbred fear. Fear that everything we've worked to build—the House system, the Presidium, the *Canon*—will be brought down by vamps who drink."

It was a good argument, and one that I could appreciate,

having seen a sample of the punishments doled out to vampires by humans. However, I reminded him, "It was Navarre that held the press conference, Morgan. It was Navarre that announced our existence."

"It was a precautionary move. Every day that passed without vampires taking the initiative was one day closer to humans doing it for us. Pushing us into the spotlight in a way we couldn't control. In a way we couldn't spin. This was about coming out on *our* terms."

I stretched my legs out on the couch and rested my head on the armrest. "And do you believe that?"

"It doesn't especially matter what I believe. I'm Celina's Second. I act as she wishes. But having said that, yes, I do believe it. The world's a different place today."

"You act as she wishes, yet here you are, conversing with the enemy."

He chuckled. "It seemed worth the minor mutiny."

"And I wasn't worth it last night when she was calling us out?"

Morgan sighed, then lifted both hands to run them through his hair. "At the risk of sounding ungrateful for your forgiveness, I already apologized for that." He let his hands fall and offered me a hopeful look. "Maybe we could talk about something else? Not vampires or drinking. Not alliances or Houses. Just pretend to be normal for a couple of hours?"

I let the smile spread slowly. "How do you feel about the Bears?"

Morgan snorted, then looked down the hallway. "Kitchen down there?"

I nodded.

"Can I get something to eat?"

Had I any interest in dating the boy—had it not evaporated last night when I'd promised never to flirt with another vampire again—I'd have decided this was the lamest second date ever. "I guess."

He popped up and walked to the threshold. "Thanks." He

disappeared down the hallway, but called back, "I'm a Packer fan. I was born in Madison."

He was rustling through a drawer when I reached the kitchen. "You have to admit it—Green Bay's a better team, especially this year. Chicago has problems with its O line, there's a quarterback issue, and you've got no defensive secondary."

I leaned back against the doorframe and crossed my arms. "You're going to stand in my kitchen, eating my food, going through my things, and bash my Bears? You're either brave or stupid."

Morgan pulled out a knife and cutting board, then moved to a stack of sandwich items he'd already arranged on the countertop—a loaf of nutty bread, mustard, mayo, ham, American cheese, Swiss cheese (an international cheese détente!), smoked turkey, a jar of bread and butter pickle slices, black olives, lettuce, and a tomato.

In other words, the contents of our refrigerator but for the sodas and blood.

Then he grabbed two cans of soda. He popped the tab on one, and offered the other to me as he sipped, one hip cocked against the cabinets.

"Thoughtful of you to offer," I drily said, accepting the soda as I joined him at the counter. "Don't they feed you at Navarre House?"

He cut off two healthy slices of bread, then went to work on the tomato, slicing as he talked. "They throw out some gruel between the indoctrination sessions and propaganda films. Then we're off for a good marching around the grounds and the recitation of sonnets to Celina's loveliness."

I chuckled and tore off a couple of lettuce leaves, then held them up for his approval. He nodded, then began the very careful process of layering meats, cheeses, vegetables, and condiments on his Dagwood.

"They put out healthy stuff in the cafeteria—I just don't

usually have a chance to make a sandwich my own way, you know?"

Having grown up with too much brie and foie gras and too few processed carbs, I knew very well. That was why I stopped him before he added the final piece of bread. I grabbed the bag of tortilla chips from the other end of the counter and handed them to him.

"Layer of chips," I solemnly explained. "Adds a good crunch."

"Genius," he said, then squished a layer of tortilla chips into his sandwich. We both looked down at it for a moment, four vertical inches of deliciousness.

"Should we take a picture?"

"It's pretty damn impressive."

He cocked his head at it. "I almost hate to ruin it by biting in, but I'm starving, so. . . ." Regrets spoken, he picked it up with two hands and bit in. His eyes closed as he crunched through the first bite. "That's a damn good sandwich."

"Told you," I said, leaning against the counter and pulling the bag of chips toward me.

"Tell me about yourself," he said between bites.

The bag crinkled noisily as I reached for a chip. "What do you want to know?"

"Origins. Interests. Why the daughter of one of the most powerful men in Chicago decided to become a vampire."

I watched him for a minute, a little disappointed that he'd asked, and wondering if the fact that my parents had money was the lodestone of his interest in me. And since he'd known, I wondered if news of my changing and my family connections was circulating through the Houses. Of course, since he thought the decision was mine, he clearly didn't know everything.

"Does it matter who my father is?"

Morgan shrugged lightly. "Not to me. To some, maybe. I wonder if Ethan cares."

He had, I ruefully thought, but that was not how I answered. "He saved my life."

Morgan's gaze shot up. "How?"

I debated what to tell him, but opted for the truth. If he really knew nothing, all the better. If he knew something, maybe the boundaries of his knowledge could help signal the guilty parties. "I was attacked. Ethan saved my life."

Morgan stared at me, then wiped his mouth with a napkin he'd taken from the stainless steel holder on the counter. "You're kidding."

I shook my head. "Someone assaulted me when I was walking across campus. He nearly tore out my throat. Ethan found me and started the change."

Morgan's gaze narrowed. "How do you know Ethan didn't set it up?"

An uncomfortable twitch arced through my stomach. I didn't know that, not for sure. I was relying on instinct and Ethan's explanation, his professions of innocence. I still wondered why he'd happened to be in that spot in the middle of the night, and his answer—something about luck—hadn't been satisfying. I didn't think he'd purposefully hurt me, not physically anyway. Emotionally, though, was a different matter, and all the more reason for me to steer clear of him. He was my boss, and I'd acquiesce as far as necessary to get my job done, whatever that might be. But he was off-limits for anything else, his (conflicted) interest beside the point.

"Merit?"

I blinked back to my kitchen, to Morgan staring at me across the countertop. "Sorry," I said. "Just thinking. I know he didn't set it up. He saved my life." I crossed my fingers under the table, hoped that it was true.

Morgan frowned. "Huh. They found that Cadogan medal at the scene of Jennifer Porter's death."

"Anyone with access to the House could have planted it there—even a Rogue trying to make the House system look bad."

He nodded. "That's a theory. Actually, it's what Celina thinks."

"She doesn't think Ethan did it? Or someone from Cadogan?"

Morgan watched me for a careful moment, then shrugged and finished the final bites of his sandwich. "It would be more accurate to say that we fear people's responses to Cadogan, not the vamps themselves. Peace is fragile."

So I'd heard, but somehow the sentiment didn't ring as true coming from Morgan as it did from Ethan.

"What did you do—before?" he asked.

Having finished the first soda, I moved back to the refrigerator and grabbed another one, popped open the top, and returned to our spot at the counter. "I was a graduate student. English lit."

"Here in Chicago?"

I nodded. "University of Chicago."

"So you wanted to, what, teach?"

"At the college level, yeah. I wanted to be a professor. Romantic medieval literature was my specialty. The Arthurian sagas, Tristan and Isolde, that kind of thing."

"Tristan and Isolde. That's interesting."

I dug into the chip bag for a single whole chip, found one, and crunched into it. "Is it? What did you do before?"

"My dad owned Red, or at least the bar it was before I rehabbed it. He died a few years before I switched, and I took it over."

"Why did you decide to become a vampire?"

Morgan frowned, rubbed the back of his neck. "I had a girlfriend. She was sick, and she was approached by someone in Navarre. We made some overtures to Carlos—he was Celina's Second at the time—and they approved our becoming Initiates. She was bright, strong, would have made a great vampire."

He paused and stared blankly at the counter, and the volume of his voice dropped. "The night came for the change.

They changed me, but she couldn't go through with it. She died about a year later."

"I'm sorry."

"She said she didn't want to live forever. I was young and stupid, felt immortal anyway—who doesn't at that age? I was with her when she died. She wasn't afraid."

We sat quietly for a few minutes, as I let him work through that memory.

"Anyway, that's my story."

"How long ago was that?"

"Nineteen seventy-two."

"So that would make you . . ."

He half chuckled, and I was glad to see a little more color in his face. "An age that will make you uncomfortable."

I leaned against the counter, crossed my arms, and gave him a good looking over. "You look about, what, twenty-eight? That would mean you were born around nineteen forty-four."

"I'm seventy-two," he offered, saving me the subtraction. "Not so old that it seems unreal enough to discount, and just old enough to think of me as . . . *old.*"

"You don't look seventy-two. You certainly don't act seventy-two. Not that there's anything wrong with that," I belatedly added, a finger in the air to emphasize the point.

Morgan laughed. "Thanks, Mer. I don't feel a day over seventy-one."

"A sprightly seventy-one."

"A sprightly seventy-one," he agreed. "There's actually some pretty serious debate out there on the impact of looking young on how we act, on the age we pretend to be."

I smiled dubiously. "Vampire philosophers?"

He smiled back. "Immortality does pose its own set of quandaries."

Immortality was a quandary *I* hadn't fully considered yet, and I wondered what the rest of the vamps were thinking about. "Like?"

Morgan reached out and grabbed the bag of chips, our arms just brushing as he pulled it away. I ignored the little shock that spilt down my arm, reminding myself that I'd sworn off boys with unusually large canines.

"Vamps change identities every sixty years or so," Morgan responded, waving a chip in the air. "And yet, to stay under the radar, we've had to operate within the system. That means we fake our deaths. We have to lie to the friends and family we accumulate in each human lifetime. We forge social security numbers, drivers' licenses, passports. Is that ethical?" He shrugged. "We justify it by saying it's necessary to protect ourselves. But it's still lying."

Thinking of my own hasty exit from academia, I wondered aloud, "Where do they work? These philosophers, I mean."

"They stay pretty cloistered. Some in academia, usually with enough tenure to get basement offices and night classes. You ever see those guys who hang out in coffeehouses— they've got their laptops and those little black notebooks? They're always there at night, scribbling furiously?"

I grinned. "I used to be one of those guys. Well, girls, anyway."

Morgan leaned forward conspiratorially and hooded his fingers into a claw, then pawed at the air. "You never know if they're vamps on the prowl."

"Good to know," I offered with a chuckle. Morgan smiled back at me. It was a nice smile, but it broke when he pulled an empty hand from the plastic chip bag, apparently realizing we'd finished it off. I took it away, crumpled it, and tossed it into the trash, a perfect arc on the shot.

"Nice," he said. "And speaking of hoops, you have something planned?"

I didn't know we'd been speaking of hoops, but I gave him the benefit of the doubt. "What did you have in mind?"

He checked his watch. "It's one fifteen. *SportsCenter*'s probably on."

"It's a date," I said with a firm nod, and led him back into the living room.

He was right. It was on. Even as late as it was, I shouldn't have doubted *SportsCenter* was rolling tape on ESPN. Was it ever *not* on in the wee hours of the morning? We settled back into the living room, watched forty-five minutes of sports-related sarcasm, and debated this year's potential NFL draft picks. When the show was over, Morgan pushed up from the couch.

"I should get going. Couple things I need to check into before dawn, and I should run by Red."

I belatedly realized that it was Saturday night, surely a big night for the club, and that he'd opted to spend it here, eating sandwiches and watching ESPN. As he went for the door, stretching his arms above his head and revealing the curve of smooth skin at the small of his back, I found myself wishing that he wasn't a vampire. We'd reached a kind of comfortable rapport, and a quiet night with ESPN and lumpy sandwiches was a nice change from political intrigue, death threats, and supernatural revelations.

"Thanks for coming by to apologize," I said, rising to walk him to the door. "It would have been nicer if you hadn't been a jackass in the first place, but a girl always appreciates a nice dose of remorse."

Morgan laughed. "Does a girl?"

I smiled back and opened the door, and we stood next to it for a minute, watching each other. Then he leaned down, one hand at my hip, and pressed his lips to mine. Morgan kissed me in slow increments, meeting my lips, then pulling back and moving in again. It was teasing by kiss, and he was incredibly good at it. But I wasn't eager to repeat the mistake of kissing a vampire, so I pushed him back with the flat of my palm.

"Morgan."

He protested with a groan, then diverted his mouth to my neck, where he trailed a line of kisses from ear to collarbone.

My eyes drifted shut, my body apparently as eager as his to push things forward.

"You're a hot single vampire," he breathily murmured. "I'm a hot single vampire. But for your unfathomable allegiance to the Bears, we should be together."

I pushed him back again, and this time he stayed upright. "I'm not up for a boyfriend right now."

Morgan's face furrowed into an exquisite frown, and he ran a hand through his hair. "Do you and Ethan have a thing?"

"Ethan? *No*," I replied, probably sounding a little more defensive than I should have. "God, no."

Still frowning, he nodded. "Okay."

"I don't do fang."

He pulled back, apparently shocked, and gazed at me. "You *are* fang."

I grinned at him. "Yeah, I get that a lot. Friends, though?" I offered a conciliatory hand.

"For now."

I rolled my eyes and pushed a hand against his chest again, pushing him over the threshold. "Good night, Morgan."

He turned and walked down the steps. When he got to the sidewalk, he turned around and began strolling backward. "I'm going to worm my way into your life, Merit."

I waggled my fingers at him. "Uh-huh. Let me know how that works out for you."

"Hey, you're missing out. I've got mad skills."

I rolled my eyes dramatically. "I'm sure you do. Find a nice, sweet Navarre girl. You're not ready for Cadogan."

He faked pulling a knife from his heart, but then winked, and crossed the street to his car—a convertible roadster. The car beeped cheerily as he approached, and in seconds he was inside and zooming down the street.

I was asleep when they came back at five thirty a.m. They fought at first—Mallory screaming at Catcher, Catcher yelling back. The topic was magic and control and whether Mallory was mature enough for Catcher to leave her to her own devices. Mallory rued his arrogance, and Catcher rued her naïveté. The argument woke me, but it was the making up that kept me awake. They slammed into her bedroom, and that was when the grunting and moaning began. I loved Mallory, and I was beginning to appreciate Catcher's sarcasm. But in no fathomable way was I interested in listening to the two of them engage in a rowdy bout of makeup sex. When she screamed out his name for the third time—Catcher was apparently a machine—I wrapped a blanket around my shoulders and stumbled groggily through the still-dark house to the living room, where I swaddled myself and fell asleep again.

The second time I woke it was almost noon. The house was quiet and dappled in sunlight, and I was just dazed enough—just stupid enough—to attempt to stumble back to my bedroom. I resituated the blanket, only one forearm, a few toes, and my face visible above the quilting, and began the trek back upstairs. I made it through the living room unscathed, unaware of how lucky that made me. With only a few days of vampiredom under my belt, I'd yet to come into contact with that terrible little vulnerability known to all who've ever seen an episode of *Buffy*—the sunlight allergy. I was just conscious enough to tread carefully through the dining room, and it wasn't until I'd made it halfway to the stairs that I felt the pinch and sudden burn. I'd walked directly across a shaft of sunlight, my uncovered forearm catching the full exposure. I gulped in air, the pain of it nearly bringing me down into the beam—it stung like a burn, but tipped to unfathomably painful levels. The heat was astounding— like punching my arm into an overheated oven—and the skin immediately began to redden and blister. I yanked it back and clutched at the blanket with my safe hand, searching frantically for some way back into the dark, realizing that I'd trapped myself in a tiny sliver of shadow. I felt behind me for the doorknob, and pulled open the door of the tiny hallway closet, careful not to push myself back into the sunlight. When I'd maneuvered it open, I stepped backward into cool darkness, hunkered down on the hardwood floor, tears streaming from my eyes from the needle-sharp pain in my arm, and fell asleep.

CHAPTER NINE

THERE'S NOT MUCH WRONG THAT
CHUNKY MONKEY CAN'T FIX.

I thought I was in a coffin. I thought I was the brunt of some horrible Navarre joke, or some horrible Cadogan hazing ritual, and I'd been stuffed into a pine box like the dead girl I'd once thought I was. Starting to hyperventilate, I clawed at the blankets around me, then pounded on the walls, screaming for someone to let me out.

I fell forward when Mallory pulled the door open, landing face-first in her poofy slippers. Face flush with embarrassment, I rose to my elbows, spitting out bits of pink polyester fuzz. So much for the hard-ass vamp.

Mallory's voice was strangled, and I could tell she was working hard not to laugh. "What. The. Hell."

"Bad night. Really bad night." I sat down on the floor, tucking my legs beneath me, and checked the status of my arm. It was lobster red from fingers to elbow, but the blisters were gone. Supernatural healing was a handy trick for an absentminded vampire, although it would make my enemies harder to kill. Tit for tat, I guess.

Mallory crouched beside me. "Jesus, Mer. What happened to your arm?"

I sighed and spent a few seconds wallowing in self-pity.

"Vampire. Sunlight. Poof." I waved my arms in the shape of a mushroom cloud. "Third-degree burns."

"Dare I ask why you were sleeping in the closet?"

I didn't want to embarrass her with a replay of her late-night antics, so I shrugged off the question. "Fell asleep, got too close to the sun, hunkered down."

"Come on," she said, taking my free elbow and helping me to my feet. "Let's at least put some aloe on your arm. Does it hurt a lot? Never mind. Don't answer that. You've got a master's degree in English and you've yet to string a subject and predicate together. I'll draw my own conclusions."

"Mallory!" Catcher's voice boomed down the stairs.

Mallory fixed her mouth into a tight line and walked me into the kitchen. "Ignore it," she advised. "Much like the bubonic plague, it'll go away if you give it enough time."

"Mallory! You weren't finished! Get back in here!"

I glanced up the stairway. "You didn't leave him handcuffed to the bed or something, did you?"

"Jesus, no." I incrementally relaxed, until she continued. "My headboard's a single piece of wood. There's nothing to handcuff him to."

I groaned and tried to wipe the image of a naked, bound Catcher writhing on the bed from my mind. Not that it was a bad image, but still . . .

Mallory kept us moving toward the kitchen. "He's pissed because he doesn't think I'm paying attention to his incessant goddamn lectures on magic." Her voice went lower, and she mimicked, "Mallory Delancey Carmichael, you're a fourth-class sorcerer with duties and obligations, blah blah blah. I think I understand now why the Order kicked him out; he was too bossy, even for them."

We went into the kitchen, and I took a seat while Mallory pulled a tube from a drawer next to the sink. She slathered cream on my arm with careful attention, then recapped the tube and set it aside. "I wonder if you need blood today."

I frowned, partly from the thought of drinking blood, partly from the realization that Mallory had become my predatory den mother. Since when had I become so needy? "I'm fine, I think."

"It's just that sometimes in the literature"—and by that she meant the occult fanzines that appeared in our mailbox with surprising frequency—"when vamps are injured, they need extra blood to supplement the healing process." Her gaze flashed up. "You are healing, aren't you?"

I nodded. "The blisters are gone."

"Good." She went to the refrigerator and pulled out a bag, and my stomach began to grumble immediately.

"I need it," I sheepishly admitted, a little ashamed that I still had so little knowledge about the workings of my post-change body. I rubbed at a crick in my neck, no doubt the result of my having slept hunkered in a ball on the closet floor. "The fact is, for all this talk about how strong I am, I'm really not very good at being a vampire."

Mallory warmed the blood, poured it into a glass, and handed it to me. But she held up a hand before I could lift it to my mouth, went back to the refrigerator, and pulled out a celery stalk and bottle of Tabasco. She dotted some pepper sauce into the glass, then slipped in the celery. "Bloody Bloody Mary."

I took a sip and nodded. "Not bad. It could use vodka and tomato juice, but not bad for all that."

Mallory snickered, but her grin faded when Catcher stomped into the kitchen. In his hands was the thick leather-bound book I'd seen him looking through the night I'd visited my grandfather's office. He was half naked, a pair of jeans that rode low on his sculpted hips the only visible bit of clothing. The man had a body to die for—all curves and angles and little delicious hollows of sculpted muscle and flesh.

While I took in the view, Mallory yelled, "Will you quit following me around? It's not even your house!"

"Someone has to follow you around! You're a danger to the goddamn city!"

A little thrilled that this piece of supernatural drama had nothing to do with me, I gave up the pretense of politely ignoring their fight, put down the glass, and gave them my full attention.

Catcher stalked through the kitchen, practically threw the book down on the kitchen counter, then pushed Mallory onto a stool. He pointed at the book. *"Read!"*

Mallory popped up and stared at him for a long time, her mouth drawn into a tight line, her hands fisted so tightly together her knuckles were white. "Who the hell do you think you are that you can order me around?"

Tension and magic rose and spiraled around the room, tangible enough to raise the hair on my arms and neck. Eddies of it dipped and flowed, the ends of Mallory's hair lifting around her face like she'd stepped into a strong breeze.

"Jesus," I muttered, staring at the two of them.

Without warning, there was a crack of light. My glass, thankfully empty of blood, shattered on the counter.

"Mallory," Catcher warned, a half growl.

"No, Catcher."

The overhead light flickered as they stared at each other, a strobe lighting the battle of the wills.

Finally, Catcher sighed, power dissipating from the room with a tangible *whoosh.* Without words or hesitation, he grabbed her arms and pulled her against the line of his body. Then he lowered his head to hers, and kissed her. She squealed and twitched, but as his mouth worked at hers, she stilled. When, moments later, he pulled back, he looked at her expectantly.

For a heartbeat, then two, she just stared at him. "I told you we were done."

"Sure you did." He kissed the top of her forehead, turned her body, and pushed her shoulders so she dropped onto the stool. Then he raised her chin to meet his gaze. "I have to get to work. Read the Key."

He walked out of the kitchen. The front door shut seconds later.

For a good five minutes, neither one of us said anything. Mallory, hands in her lap, stared blankly at the book. When I'd shaken myself out of the drama-induced stupor, I went to the freezer and grabbed the carton of Chunky Monkey. I pulled off the top, found a spoon, handed them both to Mallory, then took the stool next to hers. Reciprocal ice-cream therapy, I decided. "So. *That* happened."

Mallory nodded absently and chewed a giant spoonful of ice cream. "I hate him."

"Yeah."

Mallory dropped the spoon into the container and put her head in her hands. "How does someone that arrogant look that good? It's unfair. It's a crime against nature. He should be . . . punished for being pretentious with pockmarks and hairy warts or something."

I took up the spoon and picked through the ice cream for a square of white chocolate. "He spending the night again?"

"Probably. Not that I have anything to say about it."

I bit back a smile. There were many things I'd come to learn about Mallory. Number one among them was the fact that she rarely did anything by halves. Whatever she was involved in, be it boyfriend or career, she gave a near-obsessive level of attention. So that fake nonchalance heralded something very interesting about one Catcher Bell.

"In love with him, are you?"

"Little bit," she said, nodding. She rubbed her arms, then stared down at the table. "The thing is, Mer, he doesn't let me order him around. Like Mark—if I told Mark to climb the Matterhorn, he'd hop the next plane to Europe. Catcher stands up to me." A corner of her mouth tipped up. "I didn't realize how attractive a quality that was in a man."

Her gaze found mine, and her bright blue eyes were moist. "He doesn't give a shit if I've got a kick-ass job in the best ad firm in town, or if I've got blue hair, or if I'm pretty underneath it. He just likes me."

I stood and gathered her into a hug. "Too bad he's a pretentious asshole."

Mallory gave a watery laugh. "Yeah, it is. But he's hung like a horse, so that kinda helps."

I pulled away, grimacing, and walked toward the kitchen door. "This house is getting too small for the three of us. Seriously."

Mallory laughed, but I wasn't sure I was kidding.

After showering and dressing in an outfit I knew wouldn't meet Ethan's approval—jeans, Pumas, and a couple of layered tank tops—I decided to head for my grandfather's office. I wanted an update about the investigation, and I was also working to avoid thinking about tomorrow. Day Seven. The Commendation Ceremony, during which I'd be assigned a position in Cadogan House, would take my oaths to Ethan, and would probably be hazed within an inch of my newfound immortality.

I wasn't sure of my welcome at the Ombud's office, or even if anyone would be staffing the building on a Sunday night, so I decided to bring a bribe á la fast-food chicken. After I made the pickup, I parked in front of the Ombud's office. I took my bribe to the front door, hit the buzzer, and waited.

Minutes passed before Catcher strolled down the hall, this time having paired a black Ramones shirt with boots and jeans. He looked surprised to see me, but punched in the code to unlock the door and opened it, his gaze on the paper bucket I cradled in the crook of one arm.

"I brought chicken," I pointed out.

"I can see that. Did she kick you out, too, or is this a humanitarian visit?"

"Neither. I wanted to check on the investigation—"

"And you're scared shitless about tomorrow night."

"And I'm scared shitless about tomorrow night."

Catcher cast a wary glance at the street, then moved aside to let me in. I waited while he relocked and coded the door and grabbed a drumstick from the buckets. Then I followed him back down the hallway and into the office. Catcher immediately moved to his desk, leaning over it to press the button on a *Charlie's Angels*–era intercom system.

"Merit's here," he said into it.

Jeff jumped out of his chair and made for the bucket that I had placed on one of the empty desks after pulling out a piece for myself. Apparently lacking the gene for subtlety, he grabbed a breast, eating it only after he'd pointed at the chicken to point out the symbolism. I couldn't help but laugh, even knowing he didn't need the encouragement.

"Hello, baby girl." My grandfather shuffled into the room, a grand smile on his face. It was nice to be loved, I thought, and basked in the glow of it. "What are you doing here?"

Catcher pulled a chunk of meat from his drumstick. "She's hiding out. Commendation's tomorrow."

"Oh yeah?" Grandpa asked, picking through the bucket until he found a choice piece, then nudging a hip onto the edge of the desk. "Are you nervous?"

Jeff kicked back in his chair and crossed his ankles on his desktop next to his mutant keyboard. "Do they still make the Initiates eat a raw chicken?"

I swallowed hard and, having lost anything resembling my appetite, dropped the piece of chicken I'd selected back into the bucket.

"I think it's only half a chicken nowadays," my grandfather solemnly corrected. "They start with a whole one, but they'll stick two Initiates on it and make them tear it apart. No hands allowed. Just fangs."

"Bloody and awesome," Jeff said with approval, tearing into the breast he held between two hands.

That was nauseating, but having not yet experienced the

Commendation, I didn't get the joke until Grandpa winked at me. I should have known. Two vampires fighting over a raw chicken wasn't very Ethan-esque—it wasn't nearly dignified enough. His style was a little more European, a little less sports entertainment. He was, I imagined with a grin, more likely to make the recruits recite the English monarchs or play a complicated Chopin piece.

"Quit mooning over Sullivan," Catcher muttered, bending around me to get to the chicken bucket. He continued before I could argue the assumption. "The Commendation's gonna go fine. It's mostly ceremonial, except for the oaths. In fact," he began, before hopping onto the desk beside my grandfather, "if anything, I bet Sullivan gets a big surprise."

I frowned at him. "How so?"

Catcher shrugged. "I'm just saying. You're strong. He's strong. Should make for an interesting ceremony."

I took an empty seat. "Describe interesting."

Catcher shook his head. "You're a smart girl. You should be doing your homework. What have you learned about the ceremony so far?"

I frowned, tried to recall what I'd seen in the *Canon*. "All the vamps who live in Cadogan will be there, like witnesses. Ethan will call me forward, say my name or something, and I'm supposed to take two oaths—fealty and homage. To serve the House and be loyal to it."

"Not just the House," Catcher said, reaching over to pull more chicken from the bucket. "To the Master himself." He nibbled the edge of his drumstick, then glanced up at me. "Are you ready for that?"

How could I possibly be ready for that? I'd be twenty-eight years old in a matter of days, and hadn't even recited the Pledge of Allegiance in ten years. How could I be prepared to swear my loyalty and service to a community I'd joined as the alternative to death or to a man who didn't find me capable of loyalty, worthy of trust?

On the other hand: "Is it an option—not to take the oaths?"

"Not unless you want to live separately from them," Catcher said, picking a chunk of chicken from the bone. "Pretend you weren't made by him. Pretend you aren't what *he* made you."

You are what I made you, Ethan had told me. Hard to pretend otherwise.

"If you came at this vampire thing on your own, found your own way to it, what would you do?"

"I wouldn't have come to it," I countered. "I'm not like them, not into the vampire mystique."

His expression softened. "So, because things aren't exactly the way you want them, you're going to bail? Believe me, Merit—exile is a lonely way to live."

"Sometimes," my grandfather put in, "even if you can't be what you want, making the most of what you *can* be isn't a bad second choice. You have a chance to remake yourself, baby girl."

"But in whose image?" I drily asked.

"That's your decision," Catcher said. "You were made a vampire by Sullivan, sure, but the oaths are still yours to take. And you haven't taken them yet."

My grandfather nodded at me. "You'll know what to do when the time comes."

I hoped he was right. "Anything new in the Porter investigation?"

"Not much," he admitted, swinging a leg. "In terms of evidence, we've gathered nothing else."

"But we did get some interesting gossip," Jeff said, pausing to swallow a bite. He inclined his head toward my grandfather. "Chuck's vampire says Celina Desaulniers met with Mayor Tate this week. Apparently, she was trying to reassure the mayor that the murder couldn't have been perpetrated by a House vamp."

"Morgan told me she thinks Cadogan's innocent, that Rogues are behind the murder." I explained my newly formed friendship with the Navarre vamp.

Grandpa seemed amused and nodded, then began to tell me what little they knew about Rogue vamps in the Windy City—mainly that they were a couple dozen strong—when his cell phone rang. He slid off the desk, unclipped and opened it, and frowned at the display before raising it to his ear.

"Chuck Merit . . . When?" He made a writing motion with his hand, and Jeff passed over a pen and pad of paper. My grandfather began scribbling quickly, occasionally throwing in an "Okay" or "Yes, sir."

Mayor, Catcher mouthed to me. I nodded.

The call continued for a few minutes, my grandfather closing the phone after assuring Mayor Tate he'd make some calls. He stared down at it, a chunk of silver plastic in his hand, and when he raised his head, worry was etched on his face.

"Another murder," was all he said.

Her name was Patricia Long. We sat quietly, without jokes or sarcasm, our eyes downcast, as he passed along the details. She was twenty-seven years old. A tallish brunette. An attorney at an international firm that officed on Michigan Avenue. She'd been found in Lincoln Park this time, an anonymous phone call directing the CPD to the scene. The cause of her death had been the same—exsanguination due to the wounds on her neck and throat.

But there was an additional bit of information with this one. The caller said he'd seen a vampire leaving the scene—a man wearing a blue-and-yellow baseball jersey, fangs bared, mouth covered in blood.

Catcher swore. "The jersey's probably a Grey House shirt. It's one of Scott's signatures." He slid me a glance, explaining, "Grey's a sports fan. Doesn't do the medals like Cadogan and Navarre—they've got jerseys instead."

Grandpa nodded. "Unfortunately, you're right. Sounds like Grey House. They haven't found anything else at the scene—no medals or detritus that would link this to anyone else—but they're still processing." He reclipped the phone to his belt, his knobby fingers working to join the plastic components. "This takes the heat off Cadogan, slides it right over to Grey. Anybody wanna put money on whether there'd have been something from Navarre at the scene of Merit's attack?"

The three of them looked at me, their expressions gloomy.

"You can ask Ethan," I said. "But he didn't mention anything to me." Not that he necessarily would. He still wasn't sure of my loyalties.

"Even if there'd been something," Catcher put in, "that doesn't mean it's related to the assaults. I'll eat my right hand if Scott Grey, or anyone from Grey House, had something to do with this one. They're a tight squad and completely harmless."

"It's unlikely," my grandfather agreed.

"But there's no evidence that points specifically to a Rogue vamp, either," I pointed out.

"Actually, that's not entirely true," Grandpa said. "CPD knew the jersey linked to Grey House, so they sent a couple of uniforms over. When they got there, they found a note tacked to the front door. Scott hadn't seen it yet—they don't have guards outside, probably think the House is new enough not to have created enemies. It's barely three years old."

Catcher frowned and crossed his arms. "What did the note say?"

"It was an attempt at a rhyme: 'Blue, yellow, Grey/Who wants to pay?/The Devil is Due/The system is, too.' "

I winced. "That's truly, truly awful."

"By saying 'system'—that's a knock at the Houses?" Jeff asked. "The attacks are staged to look like House crimes, but the notes definitely read 'Rogue.' "

"Or," I suggested, "if the theory is that Rogues are responsible, the murders are for the cops, and the threats are for the House vampires."

My grandfather nodded thoughtfully. "It does play that way."

Catcher pulled over the pad, glanced at the notes my grandfather had written, and frowned. "I don't like this. It's too tidy. I never liked the medal plant, and I like this jersey thing even less. But for a Rogue to leave a note—isn't that a little suspect? They'd have to know the notes connect the Rogues, not the Houses, to the murder. Why go to all the trouble to set up the Houses in the attacks, then stab yourself in the foot with a note that pins the thing on you?"

"Depends on the Rogues," my grandfather suggested. "If the murders are supposed to be a slap at the system, the notes say, 'Hey, look what I pulled off right under your nose, affiliation or not.' Maybe they didn't think the vamps would share the notes with cops."

Catcher brushed a hand over his closely shaven head. "Whatever the fuck is going on out there, Sullivan needs to get on this. The Houses need to call the city's Rogues together, figure out who might be behind this, offer sanctions or rewards for information. They love that bargaining shit—I don't understand why they're not doing it now."

"Because talking to the Rogues would be an admission that the Rogues have power," Jeff offered. "The House vamps would have to acknowledge vamps who've bucked the system, and ask for their help. No way is Ethan or Celina going to do that. Grey maybe, but not the other two. Their memories are too long."

Grandpa picked up the notepad again and rose, then walked to the door. "You're right—they need to talk, if for no other reason than the timing of this thing. There was a week between Porter's death and Merit's attack, nine days between Merit and this girl's death. It's not a huge sample, but. . . ."

"We don't have much time," I quietly concluded. "Which means we could see another in the next ten days?"

My grandfather blew out a slow breath, then linked his hands above his head. "Maybe so, kid. I don't envy the CPD on this one." He looked over at me, gave me a sad smile. "I'm sorry to run you off, but we need to start making phone calls.

Cadogan and Navarre need to be notified, and I need to talk to my source."

"Thanks for dinner," Jeff said.

"Sure." I peeked in the bucket, looked over a handful of pieces, decided I still had no appetite for fowl. "Enjoy the rest," I said. "I'll leave it here."

"Oh, before you go," Jeff said, burrowing beneath this desk, "I got you something." He dug around underneath there for a minute making clanging and banging noises, before crawling out with an Army green canvas bag in his hands. He held it out to me, and I took it and peeked inside.

"Are you trying to tell me something, Jeff?" I asked, peering into the sack of sharpened wooden stakes.

"Just that I'd prefer you alive."

I hitched the bag over my shoulder, gave him a jaunty wink. "Then thanks."

He smiled endearingly. Jeff was a kid, but a good kid.

Catcher rose. "I'll walk you out."

I gave Grandpa a hug, and passed a final wave and smile to Jeff, then let Catcher guide me back to the front door. He uncoded it and held it open so I could walk through. "Stay close to the guards this week. Could be this maniac's going to try to finish you off, take a swipe at hit number three."

I shivered and hitched the bag of stakes a little tighter at my shoulder. "Thanks for the comfort."

"I'm not here to comfort you, babe. I'm here to keep you alive."

"And screw my roommate."

He smiled grandly, a dimple peeking from the left side of his upturned lips. "And that, assuming I can get her to see it my way."

I left him with a smile, glad that, whatever the supernatural drama, I'd found friends to help me through it. A new family, for all the genetic differences.

I got into the car and drove home with the windows down,

trying to hold on to that smile, that comfort, trying to let the spring breeze and a soft tune carry away my uncertainty.

Have you ever had a moment where you knew, beyond a shadow of a doubt, that you were in the right place? That you were on the right journey? Maybe the sense that you'd crossed a boundary, jumped a hurdle, and somehow, after facing some unconquerable mountain, found yourself suddenly on the other side of it? When the night was warm, and the wind was cool, and a song carried through the quiet streets around you. When you felt the entire world around you, and you were part of it—of the hum of it—and everything was good.

Contentment, I suppose, is the simple explanation for it. But it seems more than that, thicker than that, some unity of purpose, some sense of being truly, honestly, for that moment, at home.

Those moments never seem to last long enough. The song ends, the breeze stills, the worries and fears creep in again and you're left trying to move forward, but glancing back at the mountain behind you, wondering how you managed to cross it, afraid you really didn't—that the bulk and shadow over your shoulder might evaporate and re-form before you, and you'd be faced with the burden of crossing it again.

The song ends, and you stare at the quiet, dark house in front of you, and you grasp the doorknob and walk back into your life.

CHAPTER TEN

KEEPING WATCH IN THE NIGHT

"Time to get up, sleepyhead!"

I heard the voice, but grumbled into my pillow and pulled the comforter over my head. "Go away."

"Aw, come on, Mer. Today's your big day! It's Vampire Rush!"

I tunneled into the blankets. "I don't want to be a vampire today."

I heard a huff, and the covers were ripped from my body and thrown to the floor.

"Damn it, Mallory!" I sat up and pushed a nest of dark hair from my face. "I'm twenty-seven years old and perfectly capable of getting up on my own. Will you get out of my room? Go bother Catcher."

"Catcher has bigger issues on his mind right now, Mer." She paused in the middle of flipping through the shirts that hung in my closet. "Did you hear about this other girl? The one who was killed."

I nodded as I rubbed sleep from my eyes. "They mentioned her last night."

"Helluva time to become a vampire."

"Tell me about it. I said the same thing the other day."

Mallory began to pull clothes off hangers and drop them

into a pile on the floor. I gave her a dramatic glare she didn't bother to notice. "What are you doing?"

"I'm finding you something to wear. You've got Rush today." For all that Mallory proclaimed herself immune to the benefits of being as gorgeous and fit as she was, there were moments that she reveled in girly stuff. Her sorority sisters would have been proud.

I swung my legs over the side of the bed. "It's not Rush. It's hazing. *Vampire* hazing. I don't need to dress up so Ethan can humiliate me."

"True. He's humiliated you just fine when you were in jeans and a T-shirt." She glanced back, gave me a look over her shoulder snarky enough to reduce a pledge to tears. "But you're going to be there with, what did you say, eleven other new vamps? You need to show them what you're made of. Today's your day to start over. To reinvent yourself."

I shuddered as Mallory pulled out a pair of high black heels and a fitted white button-up blouse. They joined the trousers she'd tossed on the bed.

"That's not the kind of stuff I usually wear."

She snickered. "That's why you're wearing it tonight." She made a shooing motion with her hands. "Bathroom. Clean thyself."

Once I'd showered and dried off, Mallory took over. Nothing escaped her notice. I was perfum'd, pluck'd and powder'd within an inch of my life, my long hair brushed and sprayed until it gleamed, the long fringe of my dark bangs over my forehead. I was tucked into the trim flat-front trousers and the very snug white button-up shirt, which had cuffs at the ends of the three-quarter sleeves. The shirt was tucked in, and she twined a black belt around my waist, before unbuttoning the top couple of buttons on the shirt.

"You can see my boobs if you do that," I warned her.

"Such as they are," she snarked back. "And that's the point. You're playing the part of hot single vampire tonight."

I watched my reflection change in the mirror—from casually attractive graduate student to something a little more fierce. She chained three snug strands of thick silver beads around my right wrist, added a couple of layers of makeup—giving me, as she explained, "a dramatic, smoky eye and just-kissed lips," then slid me into the heels.

"All right," she said, wiggling her finger in a circular motion. "Turn around."

I performed like a trained circus poodle, spinning slowly in place so she could look me over.

"Nice," she complimented. "You clean up very, very nicely."

I shrugged and let her adjust the cuffs on the pant legs and collar of my shirt, then check my teeth for lipstick.

"All right. Final test. Let's go."

Because I was unused to walking in heels, she helped me downstairs, then made me stand at the foot of the stairs while she moved into the living room. "Gentlemen, I present the newest member of Cadogan House, Chicago's smartest vampire—Merit!"

I was disappointed she hadn't named me "Chicago's sexiest vampire," but took what I could get and moved forward when she motioned me to do so. Jeff and Catcher sat on the couch, Jeff nearly propelling himself off it when I stepped into the living room.

"Woot, woot!" he yelled. "You look good enough to eat!"

I slid Mallory a glance. "He's your test? He thinks anything with breasts looks good."

"Since you don't qualify, that's why I asked him over."

I gave her a juvenile face and cupped my breasts protectively. There wasn't much to them, but they were mine, damn it. I dropped my hands when Jeff stood in front of me, grinning boyishly.

"You look ho-ot. Sure you don't wanna drop this vampire business and join the Pack? We've got better . . . insurance."

I grinned at him, positive that "insurance" hadn't been the

first suggestion on his mind, but was actually prompted by the finger Catcher poked between his shoulder blades. But I thanked him and held out my arms to Catcher.

"Good luck," he offered, hugging and releasing me. "You decided yet what you're going to do about the oaths?"

"Not yet," I admitted, the question alone churning my nerves. As if on cue, a knock sounded at the door. Jeff, who was closest, pulled it open. A liveried driver tipped the cap on his head.

"Ms. Merit, please, bound for Cadogan House."

I blew out a slow breath, trying to calm the fear that was making a tangled mess of my stomach, and turned nervous eyes to Mallory. She smiled and held out her hands, and I moved into her fierce hug. "My little girl's growing up."

I couldn't help but laugh, which I'm sure was her intention. "You are so full of shit." When I let her go, Catcher moved in, putting a possessive hand at the small of her back.

"Be good tonight."

I nodded and grabbed the tiny black-and-white clutch Mallory had prepared for me. It held, she'd informed me earlier, a lipstick, my cell phone (turned off, so as not to irritate my housemates), my keys, emergency cash.

And, ahem, a condom, Mallory apparently thinking it likely I'd be caught in a vampire-sex emergency. (Could vampires even catch STDs? Bet they didn't cover that in the *Canon*.)

Purse prepared, I gave everyone a final tremulous wave and followed the driver down to the sleek black limousine that sat at the curb. During the walk to the driver-opened door, although most of my brain cells were busy trying to keep me upright in three-inch stilettos, I did take a moment to remember the last time a limo had been parked in front of our house. It had been six days ago, when I'd arrived, newly changed and stuffed into a cocktail dress, still woozy from the attack and the change.

Six days later, shape-shifters peppered Chicago, my grandfather employed a secret vampire, my roommate was dating a magician, and I was learning how to wield a Samurai-era sword.

Life definitely marched on.

The limousine trekked steadily south, halting in front of a bedecked and bedazzled Cadogan House. Torches lit the sidewalk in front of the House and the walk that led to the front door, and candles blazed in each of the House's dozens of windows. One of the guards from the front gate opened the limousine door and gave me a knowing smile as I stepped onto the sidewalk. As I walked into the grounds, I realized that the dozens of torches that lined the sidewalk weren't your garden-variety tikis. These were elegant, sculpted from wrought iron. And more important, they were wielded by a gauntlet of vampires—men and women, all dressed in chicly cut black suits—who stood shoulder to shoulder along the sidewalk.

My stomach clenched with nerves, but I forced myself to walk on, to walk through them. I wasn't sure what I expected—scorn or ridicule, maybe? Some indication that they'd seen through me and knew that I wasn't as powerful as some seemed to believe?

Their reaction was almost more frightening. Each pair, as I walked past, bowed their heads. "Sister," they quietly said, so the word fluttered behind me as I moved through them.

Goose bumps covered my arms, my lips parting as I absorbed the weight of what they were offering me—solidarity, kinship, family. I stepped up to the covered portico, glancing behind me, and inclined my head toward them, hoping that I was worth it.

Malik was at the open door, and he held out a hand in invitation. "He puts on a show," he quietly said as I walked inside. "You'll find the women upstairs in the ballroom's anteroom." He inclined his head toward the stairs. "All the way up and to the left."

I nodded again and gripped the railing when I reached the stairway, well aware that that stairs, three-inch heels, and adrenaline-rocked thighs were a dangerous combination. At the top of the stairway, I went to the left.

The sound of feminine giggling and banter echoed through the hall, and I walked toward it, stopping at an open door. There were a dozen women in a room that had been decked out to look like a pageant staging area—big mirrors, lots of light, lots of "product." Half the vamps wore traditional Cadogan black. These Novitiates helped the other five, who were dressed in a range of glamour wear (cocktail dresses, glimmery halter tops, satin-edged tuxedo pants), prepare for the ceremony. These makeupped and coiffed women were my fellow Initiates, and I suddenly felt old and fusty in my black-and-white ensemble.

As I watched them, I realized that they were all grinning. Their eyes were bright and eager, like they were preparing for the most exciting event of their lives. These were women, I thought, who'd been invited to join the House. Who'd chosen—consciously—to forgo the human world for night and blood and the political intrigue of vampires.

I felt a tight pang of jealousy. What would that have been like, to walk into Cadogan House and ask for membership, or to view the Commendation as the celebration of a profound achievement? It really was Vampire Rush for these women, former humans who believed themselves fortunate to have made the cut.

"They're like lions preparing to jump the gazelle."

I smiled in spite of my nerves, turning to find a smiling blond vamp behind me. She wore the requisite black, her long, straight hair pulled into a tidy ponytail at her nape.

"And Ethan's the gazelle?"

"Oh, yeah." She inclined her head toward the horde—now atwitter over some new shade of M.A.C. lipstick—and shook her head. "Not that they have a chance. He doesn't touch the new kids. But I don't think I'll tell them that." Her smile widened, and I decided not to think too closely about the fact that I was a new kid, and he'd certainly touched me.

"I think I'll let them stew," she decided. "It gives the older kids something to enjoy later on."

"The victory of defeat?"

"Exactly." She stuck out a hand. "Lindsey. And you're Merit."

I nodded cautiously and accepted her hand, wondering what other information she'd gleaned about me or, since it seemed to be popular vampire gossip, my paternity.

"Nothing to fear from me," she assured, without my having raised the issue.

When my eyes widened, she offered, "I'm empathic. You got really tense, and I had this sense that it was about something deep—familial maybe. But I could give a shit who your parents are. 'Sides, my dad was the pork king of Dubuque. So I know high living, *chica*."

I laughed aloud, drawing the attention of the women at the mirror, who all turned to look at me. And to appraise me. I got a series of up-and-down looks and a couple of carefully arched brows before they turned back to the mirror and set about perfecting their hair and makeup. I felt like an outsider—familiar enough with Ethan and the House to have lost that "new kid" glow, but definitely not yet one of the "older kids," whom I watched move around the newcomers with confident efficiency, offering assistance, spraying hair, calming nerves.

Lindsey suddenly clapped her hands together. "Ladies, we're ready. If you'll follow me, please?" She went for the door. My stomach in knots, I swallowed thickly and fell in line behind the other girls.

We walked back down the hallway, but this time passed the stairs. We moved, instead, toward a group of men who stood in a tense line outside a set of expansive double doors. There were six of them, all in trendy, well-cut suits, and they turned as we approached, smiling appreciatively. They were the rest of the new kids, the six male vampires who, in a matter of minutes, would become full-fledged members of Cadogan House.

We joined the line behind the guys, while the vampires who'd accompanied us formed a line beside us. I was the last vampire in line; Lindsey took the spot beside me.

We stood quietly for a little while, the twelve of us nervously adjusting clothing and smoothing hair, shuffling our feet as we waited for the doors to open, waited to swear our loyalty and allegiance to the man who'd hold the responsibility of ensuring our health, our well-being, our safety. I felt a momentary twang of sympathy for the responsibility he'd taken on, but I fought the feeling. I had enough to worry about.

With a soft *whoosh*, the doors were pulled open, revealing a ballroom that was swathed in light and thrumming with the beat of bass-heavy ambient music.

My stomach churned, and I put a hand on my abdomen to still the twitching.

"You'll be fine," Lindsey whispered. "I'll escort you in. And since you're last, you just have to do what the others do. Follow their lead."

I nodded, keeping my eyes on the short, dark hair of the woman in front of me. The line began to move, and we slowly proceeded into the space, in step with the vampires beside us.

Gigantic framed mirrors hung from both sides of the ballroom, swaths of billowy white fabric draped above them. The floor was gleaming oak, the walls a pale shade of gold. Chandeliers holding hundreds of candles gleamed, reflecting a golden glow throughout the space.

The vampires, all in black, were an odd foil against the decor. They stood in two large, tidy columns like a squadron at attention, a narrow aisle between them. We walked between the columns, Lindsey and I bringing up the rear.

At the front of the room, on a raised platform, stood

Ethan, flanked by Malik and Amber, Luc standing behind. Ethan looked piratical. He was dressed in black, this time a snug long-sleeved T-shirt that showed off every plane and curve of his torso, and black flat-front slacks. His feet were tucked into squarish black shoes, his shoulder-length blond hair tucked neatly behind his ears. His legs were spread, like he was bracing his body against the sway of the ocean, arms folded across his chest as he watched us move closer, every bit the captain surveying his crew. He also looked as confident as I'd ever seen him—his shoulders square, his jaw set, his emerald eyes glowing with lambent power.

His gaze followed the line of vamps, skipping over each one, and I watched his brow furrowing before he found me at the back of the line. Our gazes locked again, the act no less powerful than it had been when we'd met for the first time a week ago. And then, with a motion so slight I'd wonder later if I'd imagined it, he inclined his head.

I nodded back.

My gaze still on Ethan, I nearly stumbled into the woman in front of me when we stopped moving, the first of our line even with the columns of vamps beside us.

The music stopped and the room stilled. Ethan unfolded his arms and took a step forward.

"Brothers. Sisters. Vampires of Cadogan House."

The room burst into raucous applause, the vampires around us whistling and screaming until Ethan quieted them with a slight motion of his hand.

"Tonight we initiate twelve new Cadogan vampires. Twelve vampires who will become your brothers, your sisters, your roommates, your friends." He paused. "Your allies." There was nodding in the crowd.

"Tonight, twelve vampires will swear their allegiance to Cadogan House, to me, and to you. They will join us, work for us, laugh with us, love with us, and, if necessary, fight with us."

Ethan paused, then took a step forward. "My friends, my vassals, do you consent?"

They answered with action. To a one, the vampires at our sides swiveled to face us. Then, nearly simultaneously, their expressions solemn, they sank to the floor, kneeling before us. But for the group at the podium, we were the only men and women still on our feet, the rest genuflecting around us. They offered us fellowship; they offered Ethan consent, faith.

I got goose bumps all over again.

It was humbling, astounding, jolting to watch the display, to see a hundred vampires prostrate before me, to know that I was part of this, one of them. The nervousness disappeared, supplanted by a weighty kind of knowledge, a bone-deep understanding that I had become something different, something historic.

Something *more*.

I let my gaze flow across the crowd of vampires, still on their knees before us, and became aware of something else—the slow hum of power, like a subtle electric current, that moved across them, like water over a tumble of rocks.

Magic.

I let my hand lift, let my fingers feel the subtle shape of it, the curves and bows in the air. It wasn't unlike putting a hand out a car window and feeling the wind rush by; it had that same weird sense of solidity. And, like Catcher said, it wasn't that they were doing magic, performing it. It was more like they were extruding it, leaking it into the air around us. Whatever Ethan had said, being a vampire wasn't just about genetics.

Realizing that I was standing in the midst of nearly a hundred vampires, my hand floating in the air like an idiot, I snatched it back, rubbing the inside of my palm with a thumb to wipe away the residual tingles. I surveyed the vamps around me, realizing that no one else seemed to have noticed the magic. The Initiates stared a little blankly at the Housed vampires, mouths parted in surprise, their eyes flicking nervously across the men and women at our feet.

I risked a glance and looked up at Ethan, still on the platform. His gaze was on me, his expression unreadable, but his attention fixed. I wondered if he'd seen me raise my hand, feel out the current, and I wondered if I'd done something wrong by touching it.

After a moment, he turned back to his troops. "Rise, friends, as we welcome your comrades, as they swear their oaths to protect this House."

The vampires rose in concert, as if they'd choreographed and practiced the moves. They moved with such synchronicity that it was akin to watching a flock of birds in flight—and a little disconcerting in a group of men and women.

They swiveled again to face Ethan, and the tension in the room seemed to heighten incrementally, the new vamps in front of me shifting nervously. Something was about to happen.

Lindsey leaned toward me. "When he calls your name— when he calls you forward—go to him. It might scare you, but it's perfectly natural. He calls all of us."

Without warning, the Initiate vampire at the front of the line—a young man of maybe twenty-five—stumbled forward. The vampire at his side took his elbow to catch him, then escorted him the dozen-odd steps to the podium, where he kneeled before Ethan. The escort then stepped to the side. The room was silent, all eyes on the Master and Initiate before him. Ethan leaned down, said something to the boy, who nodded, then responded.

The exchange continued for a few moments, before Malik stepped forward and handed something to Ethan. It glinted in the light—a medal on a thin gold chain—and the vampire lowered his head. Ethan reached his hands around the man's neck and fastened the medal. When it was clasped, he whispered again, and the man rose.

"Joseph, Cadogan Initiate, I anoint you a full member of Cadogan House, with all the rights and duties afforded a Novitiate vampire."

The crowd applauded raucously as Joseph and Ethan embraced. Amber then stepped from the podium and led Joseph to one side, where he stood facing us, like a beauty pageant finalist.

The same sequence followed with the other ten vampires before me—kneeling, speaking, embracing, applause. Warner, Adrian, Michael, Thomas, and Connor followed Joseph into the ranks of Cadogan Novitiates, as did five women—Penny, Jennifer, Dakota, Melanie and Christine. Before I knew it, I stood at the front of the line, Lindsey at my side, Ethan before me, the host of Novitiates, new and old, watching as I waited to be called. Adrenaline began to surge.

The ballroom fell silent again. I forced myself to raise my gaze, to meet Ethan's. There was a moment of eye contact before he dropped his head.

That was when I heard it—the soft echo of his voice in my head, like a whisper from the end of a tunnel. And then I was hurtling through the tunnel, toward the sound, and I squeezed closed my eyes and tried to staunch the sudden burst of nausea. His voice called clear, my name. My full name—first, middle, last. And from his lips, it didn't sound so bad.

But I wasn't that girl anymore. Hadn't been, maybe ever, certainly not since I was old enough to claim my own identity. To be Merit, rather than the ghost of someone else.

Eyes closed, contemplating my identity, I hadn't heard him approach. I didn't know he stood before me until I felt his fingers in a viselike grip around my arms.

My lids lifted. Ethan stared down at me, nostrils flaring, silver tempering the edges of his irises. I swallowed and looked around, realized that the ballroom was graveyard silent, and that all eyes were on me. I looked to Lindsey, whose expression bore some mix of horror, shock, and awe, and I had no idea what I'd done.

I blinked and returned my gaze to Ethan. A muscle twitched in his jaw, and he leaned incrementally forward.

"What the hell kind of game are you playing?"

I opened my mouth, but was too flustered to form words. Desperate to make him understand that I hadn't, *this time*, purposely failed him, I shook my head wildly.

"I didn't," I managed to push out, willing him to understand.

Ethan blinked, his fingers loosening slightly, and his eyes tracked across my face, searched my gaze. "You didn't come forward when I called you."

"You didn't call me."

"You heard me say your name?"

I nodded.

"I pulled you forward, just as I pulled everyone else. You didn't come." Then his lips parted, his eyes suddenly widening, his expression suddenly appreciative. "You weren't fighting me?"

I shook my head. "Of course not. Not now. Not like this. I may not always be . . . pliant, but I have a pretty strong instinct for survival. I'm not going to insult you in front of your people." I offered him a little smile. "Well, not again, anyway."

"Ethan?" Malik stepped forward. "Should we release the others?"

Ethan shook his head. He uncrimped his fingers and released my arms, then turned on his heel. "Follow me."

I didn't hesitate, but fell into step behind him, let him take the couple of steps to the platform, and stopped in front of him. I didn't kneel, unsure of what he wanted me to do. Malik took the spot next to Ethan, and when his people were assembled again, he looked to the crowd.

"Friends."

The single word silenced the vampires, silenced the speculation that I knew had begun to work its way through the House: Why didn't she move forward? Was it some kind of rebellion? (Again?) Was he going to punish her this time? (Rightfully?)

"In these times, peace is tremulous. Allies are key. Power is key." His gaze slipped down to me. "I called her. It had no effect."

The murmuring began in earnest.

"She has resisted the call," Ethan continued, raising his voice over the vampires. "She has resisted the glamour. She has strength, my friends, and will be an asset to our House. For she is ours. She is a Cadogan vampire."

For the third time, the goose bumps rose.

He looked back at me and nodded slightly, and I sank to my knees before him. Then he took a step forward and gazed down at me. His eyes fairly glowed, bright green glass beneath the fringe of long, blond lashes.

This was it. The time to pledge myself, or not, in service to these vampires.

To Cadogan.

To Ethan.

"Merit, Initiate of Cadogan House, in the presence of your brothers and sisters, do you pledge fealty and allegiance to Cadogan House, to its honor, to its Lord? Do you pledge to be true and faithful to Cadogan House and to its members to the exclusion of all others, without deception? Do you pledge to uphold the liberty of your brothers and sisters?"

I kept my eyes on his and with a single word, accepted an eternity of obligation. "Yes."

"Merit, Initiate of Cadogan House, do you pledge to serve the House and its Lord without hesitation, and to never, by word or deed, seek to harm the House, its members, or its Lord? Will you help to hold and defend her against any creature, living or dead, and make this promise, gladly and without dread, and keep it for as long as you shall live?"

I opened my mouth to answer, but he stopped me with an arched brow. "Immortality makes for long life, Merit, and for an eternal promise. Think carefully before you answer."

"I will," I answered without hesitation, having already made the decision that I was, for better or worse, a Cadogan vampire.

Ethan nodded. "So be it. Daughter of Joshua, beloved of Charles"—I smiled at the mention of my grandfather's name—"you offer your faith and fidelity, and we accept you into our grace and favor."

He took the last medal from Malik, leaned closer, and clasped it around my neck. His hand, I thought, lingered for a moment before he stepped back, but before I had a chance to wonder at what that meant, his voice boomed through the ballroom.

"Merit, Cadogan Initiate, I anoint you . . . Sentinel of this House."

The crowd gasped. Ethan looked down at me, waited for my reaction.

My fingers instinctively touching the flat of the pendant, I gave him a reaction immediately—lifting wide eyes to his and staring, mouth open, at the revelation. I was shocked, partly that I actually knew what a "Sentinel" was, and partly that he'd made me one.

Like I'd explained to Mallory, the position of Sentinel, like much of the House, was feudal in origin, and wasn't used much in modern Houses. Where the House's Guard Captain, in this case Luc, stood as head of the House's small army of guards, the Sentinel was responsible for guarding the House as an entity. As Sentinel, I'd be responsible for the structure itself, and most important, for the House as a symbol.

As Mallory put it, I'd be defending the brand. And I'd be honor-bound to serve the House, any lingering distrust for Ethan completely beside the point.

In effect, he was ensuring my loyalty to Cadogan in the shrewdest way possible—by giving me the duty of defending it.

It was brilliant. A strategy worthy of applause. An Ethan-worthy strategy, for all that he prided himself on political maneuvering.

Still on my knees, I stared up at him. "Well played."

He smiled beneath hooded eyes, offered me a hand. I took it and pulled myself up.

"Yet again," he said, his eyes alight, "we see your potential to wreak havoc."

"It wasn't my intent to wreak havoc. I can't help it if I'm . . . abnormal."

Ethan smiled. "Not abnormal," he said. "Unique. And I believe we'll adjust to this development."

He was being unusually ungrumpy, and I wondered if by taking the oaths I'd crossed some important threshold for holding Ethan's trust. Maybe now that I was officially a Cadogan vamp—subject to the Master's rules and the *Canon*'s detailed scheme of discipline and sanctions—he could afford to trust me.

But Ethan kept his eyes on me, his gaze darting back and forth across my face. He still seemed to be searching for something, waiting for something, so I knew, even if we'd made progress, that we weren't quite done.

"What?"

"I want your allegiance."

I frowned, not understanding. "You have it. I just swore an oath. Two of them. Two oaths to protect you and yours against all things living and dead. I don't even know how that second part works, and I signed up for it anyway."

He shook his head. "The Houses will hear about your strength—they'll learn about your speed and agility. They'll learn you can withstand glamour." He lifted brows, and I realized he was asking for confirmation. I nodded.

"Others, when they learn of your origins, will test your loyalty, question whether you're . . . biddable. There will be doubts as to your willingness to accede to my authority." His gaze intensified, his irises now a deeper green—like cold, dark seawater. "I want the other Houses to know that you're mine."

I heard the strained note of possessiveness in his voice, but knew it wasn't personal—it had nothing to do with me, but reflected his concern that another House might lure me away. And Ethan wasn't interested in sharing his new toy. Whatever his physical attraction to me, I was a weapon, an instrument, a secret tool to be garnered in defense of his House. In defense of his vampires.

But he'd given me a weapon of my own. While I was a Cadogan vamp, subject to his dictates—and while I had no immediate plans to buck his authority—*I* was Sentinel for Cadogan House, not Ethan Sullivan. My plans for protecting the House would supersede his individual plans for me. Ironically, while he thought to reel me in further, he'd actually given me the keys to my independence.

"While it might be fun for you to show me off," I told him, "it's better for Cadogan if my strengths aren't paraded in front of the other Houses. It's better to keep them in the dark and for you to let me do my job. I'll attract less suspicion if they don't know how strong I am, especially if they don't know I have some immunity to glamour. The surprise will work to our advantage." My tone didn't allow for disagreement, just offered a strategy that I knew he'd see was right.

As I waited for an answer, as he considered what I'd said, I offered, "Unless you only wanted me to be a figurehead— and not actually employ my skills to secure the House."

Ethan shook his head, frowning as he did it. "No. You'll stand Sentinel. But they'll still question your loyalty. Word of our, let's call them, conflicts has spread."

"Then my word that all is well in Cadogan House, that I'm, let's say, committed to your service won't have much effect. They'll respect deeds, Ethan, not words."

I saw the glint of appreciation in his eyes. "Fair enough." His gaze slid to the crowd behind me, and I realized they'd been watching the entire dialogue. Our positions weren't exactly inconspicuous, standing as we were in the front of the room, scores of still-attentive vampires watching.

"Let's continue this discussion tomorrow, Sentinel."

Noting that I'd now lost my first name as well to my new title, I nodded my acquiescence. At the motion of his hand, I took my place as the twelfth addition to Cadogan House, standing directly in front of Amber. I could feel her glaring behind me, but kept my gaze open and blank and on the vampires in front of us. Their suspicious stares weren't any better, but at least they regarded me with a little less overt, Ethan-induced jealousy.

Ethan turned to the crowd. "Friends, having heard the oaths of our twelve new members, we face the dawn as a House made larger, made stronger, made more secure against its enemies. I bid you welcome your new brothers and sisters with open arms."

A male vamp in the crowd called out, "Open arms are great! Just don't forget to lock your bedroom doors!"

Ethan chuckled along with the crowd. "And on that irreverent note, I call this Commendation closed and bid you good night. Dismissed."

The crowd offered a simultaneous "Thank you, Liege," and the lines of vampires began to relax and cluster into smaller groups. The women to my left squealed happily, and began embracing one another, probably thrilled they'd finally been admitted to the House. I didn't feel comfortable joining in the celebration—for better or worse, I wasn't one of them—and instead glanced back at Ethan. He was back in the pirate-inspecting-his-crew pose, and I wondered if he felt that same sense of separateness—being both a member of Cadogan but, by virtue of being its Master, not really one of them.

I moved back to him, confident that I'd taken his measure, but needing to reassure myself about something.

"Ethan?"

Eyes on the crowd, he responded, "Hmm?"

"What do you think about the Bears?"

He slid me a glance, one blond brow arched. "That they're large hibernating predators?"

I opened my mouth to clarify, but realized the answer said enough. "Never mind," I said, and melted into the crowd.

Just outside the ballroom, the new vamps clustered together, grinning and laughing about the ceremony, patting one another on the back and sharing victorious hugs. I watched the celebration, not quite sure my joining them would be appreciated.

Something nudged my back. I turned to find Lindsey, who held out a stack of binders and thick manila folders, the topmost of which had a lumpy bulge. I took the materials, which must have weighed ten pounds, and lifted questioning eyes.

"Paperwork," she explained. "Insurance forms, House rules, all that good stuff. We've got a Cadogan Web site. Luc's security protocols are in the secure section. Log in and look through them as soon as you have a chance. You'll need to be familiar with them in a week or two. Your beeper's in there, too. Keep it with you always—no exceptions. If you're in the shower, take it into the bathroom. Luc considers all security personnel on-call twenty-four-seven. That even includes a high-and-mighty Sentinel."

In between smirks, I managed to ask, "Does that include you?"

She nodded. "I'm a guard." She nudged me with her hip. "So we'll be seeing a lot more of each other now that you're standing Sentinel. Historic move, that. Answer a question?"

I instinctively looked around, checked that we were far enough away from the other vamps that I wouldn't be giving away any state secrets by answering something honestly. The new Novitiates seemed to be arranging their celebration party, so I figured I was safe.

"Ask away."

Lindsey cocked her head at me. "Are you sleeping with Ethan?"

Why did people keep asking me that? "No. *No*. Definitely not. No."

Probably the first no had answered the question, but I couldn't seem to stop throwing them out. Was I protesting too much?

"Oh, 'cause it's just . . ."

"It's just what?"

She patted my shoulder. "Don't get your hackles up. I don't want to end up pinned to the training room floor."

I arched a brow at that, but she grinned back. I was beginning to like this girl.

"You two just seemed to have a connection." She shrugged. "It doesn't matter to me, either way. He's hot as a son of a bitch." Lindsey cast an interested glance back toward the open ballroom doors, just in time to see Ethan saunter out, deep in conversation with Malik. "Tall, blond, body of a god."

"*Ego* of a god," I put in, and watched them walk right past the newbies and toward the stairs. Ethan was apparently done playing the interested Master, and was back to playing chill and aloof. "He is pretty, though."

Lindsey giggled, a laugh that came out kind of adorably snorty. "I knew you had a thing for him. Your eyes melt when he's nearby."

I rolled my eyes. "My eyes do not melt."

"They silver."

After a pause, I allowed, "Not every time."

Lindsey snickered, and this time the sound was a little evil. "You're whipped, toots."

"I'm not whipped. Can we talk about something else, please?" Lindsey opened her mouth, and I added, "Something else that doesn't have to do with me and boys of the vampire persuasion?" When she snapped it shut it again, I was glad I'd taken the offensive.

A hand at my elbow stopped us before we could switch to a more pleasant topic. "Come out with us."

I looked over, found one of the new vamps beside me, and had to pause to remember his name. Tallish, youngish, curly, cropped brown hair, cute in a vague, East Coast blue-blood kind of way. Connor—that was it.

"What?" I asked.

"We're going out to celebrate." He inclined his head toward the knot of Novitiates heading collectively down the stairs. "You have to come out with us."

I opened my mouth to give a wavering answer, an "I don't know" that would have captured the fact that I knew I wasn't really one of them. But he stopped me with a hand.

"I'm not going to take no for an answer. It's our first official night as Cadogan vamps. We're going to Temple Bar to celebrate. There's twelve of us, and it would be wrong for only eleven to show up." He gave Lindsey an endearing smile. "Don't you think?"

"I definitely do," she agreed, and slipped her hand in the crook of my elbow. "We'll meet you at the bar."

Connor looked back at me, grinned boyishly. "Wicked. We'll see you then. And I'll have a drink ready." He stepped back, fisted hands on his hips, and looked me over. "Gin and tonic?"

I nodded.

"I knew it. You looked like a G and T girl. We'll be waiting for you," he said, then clucked me beneath the chin. Flipping his suit jacket over his shoulder, he bobbed down the stairs and out of sight.

Lindsey sighed audibly. "He's cute."

"He's a child." I hadn't meant chronologically—he was probably twenty-five, twenty-six. But he carried that sense of wealth-bred optimism shared by lots of the kids I'd grown up with. I was a little too cynical for that. Give me the jaded, slightly disillusioned boy instead.

"A little too pampered," Lindsey agreed, getting to the heart of it. "But that doesn't mean he can't pay for our drinks." She took a step forward and tugged at my arm. "Come on. Let's go spend a few hours pretending that being a vampire means partying and couture and being twenty-five forever."

We trotted down the stairs and walked by the parlor, where Malik and Ethan were still deep in discussion. Ethan's brow was drawn, hands on his hips as he stared at Malik, who looked to be explaining something. Lindsey and I paused in the doorway, watched Ethan shake his head, then deliver instructions to Malik, who nodded obligingly and tapped on a PDA.

"Come on, ladies! The alcohol awaits!"

Ethan's gaze flicked from Connor, to Lindsey, to me, and his expression blanked. *Tomorrow. My office.* We'd only just concluded the ceremony, and he was already making use of the mental connection he'd opened between us

"Come on, Merit," Lindsey said, tugging me away. I nodded back at him, and let her lead me away.

Temple Bar was housed in a narrow building squeezed into a corner in Wrigleyville. It was owned by Cadogan House and stocked with Cubs gear; it made a killing, no pun intended, during baseball season.

It was just after midnight when we arrived, and the bar was packed. A mix of vampires and humans (apparently oblivious to the predators surrounding them), filled the narrow space, the right side of which was lined by a memorabilia-laden bar, the left by a series of booths and tables. A small loft was perched in the back, which gave a handful of customers a bird's-eye view of the room and its supernatural patrons.

We saw Connor and the rest of the Novitiates around a long, narrow bar table at the edge of the seating area, drinks in their hands.

"Merit!" Connor yelled out when we made eye contact, pushing through the crowd to get to us. "I was afraid you were going to stand us up."

I started to clarify that it had only been minutes since we'd seen each other, but got an elbow in the ribs from Lindsey. I gave her a dirty look before smiling back at Connor.

"We made it!" I lightly said, and accepted the gin and tonic he handed me. He followed suit with Lindsey, and she immediately pulled the lime off the rim of her glass before taking a big sip of the drink. I bit back a smile, guessing she needed the liquid patience to get through an evening with baby vamps.

Randomly, I also wondered, given Catcher's theories about my physical and psychic strength, if I could form the same kind of bond with her that Ethan had formed with me. I stared at her, tried to reach out, to push through a mental tunnel between us, but all I got for my trouble was the beginning of a sinus headache and a weird look from Lindsey.

"What are you staring at?" she asked.

"How does Ethan do that mental connection thing?" I asked back, as we followed Connor through the throng to the other new Novitiates, holding our drinks aloft to avoid dumping them onto the people around us.

"I don't know the mechanics of it," Lindsey said, "if that's what you're asking. It's what Masters do. It's a connection to the vampires they turn."

We cut a path through prettily dressed men and women, finally emerging at the end of the bar table. The vamps who gathered there—women perched cattily on high stools, men standing between and around them—immediately stopped talking.

"Folks," Connor announced into the relative silence, "I bring you the Sentinel of Cadogan House." He lifted his glass toward me. "Merit, your brethren."

They stared at me, looked me over, evaluated, and questioned. Waiting for judgment, I raised my own glass and offered a tentative smile. "Hi."

A woman with a gleaming bob of sable hair slid a glance to the blond woman beside her, then smiled at me. "Lovely to meet you, Merit. You've made quite an impression."

Her diction was perfect, her words precise, her snug black suit cut into a low runway-worthy V. She looked vaguely familiar, and it took a moment before I realized that I'd seen her before—that I actually *knew* her. This was Christine Dupree, daughter of Dash Dupree, one of Chicago's most famous, most notorious criminal defense attorneys. Our fathers were friends, and Christine and I had been introduced years ago at a reception for a private school my father wanted me to attend. I'd begged him to keep me in public school, and he'd ultimately given in—both to my begging and to what he'd believed had been a two-day hunger strike. (I hadn't mentioned the stash of Oreos my grandfather had helped me sneak into my bedroom.)

"We've met before, Christine. You know my father."

She frowned, her delicately arched brows knitting together, but then a smile blossomed. "Oh, my *God*. You're *that* Merit! Joshua's daughter. Of course!" She turned to the girls around her, who watched us with avid curiosity, and explained our connection.

"God, sit *down*!" Christine said, waving Novitiate Warner toward an empty chair at a table behind us. "Get the girl a chair, Warner."

On command, Warner pulled over a seat and offered it with a flourish. "My lady."

To sit or not to sit? I glanced back at Lindsey, who was chatting animatedly with Connor, her eyes fluttering as she laughed at something he'd said. I decided she was fine, so I took the seat and set about getting acquainted.

I chatted with Cadogan's newest vampires for hours. They explained why they'd opted to become vampires, and the reasons were surprisingly varied—illness, nobility, immortality, family connections (Michael had a great-great-great-grandfather killed in a duel between warring houses who'd become a Cadogan vampire), and career opportunities. I told my own story, leaving out the sordid details of my transformation to vampire, and felt the wall between us begin to dissolve. They were especially thrilled by my challenging Ethan, the guys making me repeat the story until they'd milked it of every detail. Ethan, they informed me, was a notoriously good fighter, with an almost unbroken record of wins against other vamps. They were amused that I'd challenged him, impressed that I'd held my own.

Honestly, I was surprised by their reaction. Not that they were interested in my story, but that they listened regardless of the mess I'd inadvertently made of their Commendation. I'd expected anger or snobbery, not acceptance.

We swapped stories until the wee hours of the morning, until the guests slowly filtered from the bar, until Sean and Colin—the resident bartenders, also Cadogan vamps—cheerily evicted us. We walked out to our vehicles, and Lindsey gave me a ride back home. She spent the trip debating the merits of dating a baby vamp. At the end of the night, with minutes to spare before the dawn, I stepped out of the car, and laughed aloud at the giant banner that hung across Mal's and my front door.

It was a sheet of black plastic with "GUESS WHO'S OVER THE HILL!" printed in giant white letters across it. A skull and crossbones decorated one end, and the other bore cartoonish drawings of gravestones.

I snickered, guessing the culprit. The expressions of the front door guards were as blank as I'd ever seen them. I guess they weren't impressed by the joke. I stepped past them, unlocked the door, entered the house and locked up again. Inside the quiet living room, on the table next to the front door, was a note with my name on it.

Merit,

Congratulations on your Vampire Rush. Hope you had a great time and told Darth Sullivan to kiss off. Also hope you like the banner. It wasn't exactly what I wanted, but I liked *the gravestones. Hard to find a perfecter gift for the newly undead. XOXO.*

M

In a scratchy scrawl beneath Mallory's handwriting lay another message:

The banner was her idea.

CB

Smiling, I tucked the note into my pocket, fingered the pendant at my neck, and just as the sun began to push above the horizon, headed upstairs to bed.

CHAPTER ELEVEN

ADViCE FOR LiTiGATORS AND VAMPiRES: NEVER ASK A QUESTiON TO WHiCH YOU DON'T ALREADY KNOW THE ANSWER

"Get your ass out of bed."

Two nights in a row? I groaned and pulled a pillow over my head. "I'm trying to sleep."

The pillow was yanked back, and a cell phone was pressed against my ear in time to hear someone yell, "Get your ass out of bed, Sentin el, and get to the damn House! I don't know what kind of cushy job you expected, but around here, we earn our pay. You've got fifteen minutes."

Suddenly awake, and realizing who was on the phone, I grabbed the cell from Mallory's hand and fumbled through pillows and blankets until I was upright. "Luc? I can't make it across town in fifteen minutes."

There was a gravelly chuckle on the other end of the phone. "Then learn to fly, Tinkerbell, and get that pretty ass to the House." The call ended with an audible click, and I dropped it onto the bed and jumped to the floor.

"Hurry much?"

Cursing like a sailor on leave, I rifled through my closet. "I'm late," I vented. "The House vamps already think I'm a freak. And now I'm the prissy, princessy freak who can't show up to work on time. I didn't know he wanted me in at the crack of dusk."

Her voice almost irritatingly calm, Mal offered, "Check the door, hon."

"I don't have time for riddles, Mal. I'm in a hurry." I flipped through a long-sleeve T-shirt, then another, then another, and found nothing that Cadogan vamps would find even remotely acceptable.

"The door, Merit."

With a groan, I pushed back from the closet and glanced at the door. Hanging over my bedroom door was a short-sleeved black top and a pair of cuffed flat-front gray dress trousers. A pair of black high-heeled Mary Jane shoes sat in front of it. As an ensemble, it was simple, classy, and with the stiletto-heeled shoes, a little fierce. I glanced back at her. "What's this?"

"A first-day-of-work present."

My eyes filled with tears, and I wiped at them with the sleeves of the long-sleeved tee I'd slept in. "You take good care of me."

She sighed and moved closer, then pulled me into a hug. "You're on day eight of Merit's Brain Vacation. You've got until day ten. I expect you to have adjusted by then." She brushed the hair from my face, then tweaked a lock of it. "I miss brainiac Merit."

I smiled sheepishly. "I miss her, too."

She nodded. "Good. I'm going to run out and grab you a black suit. Since you've got a birthday coming up, I'm totally claiming that as your gift."

Birthday number twenty-eight was next week. And while I appreciated the thought, I wasn't crazy about the would-be present. "Not to be picky, Mal, but could I maybe get a birthday present that's not Ethan Sullivan–related?"

"Is there anything in your life right now that's not Ethan Sullivan–related?"

Hmm. She had a point.

"Now enough procrastinating! Go get in the shower, get these pretty clothes on, and go do that Sentinel thing."

I saluted her and followed the order.

*   *   *

It took twenty minutes to get dressed and in some semblance of order—to pull back my hair into a high ponytail, to brush out my bangs, to slide into the new clothes and fasten the tiny buckles on my three-inch-heeled Mary Janes, to grab my black messenger bag, to clip on my beeper—and another handful to get to Cadogan House. I threw the car into park as soon as I was near the gate and trotted in my heels—and quite a sight that was, I'm sure—down the sidewalk.

The House was quiet and empty when I finally bobbed up the front stairs and entered the foyer. I guessed the vamps were up and about, already assuming their positions and dedicating themselves to the Cadogan cause. I peeked into the front parlor, saw no one, and walked through to the second. Still no vampires.

"Looking for someone?"

Of all the luck. Ordering my face into what I hoped was a kind of meek chagrin, I spun to face Ethan. Not surprisingly, he was in black—a dark suit layered over a white shirt, no tie. He stood in the doorway, arms folded across his chest, his hair pulled back at the nape of his neck.

"I'm late," was my confession.

His brows lifted, a corner of his mouth almost, but not quite, tipped up in amusement. "On your first day? I'm shocked. I'd imagined you'd prove to be our most reliable, dependable employee."

I walked around him, peeked through a doorway that led from the parlor. It led to another hallway, also empty. "And I bet you became Master of Cadogan House because of your spectacular wit." I stopped and faced him, then put hands on my hips. "Where would I find Luc?"

"Please?"

"Please what?"

Ethan rolled his eyes. "That was your cue to show some respect to your employer."

"And you're suggesting that's you?"

In response, he lifted a single brow higher.

"The thing is," I pointed out, "since I've got the responsibility of ensuring the safety of the House, I've got some authority over you, too."

Ethan uncrossed his arms and put his hands on his hips. The posture was vaguely threatening, his tone only slightly less so. "Only if I was to act in a way that threatens the House. And I won't."

"But that's my determination to make, isn't it?"

He just stared at me. "Are you always this obstreperous?"

"I'm not obstreperous. Stubborn, arguably. And don't start in that I was causing trouble. I was only asking a question."

"You start causing trouble the minute you awaken. Case in point—you're late."

"And that brings us back full circle. Now where's Luc?" He lifted both brows, and I sighed. "God, you call me stubborn. Please, Sullivan, where's Luc?"

There was a pause as he slipped his hands into his pockets but then, finally, gave an answer that didn't involve a critique of my character. "Operations room. Down the stairs to the right. It's the first door on the left, before you get to the sparring room. If you suddenly discover you're fang deep in vampires, all intent on teaching you the manners you so obviously lack, you've gone too far."

I lightly grasped the edges of my shirt and dropped into a neat curtsy, batting my eyes coquettishly. "Thank you, Liege," I said, Gratefully Condescending.

"You're still not in Cadogan attire, you know."

I frowned, awash in the disheartening realization that I'd tried again, and failed, at playing Cadogan vampire. Was I ever going to be able to be good enough for Ethan? I doubted it, but faked a smile and cheekily offered, "You should have seen what I was *going* to wear."

Ethan rolled his eyes. "Get to work, Sentinel, but find me before you leave. I want to touch base about the murder investigations."

I nodded. Hard to be sarcastic when serial murder was the topic. "Sure."

Ethan gave me a final silent perusal, then turned and walked out of the room. I kept my eyes on the empty doorway even when he'd gone, still expecting him to pop back inside and add a final snarky comment. But silence filled the House, Ethan apparently content not to do further battle right now. Relieved, I took the stairs and veered to the right. The door he'd indicated was closed. I knocked, heard someone invite me in, opened the door and walked inside.

It was like stepping onto a movie set. The room was as handsomely decorated as the upper floors of Cadogan House, pale colors and tasteful furniture, but it was smeared with technology—screens, computers, printers. The ends of the rectangular room were anchored by long banks of computers and expensive-looking equipment, with security monitors mounted above. Black-and-white images of the Cadogan grounds flickered on the screens. An oval conference table sat in the middle of the room, a handful of vampires—including Luc and Lindsey—around it. And on the long wall behind the conference table was a seven-foot-wide display screen, projecting a series of pictures of a brunette.

Of *me*.

I stared, lips parted, at a picture of me dancing across a stage in a pale pink leotard, a whispery skirt around my thighs, hands arced above my head. There was a clicking sound, and the image changed. I was in college, wearing an NYU T-shirt. *Click*. I was at a library table, tucking a lock of hair behind an ear as I pored over a book. The picture was undisturbed by vampire glam—I sat cross-legged in jeans in a comfy chair, my hair pulled back in a messy knot, retro-punk glasses perched on my nose, Chuck Taylors on my feet.

I cocked my head to the side, staring at the text on the screen. *"Canterbury Tales,"* I announced to the room. All heads turned to look at me as I stood, not a little unsteadily, in the doorway. "I was preparing for a class, in case you were curious."

Luc, who sat at the head of the table, tapped a screen that was inlaid into the tabletop, and the images disappeared, replaced by a Cadogan House logo. He still looked cowboyish today—tousled blond hair ruffling the collar of a faded, long-sleeved denim shirt, jeans, and boots, visible because he crossed his ankles on the table in front of him. He was the only vamp in the room in jeans. Everyone else was in the requisite Cadogan black, fitted tops and shirts that, presumably, made it easier for the guards to do their jobs than the usual stiff suits.

"Doing some research?" I asked.

"You'd be amazed what you can find on the Interwebs in a week," Luc said, "and security always checks out security." He pointed me toward a seat at the table next to Lindsey, and across from a female vamp I didn't know—a tall, coltish redhead, who'd maybe topped out at twenty-two when she was turned. She grinned at me.

"Sit your ass down," Luc said. "It took you long enough to get here. You really need to consider moving into the House."

I smiled grimly at the other guards, none of whom I recognized beyond Lindsey, and took the proffered seat. "I can't imagine any way that'd be a good idea," I said, trying for a light tone. "I'd get pissed at Ethan and stake him in his sleep. No one wants that."

"Least of all Ethan," Lindsey pointed out, using a stick of what looked like beef jerky to gesture. "That's very magnanimous, Merit."

I smiled at her. "Thanks."

Luc rolled his eyes. "Before we were interrupted"—he gave me a heavy glance that made clear whom he was holding responsible for the disturbance—"I was explaining to your crew that I'm going to be testing you on the C-41 protocol, and that if you don't yet understand the four subsets of the C-41 protocol, you'll find your ass in Ethan's office explaining to him why you spent the evening partying with the baby vamps when you should have been preparing to ensure the security of your House."

Luc raised his gaze to mine. "I assume you looked through the Web site last night and can take us through the C-41 subsets?"

I swallowed down a keen sense of panic. It was like living the nightmare—the one where you're unprepared for an exam and you show up to the test completely naked? Here I was, nicely dressed, but still about to be humiliated in front of the squad of Cadogan guards. I might as well have skipped the wardrobe upgrade.

I opened my mouth to spit out some kind of response—an apology, a couple of lame sentences about the importance of House security in the days of dueling alliances (and Ethan said I never listened!)—when Luc was hit, square in the face, with a flying piece of jerky.

Lindsey snorted and nearly fell out of her chair laughing, catching herself—and the giant plastic tub of jerky that was sitting in her lap—just before she stumbled.

With the calm aplomb of a man accustomed to being hit in the face with dried beef, Luc peeled the square of jerky from his shirt, lifted it, and leveled a skewering glance at Lindsey.

"What?" she said. "You can't think I'm going to let you sit there and torture her." She glanced back at me. "He's bullshitting you. There's no such thing as a C-41 protocol." She reached into the tub and pulled out a ruler-shaped piece of meat, then looked back at Luc, as she nibbled on the end. "You're such a shit."

"And you're fired."

I'm not fired, she mouthed to me, shaking her head. She held out the tub. "Jerky?"

I'd never been a jerky fan, but the urge to nosh was undeniable. I reached in and grabbed two sticks of it, and immediately began gnawing. Weird thing about being a vampire—you never knew you were hungry until you were around food. Then the urges kicked in.

Luc grumbled at the set down, but kicked his legs off the table, motioned for the bucket, and when she offered it, grabbed some jerky of his own. He tugged at one end toothily, then said, "Folks, since our resident troublemaker has finally decided to join us, why don't you all introduce yourselves?" He put a hand on his chest. "I'm Luc. I exist to give you orders. If you question those orders, you'll find your ass on the floor." He smiled wolfishly. "Any questions, doll?"

I shook my head. "I think I'm good."

"Right. Peter, you're next."

Peter was about six foot, with a thinner build, and brown hair that fell just past his ears. He wore a gray sweater, jeans, and boots. He'd probably been made in his early thirties, and had a look of casual wealth that reminded me of the new Novitiates. But where they wore a gloss of naive optimism, Peter had the vaguely tired look of a man who'd seen too much in his life.

"Peter. I've been here thirty-seven, thirty-eight years."

"Peter's concise," Luc commented, nodding at the next guard. "Juliet."

Juliet was the feylike redhead. "Juliet. Eighty-six years, fifty-four in Cadogan. I was Commended into Taylor, transferred over. Nice to meet you, Merit."

"Kel, you're next."

"I'm Kelley," said the woman to my right. Her black hair was long and straight, her mouth a perfect cupid's bow, her skin perfectly pale, her eyes slightly uptilted. "Two hundred and fourteen years. I was made by Peter Cadogan before the House was formed. When he was killed, I stayed with Ethan. You'll stand Sentinel?"

I nodded, the only option available, as her tone brooked no argument. The energy that surrounded her was contained, intense, and almost thickly aggressive. For all that, she was lithe and slim, and was probably deceptively unfrightening to the average human.

"And last, and arguably least, we have Lindsey." He looked over at her, gave her a haughty look.

Lindsey just waved an airy hand. "You know who I am. I'm one hundred and fifteen, if it matters, originally from Iowa, but I did my time in New York—Yankees rule. I had too much to drink last night, and I have a splitting headache, but I divested a newbie of a pint."

I grinned, but caught a low-grade growl from Luc's end of the table. Some unrequited feelings there, maybe?

"Do us a favor and spare us the bloody details, Linds."

Lindsey smirked at him, smiled at me. "And I'm the resident psychic."

He snapped his fingers. "Of course. I knew there was a reason he kept you around. Everyone has their specialties—Peter's got the contacts, Juliet's slippery. She gathers data." I assumed he meant surreptitiously. "Kelley's our resident mechanical and software genius."

When he turned to look at me, the rest of the guards followed suit. I sat still while they gave me calculating, appraising glances, probably registering strengths and weaknesses, estimating powers and potentials.

"I'm strong and fast," I offered. "I don't know how I match up against everyone else, but as you probably heard, I at least gave Ethan a run for his money, so you know what I could do a couple of days out. Since then, I've been training with Catcher Bell, learning moves and sword work, and that's coming along. I seem to have some resistance to glamour, but I don't have any other psychic powers. At least, not yet."

Her wide whiskey eyes on me, Kelley offered, "I suppose that makes you a soldier."

"And I'm the fearless leader," Luc said, "haranguing this group of ragtag vampires into something greater than the sum of its parts. I like to think of it as—"

"Boss, she's in. She doesn't need the recruiting speech." Peter lifted brows expectantly at Luc.

"Right." Luc nodded. "Right. Well, in addition to the six of us, we liaise with the daylight guards, the folks who stay at the gate. They're employed by RDI—that's our external security company."

"And how do we know we can trust them?" I asked.

"Cynical," Luc said with approval. "I like it. Anyway, RDI is run by fairies. And nobody fucks with fairies. The thing is, while we protect the House—"

"Because a safe House is a safe Master," the four guards parroted together, their words ash-dry, and I guessed Luc broke out the proverb frequently.

"Jesus, you bastards *do* listen to me. I'm touched. Really." He rolled his eyes. "As I was saying, our primary loyalty is to Ethan, to the vamps. Your loyalty is first and foremost to Cadogan. I don't think that'll make too much difference in the short run, but should something arise that tests the bond between Master and House, you'll need to be aware of that." He shook his head, mouth pursed. "That'll put you in a helluva goddamn spot, having to counter Ethan about House security. But he thought you were the girl for the job, so . . . You know anything about guns?" he asked, expression suddenly tight.

I blinked. "Um, only to stay away from them?"

Luc blew out a breath, ran his hands through his hair. "Training, then. Jesus, you're green. Ballet and grad school to Cadogan fucking Sentinel. It'll take time." He nodded, then released his hands and scribbled something on a notepad that lay on the table in front of him. "You're going to need weapons training, strategy, cleaning and safety, all of it."

He was quiet for a moment, flipping an occasional page as he made notes. In the interim, Lindsey offered me another hunk of jerky, which I gratefully accepted.

"Now that we've done the tea party," Luc said, pushing

back the notepad and settling into his chair, "it's time for our annual review of Rules You Disrespectful Bastards Never Follow."

A unified disgruntled groan filled the Operations Room. Luc ignored it. "I'm explaining these rules for Merit's benefit, but since you people rarely obey them"—he gave Lindsey a pointed glance, to which she responded with a stuck-out tongue—"I'm sure you'll appreciate the refresher."

He tapped the panel in front of him. The Cadogan logo disappeared from the wall screen, replaced by a bulleted list entitled *Cadogan Guards—Expectations*.

Luc leaned back, crossed his hands behind his head, and kicked his booted feet back onto the table. "Number one, you're always on call. I don't care where you are, who you're with, or what you're doing. Sleeping, showering, making inappropriate advances toward still-pink vampires." That earned a grunt from Lindsey. "If your beeper sounds, you're on your way to the House, to the action.

"Number two, you will review the Web site, and you will learn the security protocols. If the worst happens—if there's a direct attack on Cadogan—I want everyone in place, knowing their positions, knowing their responsibilities, knowing whether you're guarding zone or man-to-man."

Lindsey leaned toward me. "He's obsessed with college ball," she whispered. "Expect him to channel Coach K whenever he thinks he can risk the analogy."

I grinned.

"Twice a week," Luc said, "we will review said protocols, focusing on developments, strategies, whatever burr I happen to have up my ass at that particular time. Every day that you are on duty, you will review the dailies, and you will review the dossiers that are placed in your particular file." He pointed at a line of hanging folders mounted to the wall, each a different color, each labeled with one of our names. The label on the bottommost folder read *Cadogan Sentinel*.

"These documents will keep you informed as to any

threats, any changes in the management of this or any other House, any guests in Cadogan, any particular instructions given by your Liege and mine. Four times a week you will train in accordance with the manual you'll find on the Web site. Train here, train with your comrades, train outside the House. I don't care. But you'll be tested periodically— strength, speed, stamina, katas, weapons. You're a Cadogan guard, and you owe your life and health to this House. You will be prepared to pay that debt, in full, if necessary."

A weighty silence fell over the room, and I watched the guards nod solemnly, some touching the Cadogan medals that lay at the base of their throats.

"Number three," Luc continued, pointing at the screen. "You're an employee of Cadogan House. That means you screw something up in the process of doing your duty— injuring bystanders, pissing off humans—and you risk drawing unwanted attention to the House, our getting sued, an increase in our insurance premiums, and your ass on the streets, where you'll end up following goth wannabe Rogue vampires around the Windy City. To use Merit's words, no one wants that, least of all Ethan. And you sure as shit don't want aspen drawn because you were careless.

"Number four, while this isn't a hard and fast rule, and Ethan would never admit to it, you should be . . . circumspect in your relations with other sups. That includes vamps from other Houses, sorcerers, shifters, and perhaps most relevant today"—Luc looked to Peter and tapped the tips of two fingers on the table—"nymphs. Malik is the only Cadogan vamp authorized to enter into alliances on the House's behalf without Ethan's stamp. Friendly is fine—we don't need to make enemies by acting like pricks from Navarre." A chuckle flowed around the room; some of the tension faded. "But alliances are for our Liege and his Second to arrange. Use your common sense. And if you lack common sense, talk to me." He grinned slowly, wolfishly, and directed that smile at Lindsey. "I'll be sure to point you in the correct direction."

She rolled her eyes.

"Number five. You work four days on, one off. On working days, unless I've assigned you elsewhere, you're in the Ops Room when you report. You'll either work here, or you'll patrol—the House, the grounds. At least one day a week, you'll guard Ethan personally, travel as his body man." He looked at me. "Technically, as Sentinel, you'll set your own schedule. But I'd suggest you work with us, learn the ropes in here, at least until you're familiar with our processes."

I nodded my agreement.

Luc's brows lifted. "Well, you're a little more biddable than we thought."

That earned another chuckle around the room. I blushed in response, but smiled at my colleagues. Luc dished it out to everyone, and I knew I needed to—and could—take it.

"I await your pleasure," I drily said, which earned an appreciative snort from Lindsey.

Luc tapped the screen again, and the image on the wall disappeared. "I'm going to give Merit the grand tour. Lindsey, since you're mentoring Merit—and my advance apologies for that, Sentinel—you'll take over babysitting when the tour's done. Everyone else who's scheduled, get to work."

Luc rose, but the vamps stayed obediently seated until he threw out, "Dismissed." Then they murmured thank-yous and rose, grabbing jerky from the tub Lindsey had placed on the table. Lindsey and Kelley both moved to the computer workstations at the edges of the room. Peter left the room; I guessed it was his day off. Juliet grabbed her jacket and headed for the door. "I'm on grounds," she announced, then touched a finger to the buff-colored shell of a device that fit around her ear. "Check."

"Check that," Kelley said. "Audio in. Dialing in RDI." There was a pause before she said, "Kelley, Cadogan House, on duty." She nodded, then looked over at Juliet. "Security transferred. Juliet on. You're good, Juliet."

She looked at me, winked jauntily, then made for the door. "Tell me about it."

His guards set to work, the next task on Luc's list was the full House tour. We began in the basement, which held the Ops Room, the sparring room, a gym, and the steel-lined arsenal that housed Cadogan's weapons—modern crossbows, bladed weapons of every shape and type, aspen stakes and pikes, and although Catcher had suggested vamps didn't use them, an entire cabinet of guns. Rifles, shotguns, handguns—weapons I could only identify after years of faithfully watching *Law & Order*.

The main floor held the front and main parlors, Ethan's office, the state dining room, the kitchen, a cafeteria area for informal meals, and a series of smaller offices, one of which belonged to Helen, who'd been given the unenviable duty of introducing me to the world of vampires. I made a mental note to find her and apologize.

As we took the stairs to the second floor, Luc explained the mansion had been built during Chicago's Gilded Age by an industrialist eager to show off his newfound wealth. Unfortunately, the house had been finished for only sixteen days when he was shot to death in a flophouse in one of the city's rougher neighborhoods, reportedly after an altercation with the boyfriend of a prostitute named Flora. The Greenwich Presidium purchased the building on Cadogan's behalf shortly thereafter—for a very good price.

The second floor, which held the ballroom I'd visited the night before, also held the library, which we didn't have time to see, a couple of informal dens, and half the dorm-style rooms that housed the Cadogan vamps who lived "on campus." The rooms were wood-floored and high-ceilinged, and each held a small bed, dresser, bookshelf and nightstand, and had been decorated to suit the personality of the vamps who lived there. The House's ninety-seven live-in vamps (which included all of last night's Novitiates, save me) were unmar-

ried and tended to work directly in the House—as administrators, guards, House staff, or other members of Ethan's
entourage.

The third floor housed the rest of the vamps' rooms, as
well as another den. Ethan's sizable apartments were also
there, as were the suite of rooms next door that Luc referred
to as the "boudoir." These were Amber's rooms, the suite
used by the reigning House Consort. We didn't look inside
the suite—the mental image of a "boudoir" was enough—but
I couldn't help but pause outside, thinking that I might have
been moving into those rooms, replacing Amber, making
myself, my body, available to Ethan.

I shivered and moved on.

Having walked through the corpus of the House, Luc took
me back to and through the first floor. Just off the cafeteria,
which was stocked with wooden tables and chairs, was a set
of wide glass doors that led to an expansive patio.

"Wow," I said when we emerged into the torch-lit back
yard. Before us was a formal hedged garden, with a huge
brick barbecue to the right, and a kidney-shaped pool to the
left. The entire area was ringed by a tall shrubbery that ob-
scured the wrought-iron fence and the street beyond.

"Nice, huh?" Luc asked as we stood on the patio and surveyed the area.

"It's beautiful."

Luc led the way to the parterre, the border of which was
made up of vibrantly green hedge interspersed with a purple-
leafed plant I couldn't name. In the middle of the garden was
a bubbling fountain. Black metal benches surrounded it.

"Formal garden," Luc said, "in the French style."

"So I see." I dipped fingers into the fountain, then flicked
cool water from my fingers.

"Not a bad place to spend some off-duty time," he said,
then led me through the path that split the garden into quad-
rants and through the other side to the pool. "We can't sun-

bathe, obviously, but the pool's nice in the heat. We'll have parties, barbecues, that kind of thing."

A copse of trees stood at one edge of the pool, and Luc pointed through them to the path that wound around the edge of the property, illuminated by tiny inground lights.

"Running path. Gives us a chance to get in a little outdoor exercise without leaving the grounds. It's heated from beneath, so you can even run in the winter, if that's your gig."

"It isn't, not in Chicago, but it'll be nice in the summer," I said.

But it wasn't summer yet, and the April night was still chilly, so Luc skipped the stone-by-stone tour of the grounds, and settled for a summary of the parts we hadn't seen. That done, we headed back into the building, this time through a side door that opened into a narrow hallway on the first floor. Luc then led me back down to the Ops Room and planted me in front of a computer.

"You know the password?"

I nodded, loaded a Web browser, and found the Cadogan log-in page, then typed it in. He patted my shoulder. "Learn the protocols," he advised, then moved to his desk and began poring through a foot-high stack of files.

Hours passed. Although security and warfare had never been my gig, vampire security was highly contextual and thus incredibly interesting. There were links to history (Vampires were screwed over yesterday!) and politics (House X screwed us over yesterday!), philosophy (Why do you think they screwed us over yesterday?) and ethics (If we didn't bite, would they have screwed us over yesterday?), and, of course, strategy (How did they screw us over? How can we keep them from screwing us over again or, better yet, screw them over first?).

While I didn't know a thing about elemental strategy beyond what I'd learned in Catcher's swordsmanship lectures,

I understood history. I understood philosophy. I knew how to read a first-person account of warfare, of loss, how to glean information from it. That was, after all, how I'd researched my dissertation. So, when quitting time came, I felt pretty satisfied with my lot. Confident that I could learn enough to supplement my physical strength, to make good decisions for Cadogan House, to protect those vampires I'd sworn two oaths to serve.

Luc dismissed us, and I followed the off-duty vampires back up the stairs, then said goodbye to Lindsey, intending to meet with Ethan as he'd requested earlier. His office was open, but empty. And while I was momentarily tempted to take the chance, to scrounge through his books and papers and discover what secrets the antiques might have to offer, that would be a breach of privacy I wasn't equipped to take on. So I paused inside the doorway, apparently just long enough to raise someone's eyebrows.

"Excuse me."

I turned, found a brunette behind me. The vamp was dressed like a secretary in a noir-era detective serial, her body perched cattily in the doorway, one hand on the jamb.

"You're in Ethan's office." Her voice was haughty.

I nodded. "He asked me to stop by. Do you know where he is?"

She crossed her arms, short, black nails tapping against the trim cuffs of her shirt, and looked me over. "I'm Gabrielle. A friend of Amber's."

Not an answer to the question I'd asked, but informative all the same. Gabrielle thought I was poaching, maybe preparing to steal the Master of the House from beneath the Consort's nose. If she only knew.

But I had no interest in telling her, or anyone else, what he'd offered me. I hadn't even told Lindsey. Instead, I smiled politely, played nice.

"It's lovely to meet you, Gabrielle. Ethan asked me to meet him about some security issues. Do you know where he is?"

For my trouble, I got another slow perusal. Territorial, was Gabrielle. Finally, she lifted her gaze, one dark, carefully plucked brow higher than the other. "Oh, he's . . . inside."

I nodded. "I know he's in the House. I saw him earlier, and he told me to stop by. Do you know where he is specifically?"

She pursed her lips as if holding a grin, and kind of bobbled her head presumptuously. "He's inside," she repeated. "And I doubt he'll be happy to see you." But she was smiling when she said it. I knew I was missing a joke, but couldn't for the life of me fathom the punch line.

I had to clench my fingers to keep from lashing out in sheer frustration. "He asked me to find him," I explained, "to talk about business?"

She delicately lifted a shoulder. "I'm really not interested. But if you're so keen to see him, then by all means . . . go see him. It'd probably do you some good. He's in his apartments."

"Thanks." She waited at the doorway until I left the office; then she closed the door behind us. I started back for the main staircase and heard her chuckle evilly as I moved down the hallway.

I took the stairs to the second floor, rounded the landing, and headed up toward the third. Tucked here and there into nooks that bore sofas and chairs, vampires were reading books or magazines or chatting together. The house quieted as I moved upward, the third floor nearly silent. I followed the long hallway back to Ethan's apartments, stopped outside the closed double doors.

I knocked and, when I got no response, put an ear to the door. I heard nothing, so I slipped the doorknob on the right-side door and pushed it slowly open.

It was a sitting room. Well-appointed, tastefully decorated. Oak paneling rose to chair rail height, and an onyx fireplace dominated one wall. The room housed a couple of conversation areas, the furniture tailored and undoubtedly expensive. Side tables bore vases of flowers, and a Bach cello sonata rang softly through the air. On the opposite wall, just beside a small desk, was another set of double doors. One was closed; the second was slightly ajar.

"Ethan?" I called his name, but the word was a whisper, completely incapable of rousing attention. I walked to the doors, put the flat of my palm on the closed one, and peeked inside the gap.

I realized, then, why Gabrielle had so deliberately pointed out that he was inside.

Ethan was inside—inside the House. Inside his apartments.

And inside Amber.

CHAPTER TWELVE

YOU CAN'T TRUST A MAN WHO EATS A HOT DOG WITH A FORK.

I clasped a hand over my mouth, stifling the gasp that rose in my throat.

But after glancing surreptitiously around the sitting room, I leaned in again and took another peek.

I saw him in profile. He was completely naked, blond hair tucked behind his ears. Amber was in front of him, crouched on her knees on his giant four-poster bed, her back to his front. Even in profile, it was easy to see that she was ecstatic—the part of her lips, her half-closed lids, the clench of her fingers told the story. Her hands were fisted in the khaki bedclothes, and but for the joggle of her breasts, she was otherwise still, apparently content to let Ethan do the work.

And work, he did. His legs were braced slightly more than shoulder length apart, the dimpled hollows at the sides of his buttocks clenching as he swiveled and pumped his hips against her body. His skin was golden, his body long, lean, and sculpted. I noted a script tattoo on the back of his right calf, but the rest of his form was pristine, his smooth golden skin gleaming with perspiration. One of his hands was at her right hip, the other splayed across her damp lower back, his gaze—intense, carnal, needy—on the rhythmic union of their bodies. He smoothed a hand along the valley at the small of her back, his tongue peeking out to wet his bottom lip as he moved.

I stared at the pair of them, completely enthralled by the sight. I felt the wisp of arousal spark in my abdomen, a sensation as unwelcome as it was familiar.

He was magnificent.

Absently, I raised fingers to my lips, then froze at the realization that I was hiding in his sitting room, peeking through an open door, watching a man that a week ago I'd decided was my mortal enemy have sex. I was completely disturbed.

And I would have left, would have walked away with nothing more than a little mortification, had Ethan not chosen that moment to lean forward, to lower his body to hers, and to bite.

His teeth grazed the spot between her neck and shoulder, then pierced. His throat began to move convulsively, his hips still pumping—more fiercely, if that was possible—now that he'd breached her throat. Two lines of red, of her blood, traced down the pale column of her neck.

Instinctively, I lifted a hand, touching the spot where I'd been bitten, the place where scars should have marred my throat. I'd experienced the bite, the self-interested violence of it, but this was different. This was vampire, *being* vampire. Truly vampire. The sex notwithstanding, this was feeding the way it was meant to be. Him and her, sharing the act, not just sipping from the plastic of a medical bag. I knew that, understood it on a genetic level. And that knowledge, witnessing the act of it, scenting it, so close—even when I wasn't hungry, certainly not for Amber's blood—woke the vampire. I quickly drew in breath, tried to force her down again, to keep myself calm.

But not fast enough.

Ethan suddenly raised his eyes, our gazes locking through

the three-inch gap in the doors. His breath caught, his eyes flashing silver.

He must have seen the look of mortification that crossed my face, and his irises faded to green fast enough. But he didn't look away. Instead, he steadied himself with a hand at her hip and drank, his eyes on me.

I jumped away, put my back to the wall, but the move was pointless. He'd already seen me, and in that second before the silver faded, I'd seen the look in his eyes. There was a kind of hope there, that I'd had a different reason for appearing at his door, that I'd come to offer myself to him the way Amber had. But he hadn't seen offering in my eyes. And he hadn't planned on my embarrassment.

That was when his eyes had turned back to green, his hope replaced by something far, far colder. Tempered humiliation maybe, because I'd said no to him two days ago, because I hadn't sought him out tonight. Because I'd rejected a four-hundred-year-old Master vampire to whom most bowed, cowed, acquiesced. If he was disgruntled about wanting me in the first place, he was downright pissed about being rejected. That was what had flattened his eyes, pulled his pupils into tiny angry pricks of black. Who was I to say no to Ethan Sullivan?

Before I could comprise an answer to my own question, my head began to spin, and I was swamped with the sensation of being hurled down a tunnel. Then he was in my head.

To have rejected me so handily, you seem oddly curious now.

I cringed, and opted for acquiescence. Now was not the time to fight. *I was coming by to talk to you, as you asked. I knocked. I didn't mean to intrude.*

The room quieted, and Amber suddenly cried out, made a pouty moue of disappointment, maybe that he'd stopped thrusting.

Downstairs. An obvious order. When he said it, when that

single word echoed through my head, I'd swear I heard it again, that tiny twinge of disappointment.

And suddenly I wanted to fix that. I wanted to heal that disappointment, to ease it. To comfort. That thought was as dangerous as any other I'd had, so I pushed away from the wall and crept back through the room. As I neared the door to the hallway, the rhythmic creak of the bed began again. I left Ethan's apartments and closed the door behind me.

I was in the foyer when he arrived. I'd taken a seat next to the fireplace—a larger version of the one in his apartments—and curled up with the copy of the *Canon* I'd stowed in my messenger bag. I flipped absently through its pages, working to wipe the images of him, the sound of him, from my mind.

At least, that was what I was trying to do.

He was back in black, skipping the suit coat for trousers and a white button-up, the top button undone to reveal the Cadogan medal around his neck. The front of his hair was pulled back in a tight band, the rest just hitting the top of his shoulders.

I dropped my gaze back to my book.

"Found something . . . productive to do?" His tone was unmistakably haughty.

"As you might have noticed," I said lightly, turning a page in the *Canon* despite the fact that I hadn't read the one before it, "my plans to talk to the boss didn't quite pan out."

I forced myself to look up at him, to offer him a smile, to play off what could easily become a profoundly embarrassing moment. Ethan didn't return the smile, but he seemed to incrementally relax. Maybe he'd expected a spectacle, a jealous rant. And maybe that wasn't so far-fetched as I might want to admit.

Beneath hooded lashes, he offered, "I believe I'm sated for the day, if you'd care to chat now."

I nodded.

"Good. Shall we discuss this upstairs?"

My head snapped up.

He smiled tightly. "A joke, Merit. I do have a sense of humor." But it hadn't sounded like a joke, still didn't sound like he was kidding.

Ethan offered his office, so I unfolded my legs and stood. We made it as far as the stairs, but stopped short when Catcher and Mallory walked through the front door. He held paper bags and what looked like a newspaper under one arm; she held a foam tray of paper cups.

I sniffed the air. Food. Meat, if my vampire instincts were correct.

"If you think that's true," Catcher was telling her, "then I've been giving you more credit than you deserve."

"Magic or no magic, you're a dillhole."

The handful of Cadogan vamps in the foyer, to a one, stopped to stare at the blue-haired woman who was swearing in their House. Catcher put his free hand at the small of her back.

"She's adjusting to her magic, folks. Just ignore her."

They chuckled and returned to their business, which I assumed was looking posh and very, very busy.

Catcher and Mallory walked toward us. "Vamps," he said in greeting.

I checked my watch, noted it was nearly four in the morning, and wondered why Mallory wasn't tucked into bed, presumably with her escort. "What are you doing here?"

"I'm taking a couple weeks off work. McGettrick owes me fourteen weeks of accumulated vacation. I figured I was due."

I looked at Catcher. "And you. Don't you have work to do?"

He gave me a sardonic glance and pushed the bags of food against my chest. "I am working," he said, then looked at Ethan. "I brought food. Let's chat."

Ethan looked dubiously at the paper bags. "Food?"

"Hot dogs." When Ethan didn't respond, Catcher cupped

his hands together. "Frankfurters. Sausages. Meat tube, surrounded by a baked mass of carbohydrates. Stop me if this
sounds familiar, Sullivan. You live in Chicago for Christ's
sake."

"I'm familiar," Ethan said drily. "My office."

The bags were filled with Chicagoland's finest—foil-wrapped
hot dogs in poppy seed buns, coated in relish and onions and
hot peppers. I took a seat on the leather couch and bit in,
closing my eyes in rapture. "If you weren't taken, I'd date you
myself."

Mallory chuckled. "Which one of us were you talking to,
hon?"

"I think she meant the dog," Catcher said, munching on a
curly fry. "It's amazing she's as small as she is when she eats
like that."

"Sick, isn't it? It's her metabolism. It has to be. She eats
like a horse, and she never exercises. Well, she never *used* to
exercise, but that was before she became Ninja Jane."

"You two are dating?" Across the room, where Ethan was
pulling a plate from his bar cabinet, he froze and stared back
at us, his face a little paler than usual.

I grinned down at my frank. "Don't choke on it, Sullivan.
She's dating Catcher, not you."

"Yes, well . . . congratulations." He joined us on the
couch, deposited a hot dog on a dinner plate of fine platinum-
banded china. Frowning, he began sawing at it with a knife
and fork, then carefully ate a chunk.

"Sullivan, just pick it up."

He glanced at me, spearing a chunk of hot dog with his
fork. "My way is more genteel."

I took another gigantic bite, and told him between chews,
"Your way is more tight ass."

"Your respect for me, Sentinel, is astounding."

I grinned at him. "I'd respect you more if you took a bite
of that dog."

"You don't respect me any."

Not entirely true, but I wasn't going to give him the satisfaction of a correction. "Like I said, I'd respect you more. More than *none*."

I smiled and turned back to Mallory and Catcher, who, heads cocked, stared at both of us. "What?"

"Nothing," they simultaneously said.

Ethan finally acquiesced, picking up the dog and taking a bite, managing not to spill condiments on his fancy pants. He chewed contemplatively, then took another bite, then another.

"Better?"

He grunted, which I took as a sound of hedonistic fulfillment.

Without raising his gaze from the dog in his hands, Ethan asked, "I assume you have some reason for showing up on my doorstep two hours before dawn?"

Catcher dusted crumbs from his hands, picked up the newspaper he'd laid beside him, and unfolded it. The headline of the *Sun-Times* read: *Second Girl Dead; Vamp Killer?*

Beside me, Ethan muttered a curse.

"Question of the hour, Sullivan—why haven't you called the Houses together?"

I didn't have to see Ethan's expression to know how he'd react to the less-than-subtle challenge to his strategy. But he played along. "For what purpose?"

Catcher rolled his eyes and shifted back into the couch, looping his arms over the back of it. "Information, to start."

"Isn't that your job? Investigating?"

"My job is to ease tensions, and that's what I'm talking about—calming nerves." He tapped the newspaper. "Celina in a busty suit isn't enough to get past murder. People are nervous. The Mayor's nervous. Hell, even Scott's nervous. I went by Grey House earlier. Scott's up in arms. Pissed, and you know how much it takes to get him riled up. The boy's Teflon to politics, usually. But someone comes at his people, and he's ready to battle. Mark of a good leader," he allowed.

Ethan wiped his mouth with a napkin, then crumpled it and let it fall to the table. "I'm not in a position to take steps, preventive or otherwise. I don't have the political capital."

Catcher shook his head. "I'm not talking about your directing the show. I'm talking about getting the communities together—or at least the Houses. Everyone's talking, and we're hearing a lot of it. Questions are being asked, fingers being pointed. You need to step out there. You could gain some capital if you do." He shrugged, scratched at the arm that lay behind Mallory's shoulders. "I know it's not my decision, and you're probably using that handy little mental link to explain to our mutual vampire friend here"—he bobbed his head at me—"how I'm meddling into affairs that aren't my own. But you also know that I wouldn't come to you with this if I didn't think it was important."

The room was quiet, mentally and otherwise, Catcher having been a little overenthusiastic about Ethan's willingness to confide in me.

Then he nodded. "I know. I take it you don't have any information other than this?"

Catcher swallowed a drink of soda, shook his head. "As far as facts go, you know what I know. As far as feelings go . . ." He trailed off, but held out his right hand, palm up, and slowly uncurled his fingers. There was a sudden pulse through the air, that sudden vibrating thickness that, I was beginning to learn, indicated magic. And in the space above Catcher's hand, the air seemed to wave, like rising heat.

Ethan shifted beside me. "What do you know?" His voice was low, earnest, cautious.

Catcher, head cocked, eyes on his palm, was quiet for a long, heavy moment. "War is coming, Ethan Sullivan, House of Cadogan. The temporary peace, born of human neglect, is at an end. She is strong. She will come, she will rise, and she will break the bonds that have held the Night together."

I swallowed, kept my gaze on Catcher. This was Mallory's boyfriend in full fourth-grade sorcerer mode, offering a creepily formal prophecy about the state of the Houses. But creepy as it was, I kept my eyes on Catcher, and ignored the urge to shift my head and look at Ethan, whose weighty stare I could feel.

"War will come. She will bring it. They will join her. Prepare to fight."

Catcher shuddered, curled his fingers back into a fist. The magic dissipated in a warm breeze, leaving the four of us blinking at each other.

A knock sounded at the door. "Liege? Everything okay? We felt magic."

"It's fine," Ethan called out. "We're fine." But when I looked over, his gaze was on me, penetrating in its intensity, and I knew—even without his voice in my head—what he was thinking: I was an unknown threat, and I might be the "she" in Catcher's prophecy. It was another mark against me, the possibility that I was the woman who would bring war to the vampires, risk the possibility of another Clearing.

I sighed and looked away. Things had become so complicated.

Catcher shook his head like a dog shaking off water, then ran a hand over his head. "That was vaguely nauseating, but at least I didn't do iambic pentameter this time."

"And no rhyming," Mallory put in, "which is an improvement."

I lifted a brow at that revelation, wondering how and when Mallory'd had a chance to see Catcher prophesizing. On the other hand, God only knew went on behind that bedroom door.

As if still recovering from the intensity of the experience, Catcher picked up a cup of soda, stripped off the plastic lid and straw, and drank deeply, his throat swallowing convulsively until he'd drained it. Magic looked to be tough work, and I was glad—even if being a vampire was still an emotional and physical ordeal—that I wasn't dealing with the weight of some kind of unseen universal power.

When he'd finished drinking, he sat back, then put a hand on Mallory's knee. He slid a glance to me, then looked at Ethan. "By the way, she's not the one."

"I know," he said, not even pausing to reflect. That drew a look from me, which he didn't meet. I opened my mouth to ask questions—*How do you know? Why don't you think I'm the one?*—but Catcher jumped in first.

"And speaking of prophesying, I hear Gabe's heading back, and sooner than we thought."

Ethan's head snapped up, so I could guess the import of that little revelation. "How reliable?"

"Reliable enough." Catcher looked at me. "You remember, this is the head of the North American Central—Jeff's pack." I nodded my understanding. "He's got people in Chicago, and he's got the convention coming up. He wants to assure himself that things are safe and secure before he brings in the pack. And I've heard Tonya's pregnant, so he'll want her and the kid safe."

"If things aren't safe," Ethan clipped out, "it's none of my doing."

Catcher's tone softened. "I realize that. But things are coming to a head. And if he wants assurances, he'll get them, or he'll skip Chicago altogether and order the pack to Aurora."

"Aurora?" I asked.

"Alaska," Catcher said. "Home base for the North American packs. They'll disappear into the wilderness and leave the vamps to fight it out alone. Again."

Ethan sat back, seemed to consider the threat, then slid me a glance. "Thoughts?"

I opened my mouth, closed it again. The master of strategy apparently wanted another bit of "canny analysis." I wasn't sure I could produce brilliant supernatural strategy off the top of my head. But I gave it a try, opting to stick with common sense, which seemed to be in notoriously short supply in the supernatural communities.

"There's little to be lost in getting people together, talking things out," I said. "Humans already know about us. If we can't work together, if we fight one another, it sets the stage for problems down the road. If worse comes to worst, and the tide turns, we'll want friends to turn to. We'll at least want honest conversation, open communication."

Ethan nodded.

"Why would it take capital for you to call the Houses together?" I asked. "What did you do to make them not trust you?"

Ethan and Catcher shared a look. "History," Catcher finally said, tearing his eyes from Ethan and leveling that green-eyed gaze on me. "It's always history."

The answer was unsatisfying, but I nodded, guessing it was the best I was going to get today.

Catcher leaned forward again, grabbed a handful of curly fries. "Well, something to think about. You'll call if you need support." The last wasn't a question, or a suggestion, more a prediction of how Ethan would act. They were definitely friends of a sort, Ethan and Catcher, although God only knew what weird history had brought these two—rebellious magical bad boy and neurotic, obsessively political vampire—together. Probably a good story, I decided.

"How was the Commendation?" Catcher asked, then leveled an amused glance at me. "Any surprises?"

"I did nothing," I said, grabbing an uneaten pickle from the flat of fries in front of Ethan.

"She wreaked havoc." A smile tipped one corner of Ethan's mouth.

I grinned at Mallory. "He's just jealous that I can withstand his call."

"I have no idea what that means," she said, grinning back, "but I'm thrilled to hear it."

"Can she?" Catcher asked Ethan.

"She can."

"And you named her Sentinel."

Ethan nodded. "On the expectation that you'll continue to work with her, to prepare her for that duty. You do have the expertise, after all. Your . . . *unique* brand of instruction would be invaluable."

Catcher paused for a moment, then nodded. "I'll work with her. Teach her. For now." He shifted his gaze to Ethan. "And that instruction will fulfill the debt I owe."

The debt he owed? There was definitely a good story there.

Another pause while Ethan considered Catcher's offer. "Agreed." He folded his arms over his chest, and slid me a dubious glance. "We'll see if she can rise to the occasion, do what needs to be done."

I gave Mallory a pointed look. "We'll see if she can manage not to kill her Liege and Master, especially if he continues talking about her like she's not in the room."

She snickered.

"Yes," Ethan drily said. "Forget the Merit money. Clearly, her worth is in her superb sense of humor."

The room went silent, Mallory's brow knitting with obvious concern. Catcher nervously cleared his throat, balled up the foil from his hot dog. It was up to me, I guessed, to ease the tension that bringing my family into the mix had fostered.

I looked over at him, saw the sudden tightness around Ethan's eyes, realized he regretted saying what he probably, on first blush, thought was a compliment. And in a way, in a twisted, completely Sullivan-esque way, it was.

"That's one of the nicest things anyone has ever said to me," I told him, realizing when the words were out that I was only barely lying.

For a second, I got no reaction.

And then he smiled, kind of a quirky half smile that tipped up only the right corner of his mouth. Because of that smile, that goddamn human smile, I had to swallow down a burst of affection that nearly brought tears to my eyes. Instead, I looked away, and hated myself—for my inability to hate him despite the things he said, the things he did, the things he expected.

I wanted to beat my fists against the floor like a child in tantrum. Why couldn't I hate him? Why, in spite of the fact that I knew, as readily as I knew that I was sitting on the sofa in his office with my best friend and her boyfriend nearby, that my inability to hate him was going to bite me right on the ass one day?

That was going to be a very, very bad day, and I wasn't sure if I was better off for knowing that it was coming.

"Well," Catcher said, suddenly rising, his voice cutting through the strain that still thickened the air in the room, "we should get back to the house." He looked at me. "It'll be dawn soon. You need a ride?"

I rose and began stuffing empty food wrappers back into the paper bags. "I drove over. But I should get back, too. I'll walk you out." I looked at Ethan. "Assuming we're done?"

He bobbed his head. "I had wanted to touch base with you about the murder investigations, their impact on the House, but I suppose this discussion has negated the need for that." His voice softened. "It's late. You're dismissed."

"I'll ride with you," Mallory lightly said, her tone making clear that she had words planned.

"Well, then," Ethan said, standing with the rest of us. "Thank you for the meal." He reached out and offered Catcher his hand, and they shook over the table and the crumpled remains of our dinner.

"Sure," Catcher said. "A word with you before we head out?"

Ethan nodded, and Catcher pressed his lips to Mallory's forehead. "I'll see you at home."

"Sure thing," she said, her hand brushing his abdomen as she reached up to press her lips to his. The goodbyes complete, she turned to me, smiled, and offered her hand. "Let's let the boys clean up the rest of this mess, shall we?"

We did, leaving them on either side of the coffee table,

napkins and paper cups and bags of trash between them. Her arm linked in mine, we left Cadogan House, walked quietly down the block to my car, and stayed quiet until we'd driven a block away.

"Merit, you've got a bad track record with guys."

"Don't start on me." I gripped the steering wheel a little harder. "I don't have a thing for Ethan."

"You've got a thing that's written all over your face. I thought this was just physical." She shook her head. "But whatever went on in there, that was more than physical, more than chemistry. He pushes some kind of button for you, and although he's doing a little better job of fighting it, I'd say you do the same for him."

"I don't like him."

"I understand that." She reached out, tapped a fingertip lightly against my temple. "But that's up here. That's logical. He's pulled you in. And it's not that I don't want to support you in whoever you've found. I'm a *Buffy* fan girl, I'm apparently a sorcerer, and I'm dating a former sorcerer . . . or whatever the hell he is. Regardless, I'm the last person who should give a lecture on weird relationships. But there's something. . . ."

"Inhuman about him?"

She clapped a hand against the dashboard. "Yes. Exactly. It's like he's not playing by the same rules at the rest of us."

"He's a vampire. *I'm* a vampire." Jesus, was I defending this? I was in a bad way.

"Yes, Mer, but you've been a vampire for, what, a week? He's been a vamp for nearly four hundred years. That's a freakin' plethora of weeks. You have to think it, I don't know, bleeds some of the human out of him."

I gnawed on my bottom lip, staring blankly at the passing houses, the side streets. "I'm not in love with him. I'm not that stupid." I scratched absently at my head. "I don't know what it is."

"Oh!" she exclaimed, so fiercely that I thought for a second we were under attack. "I've got it."

Once I was sure she was fine, that there weren't bat-winged beasts descending on the car, I slapped her arm. "Damn, girl. Don't do that when I'm driving."

"Sorry," she said, swiveling in her seat, her face alight. "But I've got an idea—maybe it's the vampire thing—the fact that he made you? They say that's supposed to create a bond."

I considered that, decided to embrace it, and felt some of the tension leave my shoulders. "Yeah. Yeah. That could be it." It did explain the connection between us, and was much more emotionally satisfying than imagining I was falling for someone so utterly, completely wrong for me. Someone so embarrassed by his interest in me.

As we pulled into the drive, I gave the thought a final hearty nod. "Yeah," I told her. "That's it."

She looked at me, waited a beat, then nodded. "Okay."

"Okay."

"Good."

She grinned at me. "Good."

I grinned back at her. "Great."

"Great, fine, wonderful, *Jesus*, let's just get out of the car." We did.

CHAPTER THIRTEEN

TWO'S COMPANY—THREE'S A MADHOUSE.

One day passed, then two, then four. It was surprisingly easy to fall into the routines of being a vampire. Sleeping during the day. Supplementing my diet with blood. Learning the ropes of Cadogan security (including the protocols) and doing my best to prepare for the responsibility of defending the House. At this early point, that generally involved pretending to be as competent as my actually skilled colleagues.

The protocols weren't difficult to understand, but there were many to learn. They were divided, much like the katas, into categories—offensive action plans, defensive action plans. The bulk of them fell into the latter category—how we were supposed to react if groups attacked the House or any particular Cadogan vampire, how we'd structure counterattacks. The maneuvers varied by the size of the band of marauders and whether they used swords or magic against us. Whoever the enemy, our first priority was to secure Ethan, then the rest of the in-house vamps and the building itself, coordinating with other allies when possible. Once Chicago was secure, we were to check in with the Cadogan vamps who didn't live in Cadogan House.

Under the House, beneath a small parking structure I was

clearly too low in the chain to have a spot in, were access points to underground tunnels that ran parallel to the city's extensive sewer system. From the tunnels, we could scramble to our assigned safe houses. Cheerily, we were only given the address of one house so the locations of the slate of them couldn't be tortured out of us. I was working on managing my panic about the fact that I was now part of an organization that had a need for secret evacuation tunnels and safe houses, an organization that had to plan around the possibility of group torture.

I also learned, after nearly a week of watching Luc and Lindsey interact, that he was seriously hung up on her. The vitriol and sarcasm he dished out on a daily basis—and there was a lot of it—was clearly a plea for her attention. A dismally unsuccessful plea. Luc may have had it bad, but Lindsey wasn't buying.

Ever curious, and that was going to burn my ass one of these days, I decided to ask her about it. We were in line, trays in hand in the first-floor cafeteria, picking from a selection of almost irritatingly healthy menu choices, when I asked her, "Do you want to tell me about you and everyone's favorite cowboy?"

Lindsey pulled three cartons of milk onto her tray, taking so long to answer me that I wondered if she'd heard the question in the first place. Eventually, she shrugged. "He's okay."

That was all I got until we were seated around a wooden table in ladder-back chairs, dark with age. "Okay, but not okay enough?"

Lindsey folded open a milk carton and took a long drink, then shrugged with more neutrality than I knew she actually felt. "Luc's great. But he's my boss. I don't think that's a good idea."

"You were goading me a few days ago about having a fling with Ethan." I lifted my sandwich and took a bite that was heavy on sprouts and light on flavor. Wrong kind of crunch, I concluded.

"Luc's great. He's just not for me."

"You get along well."

I pushed, and she broke. "And wouldn't that be lovely," she said, dropping her fork with obvious irritation, "until we broke up and then had to work together? No, thanks." Without looking up at me, she started picking absently through a pile of Cheetos.

"Okay," I said, in my most soothing voice (and wondering where she'd found the Cheetos), "so you like him." Her cheeks flushed pink. "But—what?—you're afraid to lose him, so you won't date him in the first place?"

She didn't answer, so I took her silence as implicit confirmation and let her off the hook. "Fine. We won't talk about it anymore."

Lindsey and I didn't talk about it anymore, but that didn't stop Luc from sliding in comments here and there, or her from baiting him with suggestions of rebellion. And while I really liked Lindsey, and I was glad we were on the same team, I sympathized with Luc. The girl had a sharp-edged wit, and it couldn't have been easy for him to be constantly on the receiving end of it. Sarcasm between friends is all well and good, but she risked tipping the balance toward meanness.

On the other hand, that biting sarcasm came in handy, since Amber and Gabrielle had teamed up to flaunt Amber's relationship with Ethan in my face. This time, we'd finished up our meal and were on our way back through the first floor to the stairs when they stopped in front of us.

"Hon," Gabrielle asked Amber, inspecting her nails while blocking the stairway. "You wanna grab a drink tonight?"

Amber, dressed in a black velour tracksuit with *BITE ME* written across the front in red letters, glanced up at me. "Can't. I have plans with Ethan tonight, and you know, darling"—she lifted an auburn brow—"how demanding he can be."

I wanted to gag, right after raking my nails through that

tacky velour, but was flustered enough by the message—and the fact that I'd seen Ethan take her up on the offer, slutty as it was—not to think of a quick retort.

Luckily, Captain Sassy Pants was nearby. With her usual aplomb, she plucked a Cheeto from a to-go bag and flicked it at Amber. "Scurry off, little woman."

Amber made a sound of disgust, but took Gabrielle by the hand, and they retreated down the hallway.

"And I've made the world safe for one more day," Lindsey said as we headed down the stairs.

"You're a real pal."

"I'm taking Connor out for a drink after shift. If I'm such a good pal, I think you need to join us."

I shook my head. "Training tonight. Can't." That was but the first of the good reasons not to take her up on that offer.

Lindsey stopped on the stairs and grinned over at me. "*Nice.* I'd pick a little quality Catcher Bell time over me, too. Has he let you hold his sword yet?"

"I think Mallory's got his sword well under control."

We reached the Ops Room door. Lindsey stopped, nodded with approval. "Good for her."

"For her, less so for me."

"Why's that?"

"Because he's constantly at the house, and it's beginning to feel a little small for the three of us."

"Ah. You know the obvious solution to that—move in here." She pulled open the door, and we walked inside the Ops Room and moved to the conference table while guards already at their stations tapped keys, watched screens, and talked into their headsets.

"Same answers as last time," I whispered as we took seats at the table. "No, no, and no. I can't live in the same house as Ethan. We'd kill each other."

Lindsey crossed her legs and swiveled her chair to face me. "Not if you just avoid him. And look how well you've managed to avoid him for the last week."

I gave her a look, but nodded when she lifted dubious brows. She was right—I'd avoided him, he'd avoided me, we'd avoided each other. And despite the vague sense of unease I had whenever I stepped across the threshold and into Cadogan, the fact that we had managed to avoid each other made living here at least *possible*.

"So," she said, "your continuing to avoid him shouldn't be a problem. And just think," Lindsey whispered, "it's practically the O.C. in here. You're missing out on a lot of excitement by heading back to Wicker Park every morning."

"Yeah, that's really the selling point you need to focus on. 'Cause these last few weeks have been dullsville otherwise."

To be fair, it was kind of a selling point. I did enjoy other folks' drama. I just didn't need any more of my own.

Catcher, Mallory, and Jeff were at the gym when I arrived. I wasn't sure why Jeff was there, but since he and Mal were the closest thing I had to cheerleaders, I didn't so much mind the extra bodies.

Or wouldn't have minded, had I arrived seconds later, and missed Catcher pawing my roommate next to the water fountain.

I cleared my throat loudly as I strode past, which did nothing to prompt a disentangling of their bodies.

"Cats in heat," I said to Jeff, who sat sprawled in a chair in the gym, his arms folded across his chest, his eyes closed.

"Are they still at it? It's been twenty minutes."

I caught the tiny bit of wistfulness in his voice.

"They're at it," I confirmed, realizing it was the second time in a week I'd walked in on a union of pink parts I had no desire to see.

Jeff opened blue eyes, grinned at me. "If you're feeling left out . . ."

I almost threw out an instinctive no, but I decided to throw him a bone. "Oh, Jeff. It'd be too good—you and me. Too powerful, too much emotion, too much heat. We'd come together and *boom*"—I clapped my hands together—"like a moth to a flame, there'd be nothing left."

His eyes glazed over. "Combustion?"

"Totally."

He was quiet for a moment, his index finger tracing a pattern on the knee of his jeans. Then he nodded. "Too powerful. It'd destroy us both."

I nodded solemnly. "Probably so." But I leaned over, pressed my lips to his forehead. "We'll always have Chicago."

"Chicago," he dreamily repeated. "Yeah. Definitely." He cleared his throat, seemed to regain a little composure. "When I tell this story later, you kissed me on the mouth. With tongue. And you were handsy."

I chuckled. "Fair enough."

Catcher and Mallory walked in, Catcher in the lead, Mallory behind, one hand in his, the fingers of her free hand against her lips, her cheeks flushed.

"Sword," Catcher said, before dropping her hand and continuing through the gym to the door on the other side of the room.

"Was that an instruction or an agenda, do you think?" I asked Mallory, who stopped in front of me.

She blinked, her gaze on Catcher's jeans-clad ass as he passed. "Hmm?"

I cocked an eyebrow at her. "I'm in love with Ethan Sullivan and we're going to have teethy vampire babies and buy a house in Naperville and live happily ever after."

She looked over at me, her gaze as vacant as Jeff's had been. "It's just—he does this thing with his tongue." She trailed off, lifted an index finger, crooked it back and forth. "It's kind of a flicking?"

Before I knew what I was saying, but finally at the end of my Mallory-and-Catcher rope, I spilled out a plan in a quick tumble of sound. "I love you, but I'm moving into Cadogan House."

That got her attention. Her expression cleared, her brow furrowing. "What?"

Instantly deciding it was probably for the best, I nodded. "You two need your space, and I need to be there to do my job effectively." Left unspoken: I did not need to hear or see anything else regarding Catcher's sexual prowess.

"Oh." Mallory looked down at the floor. "Oh." When she looked back up again, there was sadness in her eyes. "Jesus, Merit. Everything's changing."

I squeezed her into a hug. "We're not changing. We're just living in different places."

"We'll be living in different ZIP codes."

"And, as I've said before, you have Sexy Bell to keep you company. You'll be fine." I'd probably be fine, too, assuming I could convince myself and the other Cadogan vamps that I could live under the same roof as Ethan without impaling him on the business end of an aspen stake. That was going to require some Mallory-worthy creative thinking.

Mal squeezed me back. "You're right. You're right. I'm being ridiculous. You need to get in there, do that vampire thang, mix it up." Then she quirked up an eyebrow. "Did you say you were in love with Ethan?"

"Just to get your attention."

Probably.

Shit.

"Gotta say, Mer, I'm not loving that idea."

I nodded ruefully and began the walk toward the locker room. "Just be glad you're not me."

Minutes later, I emerged barefoot and ponytailed, ready for another night of training to protect, among others, a man I apparently had conflicting feelings about. Mallory and Jeff sat in chairs on the other side of the room. Catcher hadn't yet emerged from the back, so I moved toward the body bag that hung in one corner of the gym, curled my hands into fists, and began to wail.

In the couple of sessions I'd had with Catcher since Commendation, we'd trained with pads, practicing jabs and front kicks, guards and uppercuts. The practice was designed to increase my stamina, to give me a vocabulary of vampire fighting basics, and to ensure that I could pass the tests required of Cadogan guards. But I'd usually been too worried about learning the moves, the forms, to find therapy, solace, in the movements.

With Catcher in the back, there was no such distraction.

I aimed a bare-handed jab at the logo in the middle of the bag, *thwack*, loving the flat thud of contact and the flight of the bag in the other direction. Loving the fact that I'd made it move. Enjoying the fact that I'd imagined green eyes peering out through the logo, and had nailed the spot just between those eyes.

Thwack. Thwack. A satisfying double punch, the bag standing in for the man I'd become honor-bound to serve, whom I was becoming a little too interested in.

I stepped back, pivoted on a heel, and swiveled my hip for a side kick. It probably seemed, to the casual observer, that I was warming up, taking a few well-aimed kicks at an inanimate object.

But in my mind, *thwack*, I was kicking, *thwack*, a certain Master vampire, *thwack*, in the face.

Finally smiling, I stood straight again, planting hands on my hips as I watched the bag swing on its chain. "Therapeutic," I concluded.

The door at the back of the gym opened, and Catcher walked through, the katana, sheathed in gleaming black lacquer, in his right hand. In his left was a wooden bar in the shape of a katana—a long slice of gently curving, gleaming wood—but without the hilt or any other physical distinction between the handle and blade. This, I'd learned, was a *bokken*, a practice weapon, a tool for learning swordsmanship sans the risk of an amateur slicing through things not intended for slicing.

Catcher moved to the center of the mats, laid the *bokken* down, and with a slow, careful movement, the blade angled just so, unsheathed his katana. The naked steel caught the light, glinted and made a metallic whistle as he pulled it through the air. Then he motioned at me, and I joined him in the center of the mats. He turned the katana, and one hand near the hilt, offered it to me.

I took it, tested the weight in my hand. It felt lighter than I'd imagined it would given the complicated combination of materials—wood, steel, bumpy ray skin, corded silk. I gripped the sword in my right hand beneath the hilt and wrapped the fingers of my left hand below it, four finger spaces between my hands. It wasn't that I'd studied up. I just mimicked the hand positions he'd demonstrated with the sword he usually didn't let me hold, the sword he treated with careful reverence.

I'd asked him earlier in the week about that reverence, why he stilled when the blade was revealed, why his gaze went a little unfocused when he unsheathed it. His answer— "It's a good blade"—was less than satisfying, and, I guessed, barely the tip of that iceberg.

Sword in hand, I held it before me, waited for Catcher's direction.

He had plenty.

For all his lack of loquaciousness in discussing why he liked the sword, he had plenty to offer in how I should relate to it—the position of my hands on the handle (which wasn't quite right, despite my careful mimicry), the position of the blade relative to the rest of my body, the stance of my feet, and the carriage of body weight as I prepared to strike.

Catcher explained that this, my first time with the sword, was only to accustom me to the feel of it, the weight of it. I'd learn the actual moves with the *bokken* because, although Catcher was pleased with what I'd learned so far, he had no confidence in my ability to manage the katana. At least not to his nitpicky expectations.

When he said that, I paused in the middle of a stance he'd

been teaching me, looked over at him. "Then why do I have this katana in my hands?"

His expression went immediately serious. "Because you're a vampire, and a Cadogan vamp at that. Until you know the moves, until you're ready to wield the sword as an expert"—the tone in his voice made it obvious that he'd settle for nothing less—"you're going to need to bluff." He raised a hand, pointed at the blade of the katana. "She is, among other things, your bluff."

Then he slid a glance to Mallory, and gave her a wicked look. "If you aren't ready to truly handle the sword, at least learn how to hold it."

There was a sardonic grunt from her side of the gym.

Catcher laughed with obvious satisfaction. "It only hurts the first time."

"Where have I heard that before?" Mallory drily responded, one crossed leg swinging as she flipped through a magazine. "And if I've told you once, I've told you a thousand times—magic does *not* belong in the bedroom." But while her eyes were on the magazine in her lap, she was grinning when she said it.

Cadogan House, here I come, I thought, and adjusted my grip on the katana. I centered my weight, rolled my shoulders, and attacked.

Two hours later, the sun just preparing to peek over the horizon, I was back home in a tank top and flannel pajama bottoms. I was on my bed, cell phone in hand, replaying the message I found when I left the gym. It was from Morgan, a voice mail he'd left while I was training.

Beep. "Hey. It's Morgan. From Navarre, in case you know a lot of us. Morgans, I mean. I'm rambling. I hope the Commendation went well. Heard you were named Sentinel. Congratulations." Then he gave me a little speech on the history of the House Sentinel, and the fact that Ethan had resurrected the position.

He talked so long the cell phone cut him off.

Then he called back.

Beep. "Sorry. Got a little long-winded there. Probably not my finest moment. That was not really the suave demonstration of the mad skills I had planned." There was a pause. "I'd like to see you again." Throat clearing. "I mean, if for no other reason than to explain to you, a little more thoroughly this time, the obvious benefits of rooting for the Packers—the glory, the history—"

"The obvious humility," I muttered, listening to the message, unable to stop the grin that curled the corners of my lips.

"So, yeah. We need to talk about that. Football. 'That,' meaning football. Jesus. Just give me a call." Throat clearing. "Please."

I stared at the open shell of the phone for a long time, thinking about the phone call even as the sun pulled at the horizon, peeked above it. I finally clamped the phone closed, and when I curled into a ball, my head heavy on the pillow, I slept with the phone in my hand.

When the sun set and I opened my eyes again, I deposited the cell phone on the bedside table, and decided—it being both my day off and my twenty-eighth birthday—that I had time for a run. I stretched, donned workout gear, pulled up my hair, and headed downstairs.

I got in a run, a loop around Wicker Park, the commercial parts of the neighborhood buzzing with dinner seekers and folks seeking the solace of an after-work drink. The house was still quiet when I returned, so I was spared the sights and sounds of a Carmichael-Bell liaison. Thirsty enough to guzzle Buckingham Fountain, I headed for the kitchen and the refrigerator.

That was when I saw my father.

He sat at the kitchen island, dressed in his usual suit and expensive Italian loafers, glasses cocked at his nose as he scanned the paper.

Suddenly, it didn't seem coincidental that Mallory and Catcher were nowhere to be found.

"You've been named Sentinel."

I had to force my feet to move. Aware that his eyes were on me, I walked to the refrigerator, grabbed a carton of juice, and cracked it open. I almost reached for a glass from the cupboard, thinking it would be more polite to pour a cup than chug from the carton, but opted to chug anyway. Our house, our rules.

After a long, silent drink, I walked to the opposite side of the island, put down the carton, and looked at him. "So I have."

He made a show of loudly folding the paper, then placed it on the counter. "You've got pull now."

Word, even if fundamentally incorrect, had traveled. I wondered if my father, like my grandfather, had his own secret vampire source. "Not really," I told him. "I'm just a guard."

"But for the House. Not for Sullivan."

Damn. Maybe he did have a source. He knew a lot, but the more interesting question was why he'd bothered to find out. Potential business deals? Bring out the daughter's vampire connections to impress friends and business partners?

Whatever the source or the reason, he was right about the distinction. "For the House," I confirmed, and squeezed the top of the carton closed. "But I'm a couple of weeks old, with hardly any training, and I'm probably last on Ethan's list of trusted vamps. I have no pull." I thought of the phrase Ethan had used and added, "No political capital at all."

My father, his blue eyes so like mine, gazed at me quietly before standing. "Robert will be taking over the business soon. He'll need your support, your help with the vampires. You're a Merit, and you're now a member of this Cadogan House. You have Sullivan's ear."

That was news to me.

"You've got the in. I expect you to use it." He tapped fingers against the folded paper, as if to drive home the point. "You owe it to your family."

I managed not to remind him exactly how supportive that "family" had been when I'd discovered I was a vampire. I'd been threatened with disinheritance. "I'm not sure what service you think I could provide to you or Robert," I told him, "but I'm not for rent. I'll do my job as Sentinel, my duty, because I swore an oath. I'm not happy to be a vampire. It's not the life I'd have picked. But it's mine now, and I'll honor that. I'm not going to jeopardize my future, my position"—or my Master and his House—"by taking on whatever little project you've got in mind."

My father huffed. "You think Ethan would hesitate to use you if the opportunity arose?"

I wasn't sure what I thought about that, but Ethan was off-limits as a paternal conversation topic. So I stared down Joshua Merit, gave him back the same blue-eyed glare he leveled at me. "Was that all you needed?"

"You're a Merit."

But no longer *just* a Merit, I thought, which pushed a little grin onto my face. I repeated, my tone flat, "Was that all you needed?"

A muscle ticked in his jaw, but he backed down. Without another word to his younger daughter, birthday wishes or otherwise, he turned on his heel and walked out.

When the front door closed, I kept my place. I stood for a minute in the empty kitchen, hands clenching the edge of the island, filled with the urge to run after my father, demand that he see me for who I was, love me for who I was.

I swallowed down tears, dropped my hands away.

And as the bloodlust rose again, whether fueled by anger or grief, I went back to the refrigerator, found a bag of O positive, cradled it in my arms, and sank to the floor.

There was no intoxication this time. There was satiation, a sense of deep, earthy satisfaction, and the oblivion that accompanied the detachment I had to adopt in order to take human blood into my body. But there was no drunkenness, no stumbling. It was as if my body had accepted the thing my mind was only just becoming accustomed to—the thing that I'd admitted to my father, to Ethan, to myself.

I was a Cadogan vampire.

No—I was a *vampire*. Regardless of House, of position, and despite the fact that I didn't rave through graveyards at night, I didn't fly (or, at least, I assumed I didn't fly—I hadn't fully tested that, I guess), and I didn't cower at the sight of the crucifix pendant that hung on the mirror in the upstairs bathroom. Despite the fact that I ate garlic, that I still had a reflection, and that I could stumble groggily through the day, even if I wasn't at my best.

So I wasn't the vampire Hollywood had imagined. I was different enough. Stronger. Faster. More nimble. A sunlight allergy. The ability to heal. A taste for hemoglobin. I'd acquired a handful of new friends, a new job, a boss I studiously avoided, and a paler cast to my skin. I could handle a sword, knew a smattering of martial arts, had nearly been murdered and had discovered an entirely new side to the Windy City. I could sense magic, could feel the power that flowed through the metro, a metaphysical companion to the Chicago River. I could hear Ethan's voice in my head, had seen a bad boy sorcerer shoot magic in my direction, and had lost my best friend and roommate (and room) to that same bad boy sorcerer.

For all those changes, all that upheaval, what else was there, but to do? To act? To be Cadogan Sentinel, to take up arms and bear them for the House I'd been charged with protecting.

I pushed up off the floor, tossed the empty plastic bag in the trash, wiped at my mouth with the back of a hand, and gazed out the kitchen window and into the dark night.

Today was my twenty-eighth birthday.

I didn't look a day over twenty-seven.

*　　*　　*

Intent on making the most of the rest of my night off, I'd showered, changed, and was in my bedroom—door shut, sitting cross-legged in jeans on the comforter, a copy of Algernon Swinburne's *Tristam of Lyonesse* open before me. It was outside the context of my dissertation, Swinburne's version of Tristan and Isolde having been penned in 1852, but the despite the tragic end, the story always drew me back. I'd read and reread the prelude, Swinburne's ode to history's soul-crossed lovers, his ode to love itself:

> *. . . And always through new act and passion new*
> *Shines the divine same body and beauty through,*
> *The body spiritual of fire and light*
> *That is to worldly noon as noon to night;*
> *Love, that is flesh upon the spirit of man*
> *And spirit within the flesh whence breath began;*
> *Love, that keeps all the choir of lives in chime;*
> *Love, that is blood within the veins of time;*

Fire. Light. Blood. The veins of time. Those words had never meant as much to me as they did now. Context definitely mattered.

I was staring at the text, contemplating the metaphor, when a knock sounded at my bedroom door. It opened, and Lindsey peeked inside.

"So this is where the mysterious Cadogan Sentinel spends her free time?" She was in jeans and a black T-shirt, heavy, black leather bands at each wrist, her blond hair in a ponytail. She tucked her hands behind her back, turned around to survey the room. "I understand it's someone's birthday."

I closed the book. "Aren't you working today?"

Lindsey shrugged. "I switched with Juliet. Girl loves her guns, sleeps with that sword. She was happy to take duty."

I nodded. In the few days that I'd known Juliet, that summed up my impression. She had the look of an innocent, but she was always ready for a fight. "What brings you by?"

"You, birthday girl. Your party awaits."

I arched a brow. "My party?"

She crooked a finger at me, walked back into the hallway. Curious, I put the book aside, unfolded my legs, turned off the bedside lamp, and followed her. She trotted back down the stairs and into the living room—and into an assemblage of friends. Mallory, Catcher behind her, one hand at her waist. Jeff, quirky grin on his face and a silver-wrapped box in his hands.

Mallory stepped forward, arms outstretched. "Happy birthday, our little vampette!" I hugged her and gave Jeff a wink over her shoulder.

"We're taking you out," she said. "Well, no, actually, we're taking you in—to your grandfather's house. He's got a little something prepared."

"Okay," I said, at a loss to argue, and a little gushy-hearted that my friends had come to sweep me away to birthday festivities. It was a hell of an improvement over the mock-paternal visit earlier in the evening.

I found shoes and we gathered up purses, turned off lights, and locked the front door under the gaze of the guards who stood outside. Mallory and Catcher bundled off to the SUV that sat at the curb, a vehicle I guessed was Lindsey's when she headed toward the driver's seat. Jeff hung back, shyly offering the silver box.

I took it, looked at it, glanced up at him. "What's this?"

He grinned. "A thank-you."

I smiled and pulled off the silver gift wrap, then slid open the pale blue box beneath it. Inside was a tiny silver sculpture. It was human in form—a body genuflecting, arms outstretched. A little confused, I looked up at him, brows lifted.

"It's bowing to you. I may have"—he pulled at the collar of his dress shirt—"spread around the fact that the Sentinel of Cadogan House had a tiny crush on me."

I folded my arms and looked at him. "How tiny?"

He started for the car. I followed.

"Jeffrey. How tiny?"

He held up a hand as he walked, the fingers pinched together.

"Jeff!"

He opened the back door, but turned before he slid in, a grin lighting his eyes. "There may have been begging, and I may have turned you down because you were a little too. . . ."

I rolled my eyes, slid into the backseat beside him. "Let me guess—too clingy?"

"Something like that."

I faced forward, felt his worried gaze at my side and the sudden peppering of magic that filled the back of the car. No, not just magic—alarm. But he was a friend, so I ignored the prick of vampiric interest—predatory interest—in the sweetly astringent aroma of his fear. "Fine," I said. "But I'm not giving you underwear."

I heard a chuckle from the front seat, then felt Jeff's lips on my cheek. "You seriously kick ass."

Mallory flipped down her visor, met my gaze in the inset mirror, and winked at me.

There were cars all around my grandfather's house—at the curb, parked on the front lawn. All luxury roadsters—Lexus, Mercedes, BMW, Infiniti, Audi—all in basic colors—red, green, blue, black, white. But it was the license plates that gave them away: NORTH 1, GOOSE, SBRNCH. All divisions of the Chicago River.

"Nymphs," I concluded, when we were out of the car and Catcher had joined me on the sidewalk. I remembered the designations from the posters in my grandfather's office.

"This wasn't scheduled," he said. "They must have needed some Ombud input. A mediation, probably." He looked over at Jeff, stuck out a pointed finger. "No touching. If they're fighting, there'll be tears enough."

Jeff raised both hands, grinned. "I don't make the ladies cry, CB."

"*Don't* call me that," Catcher ground out, before looking at me. "This was not part of the birthday party."

I looked at the house, brightly lit, figures moving to and fro inside, and nodded. "So I gathered. Anything I need to be aware of?" And before he asked the obvious question, I gave the obvious answer. "And, yes, I've read the *Canon*." The book wasn't a bad fill-in for the supernatural reference guide I'd been wishing for—it had introductory sections on all the major supernatural groups, water nymphs included. They were small, slim, moody, and prone to tears. They were territorial and wielded considerable power over the river's flow and currents, and were rumored—and God only knew how to evaluate rumor in something like this—to be the granddaughters of the Naiads of Greek myth. The boundaries of the nymphs' respective areas were constantly waxing and waning, as the nymphs traded up and down for tiny bits of water and shore. And although human history books didn't mention it, there were rumors that they'd played a key role in reversing the Chicago River's flow in 1900.

"Just stay out of arm's reach," Catcher advised, and went for the door.

My grandfather's house was full of women. All of them petite and curvy, not a single one taller than five foot four. All drop-dead gorgeous. All with flowy hair, big, liquid eyes, tiny, tiny dresses. And they were screaming, screeching at one another with voices half an octave past comfortable. They were also crying, watery tears streaming down their faces.

We walked in, the five of us, and were greeted by a brief din in the silence.

"My granddaughter," my grandfather, seated in his easy chair, one elbow on the arm, hand in his chin, announced. "It's her birthday."

The nymphs blinked big eyes at me—blue and brown and translucent green—then turned back to one another, and the screaming commenced again. I caught a few snippets—

something about bascule bridges and treaties and water flow. They were clearly unimpressed that I'd arrived.

My grandfather rolled his eyes in amusement. I grinned back and gave him a finger wave—and nearly lost a chunk of hair to the snap of pink-tipped fingers before Lindsey pulled me back from the fray.

I looked over at Catcher, who offered me the Look of Disappointed Sensei. "Arm's reach," he said, inclining his head toward the nymphs, who'd moved on to clawing and hair-pulling. It was a catfight of YouTube-worthy proportions. Hems were tugged, hair yanked, bare skin clawed and raked by prettily manicured nails. And through it all, screaming and tears.

"For goodness' sake," said a voice behind me, and Jeff pushed through us to the edge of warring women. "Ladies!" he said, and when they ignored him, gave a little chuckle, before yelling again, *"Ladies!"*

To a one, the nymphs stopped in place, even while their hands were wrapped around the necks and hair of the ones nearby. Heads swiveled slowly toward us, took in the group of us, stopped when they reached Jeff. The nymphs—all nine of them—dropped their hands, began adjusting hair and bodices, and when they were set, turned batty-eyelashed smiles at Jeff.

Mallory and I stared, openmouthed, at the skinny computer programmer who'd just wooed nine busty, lusty water goddesses into submission.

Jeff rocked back on his heels, grinned at them. "That's better. Now what's all the fuss?" His voice was soothing, crooning, with an edge of playful that made the women visibly shiver.

I couldn't help but grin . . . and wonder if I hadn't been giving Jeff enough credit.

The tallest of the petite group, a blue-eyed blonde whose perfect figure was tucked into a blue cocktail dress—and who I remembered from the posters at my grandfather's office was the Goose Island nymph—looked across the group of women, smiled tentatively at Jeff, then let loose a stream of invectives about her sisters that would have made a salty sailor blush.

"Uh, earmuffs?" Mallory whispered next to me.

"Seriously," I murmured back.

The gist of Goose Island's argument, without all the cursing, was that the (slutty) raven-haired nymph on her left, North Branch, had slept with the (whorish) boyfriend of the platinum blond nymph on her right, West Fork. The reason for the betrayal, Goose suggested, was some sort of complicated political nudging of their respective boundaries.

Jeff clucked his tongue and regarded the North Branch brunette. "Cassie, darling, you're better than this."

Cassie shrugged sheepishly, looked at the ground.

"Melaina," he said to the West Fork blonde, "you need to leave him."

Melaina sniffled, her head bobbing as she toyed with a lock of hair. "He said I was pretty."

Jeff gave her a sad smile and opened his arms. Melaina practically jumped forward and into Jeff's embrace, squealing when he hugged her. As Jeff patted her back, crooned soothing whispers into her ear, Mallory, agog, slid me a dubious glance.

I could only shrug. Who knew little Jeff had this in him? Maybe it was a shifter-nymph thing? I made a mental note to check the *Canon.*

"There, there," Jeff said, and released Melaina to her sisters. "Now." He folded long-fingered hands together and looked over the group. "Are we done bothering Mr. Merit for the evening? I'm sure he's noted your concerns, and he'll pass them along to the Mayor." He looked at my grandfather for approval, and Grandpa nodded in response.

"Okay, girls?" A little more sniffling, a few brushes of hands across teary cheeks, but they all nodded. The making up was as loud as the dispute had been, all high-pitched apologies and plans for mani-pedis and spa days. Hugs were exchanged, ripped hemlines were cooed over, makeup adjusted. (Miraculously, not a mascara smudge to be seen. Indelible mascara was a river nymph necessity, I supposed.)

When the nymphs had calmed themselves, they gathered around Jeff, peppered him with kisses and sweet words, and filed out the door. Mallory and I watched through the screen door as they flipped open cell phones and climbed into their tiny roadsters, then zoomed off into the Chicago night.

We turned simultaneously back to Jeff, who was typing with his thumbs on a cell phone with a slide-out keyboard. "Warcraft tourney tonight. Who's in?"

"How long do shifters live?" I asked Catcher.

He looked at me, one eyebrow arched in puzzlement. "A hundred and twenty, a hundred and thirty years. Why?"

So he was young, even if, at twenty-one, a legal adult in human years. "Because he's going to be frighteningly good when he grows up."

Jeff looked up, pointed at his phone. "Seriously, who's in?" he asked me, his eyes wide and hopeful. "You can be my elf? I have headsets."

"When he grows up," Catcher confirmed, and slipped the cell phone from Jeff's hands and into his own pocket. "Let's eat, Einstein."

After exchanging belated hello hugs with my grandfather, I was led into the dining room. A meal fit for a king—or a cop, two vampires, a shifter, and two sorcerers—was laid out on the table. In the infield of a ring of green place mats lay bowls of green beans, corn, mashed potatoes, squash casserole, macaroni and cheese. There were baskets of rolls and on a side buffet sat the desserts—a layered white cake mounded with coconut shavings, a pan of frosting-covered brownies, and a plate of pink and white cupcakes.

But the showpiece, which sat on its own platter in the

middle of the oval table, was the biggest ketchup-topped meat loaf I'd ever seen.

I made a happy sound. I loved to eat, sure, and I'd eat nearly anything put in front of me, the pint of blood I'd downed earlier evidence enough of that, but my grandfather's meat loaf—made from my grandmother's recipe—was by far my favorite meal.

"Anyone touches the meat loaf before I get my share, you become chew toys," I said, pointing a cautionary finger at the grinning faces around the room.

My grandfather put an arm across my shoulders. "Happy birthday, baby girl. I thought you'd appreciate the gift of food. as much as anything else."

I nodded, couldn't help but laugh. "Thanks, Grandpa," I said, giving him a hug before pulling out a chair.

They moved around the table, my friends, Mallory beside me, Catcher at one end, Grandpa at the other, Lindsey and Jeff—who wore an unfortunately eager grin—on the opposite side. There was a quick moment of silence led, interestingly, by Catcher, who closed his eyes, dropped his head, and said a quick, reverential blessing over the food.

And when we all looked up again, we shared a smile and began to pass the bowls.

It was a homecoming, the family homecoming I'd always wanted. Jeff said something ridiculous; Catcher snarked back. Lindsey asked Mallory about her work; my grandfather asked me about mine. The conversation took place while we heaped meat loaf and vegetables on our plates, sprinkled salt and pepper, sipped at the iced tea that already sat in our glasses. Napkins were put into laps, forks lifted, and the meal began.

When we'd eaten our fill, leaving bowls empty but for crumbs and serving spoons, when the men had unbuttoned the tops of their pants and leaned back in their chairs, happy and sated as cats, Lindsey pushed back her chair, stood, and raised her glass.

"To Merit," she said. "May the next year of her life be full of joy and peace and AB positive and hunky boy vamps."

"Or shifters," Jeff said, raising his own glass.

Catcher rolled his eyes, but raised his glass as well. They saluted me, my family, and brought tears to my eyes. As I sniffled in my seat—and wolfed down my third helping of meat loaf—Mallory brought in a gigantic box wrapped in pink-and-purple unicorn-covered paper and topped by a big pink bow.

She squeezed my shoulders before putting it on the floor beside my chair. "Happy birthday, Mer."

I smiled at her, pushed back enough to pull the box into my lap, and pulled off the bow. The wrapping paper was next, and I complimented her juvenile taste as I dropped crumpled balls of it onto the floor. I popped open the box, pulled out the layer of tissue paper, and peered inside.

"Oh, Mal." It was black, and it was leather. Buttery soft leather. I pushed my chair all the way back, dropped the box on the seat, and pulled out the jacket. It was trim black leather with a mandarin collar. Like a motorcycle jacket, but without the branding. It wasn't unlike the jacket Morgan had worn at Navarre, and as chic as black leather came. I peeked into the box, saw that it contained matching black leather pants. Also sleek, and hot enough to make Jeff's eyes glaze over when I pulled them out.

"There's one more thing in there," Mallory said. "But you may not want to take it out right now." Her eyes glinted, so I grinned back, a little confused, and peered inside.

It could arguably have been called a "bodice," but it was closer in form to the black spandex band I had worn during training. It was leather, a rectangle of it, presumably designed to fit across my breasts, with a slat of corsetlike ties in the back. The band was maybe ten inches wide, and would reveal more skin than it covered.

"Vampire goth," Mallory said, drawing up my gaze again. I chuckled, nodded, and closed the box around the pants and "top."

"When you said you were going to buy me a black suit, I thought you meant the one you already bought." I grinned at her. "This goes above and beyond, Mal."

"Oh, I know." She stood up and came around the table, taking the jacket to help me shrug into it. "And don't think you don't owe me."

Mallory held out the leather, and I slid one arm in, then the second, and zipped up the snug, partially ribbed bodice. The arms and shoulders were segmented to give me some freedom of movement, a handy thing when I'd need, at some point in the future, to swing a sword around.

Jeff gave an appreciative whistle, and I struck a couple of ass-kicking poses, hands clenched in front of me in guard positions.

This was a new style for me. Not goth, exactly. More like Urban Vamp Soldier. Whatever it was, I liked it. I'd be able to bluff a lot better in leather than in a pretentious black suit.

While Mallory and Lindsey patted the buttery softness of the leather, Catcher rose, and, with the lifting of an imperious eyebrow, motioned me out of the dining room. I made my excuses and followed him.

In the middle of my grandfather's small fenced-in back-yard lay a square of white fabric—a linen tablecloth I remembered from dinners hosted by my grandmother. One hand at the small of my back, Catcher steered me toward it. I took a place facing him on the opposite side of the square, and when he went to his knees across from me, I did the same.

He had a katana in his hand, but this one was different. Instead of his usual black-scabbarded model, this one was sheathed in brilliant red lacquer. Handle in his right hand, scabbard in his left, Catcher slipped the sword from its home. The scabbard was laid to the side, and the sword was placed on the linen square. He bowed to it and then, his hand inches above the blade, passed the flat of his palm over the length of the sword. I'd have sworn he said words, but nothing in a language I'd heard before. It had the staccato rhythm of Latin, but it wasn't Latin. Whatever the language, it had magic in it. Enough magic to ruffle my hair, to create a breeze in the still April night.

When he was done, when goose bumps peppered my arms, he looked up at me.

"She will be yours, Merit. This sword has belonged to Cadogan since the House existed. I've been asked to prepare it for you. And prepare you for it."

Admittedly, I'd been avoiding Ethan, so it was fine by me that he wasn't here, that Catcher was commanding the arsenal. But I still didn't get why it was him, and not Ethan, who'd been charged with giving me the sword. "Why not a vampire?"

"Because a vampire can't complete the temper." Catcher lifted the sword, flipped it around so the handle was on my right, and laid it down again. Then he nodded down at my arm. "Hold out your hand. Right. Palm up."

I did as he directed, watched him pull a small squarish knife from his pocket, the handle wrapped in black cord. He took my right hand in his left, then pressed the sharp tip of the knife to the center of my palm. There was an immediate sting, as a drop of blood, then two, appeared. He gripped my hand hard against my instinctive flinch, put aside the knife, and rotated my palm so it was positioned directly above the sword.

The crimson fell. One drop, then two, three. They splashed against the flat of the steel, rolled across the sharpened edge of the blade, and dropped onto the linen beneath it.

And then it happened—the steel rippled. It looked like waving heat across hot asphalt, the steel flexing like a ribbon in the wind. It lasted only seconds, and the steel was still again.

More words were whispered in that same rhythmic chant; then Catcher released my hand. I watched the pinprick in my palm close. Props for vampire healing.

"What was that?" I asked him.

"You've given a sacrifice," he said. "Your blood to the steel, so that she can keep you from shedding it in battle. Care for her, respect her, and she'll take care of you." Then he removed a small vial and cloth from a pocket of his cargo pants, showed me how to paper and oil the blade. When the sword was clean again and lay gleaming in the light of the backyard flood lamps, he rose.

"I'll let you two get acquainted," he said. "Since you won't be wearing robes, I've left a belt inside. The scabbard fits it. From today on, you wear it. All day, every day. When you sleep, you keep it beside you. Understood?"

Having gotten the same speech about my beeper, and understanding the threat of the still-loose killer, I nodded, waited for him to rise and leave, then looked down at the sword that still lay in front of me. It was an oddly intimate moment—my first time alone with her. This was the thing—this complicated arrangement of steel and silk and ray skin and lacquered wood—that was supposed to keep me safe for the next few hundred years, the thing that would enable me to do my duty, to keep Ethan and the other Cadogan vamps alive.

Nervously, I looked around the yard, a little self-conscious about picking it up, and scratched absently at my eyebrow. I rustled my fingers, cleared my throat, and made myself look at it.

"So," I said, to the sword.

To the *sword*.

I grinned down at her. "I'm Merit, and we're going to be working together. Hopefully I won't . . . break you. Hopefully you won't get me broken. That's about it, I guess." I reached out my right hand, clenching and unclenching my fingers above the metal, somehow suddenly phobic about taking up arms for the first time, and then dropped my fingertips to the wrap around the handle, and slid them around the length of it.

My arm tingled.

I gripped the handle, lifted the sword in one hand and stood, angling the blade so that it caught the light, which ran down the steel like falling water.

My heart sped, my pupils dilated—and I felt the vampire inside me rise to the surface of my consciousness.

And, for the first time, she rose not in anger or lust or hunger, but in curiosity. She knew what I held in my hand, and she reveled in it.

And, for the first time, instead of fighting her, instead of pushing her back down, I let her stretch and move, let her look through my eyes—just a peek. Just a glimpse, as I had no illusions that if given the chance, she could overpower me, work through me, take me over.

But when I held the sword horizontally, parallel to the ground, and when I sliced it through the air, swung it in an arc around my body, and slid it back into its sheath, I felt her sigh—and felt the warmth of her languid contentment, like a woman well-satisfied.

I kissed the pommel of the sword—of my sword—then let it slip into my left hand, and went back into the house. Jeff, Catcher, Lindsey, and Grandpa were gathered around the dining room table. Mallory stood at the side table, carving up the coconut cake.

"Oh, sweet!" Jeff said, his gaze shifting from the katana in my hand to Catcher. "You gave her the sword?"

Catcher nodded, then looked at me, quirked up an eyebrow. "Let's see if it worked. Is he carrying?"

I blinked, then looked between Jeff and my grandfather. "Is who carrying what?"

"Look at Jeff," Catcher said carefully, "and tell me if he's carrying a weapon."

I arched a brow.

"Just do it," Catcher insisted, frustration in his voice.

I sighed, but looked over at Jeff, brow pinched as I scanned his body, trying to figure out what trick I was supposed to be demonstrating. "What am I trying to—"

"If you can't see it," Catcher interrupted, "then close your eyes and feel him out. Empty your mind, and allow yourself to breathe it in."

I nodded although I had no idea what he was talking about, and while facing Jeff, closed my eyes. I tried to blank my mind of extraneous information and concentrate on what was in front of me—namely, a skinny, shape-shifting computer programmer.

That's when I noticed it.

I could feel it. Just a hint. The different weight of him, feel of him. He kind of—vibrated differently.

"There's . . . There's. . . ." I opened my eyes, stared at Jeff, then turned my head to look at Catcher. "He's carrying. Steel. A knife or something," I guessed, given the weight of it.

"Jeff?"

"I don't even own a weapon," Jeff protested, but he stood up and reached into his first pocket. As we all watched, riveted, he turned it inside out. Empty.

He tried the second, and when he reached in, he pulled out a small, cord-wrapped knife, its blade covered in a black sheath. Obviously shocked, he held the knife in his palm, and looked at each of us. "This isn't mine."

Catcher, who sat next to him, clapped him on the back. "It's mine, James Bond. I slipped it into your pocket when you were ogling Mallory."

A flush rose on Jeff's cheeks as Catcher took back the knife, slipped it into his own pocket. "I wasn't ogling Mallory," he said, then glanced apologetically at Mal, who was walking back to the table, paper plate of cake in her hand. "I wasn't," he insisted, then looked back at Catcher. "Ogling's a harsh word."

Catcher chuckled. "So's 'beat down.'"

"And on that pleasant note," Mallory interrupted with a chuckle, placing the slice of cake on the table in front of me, "let's eat."

We ate until we were stuffed, until I expected my stomach to burst open like a coconut-filled piñata. The food was incomparable, deliciously homey, the sweetness of cake the perfect dessert. And when our bellies were full and my grandfather began to yawn, I prepared to take the team home. I belted the sword and grabbed the box of leather.

The car loaded with gifts and cupcakes, I slipped back inside to say a final goodbye, and inadvertently walked in on another Catcher-Mallory moment.

They were in a corner of the living room, their hands on each other's hips. Catcher gazed down at her, eyes full of such respect and adoration that the emotion of it tightened my throat. Mallory looked back, met his gaze, without coquettish eyelash batting or turning away. She met his gaze and shared his look, the expression of partnership.

And I was struck with the worst, most nauseating sense of jealousy I'd ever felt.

What would it be like, I wondered, to have someone look at me that way? To see something in me, inside me, worth that kind of admiration? That kind of attention?

Even when we were younger, Mallory had always been the one around whom men flocked. I was the smart, slightly weirder sidekick. She was the goddess. Men bought her drinks, offered their numbers, offered their bank accounts and time and rides in their BMW convertibles. All the while I sat beside her, smiled politely when they looked my way to size me up, to determine if I was a barrier to the thing they wanted—blond-haired/blue-haired, blue-eyed Mallory.

Now she had Catcher, and she was being adored anew. She'd found a partner, a companion, a protector.

I tried to force my jealousy into curiosity, to wonder at the sensation of being wanted, desired in a profound way. I tried not to begrudge my best friend her moment in the sun, her opportunity to experience true love.

Yeah, that didn't work so well.

I was jealous of my best friend, my sister in every way that mattered, who deserved nothing less than total adoration. I hated myself a little for being jealous of the happiness she deserved. But when he kissed her forehead, and they looked up and smiled at me, I couldn't help but hope.

CHAPTER FOURTEEN

LOVE IS A BATTLEFIELD.

SO IS THE CITY OF CHICAGO.

The next evening, I woke pepared for battle. But not with a serial killer. Not with warring nymphs or Rogue vampires. Not even with the Master I avoided.

This time, I prepared for Helen. I hadn't handled our first meeting well, which maybe wasn't so unusual given the nature of it—the cold, hard reality she'd been burdened with preparing me. But I was losing my house, Mallory's house, to Catcher and his roaming hands. I needed a place to crash. It was time to ask about moving into Cadogan.

Although I wasn't thrilled with that choice, the alternatives didn't seem much better. I couldn't move in with my parents. I didn't think they'd allow it, and dealing with my father was soul-sucking enough from a ZIP code away.

Getting my own place wasn't a viable option, either. My Cadogan stipend was nice, but it wasn't enough to cover rent in Chicago without a roommate. I wasn't ready for the burbs, and I certainly didn't want to bring my supernatural drama to some new roommate's door. And unless I lived in Hyde Park, having my own place didn't solve the time problem—the fact that I'd still have travel time between me and a Cadogan crisis.

I could move in with my grandfather, and there was no

question that he'd invite me in, but with me came my baggage—including being the near-victim of a serial killer, the recent recipient of a death threat, and the new guard for Cadogan House. Moving into Cadogan posed its own set of problems, its meddlesome Master key among them. But I'd never need to worry about troubling someone who couldn't handle it. If there was anything pleasant I could say about Ethan Sullivan, it was that he was equipped to deal with supernatural drama.

I hadn't, of course, informed Ethan that I was considering moving into the House. I imagined three possible responses to the news, none of which I was interested in experiencing.

At best, I figured I'd be offered cool approval that I'd finally reached the decision a proper Sentinel would have reached a week ago. At worst, I bet on vitriol, on his expressing serious concerns that I was going to spy on Cadogan or sabotage the House from the inside.

But most disturbing was the third possibility—that he'd ask me again to be his Consort. I was pretty sure we'd moved past that idea, the fact that we'd happily avoided each other for the last week evidence enough, but this boy was more stubborn than most.

So I planned to work through Helen, who, in her position as Initiate Liaison, also coordinated new vampires' moves into the House, and let word reach Ethan through channels. But working through Helen meant apologies. Big-time apologies, since the last time I'd seen her, I yelled at and insulted her, and prompted a sorceress to kick her out of our house. To fix things, I opted for a simple, classic strategy—bribery. I was going to buy my way into her good graces with a dozen pink-and-white birthday cupcakes. I'd repackaged them in a shiny pink bakery box, and I was ready to make the drop at her office as soon as I reached Cadogan.

But before I did that . . . I had my own business to attend to, namely in the form of a private vampire fashion show. After I'd showered, but before I'd slipped into the requisite Cadogan black, I slipped my birthday ensemble from its hangers and donned the leathers. The suit, such as it was, fit like a glove, like it had been molded for my body. My hair in its high ponytail, the sword in my hands, I looked pretty fierce. I looked like I was ready for serious vampire combat. That was patently untrue, of course, but it didn't make posing in front of the mirror any less fun.

I was still in front of the mirror, sword in hand, when my beeper began to vibrate. I jumped at the sound, thinking someone had walked in on the spectacle of my vampire dress-up. When I realized the source of the noise, I grabbed the beeper from the top of my bureau and scanned the screen: CADGN. BREACH. GREEN. 911.

Breach: Uninvited supernaturals on the premises.

Green: Ethan's code. He was in trouble, needed assistance, etc.

911: Quickly now, Sentinel.

There were footsteps in the hallway. Beeper in hand, I opened the bedroom door and peeked into the hall. Catcher, in jeans and a long-sleeved T-shirt, walked toward me. I had to give him credit—he didn't so much as bat an eyelash at my ensemble.

"You got the page?"

I nodded. But before I could ask how he knew about it, he continued, "The meeting we discussed, with all the vamps? The one Sullivan needed to schedule? It's happening right now, and not by invitation."

"Shit," I said, moving my left hand to the handle of the katana, and ignoring for the moment the fact that he had this information before I did. "I need to change."

Catcher shook his head. "Today's the day you bluff," he said. "I'll get your car ready."

I stared at him. "Are you kidding? Ethan will shit if I show up dressed like this in front of other Cadogan vampires, much less other Houses."

Catcher shook his head. "*You* stand Sentinel, not Ethan.

You do your job the way you do it. And if you're going to bluff your way into keeping Ethan safe, would you rather do it in leather or a suit and prissy heels? You need to show teeth today."

Because his words echoed my own thoughts, I didn't argue.

He offered me advice via cell phone the entire ride to Cadogan House: Look everyone in the eye. Keep my left hand on the handle of the sword, thumb at the guard, and only pull the right hand over if I needed to be seriously aggressive. Keep my body between Ethan and whatever pointy thing—be it blade or teeth—was threatening him. When Catcher started to repeat himself, I cut him off.

"Catcher, this isn't me. I'm not prepared for warfare. I was a grad student. But he gave me this job, presumably, after four hundred years of experience, because he thought I could bring something to the table, something he thought could trump my lack of training. I appreciate the advice, and I appreciate the training, but it's the eleventh hour, and if I haven't learned it by now, I'm not likely to learn it in the next five minutes." I swallowed, my chest tight. "I'll do what I can. It's been asked of me, and I agreed to stand Sentinel, and I'll do what I can."

I decided to confess the thought that had tickled the back of my mind, but hadn't yet voiced. That the vampire inside me had a mind of her own. That sometimes it felt like we hadn't merged, not truly, but rather like she lived inside me.

Maybe because it sounded ridiculous, I found it harder to vocalize than I'd imagined. "I think—I think—"

"What, Merit?"

"She feels kind of separate from me."

Silence, then: "She?"

He spoke the word as if it was a question, but I had the sense he knew exactly what I meant. "The vampire. My vampire. *Me.* I don't know. It's probably nothing."

Silence again, then: "Probably nothing."

Blocks passed, and then I was turning onto Woodlawn, cell phone still pinched between shoulder and ear.

"If you need to look threatening, can you silver your eyes? Pull down you fangs? On purpose, I mean?"

I hadn't tried, but imagined I'd learned enough in the last week about what silvered my eyes to be able to manufacture the effect. Method vampirism, as it was.

"I think so, yeah."

"Good. Good." I pulled the car up to the curb in front of Cadogan House. There were no guards at the gate. The House looked empty, and that foretold nothing good.

"Shit," I muttered and grabbed the door handle. "The House looks deserted."

"Merit, listen."

I paused, one hand on the door, the other wrapped around my cell phone.

"Cadogan House hasn't had a Sentinel in two centuries. You got the job because he believed in you. Do the job. Nothing more, nothing less."

I nodded, although he couldn't see it. "I'll be fine."

Or I wouldn't, I thought, as I threw the phone in the passenger seat, walked down the empty sidewalk, and tugged at the hem of the leather jacket I'd zipped over the midriff-baring bodice.

Either way, we'd find out soon enough.

The front door was partially ajar, the first floor empty of vampires. I heard rumblings upstairs and, with a hand on my sword, took the staircase. Luc stood on the landing, legs braced, arms crossed, a katana belted on his left side.

I gave him a nod, waited for him to look over my ensemble. When he'd taken me in, I asked, "Where are we?"

He inclined his head toward the ballroom, and we walked together toward it. His voice was all business. "Ethan tried to schedule a meeting about the murders. He invited representatives from Grey, Navarre. The meet was supposed to happen later tonight. Then the Rogues found out. Noah Beck—he's their rep—showed up half an hour ago."

A chunk of time had passed then, since the page. I *did* need to move into Cadogan House.

"They're pissed about not being included," he continued, his expression pulled tight, "about our existence being leaked—no, *announced*—to the press." Clearly Ethan wasn't the only one who doubted Celina's decision making in that regard.

We stopped in front of the closed ballroom doors, and I planted my hands on my hips, slid him a glance. "How many?"

"Twelve Rogues, maybe thirty vamps from Cadogan. Scott Grey and four of his people; they showed up early for the meet. Lindsey, Jules, and Kelley are in there, but they're hanging back."

I lifted brows. "You ever think the ratio of six guards to three hundred Cadogan vamps ain't quite right?"

"It's peacetime," he explained, irritation in his voice. "We hold too many swords, and we're showing animosity, risking war." He shrugged. "Too few, of course, and we risk a Rogue taking a shot at Ethan."

It took me a moment to realize he wasn't being metaphorical. "A shot? I thought vampires used blades?" I motioned to the katana at his waist, but he shook his head.

"That's House *Canon*, tradition. Rogues reject the system, reject the pretense, the rules. They'll have weapons. They've got their own Code, such as it is. They might have one blade visible, maybe more hidden. But they'll have guns—probably handguns, probably semiautomatic. Probably a forty-five. They're partial to the nineteen eleven."

I nodded, remembering the picture I'd seen in a Kimber catalog in the Ops Room. That was all I needed—stray bullets flying around the room during my first real fight.

"I can't defend shots," I told him, belatedly realizing the

weapon I was expected to use in a gunfight was my body—
between Ethan's and the racing bullets.

As if catching my concern, probably easy given the expression of sheer terror on my face, Luc offered, "Shots
won't kill him, unless they let loose a spray. Just do what you
can. And one more thing."

He paused so long I looked over, saw his brow furrowed.

"Your position," he said, before pausing again, "it's more
political than ours. We're considered field soldiers, even me.
Sentinel's still soldiering, but traditionally vamps see it as
more of a strategic position. And that means more respect."
He shrugged. "That's history, I suppose."

"Which means," I concluded, "I can get a little closer to
him than you can. I'm less a declaration of war, more a show
that the situation's being taken very, very seriously."

Luc nodded again, relief that I understood evident in his
expression. "Exactly."

I blew out a slow breath, trying to assimilate this new
information—which would have been helpful before the
crisis—and not panic at the pressure. I stroked my thumb
over the handle of the katana, prayed for calm. Two weeks
into vampiredom and I was being asked to defend the House
against a band of marauding unHoused vampires.

Lucky me.

Not that it mattered. I had a job, and while I panicked at
the thought of actually doing that job, doing it was the only
thing I could do. Enter the fray, take the step, and bluff like
my life depended on it. Because it probably did.

I accepted the tiny earpiece Luc offered, slipped it into my
ear. "Let's go."

When Luc nodded, I took a breath, put my hand on the
door, and opened it.

There were fifty people in the ballroom, but even in the giant
space, it seemed like a much larger swarm. Even the air seemed
thick. It fairly prickled with bitter magic, with a flowing energy

that called my vampire. I felt her shift, awaken, stretch, and wonder why the air felt barbed. My lashes shuddered, and I had to force my palm against the sword's handle until cording bit into my skin, to force her back, to keep my mind clear. But later, I promised her, she'd feed.

The vampires stood in a mass, backs to the door. I recognized the black-suited Cadogan vamps, but from the back, couldn't tell where anyone else, including Ethan, was standing. I glanced at Luc, mouthed, *Where is he?*

Kelley's voice sounded in my ear. "Nice of you to join us, Sentinel. Ethan's in front of the platform, facing the crowd. The Rogues are facing him, their backs to us, and the Cadogan vamps are in a circle around everyone. We're just trying to keep things calm."

I scanned the crowd, looking for an in, and saw Kelley's straight dark hair. She glanced back, slightly inclined her head at Luc and me, then turned back to the crowd.

I looked over the mass of bodies and tried to imagine where to go, where I could be close enough to see, to guard, but not so close that I, as Sentinel, escalated matters. The room was tense enough as it was, the vampires leaking energy as they dealt with the possibility that a murderer was among them.

I motioned to the left, indicated my direction, and Luc nodded, pointed to the right, then made a hand signal indicating we'd meet in the middle.

At least, I hoped that was what it meant.

I took a breath, blew it out slowly, stabilized the scabbard and stepped forward. I skirted the edge of the crowd, trying to will myself invisible as I moved to the left, as I eased around the border of Cadogan vampires. My attempt at glamour didn't help—the Cadogan vamps watched as I moved, a few nodding in quiet acknowledgment, a few giving looks that suggested something altogether different from respect—but I was glad, even in the face of bitter stares, that they played buffer between me and the rest of the interlopers.

Seconds later, I was close enough to see the action. Ethan, with Malik at his side, stood in front of the platform at which I'd been Commended into the House only days ago. Standing perpendicular to Ethan was a tall, dark-haired man in a Cubs T-shirt and jeans who I guessed from the athletic bent of his clothing was Scott Grey. Across from Ethan, striking stand-outs in a room of tidy, chic suits, and sports gear, were the Rogues.

They stood in a tight pyramidal cluster and were, just like the Cadogan vampires, clad in black. But this wasn't Michi-gan Avenue black. This was vampire warfare black. Black boots. Trim black pants. A chest piece of black leather body armor. There was enough black in the cluster of them to suck the light from the ballroom. Punctuating the look was silver—belts, rings, wristbands, wallet chains, and in the middle of each chest, a silver pendant—an anarchy symbol on a silver chain.

This was the look Morgan wanted to achieve. Urban, re-bellious, dangerous.

But this was real.

This was *actual* bad ass.

That said, all the Rogue vampires were dressed the same. Wasn't it kinda ironic that the herd mentality affected even the disaffected? That warranted pondering, but not today. To-day was business.

One of the Rogues—tall, broad-shouldered, muscled—stood point, facing Ethan. Where the rest of the vamps in the room, the Housed vamps, looked polished, he looked a little fierce. He was ruggedly handsome, a couple days' worth of stubble across his face and jaw. His brown hair was an inch or two past a haircut, and stood in kind of messy whorls. And his eyes, big and blue, were ringed with kohl. He stood with arms folded across his broad chest, head cocked slightly to the side, listening as Ethan discussed the ongoing investiga-tion.

They were definitely here for business. At their waists

were holsters with handguns snapped inside, probably the 1911s Luc had mentioned. While the feel of them was different from Housed vampires anyway—the energy a bit less focused than House vamps, a little more scattershot—it was obvious they were carrying more than just the guns. The power flowed differently around their bodies. I couldn't see it, but I could sense it, the change in the current, like rocks altering the flow of a stream.

When I was where I wanted to be, a few bodies behind the edge of the crowd and still out of the players' direct line of sight, I checked Ethan, saw that he was unharmed and managing to mask the frustration I knew he felt. His body was loose, his hands in the pockets of the ubiquitous black trousers, half of his blond hair pulled back in a tie. His gaze was on the Rogue in front of him.

"Frankly, Noah," Ethan was saying, "it wasn't an oversight that you weren't invited to talk, nor was it a sign of disrespect. It was a choice, based on my assumption, apparently incorrect, that you weren't interested in participating. The humans only know about the Houses. As far as I'm aware, your existence is still a secret, and I'd imagined you'd be happier keeping it that way."

Noah gave Ethan a flat stare. "It was an assumption of uninterest, then. The assumption that because we're not affiliated with a House, because we aren't sheep, we're unconcerned about our fellow vampires." His tone was all sarcasm.

Ethan lifted a blond brow, responded crisply, "That's not what I said."

Thinking it might be helpful to say hello, to let him know that he had backup should the worst occur, I reported in, opening my mind to Ethan. *I'm here*, I sent him.

He didn't respond, but the Rogue in front of him, Noah, did. Not, I think, because Noah heard me, but because there was scuffling behind us, which drew his eyes across the crowd. As he looked for the source of the trouble, gazed across the sea of watching vampires, he met my eyes, lifted both brows. The subtext was easy enough to read: *And who are you? Friend or foe?*

I blinked, trying to guess how I was supposed to react—was there etiquette for this? The unintroduced Sentinel responding to a flicker of interest from the spokesperson for Chicago's Rogue vampires? Unfortunately, I didn't have time to fully evaluate, so I just did what felt natural given the awkward position we were in: I gave a half smile and a shrug.

I'm not sure what I expected from him. Maybe the reaction Ethan would have given—a condescending look, a roll of the eyes.

But Noah wasn't Ethan. Noah smirked, squeezed his lips together to keep in the laugh that shook his chest, and quickly looked away, mouth curved. My first real political act, and it sparked a bubble of laughter from the man who'd allegedly breached the walls of Cadogan House. A good enough reaction, I decided, hoping his amusement would defuse the obvious strain in the room.

Unfortunately, I didn't have a chance to test that theory. Our exchange took only seconds, but that was more than enough time for trouble to call. The vampire whose shuffling we'd heard behind us revealed himself, Morgan pushing through the crowd, through the Rogues, until he stood before Ethan. Perhaps sensing his obvious anger, the waves of it radiating from his body, the other vampires moved back, gave him space.

He looked like a man possessed—hair sexily mussed, his leather jacket over a green T-shirt and jeans, black sneakers beneath the cuffs. And although he vibrated with the energy I knew he was capable of, that wasn't the only reason he roiled. He was carrying. And not a sword, not a weapon obviously belted or sheathed. This was hidden. A medium-sized blade, I guessed, by the differential weight of him. Too small to be a sword, but bigger than your average kitchen knife.

I tightened my grip on the sword's handle, my thumb on

the latch that would release the blade from its scabbard, and waited.

"You fucking son of a bitch." The words were tight, forced through his clenched jaw.

Ethan blinked, but made no other move, his stance still relaxed, confident. "Excuse me?"

"You think this is right? That you can do this?"

I flinched when Morgan lifted his arm, nearly pushed through the couple of vampires who separated Ethan and me, but held back when I saw the white paper he held in his hand. A small square of it, a black curve of handwriting across one side. Having seen something similar weeks before, I guessed what might be written on it.

Ethan probably knew, too, but bluffed. "I don't know what that is, Morgan."

Morgan fisted the note, held it in the air. "It's a fucking death threat—that's what it is. It was on Celina's bedside table. Her *bedside. Table.* She's scared to death." Morgan took a half step forward, uncurled the note, held it out for Ethan to read. Ethan gingerly took it between long fingers, his gaze traveling the length of the paper and back.

"It's a threat," Ethan announced to the crowd, his gaze still on Morgan. "Very similar to the one Merit received. I'd guess it's the same handwriting, the same paper. And it's purportedly signed by me."

The crowd rumbled. Morgan ignored it, lowered his voice to a fierce whisper that immediately quieted the crowd again.

"And that's fucking convenient, isn't it? Get Joshua Merit's daughter into the House, then take out Celina? Blame it on the Rogues, consolidate your power right under Tate's nose?" Morgan turned, surveyed the crowd, swinging out an arm dramatically. "And all of a sudden, the House that drinks is everyone's favorite."

The room went eerily quiet, and Ethan's frame finally stiffened. I watched the change in his posture, and my stomach sank as I feared, and faced, the worst—that Morgan had guessed correctly, and that Ethan was on the main quad that night for a very specific reason. That it wasn't "luck" at all.

Ethan leaned forward, eyes flaming green, and bit off, "Watch your words, Morgan, before you take steps Celina isn't ready to back up. Neither myself nor any other Cadogan vampire is responsible for that note, for any violence or threats made against Celina or Merit." He lifted his head, looked at Noah, then Scott Grey, then out over the crowd. "Cadogan is not responsible for the death of Jennifer Porter, for the death of Patricia Long, for the notes, for the evidence, for any part of those crimes." He paused, let his gaze travel. "But if someone—some vampire—is responsible, be they Grey, or Rogue, or Navarre, and if information comes to light that any vampire or sect of vampires took part—*any* part—in these crimes, we will give that information to the police, human or not. And they will answer to *me*."

He glanced back at Morgan, gave him the withering Master-to-Peon look I knew he was capable of.

"And you'd better remember your place, your age, and where you're standing, Morgan of House Navarre."

"She's afraid for her life, Sullivan," Morgan said through clenched teeth, clearly unaffected by Ethan's threat. His jaw was set, his stance aggressive—feet planted, hands clenched into fists, chin tipped down just enough so that he glared at Ethan from beneath his brow. "I'm her Second, and that is *unacceptable*."

I sympathized, understood his frustration, knew Ethan would expect the same loyalty from Malik, if not the drama that made me wonder about the relationship between Celina Desaulniers and her Second. But I also knew Ethan wasn't involved. Maybe the Rogues had some involvement, maybe Grey House, undoubtedly some vampire with access to the Cadogan grounds. But Cadogan vampire would have, could have, murdered under his watch.

I looked across the anxious crowd, met Luc's eyes, got the nod that I knew signaled action. Just as Morgan cocked back a fist, I stepped forward, pushed through the remaining veil of vampires, whipped the sword from its scabbard, and stretched out my arm just so the tip of it lay before the pulse that throbbed in his neck.

I lifted a brow at him. "I'm going to have to ask you to step back."

The ballroom went silent.

His dark eyes followed the length of the sword, surveyed the leather. He took in the jacket, the pants, the boots, the high ponytail that held back my hair. If he hadn't been completely sobered by the steel, I think he'd have complimented the ensemble. But this was business, and I'd stepped into his fight.

Morgan lifted his chin incrementally above the blade. "Put down the sword."

"I don't take orders from you." I took a step to the side, my arm outstretched, and stepped directly between Morgan and Ethan, forcing Ethan to back up behind me. It was enough to put him out of Morgan's reach, and to substitute me in Morgan's line of attack.

"But you take orders from *him*?" His voice dripped with sarcasm.

I blinked, all innocence, and let my voice ring across the room. "I stand Sentinel. I'm a vampire of his House, and I stand Sentinel. If he orders me to lower the blade, I will."

Ethan was silent behind me. But it wasn't the fact that he made no order, but my admission that I'd obey it if it came, that prompted a round of whispering. Ethan had been right: Chicago's vampires doubted my allegiance, maybe because rumors had leaked out about the nature of my change, maybe because of my father, maybe because of my strength. Whatever the reason, they had doubted.

Until now.

Now they knew. I'd joined the fight, I'd made a shield of my body, and I'd stepped between Ethan and danger, drawn steel on his behalf. I'd accepted the possibility of injury, of death, in order to protect him, and I'd publicly made clear that I was amenable to his orders, willing to submit to his authority.

I had to squeeze the handle of the katana when the tunnel rushed me, when I heard Ethan's voice. *I'd say this counts as a show of allegiance.*

I almost grinned from the sheer relief of it, of realizing that I wasn't doing this alone, facing down a hostile crowd outside the chain of command. But I kept my gaze neutral, remembered the audience around us, and knew that they were memorizing this moment, would play it back, would recall it for friends and enemies and allies—the night they first saw Cadogan's Sentinel take up arms.

I said a quick prayer not to screw it up too badly.

Oblivious to the undercurrent, Morgan barked, "This isn't your fight."

I shook my head at him. "I took my oaths. It's my fight—only my fight. He named me Sentinel, and if you bring this to Cadogan House, you bring this to me. That's the way this works."

Morgan shook his head. "This is personal, not House business."

I cocked my head at him. "Then why are you here, in someone else's House?"

That must have had some kind of impact. He growled, the sound low and predatory. If I'd been an animal, it would have raised my hackles. As it was, it called the vampire again, and I knew my eyes were silvering at the edges, but pushed, as hard as I could, to quiet her again.

"This isn't your concern," Morgan said. "You're only going to get hurt."

A corner of my mouth lifted. "Because I'm a girl?"

His lips tightened, and he leaned forward, pricked his neck against the sharpened tip of the blade. A single crimson drop slid down the edge of it. Looking back, I'd have sworn the sword instantaneously warmed as Morgan's blood traced the steel.

"First blood!" was called by someone in the crowd, and the vampires around us backed up, widening the open circle in which we stood. There was movement to my left and right, and I slid a quick glance sideways, saw Luc and Juliet take up positions at Ethan's sides.

Master secured, I grinned at Morgan beneath the fringe of my bangs and called up all the bravado I could muster. "You're here. I'm here. We gonna dance?"

I kept my sword level, saw Morgan's gaze flick behind me, then back to me again. His eyes widened in surprise, his lips parting. I had no idea what that was about. But Morgan began pulling off his jacket, then held it out to the side, revealing the straps of a sheath. A vampire, presumably one who'd arrived with him from Navarre House, stepped forward to claim his jacket, and reaching behind him, Morgan pulled a gothic-looking dagger from its mount. The blade glinted, all weird curves and angles, and I couldn't say that I was impressed by the fact that he hid it beneath clothes.

I stifled a sudden sense of panic that, at twenty-eight, I was about to be in my first real fight—not a sibling spat, but a duel, combat, my first battle on Cadogan's behalf. Honestly, I still wasn't sure Morgan would go through with it, that he would actually attempt to draw my blood in front of Ethan, Scott, the Rogues, and witnesses from Cadogan House, and on Cadogan territory. Especially because he lacked concrete evidence that Cadogan was involved in the threat, because he knew I'd received a threat of my own, and maybe most important, because he'd kissed me.

But here we were, in this circle of fifty vampires, and he'd brought this on himself, so I called his bluff. Carefully, slowly, I lowered the sword, flipped the weight of it so the pommel was up, and held it out to the right, waiting until Lindsey stepped forward to take it.

Morgan's eyes went wide when I unzipped the jacket, but not as wide as they did when I slipped it off. The only thing beneath was snug leather band, which left my abdomen and hips bare to the top of the leather pants. I extended the jacket with my left hand, felt the weight of it disappear, then held out my right to retrieve the sword. When the body-warmed handle was back in my hand, I rolled it in my wrist, getting used to its weight, and smiled at him.

"Shall we?"

His expression darkened. "I can't fight you."

I assumed the basic offensive position Catcher had taught me—legs shoulder width apart, weight on the balls of my feet, loose knees, sword up, both hands in position around the handle.

"That's unfortunate," I commented, then lunged forward slightly and sliced a stripe in the sleeve of his long-sleeved T-shirt. I pursed my lips, blinked up at him, gave him a look of doe-eyed innocence. "Oops."

"Don't push me, Merit."

This time my expression was flat. "I'm not the one who's pushing. You challenged my House. You're here to take up arms against Cadogan, against Ethan, because you think we have something to do with the deaths of these women. And you do this on the basis of a note that someone placed in the bedroom of your Master. I doubt Ethan made it into Celina's boudoir without notice." The crowd snickered appreciatively. "So how else did you expect us to respond to this, Morgan?"

"He shouldn't have called you here."

"I stand Sentinel, and this is House business. He didn't have to call me here. I'm honor-bound to fight—for the House and for him—and I will."

I don't know what I said to spark it, but Morgan's expression changed so suddenly I doubted what I thought I'd heard in his voice when he'd sought to protect Celina from her would-be attacker only moments ago. He looked at me slowly, a head-to-toe perusal that would have melted a lesser woman. He looked at me, Morgan of Navarre, and his gaze went hot, his voice dropping to a fierce whisper. "Yield, damn it. I won't fight you. A fight isn't the thing I want from you, Merit."

I felt the blush warming my cheeks. I could take threats, I could take blustering, but propositioning me in front of fifty vampires was completely uncalled for. So I leveled the sword at the height of his heart.

"Don't say it. Don't suggest it. Don't even think it. I've told you before"—I grinned up at him evilly—"I don't do fang."

The crowd gave an ironically appreciative snicker.

I took a step forward, took satisfaction in the fact that he moved a step back. "Yield, Morgan. If you want out of this, then yield. Apologize to Ethan, take your note, and leave the House. Or," I added, thinking about the strategy of it, "decide to stay, to be part of the dialogue, to figure out a solution to the problem of sudden human attention on our Houses."

I could practically feel the glow of Ethan's approval at my back. I'd given Morgan options, including at least one that would allow him to salvage his pride, to back down from the point of the sword without ruining his reputation.

And then the tunnel rushed me again. But this time, it was Morgan's voice that rang through my head, my sword trembling as I focused all my will on the blade in my hand, trying to maintain my stance and my composure. I thought telepathy was something shared only between Master and Novitiate. It seemed wrong somehow for Morgan to be inside my head. Too personal, and I wasn't comfortable knowing that he had a psychic "in."

I can't back down without a boon, he told me. *I represent my House as well, Merit, and I have my pride. His name was on the note.*

I arched a sardonic brow. *You know that no one from Cadogan is involved in this.*

He was quiet for a moment, then gave me the slightest

inclination of his head, a signal that he'd understood, was willing to admit our innocence. *Perhaps, but Ethan knows something.*

I couldn't argue with that. I already suspected Ethan knew more than he let on, but I had no more evidence for that than I did for the possibility that he'd written the note himself.

Then stay, and talk, and find out what that is, I told Morgan. *Stay and work this out with conversation, not with swords. You know that's the right thing to do. No one will condemn you for running to Celina's rescue. You're her Second.*

For what seemed like a long time, he looked at me, a smirk on his face. *A boon, then. If I back down, I want something in return.*

You brought the fight, I reminded him. *You came into my House, threatened Ethan.*

And you just took my blood.

I rolled my eyes. *You leaned into* my *blade.* God, but he would argue with a signpost.

You pulled your weapon first, Sentinel. That was threat enough to prompt a reaction.

I looked at him for a while, long enough to make the vampires around us stir nervously, as I considered his position. He was right—he'd verbally threatened Ethan, but I'd pulled steel first. I could have taken a softer approach, thumbed the guard, reached for it without unsheathing it, but I'd seen him pull back his arm and assumed he was going to throw a punch. That was when I stepped forward. And in return for my trouble, I stood in the middle of a throng of vampires, their eyes on me as I psychically negotiated with the vamp who started the scuffle in the first place.

Fine, I told him, hoping irritation carried telepathically. *I owe you a favor.*

A favor, unspecified.

There was my mistake.

I had to give him credit—he saw his opportunity, and he took it. I omitted terms, failed to identify the thing I owed him, failed to clarify that I owed him a favor equal to the one he'd given. Vampires, I belatedly realized, negotiated via a system of verbal trades and barters and, just as to overzealous attorneys, every word mattered. These were oral contracts of a sort, backed by steel rather than law, but just as binding. And I'd just handed Morgan a blank check.

He grinned wolfishly, offered a smile so possessive it made my stomach flip, and then sank to one knee. My own eyes wide, I followed him down with my sword, kept it pointed at his heart.

You made it too easy, he said, then announced to the room, "Merit, Sentinel of Cadogan House, I hereby claim the right of courtship. Do you accept?"

I stared down at him. I wasn't even sure what it meant— not the details, anyway—although the gist of it was bad enough. *You* cannot *be serious,* I told him.

Once you go fang, babe, you'll never go back.

I was about to respond with a few choice maxims of my own, but the landscape shifted, and I was hurling down another tunnel, Ethan whispering at the end of it.

Take his hand. Accept his claim.

My stomach dropped again, this time for an altogether different reason. *What?*

You heard me. Take his hand. Accept him.

I had to fight back the urge to turn on him and level my sword at the shrunken black nugget of his heart. *Tell me why. Explain to me why.* "Why you're pimping me out," was the unspoken end of that request.

Silence, until: *Because it's a chance for us. For Cadogan. If Morgan courts you, he courts Cadogan by proxy. And he has made this request before representatives of Cadogan, Navarre, Grey, and the Rogues. For Navarre to court a House that drinks, to court Cadogan so openly—it's unprecedented. This could be the gateway to an alliance between our Houses. Things are . . . unstable, Merit. If your courtship brings Navarre closer . . .*

He didn't finish the thought, the obvious implication being that I was a useful bridge between Cadogan and Navarre, a leather-clad link between the Houses. My feelings, my desires, were irrelevant.

I looked down at Morgan on his knees before me, his smile bright and hopeful even while he'd manipulated his way into a relationship, and wondered which of them was the lesser evil.

The crowd around us shuffled, getting antsy as they waited for a response. There was chatting. I heard snippets, whispered behind cupped hands:

"Do you think she'll say yes?"

"Morgan dating someone from Cadogan—that's huge."

"I didn't know they knew each other."

And the real kicker: "I thought Ethan had a thing for her?"

My eyes still on Morgan, I squeezed the handle of my sword, sent Ethan another question: *If I accept his claim, what does that mean?*

It means you accept his suit. You acknowledge that I am, and that you are, receptive to his courting you.

I locked my knees and forced out the question that needed asking, unpleasantly surprised that the answer mattered so much. *And are you? Receptive?*

Silence.

Nothing.

Ethan didn't answer.

I closed my eyes, realizing I'd made the lamentable, and incorrect, assumption that, at the least, we had reached an accord that would have prevented him from using me, from passing me to a rival to meet a political goal. Oh, how wrong I'd been. Wrong to discount the fact that he was first and foremost a strategist, weighing outcomes, considering options, debating the means that would best achieve his ends. Wrong to think that he'd make an exception for me.

While his end might have been laudable—protecting his House, protecting his vampires—he was willing to sacrifice me to meet those goals. I'd just been sent to the sacrificial altar, given to the man who only moments ago, and quite literally, wielded the ceremonial dagger.

I'd imagined myself safe from Ethan's machinations because I'd thought, naively, that he cared for me, if not as a friend, then because I was a Cadogan vampire.

I squeezed back tears of frustration. Damn it, I was supposed to be one of his vampires, to protect, to shield. Not to offer up.

But there was something worse beneath that sense of House betrayal, some undefined emotion that made my stomach ache. I didn't want to pick at it, examine it, consider why tears pricked at the corners of my eyes, why his passing me along to another vampire hurt so much.

Not because he'd given me to Morgan.

But because he hadn't wanted to keep me to himself.

I squeezed my eyes shut, lambasted my own stupidity, wondered how in God's name I'd managed to form an attachment to a man so obviously determined to push me away. It wasn't about love, maybe not even about affection, but rather some bone-deep sense that our lives were bound together in some important way. That there was—and would be— something more between us than the awkwardness of unfulfilled sexual attraction.

It would be so easy, so handy, to blame it on the vampire inside, to attribute the connection to the fact that he'd made me, turned me, that I was his to command, that he was mine to serve. But this wasn't about magic or genetics.

This was about a boy, and a girl . . .

Gently, quietly, Morgan cleared his throat.

. . . and the other boy still on his knees before me.

I opened my eyes, recalling that I was still standing in the middle of a room of anticipatory vampires, all waiting for me to act on Morgan's proposal. So I pushed down the pain of the betrayal Ethan likely hadn't known he was committing, and did my job.

I lowered my sword, smiled softly at Morgan, and took his hand. I let my voice go flat—no sense in pretending I was thrilled to play political go-between—and offered, "Morgan, Second of Navarre, I accept your claim on behalf of Cadogan House, on behalf of my Master, on behalf of myself."

The applause was hesitant at first, but soon thundered through the ballroom. Morgan rose and pressed my hand to his lips, then squeezed it. He smiled quirkily. "Is it so bad?"

I lifted my brows, unwilling to give him the satisfaction of a perky answer. "To be a pawn?"

Shaking his head, he took a step forward, bent his lips to my ear. "Whatever the political ramifications, I've told you before—I want you." When he pulled back, his eyes twinkled with an amusement I appreciated, but didn't share. "Especially now that I've seen the wardrobe change. Kudos to your stylist. When can I see you again?"

I met his eyes, was slightly mollified to see that he was sincere, and slid a glance over my shoulder to the blond who stood behind me. Ethan met my gaze, but his thoughts were unfathomable, typically blank, a tiny crease between his eyebrows the only indication that he'd witnessed anything consequential in the last few minutes.

Without thought to the consequences, I let my eyes fill with the array of emotions he'd forced me to sort through. I let all of it show—anger, betrayal, hurt, and the one I knew I'd regret most of all, the frazzle-edged bit of attachment. And then, with Morgan waiting in front of me, I waited to see what, if anything, Ethan would give back.

For a long moment, he just stared at me, need laid bare in his expression.

But then his mouth tightened, and slowly, excruciatingly, he looked away.

I stiffened, turned around again, and offered Morgan a bright smile that I hoped didn't look as forced as it was.

"Call me," I dutifully said.

*   *   *

It took minutes for Ethan to calm down the crowd again. Once he had their attention, I moved back to the edge of the crowd, close enough to defend if necessary, but outside the inner circle. I'd had my fill of attention for the night.

"Now that we've enjoyed that . . . romantic interlude," Ethan said with a smile, capitalizing on the lighter mood, "we should return to the matter of the girls."

Static buzzed in my ear, and Luc's voice echoed through the earpiece. "Thanks for the distraction, Sentinel," he whispered. "That was damn entertaining. But everyone keep eyes and ears open—we may have defused tension, but we still have a shit storm to deal with."

I bobbed my head in acknowledgment.

"That 'matter' has gotten more complicated," Noah said, arms still folded across his chest. "Navarre House has apparently been infiltrated."

"So it would appear," Ethan agreed, nodding. "We are dealing with a killer, or killers, who have access to multiple Houses, perhaps a vendetta against them."

"But they've also got a vendetta against the Rogues," Noah said. "Let's not forget that every time a House denies involvement, they implicitly accuse us."

"Implicit or not, it's hard to accuse a group no one knows about," Scott grunted, joining the conversation. "The public only knows about us—that means the shit falls on us."

"Then maybe you shouldn't have stepped forward," muttered a Rogue who stood beside Noah.

"Not my choice," Scott pointed out.

"Nor mine," Ethan said. "But it's too late to do anything about that now. The only thing we can do now is cooperate. With the CPD, the administration, the investigations. Cooperation is the only thing that will insulate us from the public relations fallout, at least until the perpetrator of these crimes has been identified."

"And our existence?" Noah quietly asked.

The room fell silent as the Masters, Ethan and Scott, likely weighed their options.

"Until we figure out who's doing the damage," Scott finally said, "there's no point embroiling other vamps." He shrugged, glanced at Ethan. "That's my take."

Ethan nodded. "I would agree."

"Then we wait," Noah pronounced, propping hands on his hips. "And if someone has information about which vampire or vampires are responsible for this cluster fuck, I suggest they come forward. We had no intention of entering the public eye, and we won't do it now. If the Houses fall, we will not step forward. We will disperse into the human world as we have before." He glanced between Ethan and Scott, then settled his gaze on Morgan. "Clean up your Houses," he said.

With that pronouncement, Noah turned and began walking through the crowd, which opened to accommodate him and the Rogues who followed.

"And we're adjourned," Ethan muttered.

*   *   *

Not privy to the private meeting between Ethan, Scott, and Morgan that followed the Rogues' departure, I went home, ignored the worried glances I received on the way in, headed straight for my bedroom, and shut the door behind me. The belted sword was placed on an armchair, and I grabbed my iPod, slipped in the ear buds, lay down on the bed, and told myself I didn't care what had happened earlier in the evening.

I'd never been a very good liar.

CHAPTER FIFTEEN

BEFORE THE FLOOD

The next night I woke exhausted, having spent most of the day rolling, staring, cursing, replaying the events of the night before, mentally reenacting every moment Ethan and I had shared, and wondering how, why it had been so easy for him to trade me in for his precious political capital.

While that mystery loomed, I had work to do, so I rose, showered, dressed, ate a bowl of cereal in the darkness of my kitchen, slipped on the leather jacket, and grabbed the belted sword and the box of cupcakes I hadn't had time to deliver last night, preparing to return to Cadogan House and report for duty.

I'd just locked the front door and turned to descend the stoop steps when I saw Morgan leaning against his car, arms and ankles crossed. He was in jeans again, a black shirt tucked into jeans snugged with a heavy black belt, and the ubiquitous leather jacket.

He was grinning. "Hi."

I stood on the stoop, blinked, then took the steps and went for the garage, hoping the obvious uninterest would send him running. Instead, he followed me, pausing at the threshold of the garage, a disarmingly cute grin on his face.

"You said I could call."

"Call," I repeated. "Not show up at dusk." I pulled open the garage door, walked inside, and unlocked the car door.

"You gave me permission to court you."

With what I thought was an impressive amount of control, I managed not to run him through with my sword, instead pulling open the driver's side door and sliding the katana into the backseat, then laying the box of cupcakes on the front. That done, I turned back to him.

"You put me on the spot in front of fifty vampires. I couldn't exactly say no." He opened his mouth to respond, but I didn't give him the chance. "Fifty vampires, Morgan. Fifty, including my Master, another Master, and the leader of the Rogue vampires."

He grinned unapologetically, shrugged. "So I wanted witnesses."

"You wanted to mark your territory."

Morgan walked through the garage, squeezed between the narrow wall and the driver's side, and before I could scramble away, trapped me in the angle between the car and the open door, hands braced to bar my exit. He leaned in. "You're right. I wanted to mark my territory."

Ego deflation time. "You don't have a chance."

"I disagree. You danced with me. You fed me. You didn't slit my throat when given the opportunity." He grinned, bright and wicked. "You may be conflicted, but you're interested. Admit it."

I gave him a withering look that didn't succeed in flattening his smile or discouraging the Come Hither look it evolved into. "Not. A. Chance."

"Liar. If Ethan ordered you to go out with me, you'd go."

I couldn't help but laugh at that. "Yeah, that's the salve your ego needs—you're only dating the Sentinel of Cadogan House because her Liege and Master forced her to meet you at a Wendy's."

He shook his head with mock solemnity. "Not Wendy's. Bennigans, at least."

I quirked up an eyebrow. "Bennigans? Big spender."

"The Windy City is at your disposal, Merit."

For a moment, we were quiet, just staring at each other, waiting for the other to back down. I considered kicking him out, reneging on my promise to let him court me, but discarded that choice as politically irresponsible. I considered saying yes while explaining that I agreed only because I was duty-bound. And then I considered the other option—saying yes, because I wanted to go. Because he was sexy and funny, because we seemed to get along, because, even if he did have some kind of weird Celina baggage, he'd tried to protect her and stepped back when he realized his method wasn't working. I could respect that, even if I didn't understand the loyalty she commanded.

I took a calming breath, looked up at him. "One date."

He smiled a smile of masculine satisfaction. "Done," he said, then leaned in and pressed his lips to mine. "No reneging."

"I don't reneg," I said against his mouth.

"Hmmph." He sounded unconvinced, but kept kissing me anyway, and for some unknown reason, I let him.

Oh—he wasn't Ethan.

Callous? Maybe. But for now, that was reason enough.

Some minutes later, surprisingly pleasant minutes, I was in the car, making my way south. But before I headed to Cadogan House, I wanted to drop by my grandfather's office. I needed a sympathetic ear, and had no doubt that Grandpa's vampire informant had already filled him in on last night's rally. I drove with the radio off, the windows down, listening to the city on the quiet spring evening, preferring the sounds of rushing vehicles to song lyrics about emotions I couldn't trust.

The neighborhood was, as usual, quiet. But there was an addition—Ethan's sleek black Mercedes parked outside. Only his car—no black SUV in sight.

More important, there was no sign at all of a security detail.

That was off. Ethan never traveled without guards, usually in the SUV that tailed his convertible; it was against protocol. I parked a little down the street, turned off the car, and grabbed my cell phone, punching in Luc's number. He answered before the second ring.

"Luc."

"It's Merit. Have you lost a Master vampire?"

He grumbled, cursed. "Where?"

"Ombud's office. The Mercedes is out front. I'm assuming there's no guard in there with him?"

"We don't force guards on him," Luc testily responded, and I heard the snapping of papers through the phone. "Normally, I can trust him not to behave like an idiot and go off alone when there's a psychopath on the loose, Rogues up in arms."

Speaking of which, I sheepishly asked, "Any additional progress made last night?"

Luc sighed, and I imagined him settling into a slouch, crossing his booted ankles on the Ops Room table. "Morgan was damn near chipper when he finally left, but that's probably your doing. I'm not sure how productive it was. Nobody's got answers, the clues point everywhere. No evidence at the murder scenes except for the trinkets someone's leaving. But they know Ethan wouldn't do it, certainly wouldn't condone it. It's not the way he operates."

I understood that. If Ethan wanted something done, taken care of, he'd make damn sure you knew it was coming from him.

"Listen," I said, "while we're on the phone." I paused, had to brace myself for the apology. "I'm sorry I bailed last night. After the thing with Morgan—"

"Forgiven," Luc quickly answered. "You handled yourself, you stepped in when you needed to, and you gave Morgan a peaceful out. You did your job. I'm fine with that. That said, the fucking look on your face when he went down on one knee." He burst into raucous laughter. "Oh, sweet Jesus, Merit," he said, hiccupping with laughter. "It was priceless. Deer in headlights."

I made a face he couldn't see, double-checked the office door to look for movement, of which there was none. "I'm glad I can be a source of amusement for you, Luc."

"Consider it your hazing ritual. Your other one, anyway."

I chuckled. "Commendation, you mean? That was more of a hazing for Ethan than for me, unfortunately."

"No—your change."

I froze in the process of flipping up the visor, my hand still on it, and frowned at the phone. "The Change? How does that count as hazing?"

His voice changed to something graver. "What do you mean, how does that count?"

"I mean, I don't remember much of it. Pain, cold, I guess."

He was quiet so long I called his name, and even then it took a moment for him to come back. "I remember every second," he finally said. "Three days of pain, of cold, of heat, of cramps. Sweating through blankets, shivering so hard I thought my heart would stop, drinking blood before I was psychologically ready to accept it. How do you not remember that?"

I played back the memory in my mind, trying to cup my hands around the fleeting images that ghosted at the edges of my vision, tried to replay the mental video of it. I got nothing more than those select memories, until the ride home, the dizziness I'd felt when I'd stepped from the car, the sluggishness, the fuzziness.

Drugs?

Had I been drugged? Spared the experience of some portion of the Change?

I was saved offering that theory to Luc, a little disconcerted by the questions it raised—who'd drugged me? and why was I spared the misery?—by Ethan emerging from the front door, the light spilling in a trapezoid on the sidewalk in front of him. Catcher stepped out behind him. "Luc, he's out."

"Keep an eye on him."

I promised I would and snapped shut the phone, then waited until Ethan and Catcher had shaken hands. Ethan walked to the Mercedes, cast a glance down the darkened street, then unlocked the door and slipped inside. Catcher stayed on the sidewalk, watched as Ethan's car pulled away. When he was a block down the road, I turned the ignition and drove forward to where Catcher stood. Motioning me to follow Ethan, Catcher raised his cell phone, then flipped it open. My phone rang almost immediately.

"What's he up to?"

"He's going to Lincoln Park," Catcher said, frustration in his voice.

"Lincoln Park? Why?"

"He got a note, same paper, same handwriting, as the ones left for you and Celina. It asked to meet him there, promised information about the murders. He had to agree to go alone."

"They won't know I'm there," I promised.

"Stay a few cars behind him. It'll help that it's night, but your car sticks out like a sore thumb."

"He doesn't know what I drive."

"I doubt that's true, but do it all the same." He explained where Ethan expected to meet his source—near the small pagoda on the west side of North Pond—which at least gave me a chance to be surreptitious. I could take another route, get there without having to keep too close a tail on the Master vampire in front of me.

"You have your sword?"

"Yes, oh captain, my captain, I have my sword. I have learned to follow orders."

"Do your job, then," he said, and the line went dead.

If Ethan knew I was tailing him, he didn't act like it. I stayed three cars behind, grateful there was enough traffic in the early evening to keep a shield between his car and mine. Ethan drove methodically, carefully, slowly. That shouldn't surprise me—it was in keeping with the way he lived his life, orchestrated his other moves. But in the Mercedes, it disappointed me. Cars like that should be *driven*.

I found the Mercedes parked on Stockton, the only car in the vicinity. I drove past it, parked, then got out of the car, belted the katana, and in a moment of uncharacteristic forethought, grabbed an aspen stake from the bag Jeff had given me, still stuffed behind the front seat. I stuck the needle-sharp stake in my belt, quietly closed the door, and began to hike back. I crept through the grass, between the trees, until I was close enough to see him, tall and lean, standing just outside the pagoda. His hands were in his pockets, his expression alert, his body relaxed.

I stopped, stared at him. Why, in God's name, would he have come here alone? Why would he have agreed to meet a source in the middle of an empty park, after dark, without a guard?

I stayed in the shadows. I could leap out if necessary, come to his rescue (again), but if his goal was to glean information from whoever had asked him to meet, I wasn't about to ruin that.

The scritch of footsteps on the path broke the silence. A tall form appeared. A woman. Red hair.

Amber.

Wait. Amber?

I saw the jolt of recognition in Ethan's face, the shock, the sudden wash of humiliation. I sympathized, felt the flash of it in the pit of my stomach.

He approached her, head snapping as he looked around him, and reached out an arm, taking hers just above the elbow. "What are you doing here?"

She looked down at his hand on her arm, blinked up at him, then pulled his fingers away. "What do you think I'm doing here?"

"Frankly, I've no idea, Amber. But I've got business—"

"Ethan, really." Her voice was flat.

He stopped, stared at her, understanding dawning, and offered the conclusion I'd reached seconds before. I knew I didn't like the little tramp. Voice defeated, he said, "You took the medals. You were in my apartments, and you took the medals."

She shrugged standoffishly.

He took her arm again, this time his grip fierce enough to make her grimace. "You took House property from my apartments. You took from *me*. Did you"—he spit out a curse—"did you kill those girls?"

Amber grunted, yanked her arm away, and took a couple of steps, put space between them. She rubbed her arm, where the red marks of his fingers—even in the dark—were obvious.

"You're—" Ethan shook his head, fisted his hands on his hips, and whipped aside his jacket in the process. "How could you do this? You had everything. I gave you *everything*."

Amber shrugged. "We're tacky, Ethan. Clichéd. Among the sups, not authentic enough. Among the vampires, a little too authentic. Cadogan House is old news." Amber looked up, and her eyes gleamed with something—hope, maybe? "We need change. Direction. She can give us that."

Ethan froze, scanned her face. "She?"

Amber shrugged and, when a car door slammed shut, popped up her head. "That's my cue to go. You should listen, love." She leaned in, brushed a kiss against his cheek, and whispered something I couldn't hear. And then she was off, and he let her go, let her walk away. Not the decision I would have made, but traipsing after her, giving her the beat down she deserved, would have given away my position. And if the car door was any indication, the fun was only just beginning.

It took only seconds for her to reach him, to walk—lithe and catlike—toward Ethan. Her black hair was up in a snug knot at the crown of her head, held by long silver pins. She was dressed like a dominatrix masquerading as a secretary—impossibly tight pencil skirt, black stockings with a back stitch that ran the length of her legs, patent black stiletto heels with ankle straps, and a tucked-in snug white blouse. I half expected a riding crop, but didn't see one. Left it in the car, maybe.

Celina walked toward Ethan, and stopped four feet in front of him, one hand on a cocked hip. And then she spoke, her voice smoky and fluid like old Scotch.

"Darling, you're out here all alone. It's dangerous at night."

Ethan didn't move. They faced each other silently for a moment, magic swirling and flaring between them, spilling its tendrils through the trees. I ignored it, had to resist the urge to brush the wispy breeze of it away with a hand.

But I used the cover of their distraction, slipped the cell phone from my pocket, and texted a phrase to Catcher and Luc: *CELINA EVIL*. God willing, they'd send out the troops.

"You look surprised to see me," she said, then chuckled. "And certainly surprised to see Amber. All women, human or vampire, are looking for something more, Ethan. Something better. It was naive of you to have forgotten that."

Wow. Nothing like a little sexism to cap off the night.

Celina sighed her disappointment, then began to circle his body. Ethan's head turned slowly, his gaze following her as she moved. She stopped next to him, her back to me.

"Chicago is at a crossroads," she said. "We are the first city with a visible vampire population. And we were the first to announce our existence. Why take the risk? Because as long as we stayed quiet, we were destined to remain in shadow, to be subservient to the human world. It was time for us to step forward. It is time for us to flourish. We can't erase history"—she paused, gazed at him solemnly—"but we can *make* it."

Celina began to move again, circling his body until she

stood on his other side.. The sound of her voice was muffled, but I caught enough.

"There are few vampires who are capable of the kind of leadership we need right now. Vampires who are disciplined. Intelligent. Cunning. Navarre fits that mold, Ethan. *I* fit that mold." Her voice became insistent. "Do you understand how powerful we could be under my leadership? If I unified vampires? If I unified the Houses?"

"The Presidium would never allow that," Ethan said.

"The Presidium is antiquated."

"You're a *member* of the Presidium, Celina." Ethan's voice was perfectly flat, perfectly modulated to hide the fury that I knew lay beneath it. Say what you wanted about his strategizing, his penchant for manipulation, the man had control. Icy control.

Celina waved off the criticism. "The GP doesn't understand our modern problems. They won't let us expand, Commend more Initiates. We're shrinking relative to the other sup populations, and they're getting braver. The nymphs are fighting. The shifters are preparing to meet *in our city*"—she punctuated the last three words with a finger pointed toward the ground—"and the fairies demand more and more each year to protect us from humans. And the angels"—she shook her head ruefully—"the bonds are breaking there, the demons loosed."

She looked up at him, chin raised defiantly. "*No.* I will not allow vampires to become less than what we are. Only the strongest will survive the coming conflict, Ethan. Being strongest means unification—vampires coming together, working together, under the guidance of a vampire with vision."

She completed her circle so that she faced him again, maybe five feet between them. Her eyes gleamed in the darkness, like a cat's caught in the light, shifting shades and colors, green and yellow. "I am that vampire, Ethan." She waved a negligent hand. "Of course, in every war there are casualties. The deaths of those humans were a messy necessity."

He spoke the words as I thought them, voice flat. "You killed them."

She held up a slender finger. "Let's be precise, Ethan. I *had* them killed. I wouldn't waste my time on the actual doing of it. Of course, that does pose certain . . . quality-control problems." She snickered, evidently pleased at her joke. "I found a Rogue. I convinced him, through no little work on my part, to do the dirty work. I had to change horses after Merit's attack." She shrugged. "I do hate sloppy work. Nevertheless, you got a Merit out of the deal. A Merit vampire, Commended into your House."

"Leave her out of this."

She chuckled without amusement. "Interesting answer. And unfortunate that we don't have time to explore your affection for your pet Sentinel."

Without warning, Celina reached behind her and whipped the pins from her hair. Or, rather, what I'd thought were pins, but were actually twin stiletto blades that gleamed in the moonlight. Her hair, released from its moorings, spilled in an inky wave down her back.

She took a step forward, angling her body so that, had Ethan not been standing between us, I'd have faced her directly.

I stepped forward, prepared to defend him, but heard a *WAIT* echo through my head.

Not yet, he told me. *Let her finish confessing it.*

He knew I was there, then. Knew I was ready. So I obeyed the order, katana handle in one hand, already slipped from its guard, halfway loosed from its scabbard, the aspen stake in the other.

"Sloppiness or not, my plan worked," she said. "Humans are now suspicious of Cadogan vampires—they think you killed Jennifer Porter. And humans are suspicious of Grey vampires, who they think killed Patricia Long. You're wicked, Ethan. All of you. All except Navarre . . ." She paused and smiled, and the effect was as lovely as it was maniacal. "If I'm the only one that humans trust, I can consolidate my influence in both worlds—human and vampire. The Houses will need me as their ambassador, and I will offer my guidance. Under my leadership we will become what we were meant to be."

"I can't allow you to do that."

"It's amusing that you believe the decision is in your hands," she said, waggling the stilettos in the air. "You'll be another sacrifice, of course, and an expensive one—a lovely one—but the cause is worth it. How many of us were staked, Ethan? You were alive during the Clearings. You *know*."

But he wouldn't be drawn into a discussion of history. "If you wanted to bring down Cadogan and Grey, why the notes? Why implicate Beck and his people?"

"The notes were only intended for vampire eyes. As for why—you've surprised me again. *Solidarity*, Ethan. It's all of us together or nothing. Rogues offer us nothing. They're warm bodies, I'll admit. They increase our numbers. But as friends, they're useless. No alliances—they're morally opposed. They certainly don't play well with others." She flicked a hand negligently in the air, and the blades glinted. "They needed cleaning out."

Ethan was silent for a long moment, his eyes on the ground, before he raised them again. "So you convinced Amber to help you, had her steal the Cadogan medal, and had someone plant them?"

Celina nodded.

"And the jersey from Grey House? How did you obtain it?"

She smiled wolfishly. "Your redhead made another friend. Another conquest."

Ethan's expression went cold. I sympathized. This was not the time to learn that your Consort had betrayed you, your House, and another.

"How could you do this?"

She sighed dramatically. "I was afraid you'd see it that

way, stake out some kind of sympathetic moral high ground. Humans are never innocent, darling. A human broke my heart once. He thought nothing of it. They're cold, callous, stupid things. And now we're forced to deal with them. We should have taken a stand centuries ago, should have banded together to fight them. It's not an option now, of course. Their numbers are too great. But we begin slowly. We make friends. We build, as you're always preaching, alliances. And while we're lulling them to sleep with our pretty faces and pretty words, we infiltrate. We plan. We get them accustomed to us, and when the time comes, we strike."

"You're talking war, Celina."

She bit out through a tightly clenched jaw, "Goddamn right. They should fear us. And they will." But her expression softened. "But first, they'll love me. And when the time comes that I can reveal my true allegiance—my love for vampires; my hatred of humans—I'll drink in that betrayal, Ethan. I will revel in it. And it will begin to make up for what he did to me."

That perfectly encapsulated Celina Desaulniers, I thought. She needed fame, attention, the focused desire of those around her. She needed friends, nearly as much as she needed enemies.

Celina razed the tip of a blade down the front of his shirt. "Centuries, Ethan. Centuries, obeying their laws, their dictates, hiding ourselves, our nature from the world. *No more.* I made this world in which we live. I decide the rules."

She drew back her arms, elbows raised, and prepared to strike. I jumped, pouring through the trees, aiming for her with a blind rage that ran like electricity through me, piqued by the thought of her injuring my Master, my Liege. *MINE.*

DOWN! I cried out, willing him to hear me, and threw the stake, pouring all my strength into the throw. Ethan ducked immediately, crouching to the ground, as the aspen whistled above him, catching Celina high in the left side of her chest. Too high. I'd missed her heart. But she dropped the blades, dropped to her knees, and screamed out at the pain, fingers clutching the stake too slippery with blood to allow her a grip. Ethan immediately jumped, grabbed her from behind, pinned her arms.

Suddenly, car doors slammed, footsteps echoed. The cavalry had arrived—Catcher, Luc, and Malik ran through the trees, accompanied by the rest of the Cadogan guards.

"Merit?"

I couldn't tear my eyes away. She screamed out blistering obscenities, berating the guards for standing in her way, for interfering with her plans, as they tried to subdue her. Her hair, the long, dark locks of it, whipped and flew around her face as she yelled.

"Merit."

I finally heard my name, looked over, saw Ethan wipe blood from his hands—Celina's blood—with a handkerchief. A red stain marred his usually impeccable white shirt. Celina's blood. Blood she'd shed because of me. I stared at the crimson stain of it, then raised my gaze to his face. "What?"

He stopped scrubbing, balled the handkerchief into a wad. "Are you okay?"

"I don't—" I shook my head. "I don't think so."

A line appeared between his eyes, and he opened his mouth to speak, but was distracted by more car doors, more footsteps. He looked away; I followed the direction of his gaze.

It was Morgan, in the same clothes in which I'd seen him an hour ago, grief and worry etched on his face. As Celina's Second, he must have gotten a call from Luc or Catcher after my text message.

Morgan stopped a few feet from us, stared at the scene before him—his Master, bleeding from an aspen stake still protruding from her shoulder, being pulled off the ground by a cadre of guards who had to work to counteract her strength, to subdue her.

He closed his eyes, turned away. After a moment, his lids lifted, and he looked at Ethan, evidently prepared for the story.

"She confessed," Ethan said. "She planned the murders, used Rogues to execute them, used Amber, of my House, to steal the medals and the jersey from Grey. She used the notes to implicate Beck's group."

"To what purpose?"

"In the short term, control. She wants Chicago's vampires. Chicago's Houses. In the long term—war."

They were quiet for a long time.

"I didn't know," Morgan finally said, the words heavy with regret.

"You couldn't have. She must have planned this for months, maybe longer. She drew me here to tell me, to kill me, maybe to take Cadogan from Malik when I was gone. She attacked first, Greer. Stilettos." Ethan pointed to where the glimmering blades lay on the ground. "Merit defended."

Morgan seemed to suddenly realize that I was there, looked down at the unsheathed katana in my hand, then up at me. "Merit?"

I wondered if she called to him, what words she was spilling into his mind. "Yes?"

"You staked her?"

I looked to Ethan, and he nodded, so I answered, "In the shoulder."

Morgan nodded, seemed to consider this, evaluate it, then nodded again, this time more firmly. A bit more composed, he offered, "I'm glad you didn't aim for her heart. That saves an inquiry for you."

An inquiry, her life, and my having committed murder. I smiled weakly, sickly, knowing that I'd aimed for her heart— but missed.

Morgan walked away, walked toward the guards, spoke with them.

"Thank you," Ethan said.

"Hmm." The guards pulled Celina to her feet, her arms pinned behind her. "What will happen to her?"

"She'll be taken before the rest of the Presidium and her fate decided. She'll likely be stripped of her authority. But she's the Master of the oldest American House. Any other punishment will likely be temporary."

There was a gentle tug on the end of my ponytail. I looked up, found Luc staring down at me, concern in his eyes. "You okay?"

I felt my stomach tighten again, nausea building as I remembered, again, that I'd nearly killed someone, had meant to do it, had wanted to do it to protect Ethan. To keep him alive, I'd selected someone for death, and only my bad aim had kept me from committing the act, from finishing the job. "I think I'm going to be sick."

His arm was suddenly around my waist. "You'll be fine. Deep breaths, and I'll get you home."

I nodded, then cast a final glance at Celina.

A serene smile on her face, she winked at me. *"Après nous, le deluge,"* she called out.

She'd spoken in French, but I'd understood what she'd said. It was an historical phrase, allegedly spoken by France's Madame de Pompadour (of big hair fame) to Louis XV.

Literal translation: After us, the flood.

Figurative translation: Things are only gonna get worse from here, *chica*.

I stifled a shiver as Luc began to lead me toward the line of cars. We passed Morgan, who was speaking authoritatively to another guard, his eyes on the woman being led away.

I realized what I'd done.

I'd given him Navarre House.

In a tenth of a second, I'd thrown aspen, catching Celina before she could kill Ethan. She'd be punished and, if Ethan was right, stripped of her House. Morgan was her Second, next in line to the throne.

I had, by proxy, made Morgan head of the oldest House of vampires in the United States. His status would rival Ethan's, even if he was younger and less skilled, because his House was older.

I wondered how much more pleased Ethan would be to have a Master of Navarre, not just its Second, seeking his Sentinel.

I looked over at Ethan, found I couldn't bear the sight of him, the bile rising in my throat. For him, I'd nearly killed someone, even if I had—thank God—failed the test in the crucial moment. Some soldier I made.

He stepped forward, but I shook my head. "Not now."

He looked at me, then looked away, and pushed a hand through his hair.

As Luc led me away, led me toward the black SUV parked along the street, the tunnel rushed me. *I owe you my life.*

My knees nearly buckled. I wanted none of it, just to be home, in my own bed, and certainly not to hold someone else's debt. *You owe me nothing.*

I wasn't sure you'd step forward. Not after last night.

I stopped, turned, looked back at him across Luc's broad shoulder.

Ethan's gaze was potent, his expression radiating incredulity that I'd protected him, reverence that I'd saved him, and that same bit of surprise I'd first seen in his office, when he'd discovered I wasn't thrilled to be a vampire of Cadogan House, that he couldn't buy my allegiance with money or art or well-tailored clothes.

He'd underestimated me again, hadn't taken me at my word even after I swore, in two oaths, that I'd protect the vampires of Cadogan House against all enemies, living or dead.

Against Morgan.

Against the Rogues.

Against Celina.

His hands were stuffed into the pockets of his trousers,

and that nearly did me in again, but I held tight to the anger, to the rage, to the disgust, and sent back to him, *I swore an oath. Last night, I proved my allegiance. You have no room to doubt me.*

He nodded. *I didn't. I don't.*

A lie, but I nodded, accepted it.

Maybe he'd learn to trust me, or maybe he wouldn't. Maybe he'd know this would change me, this first battle, this first attempt on a life. Maybe he'd know that the seed of hatred he'd planted two weeks ago would blossom, watered by the things I'd done, and would do, in his name.

He said nothing else, but turned, and walked toward Morgan.

I went home, sobbed on Mallory's shoulder, and slept like the dead.

Which I'm pretty sure I wasn't.

S he wanted control of the House. Of all the Houses. Of
Chicago's vampires, San Diego's vampires. North
America's vampires.

All vampires.

Celina confessed as much the next evening to the representatives of the Presidium who'd braved sunlight and
crossed the Atlantic to face her. She was unapologetic. Not
crazy, exactly, but without morals. Or, at best, operating on a
set of ethical standards wholly defined by her own history,
her hatred of humans and her paradoxical need to be loved
by them.

She'd worked to establish Navarre as the House of Decent
Vampires. The House of Nearly Human Vampires. And through
the murders, she'd set up Cadogan and Grey as foils, the Houses
of Evil.

Her plan, such as it was, had backfired. She'd been caught,
and now the anger and distrust she'd created and directed
toward Cadogan and Grey came to rest on Navarre. Morgan
would have an uphill climb on that one.

But while she might have temporarily lost the PR war,
she'd made enormous strides among vampires.

She as much as admitted she had no intention of killing

Ethan. She'd bluffed, taken the offensive, knowing that someone—Sentinel or guard—would step in, defend him. Rescue him. She probably knew that I'd been there the entire time, but allowed the charade to progress.

The result? She'd martyred herself. She had given up her House, her rank, her vassals, for her cause.

Not all vampires would condone her acts. Many had assimilated, lived with humans for centuries, and would decry the publicity she'd inspired, the threat she'd created to their lives and livelihoods. To the relatively peaceful status quo.

But others—angry at being pushed aside, ignored, punished, executed, made to feel less than what they were—would agree with her. They'd rally quietly at first. Secret meetings maybe, outside the purview of the GP. But their numbers would grow. They would meet in her name, call her name, ascribe to Celina any ground they gained.

Because of her, war will come. Maybe now, maybe later, after the ties with humans are forged, after their guards are dropped. I'll be asked to defend Ethan again, despite his willingness to use and manipulate, despite my broken heart.

Until then, I'll bury the anger, the betrayal.

I'll smile.

I'll tap the pommel of my sword.

I'll hop up the steps of Cadogan House, and close the door behind me, and do my job.

I'm very, very good at it.

Read on for a sneak peek at the second book in
Chloe Neill's *New York Times* bestselling
Chicagoland Vampires series,

Friday Night Bites

Available now wherever books
and e-books are sold.

Higher, Merit. Bring up that kick. Mmm-hmm. Better."
I kicked again, this time higher, trying to remember to point my toes, squeeze my core, and flutter my fingers in the "jazz hands" our instructor ceaselessly demanded.

Next to me, and considerably less enthused, my best friend and soon-to-be-ex-roommate, Mallory, growled and executed another kick. The growl was an odd accompaniment to the bob of blue hair and classically pretty face, but she was irritated enough to carry it off.

"Remind me why you dragged me into this?" she asked.

Our instructor, a busty blonde with bright pink nails and impossibly sharp cheekbones, clapped her hands together. Her breasts joggled in syncopation. It was impossible to look away.

"Fiercer, ladies! We want every eye in the club on our bodies! Let's *work* it!"

Mallory glared daggers at the instructor we'd named Aerobics Barbie. Mal's fists curled and she took a menacing step forward, but I wrapped an arm around her waist before she could pummel the woman we'd paid to grapevine us into skinny jeans.

"Ixnay on the ighting-fay," I warned, using a little of my two-month-old vampire strength to keep her in place despite her bobbing fists. Mallory grumbled, but finally stopped struggling.

Score one for the newbie vampire, I thought.

"How about a little civilized beat-down?" she asked, blowing a lock of sweaty blue hair from her forehead.

I shook my head, but let her go. "Beating down the teacher's gonna get you more attention than you need, Mal. Remember what Catcher said."

Catcher was Mallory's gruff boyfriend. And while my comment didn't merit a growl, I got a nasty, narrow-eyed snarl. Catcher loved Mallory, and Mallory loved Catcher. But that didn't mean she liked him all the time, especially since she was dealing with a supernatural perfect storm centered over our Chicago brownstone. In the span of a week, I'd been unwillingly made a vampire, and we'd learned that Mallory was a still-developing sorceress. As in, magical powers, black cats and the major and minor Keys—the divisions of magic.

So, yeah. My first few weeks as a vampire had been inordinately busy. Like *The Young and the Restless*, but with slightly dead people.

Mal was still getting used to the idea that she had paranormal drama of her own, and Catcher, already in trouble with the Order (the sorcerers' governing union), was keeping a pretty tight lid on her magical demonstrations. So Mallory was supernaturally frustrated.

Hell, we were both supernaturally frustrated, and Mallory didn't have fangs or a pretentious Master vampire to deal with.

So, given that unfortunate state of affairs, why were we letting Aerobics Barbie guilt us into using jazz hands?

Simply put, this was supposed to be quality time, bonding time, for me and Mallory.

Because I was moving out.

"Okay," Barbie continued, "let's add that combination we learned last week. One, two and three and four, and five, six and seven and eight." The music reached a pounding crescendo as she pivoted and thrusted to the bass-heavy beat. We followed as best we could, Mallory having a little harder time of not stepping on her own feet. My years of ballet classes—and the quickstep speed that vampirism gave me— were actually serving me pretty well, the humiliation of a twenty-eight-year-old vampire doing jazz hands notwithstanding.

Barbie's enthusiasm aside, the fact that we were doing jazz hands in a hip-hop dance class didn't say much for her credentials. But the class was still an improvement over my usual training. My workouts were usually *très* intense, because only a couple of months ago I'd been named Sentinel for my House.

To make a long story slightly shorter, American vampires were divided into Houses. Chicago had three, and I'd been initiated into the second oldest of those—Cadogan. Much to everyone's surprise given my background (think grad school and medieval romantic literature), I'd been named Sentinel. Although I was still learning the ropes, being Sentinel meant I was supposed to act as a kind of vampire guard. (Turns out that while I was a pretty geeky human, I was a pretty strong vampire.) Being Sentinel also meant training, and while American vampires had traded in the black velvet and lace for Armani and iPhones, they were pretty old school on a lot of issues—feudal on a lot of issues—including weapons. Put all that together, and it meant I was learning to wield the antique katana I'd been given to defend Cadogan and its vampires.

Coincidentally enough, Catcher was an expert in the Second of the Four Keys—weapons—so he'd been tasked with prepping me for vampire combat. As a newbie vampire, having Catcher as a sparring partner wasn't exactly great for the confidence.

Aerobics Barbie whipped herself into a hip-hop frenzy, leading the class in a final multistep combination that ended with the lot of us staring sassily at the mirrors that lined the dance studio. Session concluded, she applauded and made some announcements about future classes that Mallory and I would have to be dragged, kicking and screaming, to attend.

"Never again, Merit," she said, walking to the corner of the room where she'd deposited her bag and water bottle before class started. I couldn't have agreed more. Although I loved to dance, hip thrusting under Barbie's bubbly instruction and ever-bouncing bosom involved too little actual dance and too much cleavage. I needed to respect my dance master. Respect wasn't exactly the emotion Barbie inspired.

We sat down on the floor to prep for our return to the real world.

"So, Ms. Vampire," Mallory asked me, "are you nervous about moving into the House?"

I glanced around, not entirely sure how much chatting I should be doing about my vampire business. The Chicagoland Vampires had announced their existence to Chicago roughly ten months ago, and as you might guess, humans weren't thrilled to learn that we existed. Riots. Panic. Congressional investigations. And then Chicago's three Houses became wrapped up in the investigation of two murders— murders supposedly perpetrated by vampires from Cadogan and Grey, the youngest Chicago House. The Masters of those Houses, Ethan Sullivan and Scott Grey, dreaded the attention.

But the Master of the third House (that was Navarre) was conniving, manipulative, and the one that actually planned the murders. She was also drop-dead gorgeous, no pun intended. She might as well have leaped from an editorial spread in *Vogue*. Dark hair and blue eyes (just like me), but with an arrogance that put celebrities and cult leaders to shame.

Humans were entranced, *fascinated*, by Celina Desaulniers.

Her beauty, her style, and her ability to psychically manipulate those around her were an irresistible combination. Humans wanted to learn more about her, to see more, to hear more.

That she'd been responsible for the deaths of two humans—murders she'd planned and confessed to—hadn't minimized their fascination. Nor had the fact that she'd been captured (BTW, by Ethan and me) and extradited to London for incarceration by the Greenwich Presidium, the council that ruled Western European and North American vampires. And in her place, the rest of us—the exonerated majority who hadn't helped her commit those heinous crimes—became that much more interesting. Celina got her wish—she got to play the bad little martyred vampire—and we got an early Christmas present: We got to step into the vacuum of her celebrity.

T-shirts, caps, and pennants for Grey and Cadogan (and for the more morbid, Navarre) were available for sale in shops around Chicago. There were House fan sites, "I ♥ Cadogan" bumper stickers, and news updates on the city's vampires.

Still, notorious or not, I tried not to spread too many deets about the Houses around town. As Sentinel, I was part of the House's security corps, after all. So I took a look around the gym and made sure we were alone, that prying human ears weren't slipping a listen.

"If you're debating how much you can say," Mallory said, unscrewing the top of her water bottle, "I've sent out a magical pulse so that none of our little human friends can hear this conversation."

"Really?" I turned my head to look at her so quickly my neck popped, the shock of pain squinting my eyes.

She snorted. "Right. Like he'd let me use M-A-G-I-C around people," she muttered, then took a big gulp of her water.

I ignored the shot at Catcher—we'd never have a decent conversation if I took the time to react to all of them—and answered her question about the Big Move.

"I'm a little nervous. Ethan and I, you know, tend to grate on each other's nerves."

Mallory swallowed her water, then wiped her forehead with the back of her hand. "Oh, whatever. You two are BFFs."

"Just because we've managed to play Master and Sentinel for two weeks without tearing each other's throat out doesn't mean we're BFFs."

As a matter of fact, I'd had minimum contact with Cadogan's Master—and the vampire who made me—during those last two weeks, by design. I kept my head down and my fangs to the grindstone as I watched and learned how things worked in the House. The truth was, I'd had trouble with Ethan at first—I'd been made a vampire without my consent, my human life taken away because Celina planned on me being her second victim. Her minions weren't successful in killing me, but Ethan had been successful at changing me —in order to save my life.

Frankly, the transition sucked. The adjustment from human grad student to vampire guard was, to say the least, awkward. As a result, I'd pushed a lot of vitriol in Ethan's direction. I'd eventually made the decision to accept my new life as a member of Chicago's fanged community. Although I still wasn't sure I had fully come to terms with being a vampire, I was dealing.

Ethan, though, was more complicated. We shared some kind of connection, some pretty strong chemistry, and some mutual irritation toward each other. He acted like he thought I was beneath him; I generally thought he was a pretentious stick-in-the-mud. That "generally" should clue you in to my mixed feelings—Ethan was ridiculously handsome and a grade-A kisser. While I hadn't completely reconciled my feelings for him, I didn't think I hated him anymore.

Avoidance helped settle the emotions. Considerably.

"No," Mallory agreed, "but the fact that the room heats up by ten degrees every time you two get near each other says something."

"Shut up," I said, extending my legs in front of me and lowering my nose to my knees to stretch out. "I admit nothing."

"You don't have to. I've seen your eyes silver just being around him. There's your admission."

"Not necessarily," I said, pulling one foot toward me and bending into another stretch. Vampires' eyes silvered when they experienced strong emotions—hunger, anger, or, in my case, proximity to the blond cupcake that was Ethan Sullivan. "But I'll admit that he's kind of offensively delicious."

"Like salt-and-vinegar potato chips."

"Exactly," I said, then sat up again. "Here I am, an uptight vampire who owes my allegiance to a liege lord I can't stand. And it turns out you're some kind of latent sorceress who can make things happen just by wishing them. We're the free-will outliers—I have none, and you have too much."

She looked at me, then blinked and put her hand over her heart. "You, and I'm saying this with love, Mer, are really a geek." She rose and pulled the strap of her bag across one shoulder. I followed suit, and we walked to the door.

"You know," she said, "you and Ethan should get one of those necklaces, where half the heart says 'best' and the other half says 'friend.' You could wear them as a sign of your eternal devotion to each other."

I threw my sweaty towel at her. She made a yakking sound beneath it, then threw it off, her features screwed into an expression of abject girly horror. "You're so immature."

"Blue hair. That's all I'm saying."

"Bite me, dead girl."

I showed fang and winked at her. "Don't tempt me, witch."

*   *   *

An hour later, I'd showered and changed back into my Cadogan House uniform—a fitted black suit jacket, black tank, and black slim-fit pants—and was in my soon-to-be-former Wicker Park bedroom, stuffing clothes into a duffel bag. A glass of blood from one of the medical-grade plastic bags in our refrigerator—promptly delivered by Blood4You, the fanged equivalent of milkmen—sat on the nightstand beside my bed, my post-workout snack. Mallory stood in the doorway behind me, blue hair framing her face, the rest of her body covered by boxers and an oversized T-shirt, probably Catcher's, that read ONE KEY AT A TIME.

"You don't have to do this," she said. "You don't have to leave."

I shook my head. "I do have to do this. I need to do it to be Sentinel. And you two need room." To be precise, Catcher and Mallory needed *rooms*. Lots of them. Frequently, with lots of noise, and usually naked, although that wasn't a requirement. They hadn't known each other long and were smitten within days of meeting. But what they lacked in time they made up for in unmitigated, bare-assed enthusiasm. Like rabbits. Ridiculously energetic, completely unself-conscious, supernatural rabbits.

Mallory grabbed a second empty bag from the chair next to my bedroom door, dropped it onto the bed, and pulled three pair of cherished shoes—Mihara Pumas (sneakers that I adored, much to Ethan's chagrin), red ballet-style flats, and a pair of black Mary Janes she'd given me—from my closet. She raised them for my approval and, at my nod, stuffed them in. Two more pairs followed before she settled on the bed next to the bag and crossed her legs, one foot swinging impatiently.

"I can't believe you're leaving me here with him. What am I going to do without you?"

I gave her a flat stare.

She rolled her eyes. "You only caught us the one time."

"I only caught you in the *kitchen* the one time, Mallory. I eat in there. I drink in there. I could have lived a contented, happy eternity without ever catching a glimpse of Catcher's bare ass on the kitchen floor." I faked a dramatic shiver. Faked, because the boy was gorgeous—a broad-shouldered, perfectly muscled, shaved-headed, green-eyed, tattooed, bad-boy magician who'd swept my roommate off her feet (and onto her back, as it turned out).

"Not that it isn't a fine ass," she said.

I folded a pair of pants and put them into my bag. "It's a great ass, and I'm very happy for you. I just didn't need to see it naked again. Ever. For real."

She chuckled. "For realsies, even?"

"For realsies, even." My stomach twinged with hunger. I glanced at Mallory, then lifted brows toward the glass of blood on my nightstand. She rolled her eyes, then waved her hands at it.

"Drink, drink," she said. "Pretend I'm some *Buffy* fan with a wicked attraction to the paranormal."

I managed to both lift the glass and give her a sardonic look. "That's exactly what you are."

"I didn't say you had to pretend very *hard*," she pointed out.

I smiled, then sipped from my glass of slightly microwaved blood, which I'd seasoned up with Tabasco and tomato juice. I mean, it was still blood, with the weird iron tang and plastic aftertaste, but the extras perked it up. I licked an errant drop from my upper lip, then returned the glass to the nightstand.

Empty.

I must have been hungrier than I thought. I blamed Aerobics Barbie. Regardless, in order to make sure that I had future snacks (thinking a stash of actual food would increase the odds that my fangs and Ethan's neck stayed unacquainted), I stuffed a dozen granola bars into my bag.

"And speaking of Catcher," I began, since I'd cut the edge off my hunger, "where is Mr. Romance this evening?"

"Work," she said. "Your grandfather is quite the taskmaster."

Did I mention that Catcher worked for my grandfather? During that one big week when all the supernatural drama went down, I also discovered that my grandfather, Chuck Merit, the man who'd practically raised me, wasn't retired from his service with the Chicago Police Department as we'd been led to believe. Instead, four years ago he'd been asked to serve as an Ombudsman, a liaison, between the city administration—led by darkly handsome Mayor Seth Tate—and the city's supernatural population. Sups of every kind—vampires, sorcerers, shapeshifters, water nymphs, fairies, and demons—all depended on my grandfather for help. Well, him and his trio of assistants, including one Catcher Bell. I'd visited my grandfather's South Side office shortly after becoming a vamp; I'd met Catcher, then Mallory met Catcher, and the rest was naked history.

Mallory was quiet for a moment, and when I looked up, I caught her brushing a tear from her cheek. "You know I'll miss you, right?"

"Please. You'll miss the fact that I can afford to pay rent now. You were getting used to spending Ethan's money." The Cadogan stipend was one of the upshots of having been made a vampire.

"The blood money, such as it was, was a perk. It was nice not to be the only one slaving away for the man." Given her glassy office overlooking Michigan Avenue, she was exaggerating by a large degree. While I'd been in grad school reading medieval texts, Mallory had been working as an ad executive. We'd only recently discovered that her job had been her first success as an adolescent sorceress: She'd actually *willed* herself into it, which wasn't the salve to her ego that a hire based on her creativity and skills might have been. She was taking a break from the job now, using up weeks of saved vacation time to figure out how she was going to deal with her newfound magic.

I added some journals and pens to the duffel. "Think

about it this way—no more bags of blood in the refrigerator, and you'll have a muscley, sexy guy to cuddle with at night. Much better deal for you."

"He's still a narcissistic ass."

"Who you're crazy about," I pointed out while scanning my bookshelf. I grabbed a couple of reference books, a worn, leather-bound book of fairy tales I'd had since childhood, and the most important recent addition to my collection, the *Canon of the North American Houses, Desk Reference*. It had been given to me by Helen, the Cadogan Liaison burdened with the task of escorting me home after my change, and was required reading for newbie vampires. I'd read a lot of the four solid inches of text, and skimmed a good chunk of the rest. The bookmark was stuck somewhere in chapter eight: "Going All Night." (The chapter titles had apparently been drafted by a seventeen-year-old boy.)

"And he's your narcissistic ass," I reminded her.

"Yay, me!" she dryly replied, spinning a finger in the air like a party favor.

"You two will be fine. I'm sure you can manage to keep each other entertained," I said, plucking a bobble-headed Ryne Sandberg figurine from the shelf and placing it carefully in my bag. Although my new sunlight allergy kept me from enjoying sunny days at Wrigley Field, even vampirism wouldn't diminish my love for the Cubs.

I scanned my room, thinking about all the things—Cubs-related or otherwise—I'd be leaving behind. I wasn't taking everything with me to Cadogan, partly out of concern that I'd strangle Ethan and be banished from the House, and partly because leaving some of my stuff here meant that I still had a home base, a place to crash if living amongst vampires—living near Ethan—became too much to bear. Besides, it's not like her new roommate was going to need the space; Catcher had already stashed his boy stuff in Mal's bedroom.

I zipped up the bags and, hands on my hips, looked over at Mallory. "I think I'm ready."

She offered me a supportive smile, and I managed to keep the tears that suddenly brimmed at my lashes from spilling over. Silently, she stood up and wrapped her arms around me. I hugged her back—my best friend, my sister.

"I love you, you know," she said.

"I love you, too."

She released me, and we both swiped at tears. "You'll call me, right? Let me know you're okay?"

"Of course I will. And I'm only moving across town. It's not like I'm leaving for Miami." I hefted one of the bags onto my shoulder. "You know, I always figured if I moved out it would be because I got a kick-ass teaching job in some small town where everyone is super smart and quirky."

"Eureka?" she asked.

"Or Stars Hollow."

Mallory made a sound of agreement and picked up the second bag. "I assumed you'd leave after you got knocked up by a twenty-one-year-old classics major and the two of you ran away to Bora-Bora to raise your baby in the islands."

I stopped halfway to the door and glanced back at her. "That's pretty specific, Mal."

"You studied a lot," she said, edging past me into the hallway. "I had the time."

I heard her trot down the stairs, but paused in the doorway of the bedroom that had been mine since I'd returned to Chicago three years ago. I took a last look around at the old furniture, the faded comforter, the cabbage rose wallpaper, and flipped off the light.

New from *New York Times* bestselling author

CHLOE NEILL

WILD THINGS
A Chicagoland Vampires Novel

Since Merit was turned into a vampire, and the protector
of Chicago's Cadogan House, it's been a wild ride.
She and Master vampire Ethan Sullivan have helped make
Cadogan's vampires the strongest in North America, and
forged ties with paranormal folk of all breeds and creeds.

But now those alliances are about to be tested. A strange
magic has ripped through the North American Central
Pack, and Merit's closest friends are caught in the
crosshairs. The Pack Apex looks to Merit and Ethan for
help. But who—or what—could possibly be powerful
enough to out-magic a shifter?

"These books are wonderful entertainment."
—#1 *New York Times* bestselling author Charlaine Harris

Available wherever books are sold or
at penguin.com

facebook.com/ProjectParanormalBooks